THE KING WITHOUT A KINGDOM

BY MAURICE DRUON

The Accursed Kings

The Iron King

The Strangled Queen

The Poisoned Crown

The Royal Succession

The She-Wolf

The Lily and the Lion

The King Without a Kingdom

THE KING WITHOUT A KINGDOM

Book Seven of The Accursed Kings

MAURICE DRUON

Translated from French by
Andrew Simpkin

HarperCollins*Publishers*

HarperCollins*Publishers*
1 London Bridge Street
London SE1 9GF

www.harpercollins.co.uk

Published by HarperCollins*Publishers* 2015

1

ISBN: 978-0-00-749137-7

Printed and bound in Great Britain by
Clays Ltd, St Ives plc

MIX
Paper from
responsible sources
FSC
www.fsc.org FSC™ C007454

'Our longest war, the Hundred Years War,
was merely a legal debate, interspersed with
occasional bouts of armed warfare'
PAUL CLAUDEL

Foreword

GEORGE R.R. MARTIN

Over the years, more than one reviewer has described my fantasy series, *A Song of Ice and Fire*, as historical fiction about history that never happened, flavoured with a dash of sorcery and spiced with dragons. I take that as a compliment. I have always regarded historical fiction and fantasy as sisters under the skin, two genres separated at birth. My own series draws on both traditions . . . and while I undoubtedly drew much of my inspiration from Tolkien, Vance, Howard, and the other fantasists who came before me, *A Game of Thrones* and its sequels were also influenced by the works of great historical novelists like Thomas B. Costain, Mika Waltari, Howard Pyle . . . and Maurice Druon, the amazing French writer who gave us the *The Accursed Kings*, seven splendid novels that chronicle the downfall of the Capetian kings and the beginnings of the Hundred Years War.

Druon's novels have not been easy to find, especially in English translation (and the seventh and final volume was never translated into English at all). The series has *twice* been made into a television series in France, and both versions are available on DVD ... but only in French, undubbed, and without English subtitles. Very frustrating for English-speaking Druon fans like me.

The Accursed Kings has it all. Iron kings and strangled queens, battles and betrayals, lies and lust, deception, family rivalries, the curse of the Templars, babies switched at birth, she-wolves, sin, and swords, the doom of a great dynasty ... and all of it (well, most of it) straight from the pages of history. And believe me, the Starks and the Lannisters have nothing on the Capets and Plantagenets.

Whether you're a history buff or a fantasy fan, Druon's epic will keep you turning pages. This was the original game of thrones. If you like *A Song of Ice and Fire*, you will love *The Accursed Kings*.

George R.R. Martin

Author's Acknowledgements

I am most grateful to Jacques Suffel for his assistance in gathering and compiling the documentation for this book. I would also like to express my thanks to the *Bibliothèque Nationale* as well as to the *Archives de France*.

Contents

Family Tree   xiv–xv

Prologue   xvii

Part One: Misfortunes Come From Long Ago

 1 The Cardinal of Périgord thinks . . .   3

 2 The Cardinal of Périgord speaks   12

 3 Death knocks on every door   24

 4 The Cardinal and the Stars   36

 5 The Beginnings of the King they call The Good 42

 6 The Beginnings of the King they call The Bad   51

 7 News from Paris   61

 8 The Treaty of Mantes   67

 9 The Bad in Avignon   79

10 The Annus Horribilis   91

11 The Kingdom Cracks   100

Part Two: The Banquet of Rouen

1 Exemptions and Benefits   113
2 The Anger of the King   117
3 To Rouen   126
4 The Banquet   132
5 The Arrest   146
6 The Preparations   154
7 The Field of Forgiveness   164

Part Three: The Lost Spring

1 The Hound and the Fox Cub   181
2 The Nation of England   198
3 The Pope and the World   211

Part Four: The Summer of Disaster

1 The Norman Chevauchée   227
2 The Siege of Breteuil   237
3 The Homage of Phoebus   254
4 The Camp of Chartres   267
5 The Prince of Aquitaine   279
6 The Cardinal's Approach   295
7 The Hand of God   313
8 The Battalion of the King   321
9 The Prince's Supper   333

Translator's notes and historical explanations   342

Family Tree

Philip III of France   m.1   Isabella of Aragon
(1245–1285)   (1247–1271)

Marguerite   m.1   Charles,   m.2   Catherine I
of Anjou   Count of Valois,   of Courtenay,
(1273–1299)   Titular Emperor   Titular Empres
            of Constantinople, of Constantinopl
            Count of Romagna (1274–1307)
            (1270–1325)

Isabella   Philip VI
(1292–1309)   of France
m.   (1293–1350)
John III,
Duke of Brittany   m.1   m.2
(1286–1341)   Joan of Burgundy Blanche of
            (1293–1348)   Navarre
                        (1330–)

Bonne of   m.1   John II   m.2   Joan I
Luxembourg   the Good, of France,   Countess of
(1315–1349)   Count of Anjou,   Auvergne
            Count of Maine and (1326–)
            Duke of Normandy
            (1319–)

Charles,   John,
Dauphin of France   Louis I   Count of Poitiers
(1338–)   Duke of Anjou   Duke of Berry
            (1339–)   (1340–)

The House of
Valois 1350

m.3 Mahaut
of Châtillon
(1293–)

Isabella m. Peter I,
(1313–) Duke of Bourbon
(1311–)

Joan
(1294–1342)
m.
William I,
Count of Hainault
(1286–1337)

Marguerite
Countess of Blois
(1295–1342)
m.
Guy I of Châtillon,
Count of Blois
(c. 1299–1342)

Charles II,
Count of
Alençon
(1297–1346)
m.1
Jeanne de Joigny
(1290–1336)
m.2
Marie de la Cerda
(1319–)

Marie
(1326–1333)

Philip of Valois,
Duke of Orléans
(1336–)

Philip,
the Bold
(1342–)

Joan
(1343–)

Marie
(1344–)

Agnès
(1345–1350)

Marguerite
(1347–)

Isabelle
(1348–)

Prologue

HISTORY'S TRAGEDIES REVEAL great men: but those tragedies are provoked by the mediocre.

At the beginning of the fourteenth century, France was the most powerful, the most densely populated, the most dynamic, and the richest of the Christian kingdoms, whose interventions were most feared, whose arbitration was heeded and whose protection was sought after. And one could have thought that a French century was about to take hold across Europe.

How, then, did it happen that this same France forty years later came to be crushed on the battlefield by a nation it outnumbered fivefold? Why should its noblemen be split up into factions, its bourgeoisie in revolt, its people overwhelmed by excessive taxation, its provinces lawless and plagued by roving gangs engaged in pillaging and crime, all authority flouted, the currency weakened, trade at a standstill, and poverty and violence rife everywhere? Why this collapse? What caused this reversal of fortune?

It was mediocrity. The mediocrity of just a few kings, their vanity and self-importance, their frivolousness in the conduct of their affairs, their inability to attract talented advisors, their nonchalance, their presumptuousness, their failure to draw up grand designs or even to follow those already conceived.

Nothing great can be accomplished politically, and nothing can last, without the presence of men whose brilliance, character and determination inspire, rally and channel the energies of a people.

Everything falls apart when weak protagonists succeed one another at the head of the State. Unity breaks down when greatness falls away.

France is an idea that embraces history, a wilful idea, which from almost exactly the year one thousand onwards had a ruling family, the House of Capet, that passed on its rule so stubbornly from father to son that being the first-born male child of the oldest branch fast became legitimacy enough to reign.

Luck certainly played its part, as though fate had wanted to favour this burgeoning nation with a sturdy dynasty. From the election of the first Capetian up until the death of Philip the Fair, France had only eleven kings, in three and a quarter centuries, and each one left a male heir.

Oh! These sovereigns were not all blessed with genius. But the incapable or the unfortunate would so often be succeeded immediately by a monarch of great stature, or a great minister would stand in for the faltering prince and govern in his place, it was as if by the grace of God the dynasty persisted.

The fledgling France almost perished in the hands of Philip I, a man of minor vice and major incompetence. Then came the corpulent but indefatigable Louis VI, who found on his accession a country under threat just five leagues from Paris, and left it restored to its former glory, stretching as far as the Pyrenees. The undecided, inconsistent Louis VII engaged the kingdom in disastrous adventures overseas; but the Abbot Suger maintained the cohesion and activity of the country in the name of the monarch.

And France's luck, repeatedly, was to have between the end of the twelfth and the beginning of the fourteenth centuries three sovereigns of exceptional talent, each one blessed by a long reign – forty-three years, forty-one years, and twenty-nine years respectively on the throne – so that their main designs could be rendered irreversible. Three men of most different natures and virtues, but all three very much in another league compared to any other king.

Philip II Augustus, master craftsman of history, began to build the unity of his native land literally in stone, building around and beyond the royal possessions. Saint Louis, en-lightened by devotion, began to establish the unity of law, building upon royal justice. Philip the Fair, superior states-man, began to lay down the unity of the state, building on royal administration. Not one of them was overly worried about pleasing the people, but more concerned with being both active and effective. Each one of them had to swallow the bitter draught of unpopularity. But they were more sorely missed after their death than they had been disparaged, mocked or hated while they were alive. And above all, what they had strived for came to be.

A country, a judicial system, a state: the defining foundations of a nation. Under these three supreme artisans of the idea of France, the country emerged from the age of potentiality. Self-aware, France was establishing itself in the western world as an indisputable, and soon to be pre-eminent, reality.

With twenty-two million inhabitants, its borders well guarded, an army that could be called up quickly, feudal lords kept at heel, constituencies perfectly controlled, roads safe, trade flourishing; what other Christian country could compare itself to France, and which would not be envious of it? The people complained of course, feeling controlled by a hand they considered too firm; later they would moan a good deal more when delivered up to hands too soft or too deranged.

With the death of Philip the Fair, suddenly the idea of France cracked. The long succession of good fortune was broken.

The three sons of the Iron King followed each other on the throne without leaving male descent. We have previously told the story of the dramas the court of France went through as its crown was repeatedly auctioned to the most ambitious bidder.

Four kings committed to the grave in the space of fourteen years; more than enough to fill minds with dismay! France was not used to rushing to Rheims quite so often. It was as if the Capetian family tree had been struck by lightning in its very trunk. And to see the crown slip into the hands of the Valois branch, the troubled branch, would reassure no one. Ostentatious, impulsive, enormously presumptuous princes, all form and no substance, the Valois imagined that all they had to do was smile to make the kingdom happy. Their predecessors mistook themselves for France itself. They mistook France for the idea they had of themselves. After the curse of rapid demise came the curse of mediocrity.

The first of the Valois, Philip VI, called 'the found king', in other words the upstart, had a ten-year period during which he might have been able to secure his power base, but then, at the end of this time, his first cousin Edward III of England resolved to open the dynastic feud; he declared himself entitled king of France, which allowed him to rally, in Flanders, Brittany, Saintonge and Aquitaine, all those who had grounds for complaint with the new regime, including leaders of towns and feudal overlords. Faced with a more effective monarch, the Englishman would most probably have continued to dither.

But Philip of Valois was incapable of warding off impending danger and no more capable of defeating it when it came; his fleet was annihilated at the Battle of Sluys because its admiral had been selected for his ignorance of the sea; and the king himself was guilty of letting his cavalry charge trample their own infantry, carnage he saw with his own eyes when roaming through the battlefield the night after the Battle of Crécy.

When Philip the Fair introduced taxes that the people would hold against him, it was in order to build up France's defences. When Philip of Valois demanded even higher taxes, it was simply to pay the price of his defeats.

Over the last five years of his reign, exchange rates were adjusted one hundred and sixty times; the currency lost three quarters of its value. Foodstuffs, ruthlessly taxed, reached astronomic prices. An unprecedented inflation made the towns increasingly angry.

When misfortune seems to circle on cruel wings above a country, everything gets confused, and any natural disaster, let alone one of the worst in history, adds further insult to the injury of human error.

The plague, the Great Plague, having originated far away in Asia, hit France; no other part of Europe was hit harder. The streets of towns became places where the dying lay, the suburbs open graves. Here a quarter of the population succumbed, there a third perished. Entire villages were wiped out, and all that was left of them were dilapidated houses open to the winds on a wasteland of neglect.

Philip of Valois had a son that the plague, alas, was to spare.

France was to sink yet deeper into distress and ruin; this ultimate descent was to be the work of John II, erroneously called the Good.

This lineage of mediocre monarchs came close to cleaving apart the system that since the Middle Ages had trusted nature to produce within one and the same family the bearer of the sovereign's power. Are peoples any more likely to win in the lottery of democracy than in the haphazardness of genetics? Crowds, assemblies, even select councils are no less likely to be in error than nature; and anyway, Providence has always been miserly with greatness.

PART ONE

MISFORTUNES
COME FROM
LONG AGO

I

The Cardinal of Périgord thinks . . .

I SHOULD HAVE BEEN pope. How can I fail to think again and again that thrice I held the tiara in my hands; three times! As much for Benedict XII and for Clement VI as for our current pontiff, it is I who decided, as the battle drew to a close, on whose head the tiara was placed. My friend Petrarch calls me pope-maker, not such a great maker, after all, as it was never upon my own head that the tiara would be set. *Enfin*, it is God's will. Ah! What a strange thing is a conclave! I believe I am the only cardinal alive to have seen three of them. And maybe I will see a fourth, if Innocent is as ill as he makes out.

What are those rooftops yonder? Yes, I recognize them, Chancelade Abbey, in the Valley of Beauronne. The first time, admittedly, I was too young. Thirty-three, the age of Christ crucified: this fact was being whispered all over Avignon as soon as it was known John XXII (Lord, guard his soul in Your holy light; he was my benefactor) would never recover. But the cardinals weren't going to elect the youngest of the brothers in their midst; and it was most reasonable of them, I willingly confess. For this high office one needs the experience I have since been able to gather. Even so, I already possessed enough to know not to fill my head with vainglorious illusions. Whispering untiringly in the Italians' ears that never, ever would French cardinals vote for Jacques Fournier, I contrived to bring their votes upon his head, and get him elected unanimously. 'You have elected an ass!' was the thanks he shouted at us upon hearing his name proclaimed. He knew his own inadequacies. No, not an ass; but no more a lion either. A good general of the Order, who had long exercised authority at the head of the Carthusian monks and expected to be obeyed. But from there to rule over the whole of Christendom, too meticulous, overzealous, constantly prying. Overall, his reformations had done more harm than good. Only with him, one could be absolutely certain that the Holy See would not return to Rome.[1] On that he was solid as a rock, and that was the most important thing.

The second time, during the conclave of 1342 . . . ah! The second time, I would have been in with a fighting chance if only . . . if Philip of Valois hadn't wished to elect his chancellor, the Archbishop of Rouen. We in Périgord have always obeyed the French crown. Furthermore, how could I possibly have continued to be head of the French party if I had dared oppose the king? Besides, Pierre Roger was a great pope, without a shadow of doubt the best I have served. One only has to see what Avignon has become under him, the palace he built, and the influx of men of letters, scholars and artists. And he succeeded in buying Avignon outright. I personally took care of that negotiation with the Queen of Naples; I can safely say that it was my work. Eighty thousand florins, it was nothing, a beggarly sum. Queen Joan had less need for money than for indulgences for all her successive marriages, not to mention her lovers.

They must have put new harnesses on my packhorses by now. My palanquin is far too firm. It is always the way when setting off, always the way. From that moment on, God's vicar ceases to be a tenant, reluctantly seated on an uncertain throne. And the court that we had! It set an example to the world. All the kings were jostling to get in. To be pope, it is not enough to be a priest, one must also be a prince. Clement VI was a great diplomat; he was always glad to hear my advice. Ah! The maritime league that brought together the Latins of the East, the King of Cyprus, the Venetians, the Knights Hospitaller. We cleansed the Greek archipelago of the barbarians overrunning it; and we were going to do more. But then came this ridiculous war between the French and English kings; I wonder if it will ever end; it has prevented us from furthering our grand design, to bring the Church of the East back into the Roman fold. And then there was the plague, and then Clement passed away.

The third time, during the conclave four years ago, my impediment was, ironically, the fact that I was *too* princely. Too *grand seigneur*, too extravagant, it would seem, and we had just had a pope of that very ilk. I, Hélie de Talley-rand, known by my title of Cardinal of Périgord: to think it would have been an insult to the poor to choose me of all people! There are occasions when the Church is seized with a sudden passion for humility, for modesty. Which never does it any good. If we strip ourselves of all ornament, hide our chasubles, sell our golden ciboria and offer the Body of Christ in a two-denier bowl, dress ourselves like yokels, and filthy with it, we are no longer respected by anyone, least of all by the yokels themselves. Indeed! Were we to make ourselves the same as them, why on earth should they honour us? And we end up no longer even respecting ourselves. When you take a stand against this, the staunchly humble stick the gospel under your nose, as if they were the only ones who knew it, and dwell on the nativity, the crib between the ox and the ass, and then it's the carpenter's workshop they harp on about. Be like Our Saviour Jesus. But Our Lord, where is He now, my vain little clerics? Isn't He at the right hand of the Father bathed in His omnipotence? Is He not Christ in majesty enthroned in the light of stars and the music of the heavens? Is He not the king of the world, flanked by legions of seraphs and the blessed? What then is it that entitles you to decree which of these images you should, through your very self, offer to the faithful, that of His fleeting earthly existence or that of His eternal triumph?

Enough. Should I pass through any diocese where I see the bishop rather too willing to disparage God, embracing new ideas, this is what I will preach.

To walk bearing twenty pounds of woven gold, and the mitre, and the crosier, it isn't pleasant every day, especially when one has been doing so for more than thirty years. But it is necessary.

One can attract more souls with honey than with vinegar. When flea-ridden scum address other flea-ridden scum as 'my brothers', it doesn't produce a great deal of effect. Should a king say it, that is different. Bringing people a little self-esteem is the very first act of kindness, of which our Fratricelles and Gyrovagues[2] are unaware. It is precisely because the people are poor, and suffering, and sinners, and destitute, that we must give them reason to believe in the afterlife. Oh yes indeed! With frankincense, gold and music. The Church must offer the faithful a vision of the heavenly kingdom, and every priest, beginning with the pope and his cardinals, should reflect something of the image of the Pantocrator.

It is not such a bad thing after all to talk to myself this way; it helps me find arguments for my forthcoming sermons. Although I prefer to find them when in the company of others. I hope Brunet hasn't forgotten my sugared almonds. Ah! No, there they are. For that matter, he never forgets.

Although I am not a great theologian as so many of my colleagues are – theologians are thick on the ground these days – I do have responsibility for ensuring order and cleanliness in the house of the good Lord upon this earth, and I refuse to reduce the trappings of my position; not even the pope, who knows only too well what he owes me, has dared to force me to do so. He can waste away on his throne, if he so wishes, that is his own business entirely. But I, his nuncio, am careful to preserve the glory of his office.

I know there are some who scoff at my grand purple palanquin, its golden pommels and studs, and my horses upholstered with purple, and the two hundred lances of my escort, and my three lions of Périgord embroidered on my standard and on my sergeants' livery. In this I travel at present. Because of all the noble display, when I enter a town, the people rush up to bow down before me, they come to kiss my mantle. I even make kings kneel (for Thy glory, Lord, for Thy glory).

However, these qualities of leadership were simply not in the air we breathed at the last conclave, and I was made well aware of it. They wanted a man of the people; they wanted a simple soul, a humble being, a plain one. I was barely able to prevent their electing Jean Birel, a holy man – oh! most certainly, a holy man – but who hasn't an ounce of a mind suited for government and who would have been another Pietro da Morrone. I had eloquence sufficient to persuade my fellow conclavists how perilous it would be, given the state Europe found itself in, to elect another Celestine V. Ah! I certainly didn't spare the poor Birel! I spoke so highly of him, demonstrating how his admirable virtues made him unsuited to governing the Church, that he was crushed, and remained so. And I managed to have Étienne Aubert proclaimed Pope, he who was born to poverty, not far from Pompadour, and whose career lacked the lustre that would have spontaneously brought everyone around to his cause.

We are assured that the Holy Spirit lights the way for us to designate the best amongst us; in fact, more often than not we vote to keep out the worst.

Our Holy Father disappoints me. He moans and groans, he hesitates, he makes a decision, he takes it back. Ah! I would run the Church very differently! And furthermore, it was his idea to send the Cardinal Capocci with me, as if it were necessary to have two legates, as if I weren't knowledgeable and experienced enough to get things done on my own! And with what result? We fell out from the start, because I showed him the foolishness of his ways; he played the injured party, my Capocci; he withdrew; and while I race everywhere from Breteuil to Montbazon, from Montbazon to Poitiers, from Poitiers to Bordeaux, from Bordeaux to Périgueux, he merely *writes* everywhere, letters from Paris that undermine my negotiations. Ah! I sincerely hope I won't come across him in Metz before the emperor.

Périgueux, my Périgord. My God, was I seeing them for the last time?

My mother always assumed I would be pope. She made it clear to me on more than one occasion. It was why she made me wear the tonsure from the age of six, and arranged with Clement V, who was most fond of her, that I be enrolled as a papal scholar, and thus become apt to receive benefices. How old was I when she took me to him? 'Lady Brunissande, may your son, whom we most specially bless, display in the place you have chosen for him those very virtues that we should expect from such noble lineage as his, and quickly rise to the highest offices of our Holy Church.' No, no more than seven years old. He made me Canon of Saint-Front; my first cappa magna. Almost fifty years ago now . . . My mother saw me as pope. Was it a dream of maternal ambition, or a prophetic vision as women sometimes have? Alas! I do believe that I shall never be pope.

And yet, and yet, in my birth chart Jupiter is closely tied to the Sun, a beautiful culmination, the sign of domination and of a peaceful reign. No other cardinal has such favourable aspects as I. My configuration was a great deal better than Innocent's on the day of his election. But there you have it, a peacetime reign, a reign in peace; and yet we are at war, amidst turmoil and storm. My stars are too perfect for the times we are living in. Those of Innocent – which speak of difficulties, errors, setbacks – are better suited to this sombre period. God matches men and moments in the world, and calls up popes who correspond to His grand design, such a man for greatness and glory, another for shadows and downfall.

If I hadn't entered the Church, as my mother wished, I would be Count of Périgord, since my elder brother died without issue, the very same year as my first conclave, and the crown I couldn't take on was assumed by my younger brother, Roger-Bernard. Neither pope nor count. Oh well, one has to accept the place where Providence puts us, and try to do the best one can there. I will most probably be one of those men, those leading figures who play a great role in their century, but are forgotten as soon as they die. People have short memories; they remember only the names of kings (Thy will be done, Lord, Thy will be done).

Then again, there is no point in mulling over the same things I have already been through a hundred times. It was seeing the Périgueux of my childhood, and my beloved collegiate Saint-Front, and having to leave them once more, that shook my soul. Let us look rather at this landscape that I am seeing perhaps for the last time. (Thank you, Lord, for granting me this joy.)

But why am I being carried at such breakneck speed? We have already passed Château-l'Évêque; from here to Bourdeilles will take no more than two hours. The day one sets off, one should always break the journey as soon as one can. The goodbyes are trying, the last-minute petitions, the clamour for final benedictions, the forgotten piece of luggage:

one never leaves at the allotted time. But this stage of the journey is indeed brief.

Brunet! Hey! Brunet, my friend; go ahead and order that they ease the pace. Who is leading us in such haste? Is it Cunhac or La Rue? It is really unnecessary to shake my bones so. And then go and tell Monseigneur Archambaud, my nephew, to dismount. I invite him to share my palanquin. Thank you, go.

For the journey from Avignon I had my nephew Robert de Durazzo with me; he was a most agreeable travelling companion. He had the features of my sister Agnes, as well as those of our mother. Why on earth did he want to get himself slain by a gang of English louts at Poitiers, waging the wars of the King of France! Oh! I don't disapprove of his fighting, even if I had to pretend to. Who would have thought that King John would be trounced in such fashion! He lined up thirty thousand men against six thousand, and that very evening was taken prisoner. Ah! The ridiculous prince, the simpleton! When he could have seized victory without ever engaging battle! If only he had accepted the treaty that I bore him as if on a platter of offerings!

Archambaud seems neither as quick-witted nor as brilliant as Robert. He hasn't seen Italy, which frees up youth no end. Most likely it is he who will finally become Count of Périgord, God willing. It will broaden this young man's mind to travel in my company. He has everything to learn from me. Once my orisons are said, I dislike being alone.

2

The Cardinal of Périgord speaks

It is not that I am loath to ride on horseback, Archambaud, nor that old age has made me incapable of doing so. Believe me, I am fully able to cover fifteen leagues on my mount, and I know a fair few younger than I that I would leave far behind. Moreover, as you can see, I always have a palfrey following me, harnessed and saddled in case I should feel the desire or need to mount it. But I have come to realize that a full day cantering in the saddle whets the appetite but not the mind, and leads to heavy eating and drinking rather than clear thinking, of the sort I often need to engage in when I have to inspect, rule or negotiate from the moment I arrive.

Many kings, first and foremost the King of France, would run their states more profitably if they wore their backs out less and exercised their brains for a change, and if they didn't insist on conducting their most important affairs over dinner, at the end of a long journey or after the hunt. Take note that one doesn't travel any slower in a palanquin, as I do, if one has good wadding in the stretcher, and the forethought to change it often. Would you care for a sugared almond, Archambaud? In the little coffer by your side. Well, pass me one would you?

Do you know how many days it took me to travel from Avignon to Breteuil in Normandy, in order to join King John, who was laying a nonsensical siege there? Go on, have a guess? No, my nephew; less than that. We left on the twenty-first of June, the very day of the summer solstice, and none too early at that. Because you know, or rather you don't know what happens upon the departure of a nuncio, or two nuncios, as there were two of us on that occasion. It is customary for the entire College of Cardinals, following Mass, to escort the departing officials for a full league beyond the edge of town; and there is always a crowd following them, with people watching from both sides of the route. And we must advance at procession pace in order to give dignity to the cortège. Then we make a stop, and the cardinals line up in order of precedence and the Nuncio exchanges the kiss of peace with each one in turn. This whole ceremony takes up most of the morning. So we left on the twenty-first of June. And yet we were arrived in Breteuil by the ninth of July. Eighteen days. Niccola Capocci, my co-legate, was unwell. I must say, I had shaken him up no end, the spineless weakling. Never before had he travelled at such a pace. But one week later, the Holy Father had in his hands, delivered by messengers on horseback, the account of my first discussions with the king.

This time, we have no such need to rush. First, even if we are enjoying a mild spell, days are short at this time of year.

I don't recall November in Périgord being so warm, as warm as it is today. What beautiful light we have! But we are in danger of running into a storm as we advance to the north of the kingdom. I plan on taking roughly one month, so that we'll be in Metz by Christmas, God willing. No, I am not in nearly as much of a hurry as last summer; despite all my efforts, that war took place, and King John was taken prisoner.

How could such ill fortune befall us? Oh! You are not the only one to be flabbergasted, my nephew. All Europe felt not inconsiderable surprise and has since been arguing about the root causes and the reasons. The misfortunes of kings come from long ago, and often one takes for an accident of fate what is really the fatality of their very nature. And the bigger the misfortunes, the longer the roots.

This whole business, I know it all in great detail – pull that blanket over towards me a little would you? – and I might say I even expected it. I expected a great reversal of fortune, a humbling, would strike the king down, and thus, alas, bring down his kingdom with it. In Avignon, we in the Church need to know all that may interest the courts. Word of all the scheming, all the plotting, finds its way back up to us. Not a single marriage could be planned that we don't know about before the betrothed themselves. 'In the event of lady such-and-such accepting the hand of lord so-and-so, who is in fact her second cousin, would our Most Holy Father bestow upon us his permission to thus join their two crowns?' Not a single treaty would be negotiated without our receiving visits from agents of both sides; not a single crime committed without the instigator coming to us in search of absolution.

The Church provides kings and princes with their chancellors as well as most of their jurists.

For eighteen years now the houses of France and England have been in open conflict. But what is the cause of this war? King Edward's claims to the French crown most certainly! That is indeed the pretext, a fine legal pretext is how I see it, as we could debate the issue ad infinitum; but it is neither the only, nor the true motive. There are age-old ill-defined borders between Guyenne and neighbouring counties, such as ours to begin with, Périgord, borders suggested by unintelligibly written land charters, where feudal rights overlap; it is difficult for vassal and suzerain to come to an understanding when they are both kings; there is trade rivalry, primarily for wool and cloth, which was the cause of the fight for Flanders; there is the support France has always offered the Scottish, who represent a threat to the English king to the north. War didn't break out for one reason alone, but rather for the twenty that had been smouldering like embers and glowing in the night. When Robert of Artois was banished from the kingdom, with honour lost, he went to England to blow on the firebrands there. The pope at that time, Pierre Roger, that is Clement VI, did everything in his power to prevent this war, and pulled as many strings as he could to counter the malicious warmongers. He preached compromise, inviting concessions on both sides. He too dispatched a papal legate, who was by the way none other than the current pontiff, at the time Cardinal Aubert. He wanted to revive plans for a crusade in which the two kings were to participate, taking their noblemen along with them. It would have been a fine means of diverting their warring urges, with the added hope of reuniting Christendom. Instead of the crusade, we got Crécy. Your father was there; you had word from him of this disaster.

Ah! My nephew, you will see it throughout your life, there is no merit in serving a good king with all one's heart; he leads you to do your duty, and the pains one takes don't matter because one feels that they contribute to the greater good. What is difficult, however, is to serve a bad monarch well . . . or a poor pope. I saw how happy they were, those men at the time of my distant youth who served Philip the Fair. Being loyal to the vainglorious Valois requires far more effort. They are only prepared to heed advice or listen to reason when defeated and trounced.

It was not until after Crécy that Philip VI accepted a truce based on the proposals I had drawn up. Not so bad after all, or so it would seem, as the truce lasted roughly, despite a few local skirmishes, from 1347 to 1354. Seven years of peace. For many, potentially, a time of contentment. But there you are; in our accursed century, no sooner war is over than the plague takes hold.

You were spared in Périgord. Admittedly, my nephew, admittedly, you paid your tribute to the scourge; yes, indeed you have had your share of honour. But it is nothing beside the deaths that occurred in the numerous towns surrounded by populous countryside, like Florence, Avignon or Paris. Did you know that the disease came from China, via India, Tartary and Asia Minor? It spread, or so they say, as far as Arabia. It is indeed an illness for the unbeliever, sent to us to punish Europe for too many sins. From Constantinople and the shores of the Levant, ships transported the plague to the

Greek archipelago, whence it gained the ports of Italy; it crossed the Alps and came to wreak havoc upon us, ahead of countries northward, moving on to England, Holland, Denmark and finishing up in the far north, Norway, Iceland. Have you had both forms of the plague here, the one that kills in three days, with burning fever and coughing up of blood ... the unfortunate ones afflicted said they were already enduring the wrath of hell, and the other, with its more drawn-out agony, five or six days, with the same fever and great carbuncles and pustules appearing in the groin and armpits?

Seven long months we suffered this in Avignon. Retiring every evening we wondered if we would see the light of day. Every morning we would explore our underarms and crotches. To feel the faintest heat in those places was terrifying; people would be seized with dread and stare at you with mad eyes. With each breath we said to ourselves perhaps it will be with this mouthful of air that evil will enter. We never left the presence of a friend without thinking 'will it be him, will it be me, or will it be both of us?' Weavers were dying in their workshops, falling to the ground beneath their stilled looms, silversmiths dead beside their crucibles gone cold, moneychangers rotting under their counters. Children were dying on their dead mother's pallet. And the smell, Archambaud, the stench in Avignon! The streets were lined with corpses.

Half, you hear me well, half the population perished. Between January and April of the year 1348 we counted sixty-two thousand dead. The cemetery that the pope bought in haste was full within just one month; we buried eleven thousand bodies there. People departed this life without servants, and were committed to the grave without priests. The son no longer dared visit his father, nor the father his son. Seven thousand houses closed up! All those who could, fled to their properties in the country.

Clement VI stayed in town along with several cardinals including myself. 'If God wants us, He will take us.' And although he compelled most of the four hundred officers of the papal household to stay on, they were scarcely enough to organize relief operations. The pope handed out wages to all the doctors and physicians; he hired carters and gravediggers, had supplies distributed and prescribed sound enforcement measures to limit contagion. Nobody at that time accused him of recklessly squandering resources. He reprimanded monks and nuns alike who shirked their charitable duties towards the sick and the dying. Ah! I heard a few things during confession: the repentance of the high and mighty, even those of the Church, who came to cleanse their souls of all their sins and seek absolution! Even the big Florentine and Lombard bankers, who confessed through chattering teeth and suddenly discovered their generous selves. And the cardinals' mistresses . . . oh yes, oh yes, my nephew, not all, but a fair few cardinals . . . these beautiful ladies came to hang their jewels on the Holy Virgin's statue! They held handker-chiefs under their noses, impregnated with aromatic essences, and threw away their shoes before entering their homes once more. Those who accused Avignon of impiety, of being the new Babylon, didn't see it during the Great Plague. We were pious all right, I assure you!

What a strange creature is man! When everything goes his

way, when he is blooming with health, when his business is flourishing, his wife fertile and his province in peace, isn't it precisely then that he should constantly lift up his soul unto the Lord and give thanks for such blessings? Not at all; he is quick to forget his creator, proudly flying in the face of all the commandments. However, as soon as misfortune and disaster strike, then he rushes to God. And he prays, and admits his guilt, and he promises to mend his ways. God must be right to burden him, since it is the only way, or so it seems, to bring man back to Him.

I didn't choose my condition. It was my mother, perhaps you know, who designated me when I was a child. If I accepted this fate, it was, I believe, because I have always been grateful to God for all He has given me, especially, the gift of life. I remember, when I was very young, in our ancient castle in Rolphie, Périgueux, where you yourself were born, Archambaud, but which is no longer home to you since your father chose to take up residence in Montignac fifteen years back . . . well there in that huge castle, set amongst the ancient stones of a Roman arena, I remember the wonder that filled me suddenly, the wonder of being alive at the centre of the big, wide world, to breathe, to see the sky; I remember this feeling came to me on summer evenings, when the light is long and I was put to bed well before night-fall. The bees buzzed in a vine that climbed the wall beneath my room, the shadow slowly filled the oval courtyard with its enormous stones; birds flew across the still-light sky and the first star appeared amidst the rose-tinged clouds. I had a great childish need to say thank you, and my mother made it clear to me that it was to God I should give thanks, the

Organizer of all this beauty. And that thought has never left me.

On this very day, all along our route, often I feel a thank you in my heart for this warm weather, for these russet-coloured forests we ride through, for these still-green pastures, for these loyal servants who escort me, for these fine, fattened horses that I see trotting alongside my palanquin. I enjoy watching the faces of men, the movements of the beasts, the shapes of the trees, all this infinite variety that is the infinitely wonderful work of God.

All our doctors who fight over theology in closed class-rooms, and cram themselves full of empty words, and shout bitter abuse at each other, and who bore everyone to death inventing words to name otherwise what we already knew before them, all of these people would be better off con-templating nature, thereby healing their minds. I have the theology that I was taught, handed down from the fathers of the Church; and I have no desire to change it . . .

Did you know that I could have been pope? Yes, my nephew. Many tell me so, as they tell me that I could yet be pope if I outlast Innocent. It will be God's will. I do not complain about what he has made me. I thank him that he put me where he has put me, and that he has kept me on to be the age I am, an age that few attain: fifty-five years, my dear nephew, that is my age, and in as fine form as you see me. That is also the Lord's blessing. Those whom I haven't met for ten years cannot believe their eyes: that I have changed so little in appearance, my cheeks still as rosy, and my beard scarcely whitened.

The idea of being made or not being made pope only

bothers me, in truth – I confide this to you as a relative – when it occurs to me that I could act more wisely than the one who wears the papal tiara. And yet I never had that feeling with Clement VI. He fully understood that the pope should be a monarch above all monarchs, God's right-hand man. On a day when Jean Birel or some other preacher of asceticism accused him of being too extravagant, and too generous to the supplicants, he responded: 'Nobody should leave the prince's company dissatisfied.' And, turning to me, he added between his teeth: 'My predecessors didn't know how to be pope.' And during the Great Plague, as I was saying, he really proved he was the best. I don't believe, in all honesty, that I could have done as much as he, and I thanked God, once again, that He hadn't designated me to lead an ailing Christendom through this ordeal.

Not once did Clement abandon his majesty; and indeed he demonstrated that he was the Holy Father, the father of all Christians, and even father to all others, as when peoples almost everywhere, but especially in the Rhineland provinces of Mainz and Worms, turned against the Jews, accusing them of causing the scourge, he condemned such persecutions. He went further and took the Jews into his own protection; he excommunicated their tormentors; he offered asylum to the hounded Jews and relocated them within his states, where it must be said they re-established prosperity in just a few years.

But why was I going on so long about the plague? Ah, yes! Because of the dire consequences it had for the French crown, and for King John himself. Indeed, towards the end of the epidemic, during the autumn of 1349, one after the other, three queens, or rather two queens and one destined to be . . .

What are you saying, Brunet? Speak louder. Bourdeilles is in sight? Ah, yes, I want to see that. It is a stronghold indeed, and the castle well placed to monitor those approaching from afar.

There it is, Archambaud, the castle my younger brother, your father, gave up to me to thank me for liberating Périgueux. While I haven't succeeded in freeing King John from the hands of the English, at least I saved our county town from their clutches and re-established our authority here.

The English garrison, you remember, didn't want to leave. But the lances that accompany me, and which certain people make mockery of, proved themselves once again most useful. It was enough for me to appear with them, coming from Bordeaux, for the English to pack up and leave without further ado. Two hundred lances and a cardinal, it is quite something to see . . . Yes, most of my servants have been trained for combat, as well as the secretaries and the doctors of law that travel with me. And my faithful Brunet is a knight; I obtained his ennoblement not long ago.

In the end, by giving me Bourdeilles, my brother is strengthening his position. Because with the castellany of Auberoche, near Savignac, and the walled town of Bonneval, near Thenon, that I bought for twenty thousand florins from King Philip VI ten years ago . . . well I say bought, but in reality it offset in part the sums that I had loaned him . . . and with the fortified Abbey of Saint-Astier, of which I am the abbot, and my priories of Fleix and Saint Martin of Bergerac, that now makes six fortresses at a good distance all around

Périgueux which belong to a high representative of the Church, almost as if they belonged to the pope himself. And one would be reluctant to cross swords with him. That is how I keep the peace in our county.

You know Bourdeilles, of course; you have come here often. I haven't been here for a long time. Fancy that, I don't remember that great octagonal keep. It cuts a fine figure indeed. Here we are at last, this is mine, but only to spend one night and one morning, the time it takes to install the governor I have chosen, without knowing when or whether I would return. It is too short a break to enjoy. Well let us thank God for this time that he has given me here. I hope they have prepared us a good supper, travelling gives you quite an appetite, even in a palanquin.

3

Death knocks on every door

I KNEW IT, MY NEPHEW, I told you so, today we shouldn't count on going further than Nontron. And even so we will only arrive there long after evensong, in the black of night. La Rue kept on at me: 'Monseigneur is losing ground, monseigneur will not be satisfied with a stage of just eight leagues ...' Oh yes! La Rue always goes like the clappers. Which is no bad thing at all, as at least with him my escort never dozes off. But I knew that we wouldn't be able to leave Bourdeilles before midday. I had too much to do, too much to decide upon, too many signatures to dispense.

Because I love Bourdeilles, you see; I know that I could be happy there if God had assigned me not only to possess it but also to reside there. He who has just one single, unique and modest possession may enjoy it to the full. He who has vast and multifarious possessions enjoys only the idea of them. Heaven always evens out what we are honoured with.

When you return to Périgord, would you grant me the

favour of revisiting Bourdeilles, Archambaud, to see if the
roofing has been repaired as I requested earlier. And the
fireplace in my room was smoking . . . It is lucky indeed that
the English spared it. You saw Brantôme, we just passed
through: you saw the devastation they caused, a town that
used to be so lovely and so beautifully set on the banks of its
river, razed! The Prince of Wales stopped over for the night
of the ninth of August, according to what I have been told.
And in the morning, before leaving, his coutiliers and valets[3]
set the place ablaze.

I strongly condemn the way they destroy everything, burning, exiling, ruining, as they seem to be doing more and more
often. I can understand men-at-arms will slit each other's
throats in wartime; if God hadn't designated me for the
Church, I should have had to take arms and fight, and I would
have shown no mercy. Pillaging is acceptable: one must give
some of life's pleasures to those men of whom we require
the shedding of blood, including their own. But raiding for
the sole purpose of leaving behind a destitute people, burning thatch and crops to expose them to famine and chill,
consumes me with rage. I am aware of the intention; the
king can no longer draw taxes from a ruined province, and
by destroying his subjects' goods and belongings a monarch
can be weakened. However, this doesn't hold true. If the
Englishman purports to have a claim to France, why would
he lay the country to waste? And does he imagine that he
will ever be accepted, acting this way? Even if he prevails in
the signing of treaties after prevailing in the winning of
battles, does he really think that? He sows seeds of hatred.
He most probably deprives the King of France of money, but

at the same time he supplies this monarch with many souls spurred on by anger and a desire for vengeance. King Edward will inevitably manage to find a few overlords here and there willing to swear allegiance to him in pure self-interest, but the people will be set against him for ever from the time he committed these inexpiable acts of destruction. Take a look at what is happening already; good people don't resent King John for having lost in battle; they take pity on him, calling him John the Brave, or John the Good, when they should be calling him John the Fool, John the Obstinate, John the Incapable. And you will see that they will willingly bleed to pay his ransom.

You ask me why I told you yesterday that the plague had had such a disastrous effect on John and on the kingdom's fate? Ah! My nephew, for its own reasons, death, a handful of deaths in the wrong order, the deaths of women, first of all his own wife, Madame Bonne of Luxembourg, before he became king.

Madame of Luxembourg was taken by the plague in September of the year 1349. She was to have been queen, and would have been a good queen. She was, as you know, the daughter of the King of Bohemia, John the Blind, who so loved France he maintained that Paris was the only court in which one could live nobly; he was a model of chivalry, albeit not entirely of sound mind. Although he could not see a thing, he insisted stubbornly on fighting at Crécy, and in order to do so, had his horse attached to the mounts of the two knights who rode on either side of him. And that was how they flung themselves into the fray. All three of them were found dead, still tied together. Now the King of Bohemia wore three white ostrich feathers on the crest of his helmet. The young Prince of Wales was struck by his noble demise – the prince was then nearly sixteen; it was his first battle – and he did well, notwithstanding King Edward considered it politic to exaggerate the deeds of his son and heir in the matter. The Prince of Wales was thus so hard hit he begged his father to allow him to adopt the same emblem as the late, blind king from that day on. And that is why three white feathers can now be seen on the prince's helmet.

However, the most important thing about Madame Bonne was her brother, Charles of Luxembourg, whose election to the crown of the Holy Roman Empire we, Pope Clement VI and I, actively encouraged. Not that we were unaware that we would have a good deal of trouble with as sly an old fox of a yokel as he . . . Oh! You will soon see for yourself he is nothing like his father; but as we had justifiable fears that France would fall on wretched times, it could only strengthen the country to make its future king the Emperor's brother-in-law. But with the sister dead, the alliance was no more. And though troubles indeed we have had with his Bulla Aurea,[4] he has never given support to France, and that is why I am leaving for Metz.

King John, who was then still Duke of Normandy, showed little despair upon the death of Madame Bonne. They hadn't got along well, with more stormy outbursts between them than harmony and understanding. Although she possessed grace, and he had made her round with child every year, eleven in all, since he had been given to understand that it was time for him to draw closer to his wife in bed, Monseigneur John was more inclined to shower his affections upon his very own cousin, eight years his junior and of rather fine bearing. Charles de La Cerda, who was also known as Monsieur of Spain,[5] as he belonged to a supplanted branch of the throne of Castile.

No sooner was Madame Bonne buried than Duke John withdrew to Fontainebleau in the company of the handsome Charles of Spain, in flight from the epidemic. Oh! This vice is by no means rare, my nephew. I can't understand it and it annoys me no end; it is one of the vices for which I have the least indulgence. We must admit however that it is widespread, even amongst kings, to whom it does a great deal of damage. Look no further than to the case of King Edward II of England, father of the current king. It was sodomy that cost him both his throne and his life. Our King John doesn't flaunt his depravity quite so openly; but he does have many of the characteristics of a sodomite, and he revealed these traits particularly in his consuming passion for this Spanish cousin with the too-pretty face.

Whatever is the matter, Brunet? Why are we stopping? Where are we exactly? In Quinsac. This was not planned. What do these yokels want? Ah! A blessing! We shall not stop my retinue for such a thing; you know perfectly well that I only bless on foot. *In nomine patris . . . lii . . . sancti.* Go, good people, may you be blessed, go in peace. If we had to stop every time I am asked for a benediction, we would be six months in reaching Metz.

So, as I was saying, in September of the year 1349, Madame Bonne died, leaving the heir to the throne a widower. In October came the turn of the Queen of Navarre, Madame Jeanne, whom they used to call Little Joan, the daughter of

Marguerite of Burgundy and perhaps, or perhaps not, Louis Hutin,[6] the one who was kept from succession to the French throne under suspicions of illegitimacy – yes, the child of the Tower of Nesle affair – she too was taken by the plague. Neither was her demise met with many tears. She had been widowed for six years by her cousin Monseigneur Philip III of Évreux, killed fighting against the Moors somewhere in Castile. The crown of Navarre had been ceded by Philip VI upon his accession to remove any claims they could have made to the French throne. That was just part of the bargaining that ensured the throne to the Valois.

I have never approved of this Navarrese arrangement, it was neither valid *de jure* nor *de facto*.[7] But I didn't then have a say! I had just been appointed Bishop of Auxerre. And even if I *had* said something ... It just didn't make legal sense. Navarre was inherited from Louis Hutin's mother. If little Joan wasn't Louis's daughter but that of any old equerry, she would have been no more entitled to Navarre than to France. Therefore, if one acknowledged her right to one of the crowns, then *ipso facto* one substantiated her claims, and her descendants' claims, to the other. One admitted rather too easily that she had been kept from the throne, not for her alleged illegitimacy, but rather because she was a woman, and thanks to the artifice of a law invented by, and for, males.

As for the facts themselves, never would King Philip the Fair have agreed to the severing, for whatever reason, of a part of the kingdom's territory, one that he himself had annexed! One doesn't secure one's throne by sawing off one of its legs. But it was a peaceful arrangement; Joan and Philip of Navarre remained most docile, Joan still under the cloud of her mother's reputation, Philip by virtue of a dignified and thoughtful nature bequeathed him by his father, Louis of Évreux. They seemed to be happy with their rich Norman county and their small Pyrenean kingdom. Things would change when their son Charles, a boisterous young man of eighteen years, began to cast about vindictive looks, filled with condemnation for the failures evident in his family's past, filled with ambition for his own future. 'If my grandmother hadn't been such a brazen whore, if my mother had been born a man, I would be King of France by now.' I heard him say these things with my own ears. It was therefore considered advisable to show some interest in Navarre, the position of which, to the south of the kingdom, had secured the region even more importance since the English had conquered all of Aquitaine. So, as always in such circumstances, a marriage was to be arranged.

Duke John would have happily refrained from contracting a new marital union. But he was destined to be king, and the royal image required him to have a wife at his side, particularly in his case. A wife would prevent him appearing to walk too openly on the arm of Monsieur of Spain. Moreover, how could he better pander to the boisterous Charles of Évreux-Navarre, and how better tie his hands, than by choosing the future Queen of France from amongst his sisters? The eldest, Blanche, was sixteen years old. She was beautiful, and blessed with a sharp wit. Plans were coming along well, the pope's permission had been secured and the wedding was practically announced, even though during the terrible period we were living through, we were all wondering who would still be alive the next week.

Because death continued to knock on every door. At the beginning of December the plague took the Queen of France herself, Madame Joan of Burgundy, the lame one, the bad queen. For her, decorum was scarcely enough to contain the cries of joy, and the people set to dancing in the streets. She was despised; your father must have told you so. She would steal her husband's seal to have people thrown into prison; she would prepare poisoned baths for those guests she took a dislike to. She very nearly killed a bishop that way ... The king occasionally beat her black and blue with torches; but he failed to mend her behaviour. I was most wary of the bad queen. Her suspicious nature filled the court with imaginary enemies. She was quick-tempered, a liar, a horrible person; she was a murderess. Her death seemed to be a delayed manifestation of heavenly justice. What's more, immediately after her demise the scourge began to subside, as if this carnage, come from so far away, had had no other goal but to reach, at last, this harpy.

Of all the men in France, it was the king himself who was the most relieved by the news of her death. One month less one day later, in the cold of January, he remarried. Even as the widower of a universally hated woman, such haste was setting little store by social convention. But the worst was not in the timing. To whom was he wed? To his own son's fiancée, Blanche of Navarre, the slip of a girl with whom he had fallen madly in love upon her first appearance at court. Although the French are happy to turn a blind eye to bawdiness, they hate to see their sovereign let himself be ruled by it in such fashion.

Philip VI was forty years older than the beauty he had

snatched so brutally from the hand of his heir. And he couldn't invoke a tradition of poorly matched princely couples, or the greater good of empires. He was setting a stone of scandal in his own crown, while inflicting upon his successor wounds of ridicule that would assuredly leave terrible scars. Philip and Blanche married in haste near Saint-Germain-en-Laye. John of Normandy of course did not attend. He had never been particularly fond of his father, and his father had offered him little affection in return. Now the son vowed the king nothing but hate.

And one month later, the heir also remarried. He was keen to put the insult he had suffered behind him. He made out to be delighted to settle for Madame of Boulogne, widow of the Duke of Burgundy. It was my venerable brother, the Cardinal Guy of Boulogne, who arranged the marriage in the interests of his family, while not forgetting to further his own interests as well. From a financial perspective, Madame of Boulogne was an excellent match. This should have cleared up the business affairs of the prince, who was a spendthrift second to none, but in fact he was only encouraged to squander yet more.

The new Duchess of Normandy was older than her mother-in-law; the two women produced a strange effect at court receptions, all the more so as any comparison between them – in terms of beauty and bearing – was hardly to the daughter-in-law's advantage. Duke John was greatly vexed by this; he had let himself believe that he loved Madame Blanche of Navarre with all his heart, and he suffered torment seeing her, who had been so wickedly taken from him, next to his father, and being cosseted by him, in public, in the most idiotic fashion. This didn't help nocturnal matters between Duke John and Madame of Boulogne; rather, the Duke was pushed further into the arms of Monsieur of Spain. Extravagance became his revenge. One would have thought that he was buying back his honour, not vaingloriously wasting money.

Besides, after the months of terror and grief we had endured, everybody was spending like mad. Especially in Paris. In and around the court was folly after the plague. They maintained that creating an abundance of luxury would provide work for the people. And yet we were hard put to see the effects in the hovels and the garrets. Between the princes with their rising debts and the poverty-stricken common people, there were the fixers and dealers who siphoned off the profit, big merchants like the Marcels, who deal in drapery, silks and other finery, and made themselves handsomely rich. Fashion became extravagant; Duke John, although he was already thirty-one years old, could be seen, together with Monsieur of Spain, wearing laced tunics so short his buttocks showed. People laughed at them no sooner had they passed by.

Madame Blanche of Navarre had been made queen sooner than originally planned; her reign was shorter than expected. Philip of Valois had come through both the war and the plague unscathed; he wasn't to withstand love. All the years he was tied to a cantankerous, lame wife, he remained a handsome man, a little overweight but always robust, active, handling weaponry, riding fast, hunting long and hard. Six months of gallant prowess with his new, beautiful wife would undo him. It was obsession; it was frenzy. He would leave his bed with the thought uppermost in his mind of getting back in as soon as he could. He would ask his physicians for potions that would make him indefatigable in the act. What is it? Are you surprised? But of course, my nephew; despite being of the Church, or rather because we are of the Church, we need to be informed of such things, above all when they touch on the person of a king.

Madame Blanche was subjected to this obsession, the king's passion was proved to her constantly; she was consenting, worried and flattered all at the same time. The king took to proclaiming publicly and with great pride that she wearied sooner than he. He lost weight. He lost interest in governing. Each week aged him a year. He died on the twenty-second of August 1350, at the age of fifty-seven, after a twenty-two-year reign.

Beneath his splendid exterior, this sovereign, to whom I was faithful . . . he was King of France, wasn't he? And moreover I couldn't forget that he was the one who had asked for the galero[8] on my behalf . . . this monarch had been a pitiful leader and a disastrous financier. He had lost Calais, he had lost Aquitaine; he left Brittany in a state of revolt and a good many of the kingdom's strongholds in doubt or in ruin. Above all he had lost prestige. I'm afraid so! Although he had bought Dauphiny.[9] Nobody can be a perpetual catastrophe. It was I, it is good that you should know, who secured the deal, two years before Crécy. The Dauphin Humbert was so far in debt that he didn't know whom to borrow from to pay back whomever. I will tell you the story in detail another day, if you are interested, how I went about getting the eldest son of France to wear the dauphin's crown and bring Viennois back into the kingdom's fold. In this way I can safely say, without wishing to boast, that I served France better than

King Philip VI, as he only knew how to make it smaller, while I successfully expanded its borders.

Six years already! It has been six years since King Philip died and Monseigneur Duke John became King John II! Yet it still feels as if we are at the beginning of his reign, these six years have gone so quickly. Is it because our new king has achieved little one could deem noteworthy, or rather that the more one ages, the faster time seems to fly? At twenty, each month, each week, enriched with the new, seems to last for ever. You will see, Archambaud, when you get to be my age, if you do, that is, as I wish you may with all my heart, one turns around and one says to oneself: 'How is it possible? Already another year gone by? How could it go so quickly!' Perhaps it is because one takes up too many moments remembering, reliving times past.

And there it is; night has fallen. I knew we would be arriving at Nontron in the black of night.

Brunet! Brunet! Tomorrow we must leave before dawn, we have a long day's travelling ahead of us, without the luxury of making any stops. So, everyone must be stocked up with provisions and we must be harnessed up in time. Who has gone ahead to Limoges to announce my arrival? Armand de Guillermis; that's good. I send my knights on each one in turn to take care of my lodgings and the preparations for my welcome, one or two days in advance, no more. Just enough for the people to gather around eagerly, but not enough for the plaintiffs of the diocese to rush up and overwhelm me with their petitions for the king. The cardinal? Ah! We only found out the day before; alas, he is already gone. Otherwise, my nephew, I would be a veritable travelling tribunal.

4

The Cardinal and the Stars

HEY! MY NEPHEW, I can see that you are taking to my palanquin and to the meals I am served here. And to my company, and to my company, of course. Do take some of this *confit de canard* that was given to us in Nontron. It is the town's speciality. I don't know how my chef managed to keep it warm for us . . .

Brunet! Brunet, you will tell my chef how much I appreciate his keeping the dishes warm; he prepares them for me beforehand, for the journey; he is most skilful. Ah! He has hot coals in his cart . . . No, no, I don't mind being served the same food twice in a row, as long as I enjoyed it the first time. And I had found the *confit* quite delicious yesterday evening. Let us thank God that he provides for us so plentifully.

The wine is, admittedly, rather too young and thin. This is neither the Sainte-Foy nor the Bergerac, to which you are accustomed, Archambaud. Indeed, nor is it the wine of Saint-Émilion and Lussac, both of which are a delight, but which now all leave Libourne in heavily-loaded ships headed for England. French palates are not allowed them any more.

Isn't it true, Brunet, that this has nothing on a tumbler of Bergerac? The knight Aymar Brunet is from Bergerac, and finds nothing in the world better than what is grown on home soil. I mock him a little about that.

This morning, the Papal Secretary Dom Francesco Calvo is keeping me company. I want him to refresh my memory on all the matters I will have to deal with in Limoges. We will be staying there two full days, maybe three. In any case, unless I am obliged to do so by some urgent business or express summons, I avoid travelling on Sundays. I want my escort to be able to attend church services and take some rest.

Ah! I can't hide the fact that I am excited at the idea of seeing Limoges once more! It was my very first bishopric. I was ... I was ... I was younger than you are now, Archambaud; I was twenty-three years old. And I treat you like a youngster! It is a failing that comes with age, to treat youth as if it were still childhood, forgetting what one was oneself at the same age. You will have to correct me, my nephew, when you see me veering off along this path. Bishop! My first mitre! I was most proud of it, and I was soon to commit the sin of pride because of it. It was said of course that I owed my seat to favour, just as I had my first benefices, which were bestowed upon me by Clement V because he held my mother in high esteem; now it was said John XXII obtained the bishopric for me because our families had matched my last sister, your aunt Aremburge, to his grand-nephew, Jacques de la Vie. And to be totally honest, there was some truth to it. Being the pope's nephew is a happy accident, but the benefit of it doesn't last unless it be combined with nobility such as ours. Your uncle La Vie was a good man.

As for me, as young as I was, I do not believe I am remembered as a bad bishop in Limoges, or anywhere else. When I see so many hoary diocesans who know neither how to keep their flock nor their clergy in check, and who overwhelm us with their grievances and their legal proceedings, I tell myself that I did the job rather well, and without too much trouble. I had good vicars – here, pour me some more of that wine would you; I need to wash down the *confit* – and I left it up to those good vicars to govern. I ordered them never to disturb me except for the most serious matters, for which I was respected, and even a little feared. This arrangement afforded me the luxury of continuing my studies. I was already most knowledgeable in canon law; I called the finest professors to my residence to enable me to perfect my mastery of civil law. They came up from Toulouse, where I was awarded my degree, and which is as good a university as Paris, as densely populated with learned scholars. By way of recognition, I have decided ... I wanted to let you know, my nephew, as I now have the opportunity; this is recorded in my last will and testament, in case I am not able to accomplish it during my lifetime. I have decided to found, in Toulouse, a college for poor Périgordian schoolchildren. Do take that hand towel, Archambaud, and dry your fingers.

It was also in Limoges that I began my studies in astrology. For this reason: the two sciences most necessary for the exercise of authority in government are indeed the science of law and the science of the stars. The former teaches us the laws that govern the relationships between men and the

obligations they have towards each other, or with the kingdom, or with the Church, while the latter gives us knowledge
of the laws that govern the relationships men have with
Providence. The law and astrology; the laws of the earth, the
laws of the heavens. I say that there is no denying it. God
brings each of us into the world at the hour He so wishes, and
this exact time is written on the celestial clock, which by His
good grace, He has allowed us to read.

I know there are certain believers, wretched men, who
deride astrology as a science because it abounds in charlatans
and peddlers of lies. But that has always been the way; the old
books tell us that paltry fortune-tellers and false wise men,
hawking their predictions, were denounced by the ancient
Romans and by the other ancient civilizations; that never
stopped them seeking out the art of the good and the just
observers of the celestial sphere, who often practised their
skills in sacred places. Just so, it is not thought wise to close
down all the churches because there exist simoniacal or
intemperate priests.

I am so pleased to see that you share my opinions on this
matter. It is the humble attitude proper for the Christian
before the decrees of Our Lord, the Creator of all things, who
stands behind the stars.

You would like to ... but of course, my nephew, I will
be delighted to do yours. Do you know your time of birth?
Ah! That you will need to find out; send someone to your
mother and ask her to give you the exact time of your first
cry. Mothers remember such things.

As far as I am concerned, I have never received anything
but praise for my practice of astral science. It enabled me to

give useful advice to those princes who deigned to listen to me, and also to know the nature of any man I found myself up against and to be wary of those whose fate was adverse to mine. Thus I knew from the beginning that Capocci would be an opponent in all things, and I have always distrusted him. It is the stars that have guided me to the successful completion of a great many negotiations, and the making of as many favourable arrangements, such as the match for my sister in Durazzo, or the felicitous marriage of Louis of Sicily; and the grateful beneficiaries swelled my fortune accordingly. But first of all, it was to John XXII (may God preserve him; he was my benefactor) that this science was of the most invaluable service. Because Pope John himself was a great alchemist and astrologian; knowing of my devotion to the same art, and the distinction I had attained in it, impelled him to show increased favour for myself and inspired him to listen to the wishes of the King of France and make me cardinal at the age of thirty, which is a most unusual thing. And so I went to Avignon to receive my galero. You know how such a thing takes place. Don't you?

The pope gives a grand banquet for the entrance of the new recruit to the Curia, to which he invites all the cardinals. At the end of the meal, the pope sits on his throne, poses the galero upon the head of the new cardinal, who remains kneeling and kisses first his foot, then his lips. I was too young for John XXII ... he was eighty-seven at that time ... to call me *venerabilis frater*; so he chose to address me with a *dilectus filius*. And before inviting me to stand up, he whispered in my ear: 'Do you know how much your galero cost me? Six pounds, seven sols and ten deniers.' It was in the way of that pontiff to humble you, precisely at that moment when you felt the most proud, always having a word of mockery for delusions of grandeur. Of all the days of my life there is not a single one of which I have kept a sharper memory. The Holy Father, all withered and wrinkled under his white zucchetto, which hugged his cheeks ... It was the fourteenth of July of the year 1331 ...

Brunet! Have them stop my palanquin! I am going to stretch my legs a little, with my nephew, while they brush off these crumbs. This is a flat stretch, and we are graced with a ray of sunlight, you will pick us up further on. Only twelve will escort me; I would like a little peace ... Hail, Master Vigier ... hail, Volnerio ... hail, du Bousquet ... may the peace of God be with you all, my sons, my good servants.

5

The Beginnings of the King
they call The Good

KING JOHN'S BIRTH chart? Indeed, I know it; I have turned my attention to it on many an occasion . . . Had I foreseen it? Of course, I had foreseen everything; that is why I worked so hard to prevent this war, knowing full well that it would be disastrous for him, and consequently disastrous for France. But try and get a man to understand reason, particularly a king whose stars act as a barrier precisely to understanding and to reason itself!

At birth, King John II saw Saturn reach its highest point in the constellation of Aries, at the centre of the heavens. This is a dire configuration for a king, one that foretells deposed sovereigns, reigns that come to a natural end all too hastily or that tragic events cut short. Add to that, his moon rising in the sign of Cancer, itself lunar by nature, thus marking an overly feminine disposition. Finally, and to give you just the most striking features, the traits that are most obvious to any astrologer, there is a problematic grouping of the Sun, Mercury and Mars which are closely linked in Taurus. There you have a most threatening sky making up an unbalanced man, masculine and even of a thickset appearance, but for whom all that should be virile is as if castrated, up to and including understanding; at the same time a brutal and violent man, possessed by dreams and secret fears that provoke sudden and murderous fits of rage, incapable of listening to advice or of the slightest self-control, hiding his weaknesses under an exterior of grand ostentation; yet at the core, a fool, the exact opposite of a conqueror, his soul the opposite of the soul of a commander.

For certain people it would seem that defeat was their main preoccupation, they have a secret craving for it, and will not rest until they have found it. Defeat pleases the depths of their souls, the spleen of failure is their favourite beverage, as the mead of victory is to others; they long for subordination, and nothing suits them better than to contemplate themselves in a state of imposed submission. It is a great misfortune when such predispositions hang over the head of a king from the moment of his birth.

So long as John II had been Monseigneur of Normandy, living under the thumb of a father he didn't care for, he had seemed an acceptable prince, and the ignorant believed his reign would be a happy one. For that matter, the people and even the court, forever inclined to succumb to delusion, always expect the new king to be better than his predecessor, as if novelty intrinsically carried miraculous virtue. No sooner did John have the sceptre in his hands than he began to show his true colours; the stars and his nature, in their unfortunate alliance, were bent on defeat.

He had only been king ten days when Monsieur of Spain, in the month of August 1350, was defeated at sea, off the coast of Winchelsea, by King Edward III. Charles of Spain was in command of a Castilian fleet, and our Sire John was not responsible for the expedition. However, since the victor was from England, and the vanquished a very close friend of the King of France, it was a poor start for the French monarch.

The coronation took place at the end of September. By then Monsieur of Spain had returned, and in Rheims they showed the vanquished man a good deal of sympathy, thus consoling him in his defeat.

In November the constable of France, Raoul II of Brienne, Count of Eu, returned to France. Though he had been taken prisoner four years earlier by King Edward, as a captive he had been free to do almost as he pleased, even to travel between the two countries, since he was involved in the negotiations for a peace treaty. We had been working very hard for this in Avignon and I myself had corresponded with the constable. On this occasion he had returned in order to raise money for his ransom payment. I certainly shouldn't need to tell you that Raoul of Brienne was a high-ranking, great and powerful character, and one might say the second in command in the kingdom. He had taken over his father Raoul V's charge, upon the latter's death in a tournament. He held vast fiefs in Normandy, others in Touraine, including Bourgueil and Chinon, others in Burgundy, still others in Artois. He possessed land in England and in Ireland, but that was for the time being confiscated; he owned other land in the Barony of Vaud. He was the cousin by marriage of Count Amadeus of Savoy. Such a man one treats with a certain respect, when one has only just sat oneself upon the throne, wouldn't you think, Archambaud? Well, our John II, after hurling furious but wholly unclear reproaches upon Raoul on the night of his arrival, immediately ordered that he be taken prisoner. And on the morning of the next day but one, had him decapitated, without trial . . . No; no grounds were given. We weren't able to find out anything more, even at the Curia, no more than you heard in Périgueux. And yet, this was not for want of effort; certainly we went to great lengths to shed some light on the affair, believe me! To explain away this hasty execution, King John claimed to have in his possession written proof of the constable's treachery; but he never produced it, never. Not even the pope, who urged him, in his own interests, to reveal the famous proof, was offered anything but stubborn silence.

It was then that the whispering began in all the courts of Europe, assumptions were made . . . The talk was of love letters that had fallen into the hands of the king upon the death of Madame Bonne of Luxembourg, love letters from the constable, to which his queen evidently had responded in kind . . . Ah! You too have heard this fable! A strange liaison indeed, and one where it is difficult to see any opportunity, in any event, for it to have taken a criminal turn, between a woman who was forever pregnant and a man who was almost constantly in jail for four long years! Perhaps there were some painful things for the king to read in the letters of Messire of Brienne; but if this were true, they would certainly concern his own behaviour and not that of Madame Bonne

... No, nothing of any substance could have explained the execution, nothing except the new king's murderous and hateful nature, somewhat akin to that of his mother, the lame and wicked one. The real motive was revealed shortly after, when the constable's charge was passed on ... you well know to whom ... indeed! To Monsieur of Spain, with part of the deceased's estate ... all the land and possessions of Raoul of Brienne were shared out amongst the king's closest friends and allies. That is when Count John of Artois obtained the County of Eu, a large part of the estate.

Such largesse makes fewer friends than it creates enemies. Messire of Brienne had any number of friends and relatives, vassals and servants; he had a whole circle of supporters who had been sincerely attached to him and instantly became a network of malcontents when he was beheaded. In addition to them, in the ranks of the alienated, we should include those of the royal entourage who received neither bread nor crumb of the spoils, and became bitter and jealous.

Ah! We have a good view from here of Châlus and its two castles. How beautifully those two tall keeps match each other, separated by such a slender stream! And the countryside is pleasant on the eye, under these fast-moving clouds ...

La Rue! La Rue, if I am not mistaken; it was before the tower on the right, up on the hill, that Messire Richard the Lionheart was struck most sorely by an arrow that took his life? It is nothing new for the people of our country to be attacked by the Englishman, and to defend themselves ...

No, La Rue, I am not at all tired; I am only stopping to admire the view ... And I most certainly do walk at a brisk pace! I will walk on a little further, and my palanquin will pick me up ahead. We are in no particular hurry. If my memory serves me well there are fewer than nine leagues between Châlus and Limoges. Three and a half hours will suffice without straining the horses . . . So be it! Four hours. Let me enjoy these last days of fine weather that God has granted us. I will be long enough closed up behind my curtains when the rain comes . . .

So, I was telling you, Archambaud, how King John managed to make his first circle of enemies, at the heart of the kingdom itself. He resolved to make some friends, loyal supporters, men entirely devoted to him, tied to him by a new bond, who would help him in war as in peace, and who would cover his reign with glory. And to this end, at the dawn of the following year, he founded the Order of the Star, to which he gave the purpose of the raising of chivalry, the heightening of honour. This great novelty was, in fact, nothing new, as King Edward of England had already established the Garter. But King John laughed at this Order named for a trophy around a woman's thigh. The Star would be something else altogether, quite other. There you can take note of one of John's most predictable personality traits. He only knows how to copy, while always pretending to have thought it up himself.

Five hundred knights, no less, that were to swear on the Holy Scriptures to never retreat from the enemy, not one foot, and never to give themselves up. So much of the sublime needed to be signalled by visible signs. As far as ostentation was concerned, John II used all the means at his disposal; and funds began to leak from his already-compromised Treasury, like wine from a barrel full of holes. To lodge the Order he had the house of Saint-Ouen fitted out. From then on, the house was known only as the Noble House, a grand house fretted and sculpted, incrusted with ivory and other precious substances, filled with magnificent furniture. I myself have never seen the Noble House, but it has been described to me. Its walls are, or rather *were*, hung with gold and silver cloth, or with velvet sewn with gleaming stars and golden fleurs-de-lis. For each of his knights the king had made a coat of arms, white silk, a surcoat half white, half vermilion, a vermilion hood with a golden clasp in the shape of a star. They also received a white banner embroidered with stars, and all were presented with a heavy ring of gold and enamel, to show that they were all as if married to the king ... which brought smiles to some lips. Five hundred clasps, five hundred banners, five hundred rings; just figure the expense! It would seem that the king designed and discussed each piece of this glorious paraphernalia. He really believed in his Order of the Star! With as mediocre stars as his, he would have been better advised to choose a different emblem altogether.

Once a year, according to the rule that he had himself drawn up, all knights were to meet up at a great feast, where each by turn would tell the story of his heroic deeds and the feats of arms he had accomplished over the year; two scribes would keep a register and chronicle. The Round Table would live again, and King John's renown would surpass that of King Arthur of Britain! He developed projects as great as they were vague. There was once again talk of crusades ...

The first Assembly of the Star, convened on the Day of the Kings, 1352, was somewhat disappointing. The valiant knights-to-be didn't have many great exploits to tell of. Time had been too short for there to be Janissaries[10] cleaved in two, from the helmet down to the tree of their saddles, or virgins delivered from barbaric jails; these would be tales for another year. The two scribes commissioned to take down the Order's chronicles in 1352 had little use for ink, unless of course the drunkenness and debauchery manifested within the Noble House counted as an exploit. Because the Noble House was the scene of the biggest drinking binge seen in France since Dagobert. The knights in their white and vermilion threw themselves upon the feast with great abandon; before dessert they were shouting, singing, screaming, blind drunk, only leaving the table to piss or throw up, then back to pick from the dishes, challenge each other fervently as to who could empty the most flagons, deserving only to be appointed Knights of Revelry. The fine golden dishes, beautifully worked for them, were crumpled or broken; they threw them across the tables like children, or crushed them with their fists. The fine open-worked and embellished furniture was reduced to debris. Some in their drunken state seemed to believe that they were already at war, as they went about plundering the very house they were in. This was how the gold and silver cloth drapery hung on the walls was stolen.

And yet further disaster, on that same day the English seized the Citadel of Guines, which was delivered treacherously to them while the captain commanding that fortress was to be found feasting at Saint-Ouen.

The king was greatly vexed by all this and began to wallow in the idea that his greatest schemes were, by some terrible twist of fate, doomed to failure.

Shortly after came the first battle in which the Knights of

the Star would take part, not in the far reaches of some imagined Orient, but in a wood in Lower Brittany. Fifteen of them, to prove that they were capable of great deeds other than drinking, respected their pledge to never back off and never retreat; and rather than pulling out while they could, as any sensible person would have done, they let themselves be encircled by an enemy whose numbers left them not the slightest chance. Not one of them returned to tell the tale. But the relatives of the dead knights didn't hesitate to condemn the oath, and called into question the new king's mental state, saying he must have a most disturbed mind to impose upon his bannerets such an insane oath, and if all of them were to abide by it, then he would soon be very much alone at his assembly in the Noble House . . .

Ah! Here comes my palanquin . . . Would you prefer to return to the saddle? I think I will sleep a little so as to be refreshed upon arrival . . . But you understand now, Archambaud, why the Order of the Star rapidly came to almost nothing, and was spoken of less and less as the years went by.

6

The Beginnings of the King
they call The Bad

HAVE YOU NOTICED, my nephew, that wherever we stop for the night, be it at Limoges, Nontron or elsewhere, everyone asks us for news of the King of Navarre, as if our kingdom's fate depended on this prince? In truth, the situation in which we find ourselves is a strange one indeed. The King of Navarre is being held prisoner in an Artois castle by his cousin the King of France. The King of France is in turn being held prisoner in a Bordeaux house by *his* cousin, the heir to the throne of England. The dauphin, heir to the French throne, struggles with his restless bourgeoisie and his remonstrating Estates-General in Paris. And yet it is the King of Navarre that everyone seems to be worrying about. You heard the bishop himself say: 'They said that the dauphin was a great friend of Monseigneur of Navarre. Isn't he going to release him?' Good Lord! I sincerely hope not. This young man has been well advised to do nothing of the sort thus far. And I am concerned about that attempted escape that the knights of the Navarre clan put together to deliver their leader. It failed; of that we should be thankful. But there is good reason to believe that they will soon try again.

Yes, yes, I learned a good many things during our stay in Limoges. And I am preparing to write to the pope about them as soon as we arrive in La Péruse this evening. If it was pure stupidity on the part of King John to lock up his Monseigneur of Navarre, it would be more pure stupidity on the part of the dauphin to release him today. I know of no greater meddler than the Charles they call the Bad; and they certainly couldn't have done better if they'd tried, King John and he, through their feud, to throw France into its current misfortune. Do you know where his name comes from? From the very first months of his reign. He lost no time at all in earning it.

His mother, Louis Hutin's daughter, died, as I was telling you the other day, during the autumn of '49. In the summer of 1350 Charles went to be crowned in his capital city of Pamplona, where he had never once set foot in all the eighteen years since his birth in Évreux. Wanting to make himself known, he travelled the length and breadth of his State, which required no great travelling, then he went to visit his neighbours and relations, his brother-in-law, the Count of Foix and of Béarn, the one who calls himself Phoebus, and his other brother-in-law, the King of Aragon, Peter the Ceremonious, and also the King of Castile.

Now, one day, back in Pamplona, he was crossing a bridge on horseback when he met a delegation of Navarrese noblemen who had come to the city to bring him their grievances, as he had allowed their rights and privileges to be flouted. When Charles refused to hear them, things began to get a little heated; the new king then ordered his soldiers to seize those who were shouting closest to him, and, saying that one must be prompt in dealing out punishment if one wishes to command respect, further ordered that they be hanged immediately on the trees nearby.

I have noticed that when a prince resorts to capital punishment too quickly he is often giving in to fits of panic. In this Charles was no exception, as I believe his words are braver than his deeds. These brutal hangings would plunge Navarre into mourning, and soon by common consent he had earned the right to be called *el Malo* by his subjects, the Bad. He didn't delay in moving away from his kingdom, whose government he left to his youngest brother Louis, only fifteen at the time, preferring to return to the bustle of the French court accompanied by his other brother Philip.

So, you may say, how can the Navarrese contingent have become so powerful and thick on the ground when in Navarre itself the king is widely hated, and even opposed by many of the nobility? Heh! My nephew, it is because this contingent is mostly made up of Norman knights from the county of Évreux. And what really makes Charles of Navarre dangerous for the French crown, more than his possessions in the south of the kingdom, are the lands he holds, or that he held, near Paris, such as the seigniories of Mantes, Pacy, Meulan, or Nonancourt, which command access to the capital from the westerly quarter of the country.

That danger King John understood well, or was made to understand; and for once in his life he showed proof of some common sense, endeavouring to make amends and reach an understanding with his Navarrese cousin. By which bond could he best tie his cousin's hands? By a marriage. And what marriage could one offer him that would bind him to the throne as tightly as the union that had, six months long, made his sister Blanche Queen of France? Why, marriage with the eldest of the daughters of the king himself, little Joan of Valois. She was only eight years old, but it was a match worth the wait before it could be consummated. For that matter, Charles of Navarre had no shortage of lady friends to help him bide his time. Amongst others a certain demoiselle[11] Gracieuse ... yes, that is her name, or the one she answers to ... The bride, little Joan of Valois, was herself already a widow, as she had been married once before, at the age of three, to a relative of her mother's that God wasn't long in taking back.

In Avignon, we looked favourably upon this betrothal, which seemed to us a strong enough bond to secure peace. This was because the contract resolved all the outstanding business between the two branches of the French royal family. First of all, the matter of the Count of Angoulême, betrothed for such a long time already to Charles's mother, in exchange for his relinquishing the counties of Brie and Champagne, and exchanging them in turn for Pontoise and Beaumont, but it was an arrangement that was never executed. In the new agreement, the initial agreement was reverted to; Navarre would get Angoumois as well as several major strongholds and castellanies[12] that would make up the dowry. King John made a forthright show of his own power in showering his future son-in-law with gifts. 'You shall have this, it is my will; I shall give you that, it is my word ...'

Navarre joked in intimate circles about his new relationship with King John. 'We were cousins by birth; at one time we were going to be brothers-in-law, but as his father married my sister instead, I ended up being his uncle; and now I am to become his son-in-law.' But while negotiating the contract, he proved most effective in expanding his prize. No particular contribution was asked of him, beyond an advance: one hundred thousand écus[13] that were owed by King John to Parisian merchants, and were by the good grace of Charles to be paid back. However, he did not have the necessary liquid assets, either; the sum was procured for him from Flemish bankers, with whom he consented to leave some of his jewellery as guarantee. It was an easier thing to do for the king's son-in-law than for the king himself . . .

It was during this transaction, I realize now, that Navarre must have made contact with the Prevost Marcel . . . about whom I should also write to the pope, to alert his holiness to the man's scheming, which at present is something of a cause for concern. But that is another matter . . .

The sum of one hundred thousand écus was acknowledged in the marriage contract as being due to Navarre; it was to be paid to him in instalments, beginning straight away. Furthermore, he was made knight of the Order of the Star, and was even led to believe that he might become constable, though he was barely twenty years old. The marriage was celebrated in great style and jubilation.

And yet this exuberant friendship between the king and his son-in-law was soon to be soured and the two set at odds. Who caused this falling out? The other Charles, Monsieur of Spain, the handsome La Cerda, inevitably jealous of the favour surrounding Navarre, and worried to see the new star rising so high in the court's firmament. Charles of Navarre has a failing that many young men share ... and I strongly entreat you to guard against it, Archambaud ... which consists in talking too much when fortune smiles on them; a demon seems to make them say wicked words that reveal far too much. La Cerda made sure he told King John of his son-in-law's dubious character traits, spicing them up with his very own sauce. 'He taunts you, my good sire; he thinks he can say exactly what he likes. You can no longer tolerate such offences to your majesty; and if you do put up with them, it is I who will not bear them, for your sake.' He would drip poison into the king's ear day after day. Navarre had said this, Navarre had done that; Navarre was drawing too close to the dauphin; Navarre was scheming with such and such an officer of the Great Council. No man is quicker than King John to fall for a bad idea about somebody else; nor more begrudging to abandon it. He is both gullible and stubborn, all at the same time. Nothing is easier than inventing enemies for him.

Soon he had the role of Lieutenant General of Languedoc, one of his gifts to Charles of Navarre, withdrawn. To whose benefit? To that of Charles of Spain. Then the high office of constable, left vacant since the beheading of Raoul of Brienne, was at long last to be filled: it was handed not to Charles of Navarre, but to Charles of Spain. Of the one hundred thousand écus that he should have been paid back, Navarre saw not a single one, while the king's avowed friend was showered with presents and benefits. Lastly, lastly, the County of Angoulême, in spite of all the arrangements, was given to Monsieur of Spain, Navarre once more having to make do with a vague promise of a future trade-off.

Thus, where at first there was but coolness between Charles the Bad and Charles of Spain, there grew up abhorrence, and, soon after, open hatred. It was all too easy for Monsieur of Spain to point to Navarre's behaviour and say to the king: 'You see how true were my words, my good sire! Your son-in-law, whose evil plans I have unravelled, is taking a stand against your wishes. He takes it out on me, as he can see that I serve you only too well.'

Other times, when he was at the height of favour, he feigned a desire to go into exile from the court should the Navarrese brothers continue to speak ill of him. He spoke like a mistress: 'I will leave for a deserted region, far from your kingdom, to live on the memory of the love that you have shown me. Or to die there! Because far from you, my soul will leave my body.' They saw the king shed tears for his constable's most strange devotion.

And as King John's head was in a whirl with the Spaniard, and as he could only see the world through his eyes, he was most persistent in making an implacable enemy of the cousin that he had chosen as son-in-law in order to secure himself an ally.

I have already said this: a greater fool than this king is not to be found, nor one more injurious to himself ... this would be of little harm if at the same time it had not been so damaging for his kingdom.

The court buzzed with nothing other than this quarrel. The queen, a deserted wife, huddled up to Madame of Spain ... for the constable was married, a marriage of appearances, to the king's cousin, Madame of Blois.

The conseillers du roi, who were the king's advisors, all

acted as if they adored their lord and master, although they were very much divided by the feud, some thinking it best to tie their fate to the constable's star, others to gamble on the ability of the son-in-law to strike back. And the muffled struggles that divided them were all the more intense in that the king, despite wanting to appear to be the only one to make decisions, had always left the most important decisions to his entourage.

You see, my dear nephew, scheming takes place around all kings. But conspiracies and plots only happen around the weak kings, or around those whom a vice or the effects of illness have weakened. I would have liked to see them conspiring around Philip the Fair! Nobody dreamed of doing such a thing, nobody would have dared. This does not mean that strong kings are safe from conspiracies; but in that case, there have to be real traitors. Whereas around weak princes, it becomes natural even for honest people to become conspirators themselves.

The day before Christmas, 1354, in a Parisian town house, such strong words and insults were being bandied about between Charles of Spain and Philip of Navarre, brother of the king's son-in-law, that the latter drew his dagger and came this close, if he hadn't been surrounded, to stabbing the constable! The constable feigned laughter, and shouted at the young Navarre that he would have shown himself rather less threatening if there hadn't been so many others around to hold him back. Philip is nowhere near as astute as his elder brother, but he is more impassioned in combat. No sooner had he been pulled from the room than he proffered the threat that he would exact prompt vengeance on this enemy of his family, and would make him take back his insult. And this threat he would carry out just two weeks later during the night of the feast of the Magi.

Monsieur of Spain was to visit his cousin, the Countess of Alençon. He stopped for the night at Laigle, at an inn whose name is difficult to forget, the Spinning Sow.[14] Overly confident of the respect that was inspired, or so he thought, by his title and the king's friendship, he thought he had nothing to fear when travelling around the kingdom, and had taken with him but a small escort. Now the market town of Laigle is located in the County of Évreux, just a few leagues away from where the Évreux-Navarre brothers were staying in their vast castle. Forewarned of the constable's impending visit, the brothers readied themselves and prepared an ambush.

Around midnight, twenty Norman soldiers, all tough noblemen, the Sire of Graville, the Sire of Clères, the Sire of Mainemares, the Sire of Morbecque, the Knight of Aunay . . . yes! the descendant of one of the suitors of the Tower of Nesle; it wasn't at all surprising that he would be found on the side of Navarre . . . In short, I'm telling you, a good twenty armed knights, whose names are well known since the king had later to sign, against his better judgement, their letters of remission . . . sprang up in the town from nowhere, led by Philip of Navarre, broke down the doors of the Spinning Sow and stormed the stairs up to the constable's accommodations.

The King of Navarre was not with them. In case things went awry he had chosen to wait on the outskirts of the town, beside a barn, in the company of his horse guards. Oh! I can see him now, my Charles the Bad, wound up in his coat, bounding backwards and forwards like a wisp of hell's smoke the length and breadth of the frozen ground, like the devil who never touches the earth. He waits. He looks at the winter sky. The cold nips his fingers. His soul is twisted with both fear and hatred. He listens intently. He resumes his worried pacing up and down.

First to appear from the direction of the town is John of Fricamps, known as Friquet, the Governor of Caen, his advisor and most zealous machine[15] builder, who tells him, gasping for breath: 'The deed is done, monseigneur!'

Then Graville, Mainemares, Morbecque arrive, and Philip of Navarre himself, and all the conspirators with him. At the inn, they pulled the handsome Charles of Spain out from under his bed where he had taken refuge, and now he was indeed dead, still dressed in his nightgown. They had wickedly run him through, stabbed him eighty times over; eighty body wounds would later be found on him. Each of Navarre's men had wanted to stick his sword in four times ... That is how, messire my nephew, King John was to lose his good friend, and how Monseigneur of Navarre would fall into rebellion ...

Now would you please give up your seat for Dom Francesco Calvo, my papal secretary, with whom I wish to converse before we reach our next stop.

7

News from Paris

Dom Calvo, as I will be most busy upon my arrival in La Péruse, inspecting the Abbey to see if it has indeed been so badly laid to waste by the English as to justify the exemption the monks have asked of me, from paying me my prior's benefices for a full year, I want to tell you forthwith what should appear in my letter to the Holy Father. I should be obliged if you would prepare the letter as soon as we arrive, with the fine turn of phrase that you are accustomed to using.

We must let the Holy Father know of the news from Paris that reached me in Limoges, and that has been worrying me since.

First of all, the scheming of the prevost of the merchants of Paris, Master Étienne Marcel. I learned that for the last month the prevost has been building fortifications and digging ditches around the town, beyond the old walls, as if he were preparing against a siege. And yet at the present juncture in the never-ending peace talks, the English have shown no intention nor sign whatsoever of threatening Paris, and such haste in building defences is beyond comprehension. But besides that, the prevost has been organizing his bourgeois into corps of municipal officers, whom he has armed and trained, with district commanders and their officers and their NCOs[16] to ensure that orders are followed, exactly in the image of the Flemish militia who take it upon themselves to govern their own cities. He imposed upon monseigneur the dauphin, the king's lieutenant, to agree to the constitution of this militia, and, what's more, while all royal taxes and tallage are generally the object of complaint and refusal, the prevost, in order to equip his men, managed to put into effect a levy on drink that is paid directly to him.

Ever since the misfortune of Poitiers, this Master Marcel, who formerly made himself rich provisioning the king, but who was piqued four years ago when he lost this role as royalty's most prestigious supplier, has been meddling in all of the kingdom's affairs. It is difficult to gauge his designs, beyond making himself important; but he is hardly heading down the path of appeasement that our Holy Father wishes for. Also my pious duty is to advise the pope that, should any request from that party reach him, he should show himself most haughty and give no support whatsoever, not even the semblance of support, to the Prevost of Paris and his undertakings.

You have already understood me, Dom Calvo. The Cardinal Capocci is in Paris. He could well, impulsive as he is and never failing to blunder, think himself clever in hatching plots with this prevost ... No, nothing specific has been reported to me; but my instinct tells me there is one of those twisted schemes afoot in which my fellow legate never fails to get involved.

Secondly, I would like to invite the supreme pontiff to be informed in detail about the strange events that went on at the Estates-General of the Langue d'Oil[17] which ended in Paris at the beginning of the month, and to shed on them some light of his holy attention.

Convocation of these Assemblies had been promised by King John to take place in December; but due to the turmoil, disorder and despondency the kingdom found itself in following the defeat at Poitiers, the Dauphin Charles thought himself to be acting wisely when he brought forward the meeting to October. In truth, he had no choice but to try to strengthen his authority, which had come to him in this misfortune, young as he was, with an army in tatters from military setbacks, and a Treasury in dire straits.

But the eight hundred deputies of the Langue d'Oil, of which four hundred were bourgeois, didn't deliberate on the issues they were invited to discuss.

The Church has long experience of councils that elude the intentions of those who first set them up. I would like to tell the pope that this assembly looks exactly like a council that has lost its way and assumed the right to rule over everything, hurling itself recklessly into reform, taking advantage of the weakness of the supreme power.

Instead of busying themselves with the release of the King of France, our people in Paris immediately showed more concern for the release of the King of Navarre, which clearly indicates which side their leaders are on.

In addition, the eight hundred appointed an eighty-strong

commission: this began to toil away in secret to produce a long list of remonstrances containing a little that is right, and a great deal that is wrong. Firstly, they demanded the dismissal and judicial trial of the principal advisors of the king, whom they accuse of misappropriating funds, and whom they hold responsible for the defeat . . .

On that point, I must say, Calvo . . . this is not to go in the letter, but just to share my thoughts with you . . . the remonstrances are not totally unjustified. Amongst those appointed by King John to his government, I know there are some who are worthless, and even downright scoundrels. It is natural that a man should increase his own fortune when in high office, otherwise nobody would take on the burden or the risk. But one should be careful not to overstep the limits of dishonesty and look after one's own affairs at the expense of public interest. And above all, one must be capable. And King John, not being that capable himself, wilfully chooses people who are not capable at all . . .

But from that time on, armed with the remonstrances, the deputies increasingly made excessive demands. They demanded that the king, or for the time being the dauphin, govern only with advisors approved by the three estates: four prelates, twelve knights, twelve bourgeois. This council was to have the power to organize and carry through everything that the king had always done previously on his own authority; it would appoint all offices, would be entitled to reform the Court of Accounts[18] and any other of the kingdom's legally appointed bodies, could decide on a prisoner's ransom, and on many other things as well. In truth, its aim was nothing less than stripping the king of all the attributes of sovereignty.

In this way the kingdom would no longer be governed by the one anointed and consecrated according to our Holy Religion; its helm would be entrusted to this council, deriving its entitlement only from a chattering assembly, and the whole governance of the kingdom would be entirely dependent upon it. What weakness and what confusion! Its supposed reformations . . . you must understand me, Dom Calvo; and I want to insist on this, as the Holy Father mustn't be able to say that he hadn't been warned . . . these supposed reforms are an insult to common sense and are redolent even of heresy.

And that men of the cloth should side with the Assembly is most regrettable, take the Bishop of Laon for example, Robert Le Coq, who like Marcel had also lost favour with the king, and is thus in close accord with the prevost. He is one of the most vehement.

The Holy Father must see that behind all this agitation is to be found the King of Navarre who seems to be leading the dance from his prison cell, and who will be making matters yet worse should he continue. The Holy Father, in his infinite wisdom, will judge it necessary to avoid intervening in any way whatever to get Charles the Bad, I mean, Monseigneur of Navarre, released from jail, as so many petitions coming from all sides must be begging him to do.

As far as I am concerned, using my prerogatives of papal legate and nuncio . . . are you listening to me, Calvo? I have commanded that the Bishop of Limoges be part of my retinue to be presented in Metz. He will join me in Bourges. And I have resolved to do as much with all the other bishops en route, including the dioceses pillaged and devastated by the raids of the Prince of Wales, so that they may bear witness before the emperor. I will thus strengthen my case and demonstrate how pernicious the alliance between the Kings of Navarre and England may prove to be . . .

But why on earth must you keep looking out of the window, Dom Calvo? Ah! It is the swaying motion of my palanquin that turns your stomach! I myself am used to it, and would even dare to say that it stimulates my mind; and I see that my nephew, Messire of Périgord, who has often kept me company since we set out, is not at all adversely affected by it. You do indeed look a little queasy. Very well, you shall get to step down. But don't forget any of what I have told you when you take up your quill.

8

The Treaty of Mantes

WHERE ARE WE NOW? Have we passed Mortemart? Not yet!
It would seem that I have slept a little ... Oh! How the sky
darkens and how the days are shortening! I was dreaming,
you see, my nephew, I was dreaming of a blossoming plum
tree, a big plum tree, round and white, laden with birds, as if
each flower were singing. And the sky was blue, the same
blue as the Virgin's mantle. An angelic vision, a true corner of
paradise. What strange things are dreams! Have you noticed
that in the gospel, no dreams are recounted, except for
Joseph's at the beginning of Saint Matthew? It is the only one.
Whereas in the Old Testament, the patriarchs are forever
having dreams, in the New, no one dreams at all. I have often
wondered why, without being able to find an answer ...
Has that never struck you as rather odd? It is because you
are no great reader of the Holy Scriptures, Archambaud ... I
see a fine subject for our brilliant scholars in Paris or Oxford
to fight over amongst themselves and to provide us with

voluminous treatises and discourses in a Latin so impenetrable nobody could understand a word . . .

In any case, the Holy Spirit advised me well in taking me out of my way via La Péruse. You saw those good Benedictine monks who wanted to take advantage of the English raid to avoid paying their prior's commendams? I will get the enamel crucifix replaced and the three golden chalices that they hurriedly gave the English in order to avoid being pillaged; and they will settle up their annual payments.

They were naively looking to get themselves confused with the inhabitants of the other bank of the River Vienne, where the Prince of Wales's rovers wreaked havoc, pillaging and burning, as we saw only too well this morning in Chirac and in Saint-Maurice-des-Lions. And especially in the Abbey of Lesterps where the Canons Regular[19] showed great valour. 'Our abbey is fortified; we will defend it.' And they fought, those canons, as good and brave men that refuse to be taken. Several perished in the attack, who acted more nobly, to my knowledge, than many a knight at Poitiers.

If only all the people of France had as much heart . . . even so they found the means, those honest canons in their charred monastery, to offer us a copious and well-prepared dinner, which helped me sleep soundly that night. And have you noticed the look of holy cheer they wear upon their faces? 'Our brothers were killed? They are now in peace; God has welcomed them in His leniency . . . If He left us here on earth it is so that we can accomplish good works . . . Our monastery is half destroyed? We have the chance to rebuild it and make it even more beautiful than before . . .'

Good men of the cloth are joyous, my nephew, remember

that. I am wary of overly severe fasters with their long faces and their burning, close-set eyes, as if they had spent too long squinting at hell. Those God honours most highly by calling them to His service have an obligation to show in their manner the joy this brings them; it is an example and a courtesy that they owe to other mortals.

In the same way as kings, since God has elevated them over and above all other men, they have the duty to show self-control. Messire Philip the Fair who was a paragon of true majesty, condemned without showing anger; and he mourned without shedding a tear.

On the occasion of Monsieur of Spain's murder, that I was telling you about yesterday, King John showed all too well, and in the most pitiful fashion, that he was incapable of the slightest restraint in his passions. Pity is not what a king should inspire; it is better that one believes him impervious to pain. Four long days our king refrained from speaking a word, not even to say if he wanted to eat or drink. He kept to his rooms, acknowledging nobody, abandoning control of himself, eyes reddened and brimming, stopping suddenly to burst into tears. It was pointless talking to him about any business. Had the enemy invaded his palace, he would have let himself be taken by the hand. He hadn't shown a quarter of such grief when the mother of his children, Madame of Luxembourg, passed away, something that the Dauphin Charles didn't fail to mention. It was in fact the very first time that he was seen to show contempt for his father, going so far as to tell him that it was indecent to let himself go like this. But the king would hear nothing.

He would emerge from his state of despondency only to

start screaming . . . that his charger be saddled immediately; screaming that his army should be mustered; screaming that he would speed to Évreux to take his revenge, and that everyone would be trembling with fear . . . Those close to him had great difficulty in bringing him to his senses and explaining to him that to get together his army, even without his arrièreban,[20] would take at least one month; that if he really wanted to attack Évreux, he would inevitably force a rift with Normandy; he should recall, as a counter-argument for this, that the truce with the King of England was about to expire, and that monarch might be tempted to take advantage of the chaos, the kingdom could be jeopardized.

He was also shown that, perhaps if he had simply respected his daughter's marriage contract and kept his promise to give Angoulême to Charles of Navarre, instead of offering it as a gift to his dear constable . . .

John II stretched out his arms wide and proclaimed: 'Who am I then, if I can do nothing? I can clearly see that not one of you loves me, and that I have lost my support.' But in the end, he stayed at home, swearing to God that never would he know joy until he had been avenged.

Meanwhile, Charles the Bad didn't remain idle. He wrote to the pope, he wrote to the emperor, he wrote to all the Christian princes, explaining to them that he hadn't wanted Charles of Spain's death, but only to seize him for insults received, and the harm he had suffered at his hand; truly his men had overstepped his orders, but he was prepared to assume responsibility for it all and stand up for his relatives, friends and servants who had been driven, in the tumult of Laigle, by an overzealous concern for his well-being.

Having set up the ambush like a highway brigand, this is how he portrayed himself, wearing the gloves of a knight.

And most importantly he wrote to the Duke of Lancaster, who was to be found in Malines, and also to the King of England himself. We got wind of these letters when things began to turn sour. The Bad One certainly didn't beat about the bush. 'If you summon your captains in Brittany to ready themselves, as soon as I send for them, to enter in Normandy, I will grant them good and sure passage. You should know, dearest cousin, that all the nobles of Normandy are with me in death as in life.' With the murder of Monsieur of Spain, our man had chosen rebellion; now he was moving towards treason. But at the same time, he cast upon King John the Ladies of Melun.

You don't know whom we mean by that name? Ah! It's raining. It was to be expected; this rain has been threatening us from the outset. Now you will bless my palanquin, Archambaud, rather than having water running down your neck, beneath your coathardy, and mud caking you to the waist . . .

The Ladies of Melun? They are the two queens dowager, and Joan of Valois, Charles's child-bride, who is awaiting puberty. All three live in the Castle of Melun, that is called the Castle of the Three Queens, or even the Widows' Court.

First of all there is Madame Joan of Évreux, King Charles IV's widow and aunt to our Bad One. Yes, yes, she is still alive; she isn't at all as old as one would think. She is barely a day over fifty; she is four or five years younger than me. She has been a widow for twenty-eight years already, twenty-eight years of wearing white. She shared the throne just three years. But she has remained an influence in the kingdom. She is the most senior, the very last queen of the great Capetian dynasty. Yes, of the three confinements she went through . . . three girls, of which only one, the one birthed after the king's death, is still living . . . had she given birth to a boy, she would have been queen mother and regent. The dynasty came to an end in her womb. When she says: 'Monseigneur of Évreux, my father . . . my uncle Philip the Fair . . . my brother-in-law Philip the Tall . . .' a hush descends. She is the survivor of an undisputed monarchy, and of a time when France was infinitely more powerful and glorious than today. She is guarantor for the new breed. So, there are things that are not done because Madame of Évreux would disapprove of them.

In addition to this, it is said around her: 'She is a saint.' You have to admit that it doesn't take much when one is queen, to be looked upon as a saint by a small and idle court where singing others' praises passes as an occupation. Madame Joan of Évreux gets up before dawn; she lights her candle herself so as not to disturb her ladies-in-waiting. Then she begins to read her book of hours, the smallest in the world so we are led to believe, a gift from her husband who had commissioned it from a master limner,[21] Jean Pucelle. She spends much time in prayer and regularly gives alms. She has spent twenty-eight years repeating that, as she had been unable to give birth to a son, she had no future. Widows live on obsessions. She could have carried more weight in the kingdom if she had been blessed with intelligence in proportion to her virtue.

Then there is Madame Blanche, Charles of Navarre's sister,

second wife of Philip VI, a queen for just six months, barely time enough to get accustomed to wearing a crown. She has the reputation of being the most beautiful woman of the kingdom. I saw her, not long ago, and can willingly confirm this judgement. She is now twenty-four, and for the last six years has been wondering what the whiteness of her skin, her enamel eyes and her perfect body are all for. Had nature endowed her with a less splendid appearance, she would be queen now, since she was intended for King John! The father only took her for himself because he was transfixed by her beauty.

Not long after she had accompanied her husband's body to the grave that was prepared, she was proposed to by the King of Castile, Don Pedro, whose subjects had named the Cruel. She responded, rather hastily perhaps, that: 'A Queen of France does not remarry.' She was much praised for this display of grandeur. But she wonders to this day if it is not too great a sacrifice she has made for the sake of her title and whatever rights she still has to her former magnificence. The domain of Melun is her dower. She has made many improvements to it, but she can well change the carpets and tapestries that make up her bedroom at Christmas and Easter; she will always sleep there alone.

Finally, there is the other Joan, King John's daughter, whose marriage had the effect of bringing on only storms. Charles of Navarre entrusted her to his aunt and his sister, until she was of an age to consummate the bond. That Joan is a little minx, as a girl of twelve can be, who remembers being a widow at six, and who knows herself to be queen without yet being powerful, for the while. She has nothing else to do but wait until she grows up, when she will be taking up the role; and she sorely lacks patience, baulking at everything she is commanded to do, demanding everything that is refused her, harrying her handmaidens to their wits' end, promising them a thousand torments on the day of her puberty. Madame of Évreux, who does not take bad behaviour lightly, has often had to slap her face.

Our three ladies maintain in Melun and in Meaux . . . Meaux is the dower of Madame of Évreux . . . a semblance of a court. They have a chancellor, treasurer, master of the household. Most lofty titles for such reduced functions. One is often surprised to find there people that were thought dead by all but themselves, so forgotten were they. Ageing servants, survivors from former reigns, old confessors of late kings, secretaries, keepers of secrets all too well known, men who had felt powerful for a moment when they were so close to power; now they trudge through their memories, attributing importance to themselves for having taken part in events which no longer have the slightest importance. When one of them begins: 'The day the king told me . . .' you have to guess which king he is talking about, amongst the six that have occupied the throne since the turn of the century. And what the king said is ordinarily some grave and memorable confidence like: 'What fine weather we are having today, Gros-Pierre . . .'

Therefore it is almost a godsend when a dramatic affair occurs such as that of the King of Navarre's imprisonment, the Widows' Court is suddenly awoken from its slumber. The hour arrives for everyone to rouse, murmur, bustle and stir . . . We should add that for the three queens, Monseigneur of Navarre, amongst all the living, is uppermost in their thoughts. He is the beloved nephew, the cherished brother, the adored husband. No matter that in Navarre they call him the Bad! Incidentally, he does everything he can to stay in their good graces, visiting them often, showering them with presents . . . at least, he did before he was walled up . . . cheering them with his tales, speaking to them of his troubles, fascinating them with his ventures, charming as he can be, playing the respectful young man with his aunt, the affection-ate equal with his sister, the man in love with his little girl of a wife, and all out of calculated self-interest; to keep them like pawns on his chessboard.

After the assassination of the constable, and as soon as King John appeared to have calmed down a little, the queens left together for Paris, at Monseigneur of Navarre's request.

Little Joan of Navarre, throwing herself at the king's feet, recited in fine fashion the lesson that she had learned: 'Sire my father, it cannot be that my husband could have committed the slightest treachery against you. If he has acted badly, it is because traitors took advantage of him. I beseech you, for my sake, to forgive him.'

Madame of Évreux, shot through with sadness and with the authority that age conferred on her, said: 'Sire my cousin, as the eldest to have worn the crown in this kingdom, I dare to offer you advice, and ask you to adapt your thinking to the special case of my nephew. If he has accumulated wrong-doing towards you, it is because certain people in your service have greatly harmed him, and he must have thought you had abandoned him to his enemies. But he himself harbours only fine thoughts and loyal affection towards you, I assure you. It would be damaging to you both to pursue with this discord . . .'

Madame Blanche said nothing at all. She just stared at King John. She knew that he couldn't have forgotten that she should have been his wife. Before her, this tall and thickset man, usually so curt, began to falter. His eyes avoided her, his words got tied up in knots. And still in her presence, he decided on the opposite of what he believed he wanted.

As soon as the audience was over, he delegated the Cardinal of Boulogne, the Bishop of Laon, Robert Le Coq, and his chamberlain Robert of Lorris to go and negotiate peace with his son-in-law. He commanded that the matter should be handled quickly and effectively. It was indeed so handled, since one week before the end of February, the two parties signed an agreement, in Mantes. Never, as far as I can remember, was a treaty seen to be so easily and rapidly concluded.

King John displayed, on this occasion, all the strangeness of his character and the lack of coherence of his mind in the handling of his affairs. The month before, he could dream of nothing other than seizing and slaying Monseigneur of Navarre; yet now he consented to everything asked of him. Should they come to him and say that his son-in-law was asking for the Clos de Cotentin, with Valognes, Coutances and Carentan, he would reply: 'Give him them, give him them!' The Viscounties of Pont-Audemer and Orbec? 'Give them to him because it is asked of me to adapt myself to him.' In this way Charles the Bad also received the sizeable county of Beaumont, with the castellanies of Breteuil and Conches, all that had made up the lands of Count Robert of Artois. Revenge was sweet after all for Marguerite of Burgundy;

her grandson was thus to take back the possessions of the man who had lost them for her. The Count of Beaumont! The young Navarre exulted. He himself was giving almost nothing away in the treaty; he was to return to Pontoise, and he solemnly confirmed that he would abandon Champagne, a dispute which had been settled for more than twenty-five years already.

Not a single word more was spoken about the assassination of Charles of Spain. No punishment, not even for the collaborators, and no reparations. All the accomplices of the Spinning Sow, and those who didn't hesitate in coming forward from that moment on, received letters of acquittal and remission.

Ah! That Treaty of Mantes did little to improve the reputation of King John. 'They kill his constable; he gives away half of Normandy. Should they kill his brother or his son, he would hand over France itself.' That is what the people were saying.

The less significant King of Navarre had proven himself far from inept. With Beaumont, in addition to Mantes and Évreux, he was now able to isolate Paris from Brittany; with the Cotentin, he controlled direct access routes to England.

And besides, when he came to Paris to receive his pardon, it was as if he were the one granting it.

Yes; what are you saying, Brunet? Oh! This rain! My curtain is wet through ... We are arriving in Bellac? Excellent. Here at least we are sure to find comfortable board and lodgings, and they can have no excuse for not preparing us a fine reception. The English raid spared Bellac, upon the orders of the Prince of Wales, as it is the dower of the

Countess of Pembroke, who is a Châtillon-Lusignan. Men at war are capable of certain kindnesses . . .

So the story, my nephew, of the Treaty of Mantes draws to a close. The King of Navarre appeared in Paris as if he had won a war, and King John, in welcoming him, was to be seen to be holding a session of Parliament, the two queens dowager seated by his side. One of the king's counsel came and kneeled before the throne . . . Oh! It was all rather grand . . . 'My most formidable lord, my ladies Queens Joan and Blanche beseech you to forgive Monsieur of Navarre, whom they understand to be in your malgrace . . .'

Thereupon, the new constable, Gautier of Brienne, Duke of Athens . . . Yes, a cousin of Raoul's, the other branch of the Briennes; and this time, the chosen man was no youngster . . . went to take Navarre by the hand . . . 'The king forgives you, out of kindness for the queens, with good heart and good grace.'

To which the Cardinal of Boulogne had the duty of adding loud and clear: 'May not one of the king's lineage venture such actions again, as, be he the king's son, justice will be done.'

Fine justice indeed, while in reality everyone laughed surreptitiously. And before the entire court, the father- and son-in-law embraced each other. I will tell you the rest tomorrow.

9

The Bad in Avignon

To tell you the truth, my nephew, I prefer the way churches used to be built, like the one in Le Dorat we just passed through; the churches built in the last one hundred and fifty or two hundred years may be technical feats in stone, but the shadow is so dense, the ornamentation so profuse and often so frightening, that one's heart tightens with fear, as much as if one had got lost at night in the middle of the forest. It is not thought well of to have such taste as mine, I know, but it is the taste I have and I will stand by it. Perhaps it comes from my growing up in our old castle in Périgueux, built within the ruins of a monument from Ancient Rome; nearby our venerable Saint-Front, our Saint-Étienne down the road, how I love to come across forms that remind me of them, those beautiful pillars, simple and regular, those high, rounded arches under which light scatters so effortlessly.

Previous generations of monks were very good at building such sanctuaries, where sunlight pours in so abundantly the stone walls seem softly golden under the high vaulted ceilings, where the heavens are represented, and the choirs surge up magnificently, voices rising up like angels to Paradise.

By the grace of God, the English, even if they have pillaged Le Dorat, didn't destroy this masterpiece amongst masterpieces, not badly enough for it to need rebuilding. Otherwise, I wager that our Northern architects would have enjoyed putting up some stone monstrosity of their own making, a top-heavy vessel standing on stone legs like some fantastical beast, where, upon entering, one could almost believe that the house of God is the antechamber of hell. And they would have replaced the angel of gilded copper, at the tip of the spire, which gave its name to the parish ... oh yes, *lou dorat* ... by a grimacing devil with a cloven hoof...

Hell ... My benefactor, John XXII, my very first pope, didn't believe in it, or rather he professed that it was empty. That was going a little too far. If people no longer fear hell, then how can we draw almsgiving and penitences, to redeem their sins? Without hell, the Church could go out of business. It was the hare-brained idea of a great old man. We were forced to make him retract on his deathbed. I was there ...

Oh! The weather is really getting colder. One can well feel that in two days we will be entering December. A damp cold, the worst kind.

Brunet! Aymar Brunet, go and see, my friend, if there isn't a warming pan in the food supplies cart we could put in my palanquin. The furs are no longer enough, and if we carry on this way, it will be a shivering cardinal that will be getting out at Saint-Benoît-du-Sault. There too, I have been told, the Englishman has wreaked havoc ... And if there are not enough hot coals in the chef's cart, as I will need far more than that required to keep a ragout warm, you are to go in quest of them at the first hamlet we pass through ... No, I don't need Master Vigier. Let him continue to wend his way. Whenever I call my doctor to my side, the entire escort imagines that I am at death's door. I am in excellent health. I need coals, that is all ...

So you want to know, Archambaud, what ensued after the Treaty of Mantes, that I told you about yesterday ... You are a good listener, my nephew, and it is a pleasure to educate you in what one knows. I suspect that you even take notes whenever we make a stop; is this not true? Very well, I thought as much. It is the Northern lords who glorify themselves by being more ignorant than an ass, as if reading and writing were work for a mere cleric, or pauper. They require a servant to understand the smallest note addressed to them. We, in the south of the kingdom, have always rubbed shoulders with the Roman civilizations, we have every respect for learning. Which gives us the upper hand in a great many matters.

So you take notes. That is a good thing indeed. As, for my part, I will scarcely be able to bear witness of all that I have seen and all that I have done. All my letters and writings are or will be deposited in the papal registers never to be released again, as is the rule. But you will be there, Archambaud, and will be able to, at least for the business related to France, say what you know, and do justice to my memory if certain others, as I have no doubt that Capocci will ... (may God keep me on this earth just one day longer than him) ... attempt to conspire to.

So, very soon after the Treaty of Mantes, where he had shown himself so inexplicably generous towards his son-in-law, King John accused his negotiators, Robert Le Coq, Robert of Lorris and even his wife's uncle, the Cardinal of Boulogne, of having sold out to Charles of Navarre.

Let it be said between us, I believe he was not far from the truth. Robert Le Coq is a young bishop burning with ambition, who excels in scheming and revels in intrigue, and who since his quarrel with the king had openly joined Navarrese circles, quick to see his own advantage in joining forces with them. Robert of Lorris, the chamberlain, is certainly devoted to his master; however, he is from a banking family where one can never resist making a few fistfuls of gold in passing. I got to know him, this Lorris, when he came to Avignon around ten years ago to negotiate the loan of three hundred thousand florins King Philip VI had extended to the pope at that time. I, myself, merely took an honest thousand florins for having put the bankers of Clement VI, the Raimondi of Avignon and the Matteis of Florence in contact with each other; but *he* was rather more generous to himself. As far as Boulogne is concerned, as close a relative of the king as he is . . .

I fully understand that it is accepted that we, as cardinals, be fairly compensated for our intercessions on our princes' behalf. Otherwise we would never be able to carry out our duties. I have never made a secret of it, and even consider it an honour, to have received twenty-two thousand florins from my sister of Durazzo for the care of her ducal affairs that I took, twenty years ago . . . twenty years already! They were severely compromised at the time. And just last year, for the necessary exemption for the marriage of Louis of Sicily and Constance of Avignon, I was duly thanked with five thousand florins. But I have only ever accepted recompense from those who put their cause in the hands of my talent or my influence. Dishonesty begins when one is paid by the enemy. And I believe that Boulogne could not resist this temptation. Since then, the friendship between him and King John II has considerably cooled off.

Lorris, by withdrawing for a while, once more returned to favour, as is always the way with the Lorrises. He threw himself at the king's feet, last Good Friday, swore his unfailing loyalty, and cast all duplicity and connivance onto Le Coq, who remained on bad terms with the king and was banished from the court.

It is an advantageous thing to disavow one's negotiators. It serves as justification when not applying the terms of a treaty. And the king did just that. When he was told that he should have kept his deputies under tighter control, and given away a good deal less than he had, he replied irritably: 'Negotiating, debating, arguing are no business for a knight.' He has always affected contempt for negotiation and diplomacy, which has allowed him to renege on any commitments.

In fact he had only promised so much because he counted on respecting nothing at all.

But at the same time, he overwhelmed his son-in-law with a thousand feigned courtesies, always wanting him close by at court, and not only him, but his younger brother, Philip, and even the youngest, Louis, whose return from Navarre he keenly insisted upon. He proclaimed himself the protector of the three brothers and encouraged the dauphin to profess friendship to them.

The Bad didn't submit himself without arrogance to such excessive consideration, to so much incredible solicitude, going so far as to say to the king, in the middle of dinner: 'Admit that I did you a favour ridding you of Charles of Spain, who wanted to run everything in the kingdom. You won't say it, but I relieved you of a burden.' You can imagine how much King John enjoyed being reminded of such kindnesses.

Then one summer's day when Charles of Navarre and his brothers were on their way to attend a feast at the palace, the Cardinal of Boulogne rushed up to Charles and said: 'Turn back and stay in your house, if you value your life. The king has resolved to have you slain later today, all three of you, during the feast.'

This was no figment of his imagination, nor the result of vague rumours. King John had indeed taken such a decision, that very morning, during his State Council, in which Boulogne had taken part . . . 'I have been waiting for the three brothers to be together, as I want all three of them slain so that there be no further male offspring of that evil breed.'

For my part, I don't blame Boulogne for having warned the Navarrese, even though that must have given credence to the idea that he had been bought. As a priest of the Holy Church . . . and who, what's more, is a member of the pontifical Curia, a brother of the pope before the Lord . . . cannot hear that a triple murder will be perpetrated in cold blood, and accept that it should take place without attempting in the slightest to prevent it. It was to let oneself become an accessory to the crime by remaining silent. Why on earth did King John have to speak in front of Boulogne? He only had to give the order to his sergeants . . . But no, he thought he was being clever. Ah, that king, when he tries to be crafty! He has never been able to see three moves ahead. He must have thought that when the pope remonstrated with him about how he had bloodied his palace, as he surely would, he could always argue: 'But your cardinal was there, and he didn't disapprove of my actions.' Boulogne is no partridge born of the last brood to walk into such an obvious trap.

Charles of Navarre, thus forewarned, withdrew in haste to his house where he had his escort made ready. King John, when none of the brothers turned up at his feast, summoned them urgently. But his messenger received no response, there was only the thumping of horses' hooves as, at that very moment, the Navarrese were headed back towards Normandy.

King John entered into an acute rage whereupon he hid his vexation by playing the injured party. 'Look at that bad son, that traitor who turns his back on the friendship of the king, and exiles himself from my court! He must have many a wicked plan to conceal.'

And from that came his pretext to proclaim he would suspend the terms and effects of the Treaty of Mantes, that anyway he had not even begun to execute.

Upon learning this, Charles sent his brother Louis back to Navarre and dispatched his brother Philip to Cotentin to raise an army, he himself choosing not to stay in Évreux any longer.

Because meanwhile our Holy Father, the Pope Innocent, had called a conference in Avignon . . . the third, the fourth, or rather, simply the same one begun again ... between the envoys of France and England in order to negotiate, not just an extended truce, but a real and lasting peace. This time, Innocent wanted, so he said, to see the work of his predecessor through to a successful conclusion, flattering himself he would succeed where Clement VI had failed. Presumptuousness, Archambaud, lies deep even in a pontiff's heart.

The Cardinal of Boulogne had presided over the previous negotiations; Innocent reappointed him to this office. King Edward of England had always been suspicious of Boulogne, as he had been of me, believing him too close to the interests of France. And yet, since the Treaty of Mantes and the flight of Charles the Bad, King John was also suspicious of him. Perhaps it was for that reason that Boulogne ran the meeting in Avignon far better than anticipated; he had nobody to mollycoddle. He got along well enough with the Bishops of London and of Norwich, and particularly well with the Duke of Lancaster, who is a fine military leader and veritable lord. And meanwhile, behind the scenes, I myself set about playing my part. Little Navarre must have got wind of ...

Ah! Here come the coals! Brunet, slide the pan under my robes, would you? It is well sealed I trust, so that I don't get burned! Yes, that is fine like that ...

So, Charles of Navarre must have got wind of the fact that we were moving towards peace, which would certainly not have helped his cause, because one fine November day ... just two years ago ... there he was, suddenly, in Avignon, where nobody was expecting him.

This was when I saw him for the first time. Twenty-four

years old, but with his diminutive stature not looking a day older than eighteen, really very short, the smallest of the kings of Europe; but so well proportioned, so upright in his posture, so agile, so quick-witted that no one dared dream of making him aware of this. Add to that a charming face that well sets off a nose a little on the large side, handsome fox-like eyes, with corners already creased into crow's feet by shrewdness. His exterior is so affable, his manners at the same time so polite and light of touch, his speech so fluent, assured and spontaneous, quick to compliment, passing so nimbly from solemnity to bawdiness and from amusement to seriousness, and he appears so openly to offer his friendship to people it is easy to understand why women can't resist him, and men fall prey to his schemes. No, really, I have never heard a more valiant gabber than that little king there! Listening to him, one tended to forget the wickedness that hid behind so much good grace, and that he was already a hardened liar, criminal and master of stratagems. The personal impression he leaves you with make you forgive the secret blackness of his soul.

When he made his appearance in Avignon, his situation was not of the best. He was insubordinate vis-à-vis the King of France, who went about seizing his castles, and he had seriously offended the King of England by signing the Treaty of Mantes without giving him the slightest warning. 'Here is a man who calls upon my help, and offers me a clear passage through Normandy. I mobilize my troops in Brittany; I make ready even more for landing; and no sooner has he gained enough strength, through my support, to be able to intimi-date his enemy, than he begins negotiations without a word to me ... From now on, he may address whomever he sees fit; let him turn to the pope ...'

Well, it was precisely to the pope that Charles of Navarre had come to speak. And in just one week, he had brought everyone around to his cause.

In the presence of the Holy Father, and before several cardinals of which I was one, he swore, putting all of his heart into it, that he wanted nothing more than to be reconciled with the King of France, and everyone believed him. With the delegates of John II, the Chancellor Pierre de La Forêt and the Duke of Bourbon, he went further still, leading them to believe that for the price of renewed friendship, that friendship he wished to restore with the king, he would raise an army in Navarre in order to attack the English in Brittany or on their own shores.

He pretended to leave the town with his escort, but over the following days, he came back several times at night, and in stealth, to confer with the Duke of Lancaster and the English emissaries. He chose to hold his secret meetings either at the residence of Pierre Bertrand, the Cardinal of Arras, or at the home of Guy of Boulogne himself. By the way, I later raised the matter with Boulogne, who was eating at every table. 'I wanted to find out what they were up to,' he replied. 'By lending them my house I could have my spies listen in on them.' His spies must have been stone deaf, as he was to find out nothing at all, or he simply pretended not to know the first thing about it. If they weren't in league with each other, then it is the King of Navarre who must have pulled the rug right out from under him.

I was in the know. And would you like to know, my

nephew, how Navarre went about winning over Lancaster? Well now! He proudly proposed to recognize King Edward of England as the rightful King of France. Nothing less than that. The two of them even went so far as to draw up a treaty of understanding between the two countries.

Firstly: Navarre would thus have recognized Edward as King of France. Secondly: they agreed to wage war together against King John. Thirdly: Edward acknowledged Charles of Navarre's right to the duchies of Normandy, Champagne, Brie, Chartres, and also the Lieutenancy of Languedoc, in addition of course to his kingdom of Navarre and his county of Évreux. Suffice to say that they were dividing up France between them. I will spare you the rest.

How did I get to know of these plans? Ah! I can tell you that an account of them was noted down in person by the Bishop of London, who was travelling with Messire of Lancaster. But don't ask me who passed on the information at a later date. You must remember that I am Canon of the Cathedral of York and that, as poorly looked upon as I am in court on the other side of the Channel, still I have maintained several informants.

I fear there is little need to assure you that if we had started out with several opportunities to work towards peace between France and England, they were all undermined by the incursion of the spirited little king.

How could the ambassadors have ever been able to consider any form of agreement when each party was obliged to go to war by the promises of Monseigneur of Navarre? In Bourbon he would say: 'I speak to Lancaster, but I lie to him in order to serve your best interests.' Then he would whisper in Lancaster's ear: 'Indeed I saw Bourbon, but to mislead him. I am your man.' And one must admire him for being able to make both sides believe him.

So much so that when he finally left Avignon, to set out for the Pyrenees, people on both sides were all convinced, while taking great care to say nothing of the sort, that they were seeing off a friend.

Then it was the conference took an acrimonious turn; nothing more would be conceded. And the town fell into a slumber. For three weeks, the only concern had been Charles the Bad. The pope himself surprised us by becoming morose, sullen and moaning; the wicked charmer had entertained him for a while . . .

Ah! I am much warmer again now. Your turn, my nephew; pull the pan of embers towards you, and warm yourself up a little.

10

The Annus Horribilis

HOW RIGHT YOU are, how right you are, Archambaud, and I feel the same way. We have only been gone from Périgueux ten days, and yet it seems that we have already been travelling for a month. Travel makes time go by more slowly. Tonight we will sleep at Châteauroux. I make no secret of the fact that I would not be unhappy to reach Bourges tomorrow, God willing, and to rest there at least three whole days, maybe even four. I am beginning to tire of these abbeys where we are served poor fare and where my bed is scarcely warmed, deliberately, so that I am made aware how the war has brought them to ruin. They should not think, these little abbots, that it is by starving me and having me sleep in a draught that they will save themselves from paying their dues! And my escort too needs to rest, to dry off their clothes and to repair the harnesses. Because this rain doesn't make their life any easier. Listening to my gentlemen sneeze on all sides of my palanquin, I wager that more than one of them will spend his stay in Bourges getting treated with cinnamon, cloves and mulled wine. As for me, I will hardly have time to dawdle. Going through the correspondence from Avignon, dictating my missives by way of reply . . .

Perhaps you will be surprised, Archambaud, by the impatient words that I let slip sometimes regarding the Holy Father. It is true that I can be quick-tempered and show my vexation a little too much. It is because he gives me much to chew on. But you must believe me that I have no hesitation in showing him his foolishness. And more than once I have said to him: 'May the grace of God, most Holy Father, enlighten you on the blunder you have just made.'

Ah! If only the French cardinals hadn't suddenly dug their heels in over the idea that a man of such good birth would be unsuited for the office . . . humility, one needed to be born into humility . . . and if only, in addition to this, the Italian cardinals, Capocci and the others, had been less stubborn on the return of the Holy See to Rome . . . All they can think of are their Italian states; and Rome, Rome! The Capitol blocks their view of God.

What annoys me the most about our Innocent is his policy towards the emperor. With Pierre Roger, I mean Clement VI, we pushed six years long to prevent the emperor from being crowned. That he was elected was all very well. That he may govern, we give our consent. But we had to keep his crowning in reserve so long as he hadn't subscribed to the causes we wanted him to. I knew all too well that that emperor, no sooner anointed, would bring us bad luck.

Then our Aubert puts on the tiara and begins to sing: 'Reconciliation, reconciliation.' And in the spring of last year, he achieved his aims. 'The Emperor Charles IV will be crowned; that is an order!' he ended up telling me. Pope Innocent is one of those sovereigns who can muster energy only to beat a hasty retreat. We have any number of such people. He imagined he had pulled off a great victory as the emperor had accepted the condition that he enter Rome only on the morning of his coronation and leave again that same evening, not sleeping in the city. Mere trifles! The Cardinal Bertrand of Colombiers ... 'You see, I am appointing a Frenchman; you should be satisfied ...' was sent to place the crown of Charlemagne upon the brow of the Bohemian. Six months later, in return for this kindness, Charles IV honoured us with the Bulla Aurea, according to which the papacy no longer has the slightest say nor vote in the imperial election.

From now on, the Empire is to be formally organized by an electoral college of seven Germans so as to confederate their states ... or put another way, would turn their beautiful anarchy into a permanent state of affairs. However, nothing has been settled for Italy and no one really knows by whom nor in what way the country will be governed. The most serious thing about the Bulla, something Innocent hadn't appreciated, is that it separates temporal and spiritual power and sets in stone the independence of nations vis-à-vis the papacy. It is the end, it is the eradication of the principle of the universal monarchy as exercised by the successor of Saint Peter, in the name of Our Lord God Almighty. God is thus sent back to heaven, and we are left to do whatever we please here on earth. They call this 'the modern mentality', and they make a show of it. I choose to call it, forgive me, my nephew, having shit in one's eyes.

There is no such thing as an ancient mentality or a modern mentality. There is just the mind on the one hand, and stupidity on the other. And what did our pope do? Did he rant and rail? Did he excommunicate? He sent the emperor the softest and friendliest of missives replete with his blessings ... Oh! No, oh! No, I didn't draft it. But I am the one who, at the Diet of Metz, will have to hear them solemnly proclaim this Bulla that renounces the supreme power of the Holy See and can only bring turmoil, unrest and misfortune to all Europe.

It is indeed a bitter pill that I have to swallow, and with good grace to boot, since now that Germany has pulled away from us, we need more than ever to work to save France, otherwise there will be nothing left, for God will have nothing left. Ah! The future may well curse this year 1355! We haven't finished harvesting its prickly fruit.

And the Navarrese during all this time? Well now! He, the little king, was in Navarre, absolutely delighted to learn that in addition to all the mayhem and quarrelling he had started, came yet more troubles from the imperial front.

Firstly, he waited for the return of his man Friquet of Fricamps, who had left for England with the Duke of Lancaster, and who was coming back with one of his chamberlains, bearer of the opinions of King Edward on the project of a treaty drawn up in Avignon. And the chamberlain was to return to London, this time accompanied by Colin Doublel, one of his equerries and one of the murderers of Monsieur of Spain, who was to present the observations of his master.

Charles of Navarre is the exact opposite of King John. He is better than a notary at fighting over every article, every full stop, every comma of an agreement. And invoking this and anticipating that. And using such and such a custom that is deemed authoritative, and always looking to grind his own obligations down a little while increasing the other party's . . . And, in taking his time to bake his bread with the Englishman, he gave himself the luxury of keeping an eye on what was cooking over in France.

This should have been the time for King John to show tolerance and present himself in a good light. But that man always chooses to act against the grain. He chose sabre-rattling; he prepared himself for war, ready to rush upon an absent enemy; and, racing to Caen, he commanded that all of his son-in-law's Norman castles be seized, save Évreux. A fine campaign indeed, which, for want of an enemy, quickly turned into a campaign of feasting, and this greatly upset the Normans who watched the royal archers pillage their salting-rooms and larders.

Meanwhile, the Navarrese king quietly raised an army in his native Navarre, while his brother-in-law, the Count of Foix, Phoebus . . . I will tell you about him another day; that one is no mean lord . . . went to wreak havoc in the County of Armagnac just to be a nuisance to the King of France.

Having waited until summer so that they might take to the seas with the least possible risk, our young Charles landed in Cherbourg on a fine August day, accompanied by two thousand men.

And John II was flabbergasted to learn that at the same time, the Prince of Wales, who in April had been made Prince of Aquitaine and Lieutenant of the King of England in Guyenne, had boarded five thousand warriors onto his ships and was headed full sail for Bordeaux. And even though it was summer they had to wait for favourable winds. Ah! At least King John's informants were doing their jobs! We in Avignon saw this well-planned two-pronged attack looming up over the water, aiming to catch France in a pincer movement. At one point the imminent arrival of King Edward himself was announced, he was scheduled to have landed already in Jersey, only the storm forced him back to Portsmouth. We can safely say that it was the wind, and nothing else, that saved France last year.

Being unable to fight on three fronts simultaneously, King John chose to defend none at all. Once more he headed for Caen, but this time to negotiate. Travelling with him were his two cousins from Bourbon, Pierre and Jacques, as well as Robert of Lorris, recently returned to favour as I explained. But Charles of Navarre didn't come. He sent Messires of Lor and of Couillarville, two of his lords, to negotiate on his behalf. King John had no choice but to depart, and the two Bourbons were left behind, with instructions to come to an agreement as quickly as possible.

This was concluded at Valognes on the tenth of September. Charles of Navarre recovered all that had been acknowledged to him in the Treaty of Mantes, and a little more into the bargain.

And two weeks later, at the Louvre, another ceremonious reconciliation took place between king and son-in-law, in the presence of course of the Widowed Queens, Madame Joan and Madame Blanche . . . 'Sire my cousin, here is our nephew and brother that we beg you for our sakes . . .' And the king's arms were opened wide, and he kissed while longing to bite the Navarrese cheeks, and forgiveness and faithful friendship were sworn . . .

Ah! I am forgetting a detail which in fact has every importance. John II had, in order to reassure the escort of honour for the King of Navarre, dispatched his son, the Dauphin Charles, newly appointed Lieutenant General in Normandy, to go and meet him. From Vaudreuil on the Eure River, where they spent four days, all the way to Paris, the brothers-in-law travelled together. It was the first time that they had seen each other for such a long time, they got to know each other again, riding, conversing, dawdling, dining and sleeping side by side. Monseigneur the dauphin is the exact opposite of the Navarrese, as long as the other is brief, as slow as the other is quick, as quiet as the other is talkative. And with that, six years younger, and no precocity in anything at all. In addition, the dauphin is afflicted with a condition that, strictly speaking, would seem to be an infirmity; his right hand swells and becomes purple whenever he tries to lift a heavy weight or hold on to an object tightly. He is unable to wield a sword. His father and his mother begot him very early, and at a time when they were both recovering from illness; and the fruit showed the signs.

But you mustn't conclude that from all this, as do certain people rather too hastily, beginning with King John himself, that the dauphin is an idiot and would make a bad king. I took great care to study his birth charts . . . the twenty-first of January 1338 . . . The Sun is still in Capricorn, just before entering Aquarius . . . those born in Capricorn triumph late in life, but they triumph nonetheless, as long as they possess intelligence. Winter plants grow slowly . . . I am willing to wager on that prince over many others who offer a better aspect. If he gets through the dangers that threaten him in these critical times . . . he has already overcome a good many; but the worst is yet to come . . . he will know how to make himself heard in government. But it has to be said that his appearance doesn't work in his favour . . .

Ah! And now the wind is driving the showers in gusts. Undo the silk ties that hold the curtains, would you, Archambaud. It is better to continue to chat in darkness than to get wet. And we will thus muffle the splashing of the horses' hooves that will end up deafening us. And tell Brunet, this evening, to fit my palanquin with oilskins under the coloured cloth. It is a bit heavier for the horses, I know. We will change them more often . . .

Yes, I was telling you that I can imagine only too well how Monseigneur of Navarre, during the trip from Vaudreuil to Paris . . . Vaudreuil benefits from one of the finest situations in all Normandy; King John wanted to make it one of his residences; they say that the palace he had built there is a wonder; I myself have never seen it, but I know that it cost the Treasury a fortune; there are pictures painted on the walls in pure gold . . . I can imagine how Monseigneur Charles of Navarre, with all his eloquence and the ease with which he professes friendship, must have applied himself to winning over Dauphin Charles of France. Young people like to model themselves on others. And for the dauphin, what an amiable companion, his elder by six years, who was already so well travelled, had seen and done so much, and who told so many secrets and entertained him with his gibing at those surrounding his father at court . . . 'Your father, our sire, must have painted a very different picture of me than I really am ... Let's be allies, let's be friends, let us truly be the brothers that we are.' The dauphin, most pleased to find himself appreciated by a relative much further advanced in life than he, already reigning and yet so agreeable, was easily taken in.

This rapprochement was not without consequence for future developments, and contributed heavily to the misadventures and confrontations that were to take place.

But I can hear the escort drawing in, preparing to parade. Pull back the curtain a little ... Yes, I can see the outskirts of the town. We are entering Châteauroux. We won't have much of a welcoming committee. Only a truly great Christian, or truly inquisitive, would get soaked in this heavy rain for the sole purpose of watching a cardinal's palanquin go past.

II

The Kingdom cracks

THESE ROADS OF Berry have always had a bad reputation. But I see that the war has hardly improved them . . . Hey! Brunet, La Rue! Slow down, by the grace of God. I know full well that everyone is in a hurry to reach Bourges. But it is no reason to rattle my bones in this crate. Stop, stop right here! And stop the front-runners too. All right . . . no, it is not at all my horses' fault. You are all to blame, you who push your mounts as if you had burning tow on your saddles . . . Now let us start off again, and may you be mindful, I beseech you, of driving me at a cardinal's pace. Otherwise I will oblige you to fill in the ruts before me.

They would break my bones, these wicked devils, to get to bed an hour earlier! At last the rain has stopped . . . Look, Archambaud, another scorched hamlet. The English came to romp as far as the outskirts of Bourges, where they proceeded to set fire to the city, and they even sent on a party that showed up at the walls of Nevers.

You see, I don't hold it against the Welsh archers, Irish coutiliers and other such bawdy fellows that the Prince of Wales employs to this end. They are miserable souls before whom he dangled the promise of fortune. They are poor, ignorant, and are led with an iron hand. War for them means ransack, pillaging and wasteful destruction. At the first sight of them the villagers flee, screaming, 'The English, the English, God help us!', children in their arms. How villains enjoy scaring villeins! They feel their strength. They feed it, they eat poultry and fattened pork every day; they broach all the barrels they can find to quench their thirst, and what they are not able to eat or drink, they spoil before leaving. Mounting stolen horses, they seek out and slit the throats of anything that lows or bleats in cowsheds or along the roadside. And then, drunk and demon-faced, black-handed, laughing, they hurl their lit torches onto the haystacks and barns and anything else they can burn. Ah! What good fun it must be for this army of drunkards and churls to obey such orders! They are like wicked children invited to do wrong.

And I don't even blame the English knights. After all, they are far from home; they were called up to go to war. And the Black Prince sets a fine example, pillaging the most beautiful objects brought to him, in gold, ivory and silver, the most beautiful fabrics, to fill up his carts or to present to his captains. He strips innocents bare of all their belongings in order to gratify his friends, therein lies the greatness of that man.

No, those for whom I wish a truly horrible death and damnation for eternity roasting in Gehenna . . . yes, yes, good Christian that I am . . . are the knights of Gascony, Aquitaine, Poitou, and even certain of our lesser nobles in Périgord, who prefer to follow the English duke over and above their French king, and who occupy themselves laying their own country to waste, through a taste for plundering or by sheer evil pride, or through jealousy of their neighbour, or because they have failed to digest some travesty of justice. No, those men, I pray to God, may He forgive them not.

There is only one thing to be said in their defence; they had been subjected to the foolishness of King John, who hardly showed he was the man to lead them, always raising his banners too late and stubbornly sending them where the enemy was no longer. Ah! What a scandal it is that God should allow such a disappointing prince into this world!

Why then did he consent to the Treaty of Valognes that I conversed with you about yesterday, and receivè another terrible kiss of Judas from his son-in-law of Navarre? Simply because Prince Edward of England's army had set sail for Bordeaux and he was filled with dread. Now common sense would have it that, having freed his hands on the Norman front, he would be heading full tilt for Aquitaine. One doesn't need to be a cardinal to figure that one out. But no. Our pathetic king dawdled, issuing important-sounding orders for the tiniest of things. He let the Prince of Wales land on the Gironde and make his triumphant entry into Bordeaux. He knew, from reports of spies and travellers, that the prince was preparing his troops, swelling their number with Gascons and Poitevins . . . those whom I was telling you earlier I hold in little esteem. Everything thus indicated that a tough expedition should be urgently under way. And another would have swept down like an eagle to defend his kingdom and his subjects. But this paragon of chivalry didn't move an inch.

It has to be said that he had financial troubles at the time, at the end of September last year, even more than usual. And it was precisely then, while Prince Edward was equipping his troops, that King John announced he would have to defer payment of his debts and officers' wages by six months.

It is often when a king is short of money that he sends his people to war. 'Be victorious and you will make yourselves rich! Claim your spoils, demand your ransoms . . .' King John preferred to let the Englishman ruin the southern part of his kingdom and himself be further impoverished.

Ah! The *chevauchée* was good and easy for the Prince of England! He took just one month to lead his army from the banks of the Garonne down to Narbonne and the coast, delighting in shaking Toulouse to its foundations, burning Carcassonne, devastating Béziers. He left behind him a long swathe of fear, and earned himself quite a reputation at little personal expense.

His art of war is simple, and our Périgord suffered greatly this year from his tactics; he attacks only that which is un-defended. He sends a vanguard well ahead to scout out the route and reconnoitre the villages and castles. Those that are securely held he bypasses. As for the others, he sends in heavy corps of knights and men-at-arms that swoop down on towns and villages with a roar worthy of doomsday, scattering the inhabitants, crushing against the walls those who are not fast enough, while their lances and maces pierce and batter to death whosoever should in panic offer themselves as targets; then they head off in different directions for the neighbouring hamlets, manors or monasteries.

Then come the archers, who grab supplies, subsistence

enough for the army to live on, and loot the houses before setting fire to them; then the coutiliers and the batmen who pile up the spoils in their carts and finish off the dirty work of burning the place down.

As the *chevauchée* progresses, by three to five leagues per day, all of them drinking until they can drink no more, the fear of them precedes them considerably.

And the Black Knight's aim in all this? I have already told you: to weaken the King of France. One has to admit that his objective has been achieved.

The chief beneficiaries of all this are the Bordelais and those from the vineyards, and one can understand why they readily accepted their English duke's leadership. These last years they have lived through a string of misfortunes: the devastation of war, the vines trampled in the fighting, trade routes increasingly risky, a slump in sales; add to this the coming of the Great Plague, which had forced Bordeaux to raze to the ground an entire neighbourhood so as to decontaminate the town. And now it was the turn of others to suffer the disasters of war, they said, and they would laugh. So each one should suffer in turn, shouldn't he?!

No sooner had he landed, than the Prince of Wales minted coinage and put into circulation fine gold coins bearing the lily and the lion … the leopard as the English would have it … much thicker and heavier coins than those of France, which furthermore bore the image of a lamb. 'The lion has eaten the lamb.' So say the people by way of a joke. The vines yield good fruit. The province is guarded. Activity in the port is brisk and profitable; in just a few months, twenty thousand casks of wine were shipped, almost exclusively to England.

So much so that the bourgeois of Bordeaux display only joyful faces and bellies as round as their barrels. Their wives fight to get into the draper's, the silversmith's and the jeweller's. Life in the town is a succession of feasts, and each time the prince returns in the black armour he so favours, and which indeed gave him his name, he is welcomed with merrymaking. All the bourgeois women are dizzy with prosperity. The soldiers, who have made themselves rich through pillaging, spend like there was no tomorrow. The loose morals of the Captains of Wales and Cornwall hold sway; many husbands and wives have been deceived in Bordeaux during this period, as fortune does not favour virtue.

It could be said that for a year now France has had two capital cities, which is the worst thing that can happen to a kingdom. In Bordeaux, opulence and power; in Paris, shortages and weakness. What do you expect? Parisian currency has been devalued eighty times since the beginning of the reign. Yes, Archambaud, eighty times! The Tournois pound[22] has retained but a tenth of its value from the time the king came to the throne. How can one possibly govern a state with such finances? When one allows prices of all commodities to rise out of all proportion while at the same time weakening the currency, great unrest and reversals of fortune are inevitable. Setbacks, France has already witnessed, and it is now heading for ruin.

So what did our brilliant king do, this last winter, to ward off the perils that everyone could see coming? No longer able to obtain support from the Langue d'Oc after the English raid, he convened the Estates-General of the Langue d'Oil. The meeting did not turn out at all to his satisfaction.

The deputies insisted on stringent conditions and made extraordinary demands of the king before they could be persuaded to accept the ruling that an exceptional levy of eight deniers in the pound be imposed on every sale, which constitutes a weighty tax on all trades and businesses, in addition to a special gabelle on salt. Tax revenues were to be collected by agents chosen specifically by themselves; this money would not end up either in the king's pockets or his soldiers'; no further raising of new taxes should be made without their consideration, even should there be another war ... What else? The people of the third estate[23] were the most vehement. They put forward examples of bourgeois successes in the counties of Flanders, where they have established a system of self-government, and in the English Parliament, which has a much stronger hold over its king than the States of France has over ours. 'Let's do as the English, it has brought them success.' It is a failing of the French, whenever they are in political difficulties, to look to foreign models rather than applying scrupulously, and in a timely manner, the laws that are their own ... We shouldn't be surprised that the latest meeting of the States, that the dauphin brought forward, turned out badly, as I told you the other day. The Prevost Marcel had already tested the power of his voice last year ... It wasn't you I told? Ah no, it was indeed Dom Calvo ... I haven't invited him back with me since; he gets sick in a palanquin ...

And the Navarrese king, you may ask, the one called the Bad, what of him during all this time? Charles the Bad endeavoured to convince King Edward that his feelings for him were still the same, that he hadn't been duped, the treaty negotiated with John II in Valognes was not what it seemed, Charles had only feigned agreement with the King of France, to better serve their shared plans, and that it would not be long before Edward would see it. In other words, he was waiting for the first occasion to betray him.

Meanwhile, he was working to consolidate his friendship with the dauphin through all manner of cajoling and flattery, and using the lure of pleasure, even women, as I have learned from the demoiselles themselves ... of the Gracious one I must already have made mention, and also a certain Biette Cassinel, both totally devoted to the King of Navarre ... and I have heard it said they liven up no end the little parties Charles gives for his brother-in-law. Thanks to this, and having made himself his master in sin, the Navarrese proceeded to secretly turn the dauphin against his father.

He pointed to evidence proving that King John did not love him at all, though he was his eldest son. And this much was true. He declared that he was a paltry king. And this was also the case. He professed to believe that, after all, it would be a pious deed if, without going so far as to put an end to his life, he helped God to at least drive him from the throne. 'My brother, you would make a better king than he. Don't wait until the kingdom he will leave you is in a state of collapse.' A young man is easily beguiled by such a refrain. 'Together we will prevail, I assure you. But first we will have to gain support in Europe.' Imagine, it was suggested they seek out the Emperor Charles IV, the dauphin's uncle, to call on his support and ask him for troops. Nothing less. Who do you think could have had this fine idea to look abroad for help in resolving the kingdom's problems, thus offering the emperor, who was already making life difficult enough for the papacy, the chance to decide the fate of France? Perhaps Bishop Le Coq, that bad prelate, brought by Navarre into the dauphin's entourage. The fact remains that the matter was well thought out and most sophisticated . . .

What? Why are we stopping when I have given no such order? Ah! Fardiers[24] are obstructing the road. It must be we are entering the outskirts of town. Clear the way. I dislike these unplanned stops. One never knows . . . Should they occur, may my escort close ranks around my palanquin. There are most daring rovers who are not at all afraid of sacrilege, and for whom a cardinal would be a fine catch . . .

So, the journey of the two Charleses, he of France and he of Navarre, was decided upon in secret; and we have since even found out who was to be part of the venture that would take them to Metz: the Count of Namur, the Count John of Harcourt, the fat one, whom misfortune was soon to strike, as I will tell you in due course, and a Boulogne too, Godfrey, and Gaucher of Lor, and of course the Sires of Graville, Clères and Aunay, Maubué of Mainemares, Colin Doublel and the inevitable Friquet of Fricamps, that is to say the conspirators of the Spinning Sow. And another fact is of interest, as I think they were the backers who funded the expedition, with them were to be Jean and William Marcel, nephews of the prevost, who counted themselves amongst the King of Navarre's friends and were always invited to his festivities. Plotting with a king unfailingly dazzles young and rich bourgeois!

They were due to set off on the feast of Saint Ambrose. Thirty Navarrese were to await the dauphin at the Saint-Cloud tollgate at nightfall, to take him to his cousin's estate in

Mantes; and from there this fine crowd would head off for the seat of Empire.

And then, and then ... even the most foolish of kings fails to make a mess of all he undertakes, and not everything always goes wrong for a man plagued by bad luck ... The day before, on the feast of Saint Nicholas, our John II got wind of the affair. He summoned his son, cross-examined him effectively enough to obtain a confession, and the dauphin realized for himself that he had been led astray, and not only his own interests but also the kingdom's were at risk.

There, I have to admit that King John acted more skilfully than usual. The only charge he held against his son was that of planning to leave the kingdom without his permission; in return for his frankness, John showed him benevolence, granting him his forgiveness and remission of any punishment for this lapse, and, having thus discovered that his son and heir had the ability to make his own decisions, he declared a desire to engage him more closely with the duties of the throne by making him Duke of Normandy. This was of course setting a trap for his son, by giving him a duchy so densely populated with partisans of the Évreux-Navarre clan! But it was well played indeed.

Monseigneur the dauphin had just to warn the Bad that he was releasing all those who were party to their secret designs.

You can imagine that this affair didn't strengthen the father's love for his son, even if his bitterness was concealed beneath the noble gift of the duchy. But most of all, the king's hatred for his son-in-law was becoming as hard as bread baked six times in the oven. Killing his constable, stirring up trouble, disembarking troops, engaging in talks with the English enemy . . . and he was yet to find out just how far he had gone! Finally, turning his own son against him; it was just the last straw; King John would wait for the right moment to make the Navarrese pay for this flood of sins.

For those of us watching all this from Avignon, worry was growing, and we could see extreme circumstances approaching. Some provinces devastated, others breaking away from France, the currency dwindling, State coffers empty, growing debt, deputies rebellious and vehement, important vassals persisting in their factions, a king served only by his closest advisors, and lastly, to top it all, an heir to the throne willing to call upon foreign help to overthrow his own dynasty . . . I said to the pope: 'Most Holy Father, France is cracking.' I wasn't at all wrong. I only misjudged the timing.

I gave it two years until the collapse would take place. Not even one was necessary. And we have yet to see the worst. What do you expect? When the head is not resolute, how could we hope that the limbs would be? Now is the time for us to attempt to patch things up somehow, and that is why we need to resort to the good offices of Germany and thus accord the emperor even more authority, he whose arrogance we would have preferred to muzzle. Admit that there is good reason to curse!

Go on, Archambaud, take up your mount once more and resume your position at the head of the retinue. For our entry into Bourges, however late it may be, I would like your pennon of Périgord to fly next to that of the Holy See. And have my curtains pulled back for the benedictions.

PART TWO

THE BANQUET
OF ROUEN

I

Exemptions and Benefits

OH! MONSEIGNEUR OF Bourges really got on my nerves over the three days we spent at his palace. Now there is a prelate whose hospitality is overbearing and beggarly! Constantly pulling on your robe to get something or other. And he has so many protégés and clients, to whom he has promised so much, he blithely passes them on to you. 'May I introduce you to His Most Holy Eminence, a cleric of great merit . . . Would His Most Holy Eminence deign to cast his benevolent eye upon the canon of wherever . . . May I be so bold as to recommend to Your Most Holy Eminence's good graces . . .' I really had to bite my lip, yesterday evening, to avoid letting out a cry: 'Be gone, rid us of yourself, bishop, and . . . yes, at last peace descends upon My Holy Eminence!'

I took you with me this morning, Calvo . . . I hope you are beginning to put up with the rocking of my palanquin a little better; furthermore I shall be brief . . . so that we may recap in detail exactly what I granted him, and nothing more. Because, now that he is party to our journey, he won't hesitate to come and bore you with the supposed consent that he will say I have given to all of his requests. He has already told me: 'For minor exemptions, I have no wish to bother Your Most Holy Eminence; I will present them to Messire Francesco Calvo, who is certainly a most knowledgeable person, or to Messire du Bousquet . . .' Hah! I didn't bring a papal auditor, two doctors, two bachelors of law and four knights with me just to release from their illegitimacy all the sons of those guilty priests who celebrate Mass in this diocese, or who own benefices there. Moreover, it is a wonder to see that after all the exemptions granted by my holy protector, Pope John XXII, during his pontificate . . . almost five thousand, of which more than half to priests' bastards, and in return, of course, for a monetary penance, which helped to replenish the coffers of the Holy See no end . . . thus today there are to be found as many monks, all in fact the fruits of sin.

As papal legate, I have the latitude to give out up to ten exemptions during the course of my mission, no more. I granted two to Monseigneur of Bourges and that was too many to begin with. I am allowed to confer twenty-five for the notaries' offices, and then only to clerks who have done me personal favours, not to those who have slipped into the good books of Monseigneur of Bourges. You shall give him one, choosing the most stupid and the least deserving, so as to bring him nothing but trouble. Should he be surprised, you will reply: 'Ah! Monseigneur expressly recommended this . . .' Of those benefices that are unoccupied, in other words, the commendams, whether they be clerical or otherwise, not a single one is to be handed out. Say, 'Monseigneur of Bourges asked for too much.' Or, 'But monseigneur did not wish to make people jealous . . .' And, by the way, I want you to add one or two commendams for Monseigneur of Limoges, who has proved himself more discreet. With this bishop, wouldn't people say that I had come all the way from Avignon only to lavish favours and benefits around Monseigneur of Bourges? I don't appreciate those who make their way in the world by flaunting their many obligés, and if he thinks that I will put in a word for his mitre, he is deluding himself.

And besides, I found him rather too lenient with the Fraticelli, of whom I saw many lurking about his palace. I was obliged to remind him of the Holy Father's letter against these stray Franciscans . . . I know it all the better as it was I who wrote it . . . who falsely claim the ministry of preaching for themselves, win over the simpletons with habits of a feigned humility and make dangerous speeches against the faith that undermine the respect the Holy See is due. I refreshed his memory of the commandment sent to him to correct and punish these evildoers according to the canon laws, and further, if need be, to call upon the help of the secular arm of justice, as did Innocent VI the other year in the burning at the stake of John of Châtillon and François of Arquate for the crime of upholding heresy . . . 'Heresies, heresies . . . most certainly mistakes, but we must understand them. They are not wrong on all counts. And besides, times are changing . . .' This was how he answered me, Monseigneur of Bourges. I really don't like these prelates who show far too much understanding towards bad preachers, and prefer to court popularity by first seeing which way the wind blows rather than acting ruthlessly.

I would therefore be most grateful, Dom Calvo, if you would keep an eye on that fellow during the voyage, and prevent him from indoctrinating my knights, or from pouring forth to Monseigneur of Limoges or to the other bishops that will join us on the way.

Make his journey hard, even though, as the days are shortening and the cold biting, we will have but short stages. Ten to twelve leagues per day, no more. I do not want us to travel by night. That is the reason why we will go no further than Sancerre today. We will have a long evening there. Beware of the wine that is drunk there. It is fruity and most drinkable, but stronger than it seems. Let La Rue know this, and might he stand watch over the escort. I will have no drunkards in the pope's livery . . . But you are looking pale, Calvo. You clearly can't put up with the palanquin . . . No, step down, step down quickly, would you.

2

The Anger of the King

So, the German venture came to an abrupt end, leaving the Navarrese greatly vexed. He had left for Évreux and was becoming increasingly restless. Three months passed; it was the end of March last year ... yes, I am right in saying last year ... or the present year, if you like ... but as this year Easter falls on the twenty-fourth of April, it was still last year ...

Yes; I know, my nephew; it is a rather stupid custom in France according to which, while we celebrate the New Year on the first of January, for registers, treaties and all things to be recollected, we only change the number of the year from Easter. Most foolish of all, however, and the thing which creates much confusion, is to have aligned the legal beginning of the year to a moveable feast day. In such a way that some years count two months of March, while others are deprived of April ... That, we will certainly have to change, I fully agree with you.

We have already been talking about it for a very long time, but nothing has been resolved. It is up to the Holy Father to decide for the whole of Christendom. And I assure you that in Avignon, as the hub of world events, we have the biggest muddle of all; in Spain, as in Germany, the year begins on Christmas Day; in Venice, on the first of March; in England, on the twenty-fifth. Such that if a treaty involving several countries is concluded in the spring, we can never know which year we are talking about. Imagine that a truce between France and England were signed in the days leading up to Easter; for King John, it would be dated in the year of 1355 and for the English 1356. Oh! It is the most stupid thing, I'll give you that; but nobody wants to change their habits, however bungling, and one might even think that the notaries, lawyers, prevosts and other members of the administration took pleasure in entrenching themselves in difficulties to waylay the common people.

We were approaching the end of March, as I was telling you, when King John flew into a fit of rage ... About his son-in-law, of course. Oh! We must admit that he had good cause for annoyance. At the Estates of Normandy, gathered in Vaudreuil before his son, the recently appointed Duke, strong words like none ever heard before were said about him, and it was the deputies of the nobility, stirred up by the Évreux-Navarre clan, who voiced them. The two Harcourts, the uncle and the nephew, were the most violent in their language, or so I was told; and the nephew, fat Count John, got so carried away he shouted: 'By God, this king is a bad man; he is not a good king, and I shall be wary of him.' That got back to John II, as you can imagine. Shortly afterwards the new Estates of Langue d'Oil were held: the deputies of Normandy didn't show up at all. Quite simply refused to appear. They no longer wished to have a share in the grants and aides, nor did they wish to pay for them. Moreover, the assembly was forced to note that the gabelle and the sales tax had failed to produce the revenues anticipated. So it was decided to replace them with an income tax at the end of the year we were in.

I will let you imagine how warmly the measure was welcomed, to be compelled to pay the king a part of all the income they had received, collected or earned during the year, and often already spent . . . No, it was not applied in Périgord, nor anywhere else in Langue d'Oc. But I know of people from our parts who went over to the Englishman, for fear that the measure be extended to themselves. This income tax, added to the increase in the cost of provisions, sparked riots in various places, in particular at Arras, where the humble folk revolted; and King John had to send in his constable with several companies of men-at-arms to charge the agitators . . . No, of course none of this provided him with any reason to rejoice; but however great his troubles, a king must always maintain his self-control. Something he failed to do on this occasion.

He was at the Abbey of Beaupré-en-Beauvais to celebrate the baptism of the firstborn of Monseigneur John of Artois, Count of Eu since he had been presented with the possessions and titles of Raoul of Brienne, the beheaded constable . . . Yes, the very same, the son of Count Robert of Artois, whom he very much takes after in his bearing. Upon seeing him, one is struck by the resemblance; one would think one beheld the father at his age. A giant, a walking tower. Red hair, short nose, cheeks prickling with bristles, and a thick, muscular neck linking his jaw and shoulder in a straight line. He can have only dray horses for his mount, and when he charges, decked out for battle, he makes holes in any army. But that is where the resemblance ends. As for his mind, he is quite the opposite. The father was ingenious, astute, quick-witted, shrewd, too shrewd by half. This one has a brain like mortar that has begun to set. Count Robert was litigious, a plotter, forger, traitor, a murderer. Count John, as if wishing to atone for the sins of his father, likes to think of himself as a model of honour, loyalty and fidelity. Having seen his father deposed and banished and spent time in prison himself during his childhood, with his mother and brothers, he is, I believe, quite overwhelmed by the pardon he received, and his return to grace. He looks on King John as the Redeemer himself. Besides, he is dazzled to bear the same Christian name. 'My cousin John . . . my cousin John . . .'

These three words would be bandied about by cousin John all the time. Those of us who remember Robert of Artois, men of my age, even those who suffered under his infamy, cannot fail to feel a certain regret upon seeing the feeble-minded copy of himself that he left us. Ah! Count Robert was indeed a strapping fellow, and a great noise! He filled his epoch with his unruliness. When he died, one might say the century fell silent. Even the war seemed to lose its rumble. How old would he be now? Let's see . . . um . . . about seventy. Oh! He had the strength to live that long, had a stray arrow not killed him, in the English camp, during the siege of Vannes . . . We can but say that all the perpetual proof of the younger Artois' loyalty didn't make the crown feel any happier than the father's treachery had.

Because it was John of Artois, who, just before the baptism, and as if to thank the king for his patronage, revealed the conspiracy of Conches, or rather what he thought to be a conspiracy.

Conches . . . yes, that is what I said . . . one of the castles confiscated from Robert of Artois and that Monseigneur of Navarre was given in the Treaty of Valognes. But some old servants remain there who are still attached to the memory of the Artois.

This is how John of Artois was able to whisper in the king's ear . . . a whisper that could be heard at the other end of the bailiwick . . . that the King of Navarre had met up in Conches with his brother Philip, both the Harcourts, the Bishop Le Coq, Friquet of Fricamps, several Norman sires of old acquaintance, as well as Guillaume Marcel, or Jean . . . well, one of the Marcel nephews . . . and a lord arriving from Pamplona, Miguel of Espelette . . . and all of them were since plotting to attack King John, by ambush, and slaughter him, on the first occasion that brought him to Normandy. Was it true, was it false? I would be inclined to believe that there was some truth to it, and that without having gone so far as to set up the conspiracy, they had considered doing the deed. Because it is very much in the manner of Charles the Bad, having failed to pull off the operation with grandeur by obtaining the support of the Emperor of Germany, to go about accomplishing it with villainy, doubtless without a qualm, repeating the ambush of the Spinning Sow. We will have to wait to appear before the judgement seat of God to find out the whole truth.

What is certain, however, is that there was much discussion in Conches as to whether they would make their way to Rouen, one week later, the Tuesday before the feast of the Third Thursday of Lent, to which the dauphin, Duke of Normandy, had invited all the most important Norman knights to attempt to reach an agreement with them. Philip of Navarre advised that they refuse; Charles, on the other hand, was inclined to accept. Old Godfrey of Harcourt, the one with a limp, was against, and loudly said so. Moreover, he who had fallen out with the late King Philip VI over a marriage where his love had been thwarted, considered himself no longer tied to the crown by any bond of vassalage whatsoever. 'My king is the Englishman' he would say.

His nephew, the obese Count John, whom the scent of a banquet would have dragged to the other end of the kingdom, was inclined to go. In the end, Charles of Navarre said that everyone should do as they pleased, that he would himself be going, alongside whosoever wished to join him, but at the same time he approved the decision of others who did not wish to appear before the dauphin, and pointed out that there was wisdom in their retreat, as one should never put all one's hounds down the same rabbit hole.

One more thing was reported to the king that could have substantiated the suspicion of a plot. Charles of Navarre may have said that were King John to die, then he would immediately make his treaty passed with the King of England public, by which he recognized him as the King of France, and that he would behave in every way as his lieutenant in the kingdom.

King John asked for no proof. And yet the first concern of a prince must be to always establish the truth of the denunciation, from the most plausible to the most incredible. But our king isn't nearly so careful. He swallows like fresh eggs anything that feeds his grudges. A more composed mind would have listened, and then sought out and gathered together information and evidence regarding this secret treaty that had just been revealed to him. And if, from this presumption, he had been able to expose the truth, he would have found himself in a much stronger position vis-à-vis his son-in-law.

But he immediately took the matter as certified truth; and he entered the church for the baptizing of Count John's firstborn ablaze with rage. He displayed, so I was told, the strangest of behaviours, not hearing the prayers at all, pronouncing his responses all the wrong way, looking at everyone furiously and sending the embers of a censer he had collided with flying onto the surplice of a deacon. I really don't know how the Artois child was baptized; but with such a godfather, I think that they will soon have to renew the vows of that little Christian, if we want God to have mercy on his soul.

And as soon as the ceremony was over, all hell broke loose. Never had the monks of Beaupré heard such terrible cursing, as if the Devil had lodged himself in the king's throat. It was raining, but John II paid no attention. For over an hour and although dinner had already been called, he got himself soaked pacing up and down the monks' garden, splashing in puddles with his poulaines ... those ridiculous shoes that handsome Monsieur of Spain brought into fashion for him . . . and forcing all of his suite, Messire Nicolas Braque, his butler, and Messire of Lorris, and the other chamberlains, and the Marshal of Audrehem and the huge John of Artois, dumbfounded and contrite, to get wet with him. Thereupon he was to waste thousands of pounds in velvet, embroidery and furs.

'There is no other ruler in France but me,' screamed the king. 'I will kill him, this bad seed, this vermin, this rotten badger who plots my end with all my enemies. I will go and slay him with my own hands. I will tear out his heart, and cut his stinking body up into so many pieces, do you hear me, there will be enough to hang one on the door of each of the castles I bestowed upon him in my weakness. And may no one ever come again to intercede on his behalf, and may none of you dare to advocate coming to any more arrangements. Moreover, Blanche and Joan can cry themselves dry of their tears, there will be no more pleading this traitor's cause, and they will learn that there is no other ruler in France but me,' as if he needed to persuade himself that he was indeed king.

He calmed down enough to ask when the banquet would take place that his ass of a son was to give so courteously to his snake of a son-in-law. He was told the fifth of April, Saint Irene's day, and he repeated this as if he had trouble putting such a simple thing into his mind. He stayed a moment shaking his head like a horse, scattering drops from his rain-soaked yellow hair. 'On that day, I will go hunting in Gisors,' he said.

His entourage was used to his sudden changes of mood; everyone thought that the king's anger had worn itself out in words and that the matter would go no further. And then came the banquet of Rouen, and what happened there ... Yes, but you don't know it in detail. I will tell you that tale, but it must wait until tomorrow; as for today, time is getting on, we should almost be there.

You see, the route seems shorter when we chat this way. This evening, all we have to do is to dine and to sleep. Tomorrow we will arrive in Auxerre, where I will receive news from Avignon and Paris. Ah! One more thing, Archambaud. Be cautious around Monseigneur of Bourges, who is travelling with us, should he ever try to tackle you. I dislike him immensely, and I really don't know why, I suspect the man of having a secret understanding with Capocci. Toss him the name, without appearing to dwell on it, and you will tell me your opinion.

3

To Rouen

KING JOHN INDEED went to Gisors, but he only stayed there long enough to collect one hundred pikemen from the garrison. Then he left ostentatiously by the road to Chaumont and Pontoise so that all could believe he was returning to Paris. He took with him his second son, the Duke of Anjou, and his brother, the Duke of Orléans, who looks more like one of his sons, as Monseigneur of Orléans, who is twenty years old counts seventeen years difference with the king, and only two with the dauphin.

The king had been escorted by the Marshal of Audrehem, by his second chamberlains, Jean of Andrisel and Guy de la Roche, as he had sent Lorris and Nicolas Braque to Rouen several days earlier under the pretext that he was lending them to the dauphin to supervise his banquet preparations.

Who else was behind the king? Oh! He had put together quite an army. He was taking with him the Artois brothers, Charles and the other one . . . 'my cousin John' . . . who never left his side and who rose head and shoulders above the rest of the expedition, and also Louis of Harcourt who had fallen out with his brother and his uncle Godfrey, and had taken sides with the king as a result. I will spare you the equerries and huntsmen, the Corquillerays, Huet des Ventes and other Maudétours. Indeed! The king was going hunting and wanted it to appear that way; he mounted his hunting horse, a fast, brave and well-foddered Napoletano that he was particularly fond of. Nobody could be surprised to see him followed by the sergeant of his personal guard, which was commanded by Enguerrand Lalemant and Perrinet le Buffle,[25] two fellows famous for the size of their muscles; those two can flip a man over by just taking his hand . . . It is a good thing for a king to always have bodyguards around him. The Holy Father has his own. I too have my close protection, men who ride either side of my palanquin, as you must have seen. I am so used to them now that I often don't notice them at all; but I am never out of their sight.

What may have surprised some, but you needed to have your eyes wide open to see it, was that the king's men-servants, most probably Tassin and Poupart le Barbier, wore hanging from their saddles the helmet, the cervellière,[26] the great sword, all the battle attire of the king. And also amongst them the presence of the King of the Ribald, a fellow named . . . Guillaume . . . Guillaume something or other . . . who not only watches over the brothel police in the towns where the king resides, but also takes charge of all legal matters that directly concern the king. There is significantly more work to do in this role since John II came to the throne.

With the equerries of dukes, knights' pages, all the lords'

domestics and the pikemen collected in Gisors, that made at least two hundred men on horseback, of which many bristled with lances, too big an equipage to go beating the bushes for game.

The king had taken the direction of Chaumont-en-Vexin but nobody ever saw him pass through the town. His army disappeared en route as if by magic. He had headed off due north across country, for Gournay-en-Bray where he made a brief stop, just long enough to pick up the Count of Tancarville, one of the few great Norman lords who had remained a loyal supporter, because of his hatred for the Harcourts. At Gournay-en-Bray, an astounded Tancarville, surrounded by twenty knights of his banner, met him; he had been expecting the Marshal of Audrehem, but absolutely not the king himself.

'Hasn't my son the dauphin invited you to Rouen tomorrow, messire the count?'

'Yes, sire; but I received a mandate from messire the marshal, when he was here to inspect the county's fortresses, exempting me from any obligation to appear in company where a great many faces would have met with my disapproval.'

'Well now! You will nevertheless go to Rouen, Tancarville, and I will inform you of what we shall be doing there.'

Whereupon, the entire expedition turned sharply south, a short ride since night was falling, only three or four leagues, but which were on top of the eighteen travelled that day already, to go and sleep in an out-of-the-way castle on the edge of the Forest of Lyons.

If there were spies in the locality working for the King of

Navarre, they would have found it difficult to tell their master where the King of France was heading on this roundabout route, and what he planned to do there . . . The king was seen leaving for the hunt . . . The king is inspecting fortresses . . .

The king was up before dawn, hasty, feverish, urging his people on, and already saddled up and ready to charge, this time straight as an arrow, through the Forest of Lyons. Those who wanted to eat a crust of bread and a slice of bacon had to do it maintaining a steady trot and with just one hand, while holding the reins in the crook of their arm and a lance in their other hand.

The Forest of Lyons is dense and long; it measures more than seven leagues and yet one can almost get across it in two hours. The Marshal of Audrehem thought that riding at such a pace, they would certainly arrive too soon . . . It was the marshal himself who told me. 'We could well stop a moment, if only to let the horses piss,' he said. Not to mention, for his own part, 'An urge, may Your Eminence forgive me, that splits my sides.' Now, a marshal of the king's army cannot just relieve himself from high up on his mount, as simple archers would do whenever they feel the need, and too bad if they spray the saddle's leather. He said to the king: 'Sire, there is no point in rushing so; that doesn't make the sun go any faster . . . Furthermore, the horses need to take on water.' And the king replied: 'Here is the letter I will write to the pope, to explain my justice and forestall the false accounts that he could be given . . . "Most Holy Father, for far too long now, the indulgences I have granted that wicked relation and the compromises that through Christian charity I have agreed have only encouraged his treachery, and because of him calamity and misfortune have come to the kingdom. An even greater crime was in preparation, whereby he would deprive me of my life; and it is to prevent him accomplishing this foul assassination . . .'''

And straight ahead at full tilt, without noticing a thing, he left the Forest of Lyons and broke cover in the plains, before entering another forest. Audrehem told me he had never seen such an expression on the king's face, mad-eyed; he could see his heavy chin trembling under his thin beard.

Abruptly, Tancarville pushed his mount on to draw level with the king and asked him politely if he wished to head for Pont-de-l'Arche.

'Of course not,' cried the king. 'I am going to Rouen!'

'In that case, sire, I fear that you will not get there by this route. We should have turned right at the last fork in the road.'

And the king turned his Napoletano horse around on the spot and rode back past the entire procession, commanding in fits of anger that they all follow him, and his will was done, but not without a good deal of commotion, and still, to the great suffering of the marshal, without stopping to take a piss . . .

Tell me, my nephew, don't you feel anything strange in our gait? . . . Well, I do.

Brunet, hey! Brunet! One of my packhorses is limping . . . Don't tell me, 'No, monseigneur'. Go and have a look. The one bringing up the rear. And I even think it is his right fore-foot that is lame. Have them stop . . . And? Ah! He has lost his shoe? And which hoof . . .? So, who was right? My back is more alert than your eyes.

Come on, Archambaud, let's step down. We will take a short walk while they change the horses. The air is cool, but not at all unpleasant. What can we see from here? Do you know, Brunet? Saint-Amand-en-Puisaye . . . Archambaud, this is how King John must have first caught sight of Rouen on the morning of the fifth of April.

4

The Banquet

So you don't know Rouen, Archambaud, nor the Castle of Bouvreuil. Oh! It is a big castle with six or seven towers set in a circle around a large central courtyard. It was built one hundred and fifty years ago by King Philip II Augustus, to keep watch over the town and its port, and to command the fastest-flowing course of the lower Seine. Rouen is an important stronghold indeed, one of the openings of the kingdom to the English side, and thus a cut-off point as well. The sea comes in as far as its stone bridge which links the two halves of the duchy of Normandy.

The keep is not at the centre of the castle; it is in fact one of the towers, somewhat taller and broader than the others. We have similar castles in Périgord, but they usually have a more extravagant appearance.

The flower of Normandy's chivalry was there assembled, as richly dressed as it was possible to be. Sixty sires had come, each with at least one equerry. The buglers had just sounded the call for dinner when one of Messire Godfrey of Harcourt's equerries, sweating heavily from a long gallop, came to warn Count John that his uncle summoned him post-haste and urged him to leave Rouen immediately. The message was most imperious, as if Messire Godfrey had got wind of something. John of Harcourt hastened to comply with Godfrey's command, slipping away from the company and descending the keep's stairwell, his body obstructing everything in its path, he was so fat, a veritable barrel of a man, but reaching the foot of the stairs there he fell face to face with Robert of Lorris, who stood in his way with a most affable air about him. 'Messire the count, messire, are you leaving? But monseigneur the dauphin is expecting you at dinner! Your place is on his left.' Not daring to offend the dauphin, the glutton Harcourt resigned himself to delaying his departure. He would leave after the meal. And he went back up the stairs without too much regret. After all, the dauphin's table had a fine reputation; it was known that wonders were served there, and John of Harcourt hadn't acquired all the fat that he was larded with by sucking on blades of grass.

And indeed, what a feast! It had not been in vain that Nicolas Braque had helped the dauphin prepare it. Those who were there, and who lived to tell the tale, haven't forgotten a thing. Six tables were spread out in the great round room. Tapestries of verdure, so richly coloured that one would have thought oneself in the middle of a forest. Near the windows, clusters of candles, to enhance the light of day coming through the embrasures,[27] like the sun through the trees. Behind each guest, a carving equerry, either their own, for the great lords, or someone from the dauphin's service for the others. They used ebony-handled knives, gilded and enamelled with the French coat of arms, especially reserved for the duration of Lent. It is the custom at court to only bring out the ivory-handled knives from Easter onwards.

As Lent was observed, fish pâtés and stews, carp, pike, tench, bream, salmon and bass, plates of eggs, poultry, game birds; the fishponds and farmyards had been emptied, the rivers cleaned out. The kitchen pages formed a human chain in the stairwell, sending up platters of silver and vermeil on which roast-chefs, sauce-chefs and other cooks had set, arranged, dressed the dishes prepared in the hearths of the kitchens' tower. Six cupbearers poured wines from Beaune, Meursault, Arbois and Touraine ... Ah! All that whets your appetite too, Archambaud! I do hope that they will prepare a good meal for us later on in Saint-Sauveur ...

The dauphin, in the middle of the table of honour, had Charles of Navarre on his right and John of Harcourt on his left. He was dressed in a marbled blue cloak from Brussels and wore a hood of the same cloth, decorated with embroidered pearls arranged in leaf-patterns. I haven't yet described monseigneur the dauphin to you ... He's broad, but with a drawn-out body, lean shoulders, his face is elongated, a big nose with a slight bump in the middle, a look in his eye by which you never know whether he is being attentive or pensive, a thin upper lip, the lower fleshy, a receding chin.

It is said, as far as one can tell, that he rather takes after his ancestor Saint Louis, who like him was very long and a little stooped. Such a bearing, next to very upright, fiery men, appears from time to time in the French royal family.

Ushers came and went, stiffly formal with the kitchen pages, to present the dishes one after the other; and the dauphin indicated with a gesture of his hand to which table they should be carried, thus honouring each of his guests in turn, the Count of Étampes, Sire de la Ferté, the Mayor of Rouen, with a smile and much courteous dignity accompanying the gesture . . . always made with his left hand. Because, as I told you I believe, his right hand is swollen red and causes him pain; he uses it as little as possible. He can scarcely play real tennis for half an hour and his hand immediately swells up. Ah! What a weakness for a prince . . . neither hunting nor fighting. His father makes no secret of his disgust, pouring scorn upon him for it. How the poor dauphin must have envied all the well-built noblemen he dealt with, the Sires of Clères, Graville, Bec Thomas, Mainemares, Braquemont, Saint-Beuve or Houdetot, those steadfast knights, sure of themselves, rowdy, proud of their exploits in battle. He must have envied even the fat Harcourt, whose quintal[28] of blubber didn't prevent him from handling a horse, nor from being a formidable tourneyer, and particularly he envied the Sire of Biville, a man famous across France who is quickly surrounded whenever he appears in society and asked to tell of his feat . . . It is one and the same . . . You see, his name has made its way to you . . . yes, in one single blow of a sword, a Turk cut in half, before the very eyes of the King of Cyprus. Every time he repeats his story, the gash lengthens by an inch. One day he will have also managed to split the horse in two . . .

But let me come back to the Dauphin Charles. This boy knows what his birth and his station require of him; he knows why God brought him into this world, the place that Providence had assigned to him, in the highest rank of men, and that, unless he were to die before his father, he would be king. He knows that he will have sovereign power with which to govern over the kingdom; he knows that he will personify France. And even if he is secretly grieved that God hasn't given him, along with his charge, the strength that will help him to bear it successfully, he knows that he must make up for the inadequacies of his body with a good grace, an attention to others, a mastery of his expressions and his words, an air of benevolence and certainty that never let anyone forget who he is, including himself, and thus he creates for himself a means to majesty. That is no mean feat, when one is but eighteen years old and one's beard has scarcely begun to grow!

It has to be said that he was prepared from an early age. He was just eleven years old when his grandfather, King Philip VI, finally managed to buy the Dauphiny from Humbert II of Vienna. That somewhat made up for the defeat at Crécy and the loss of Calais. I told you after which negotiations . . . Ah! I thought . . . So you want to know about it in detail?

The Dauphin Humbert was as swollen with pride as he was crippled with debt. He wanted to sell, while continuing to govern parts of the territory he was handing over, and wanted his states to remain independent upon his death. At first he had wanted to deal with the Count of Provence, King of Sicily; but he had set his price too high. He then turned to France, and it was then that I was called upon to take care of negotiations. In an early agreement, he was to give up his crown, but only after his demise . . . he had lost his only son . . . a part in cash, one hundred and twenty thousand florins if you please, and the rest in a pension. He could have lived comfortably on that for the rest of his days. But instead of clearing his debts, he squandered everything in seeking glory fighting the Turks. Hounded by his creditors, he was forced to sell all he had left, that is, his lifelong pension rights. This he ended up accepting for two hundred thousand florins more and an allowance of twenty-four thousand pounds, while continuing to play the high and mighty. Thankfully for us, he no longer had any friends.

It was I, and I say this modestly, who found the compromise that was able to satisfy the honour of Humbert and his subjects. The title of Dauphin of Viennois would not be borne by the King of France, but by the eldest of the grandsons of Philip VI and then, in turn, by his eldest son. In this way the dauphin's subjects, who had been hitherto independent, maintained the illusion of having a prince who reigned only over them. That was why the young Charles of France, having received his investiture in Lyons, had to accomplish throughout the winter of 1349 and spring 1350, a tour of his new states. Processions, receptions, fairs. I repeat, he was only eleven years old. By virtue of that ease with which children get into character, he became used to the cheers of the crowds welcoming him in the towns, the bowed heads he walked between, he sat gracefully on a throne while officials rushed to pile silk hassocks under his feet . . . enough so that they didn't dangle in the air . . . he received suzerains' tributes in his hands, listened solemnly to local grievances. He surprised by his dignity, his affability, the common sense behind his questions. People were touched by his earnestness; tears welled up in the eyes of old knights and their old wives when he assured them of his love and his friendship, praising them for their merits and counting on their loyalty. The slightest word of any prince is the object of infinite gossip which conveys self-importance upon the one who received it. But coming from such a young boy, from this miniature of a prince, the simplest of phrases inspired such moving tales! 'One cannot pretend at that age.' But of course he was pretending, and even enjoying pretending, like all children do. Pretending to be interested in someone he was seeing, even if he was offered a cross-eyed gaze and a toothless grin, pretending to be happy with whatever gift that was presented, even if he had already received four of the same, feigning authority when the moment came, after having listened to representatives of a town council complain about a matter of a toll or some such narrow dispute ... 'Your rights will be restored, if you have been done wrong by. I want an enquiry to be made post-haste.' He had quickly understood how effective it was to command, in a determined tone of voice, an investigation, to be led diligently ... this produced great impression without committing him to anything.

He was yet to find out that he would be overtaken by such fragile health, although he had fallen ill for several weeks in Grenoble. It was while at Grenoble he learned of his mother's death, then his grandmother's, and shortly after, the remarriage of both his grandfather and of his father, one after the other, before it was announced to him that he himself was soon to marry Madame Joan of Bourbon, his cousin, who was the same age as he. This took place at Tain-l'Hermitage at the beginning of April, with great pomp and affluence from the Church and nobility. Just six years ago.

It is a miracle that it didn't go to his head, or that he wasn't disturbed by all that pomp and vanity. He had simply revealed the penchant shared by all the princes of his family for spending and luxury. Spendthrifts. Acquire everything that takes their fancy, immediately. I want this, I want that. Buying, possessing the most beautiful things, the rarest, most curious, and above all the most expensive, menagerie animals, sumptuous silverware, illuminated manuscripts, spending, living in rooms hung with silk and gold drapery from Cyprus, their clothes sewn with fortunes in gemstones that brightly glisten in the candlelight. This, for the dauphin, as for all his lineage, is the symbol of power and proof, in his own eyes, of majesty. A naivety that comes down to the family from the grandfather, the first of the Charleses, Philip the Fair's brother, titular Emperor of Constantinople, that great idiot who bumbled about, shaking up Europe, and even for a moment thought about the Empire of Germany. A profligate one if ever there was . . . they all have it in their blood. When they order shoes for the family, it is by the two-dozen, forty or fifty-five pairs at a time, for the king, for the dauphin, for Monseigneur of Orléans. To be sure, their stupid poulaines get saturated with mud, especially the long tips, which lose their shape, the embroidery gets dulled, and in three days they're ruined, that each took a month for the best Paris artisans, who are in Guillaume Loisel's boutique, to make. I know this because my own red slippers come from there too; but I make do with just eight pairs a year. And look, am I not always properly attired?

As the court sets the tone, nobles and bourgeois spend a fortune on passementerie,[29] furs, jewels, vanity spending. They vie with each other for ostentation. Consider alone the hood worn by monseigneur the dauphin on that day in Rouen, a mark[30] of large pearls and a mark of small ones were used, all ordered from Belhommet Thurel for the sum of three hundred or three hundred and twenty écus! Should you really be surprised that the coffers are empty when each one spends more money than he has left?

Ah! There is my palanquin returning. They have changed the equipage. Well then, let's get back in . . .

In any case, there is one man that takes advantage of financial difficulties, and who makes good business from shortfalls in the royal coffers; and that is Messire Nicolas Braque, Grand Master of France, who is also Treasurer and Governor of Finance. He set up a small banking company, I should say a company just for show, which buys back at two-thirds the price, sometimes half, sometimes even at a third of the price, the king's and his family's debts. The mechanism is simple. A court supplier is in desperate trouble because for two years now nobody has paid him a thing and he no longer knows how he is going to pay his journeymen or buy his supplies. He comes looking for Messire Braque, and waves the unpaid bills under his nose. Messire Braque is most impressive; he is a handsome man, always severely dressed, and never lets past his lips any more words than are absolutely necessary. No one can put people in their place like he does. Such as those who turn up ranting and raving . . . 'This time I'll give him a piece of my mind; there is much to be said and I will not mince my words . . .' The angry court supplier finds himself quick as a flash turned into a stammering, imploring wreck. Messire Braque drops on him, like a shower from a drainpipe, a few cold, stiff words: 'Your prices are inflated as is always the case with work done for the king . . . the clientele of the court brings you a great many customers from whom you earn a good living . . . if the king has trouble paying, it is because all the monies from his Treasury go to covering the costs of the war . . . you should inform the bourgeois, such as Master Marcel, who baulk at granting aid . . . since you are having so much trouble supplying the king, we will withdraw our orders . . .' And when the plaintiff has quietened down, most grieved and shivering, Braque tells him: 'If you are truly in financial difficulties, I am willing to come to your aid. I can bring to bear my influence on your behalf with a bank, where I can count on some friends to buy back your debts. I will attempt, I repeat, I will attempt to have them redeemed at four-sixths of their value; and I will acquit you of that sum. The company will be paid back whenever, if ever, God is willing to replenish the Treasury. But don't speak a word of this, otherwise everyone in the kingdom will ask the same of me. It is a great favour indeed that I am granting you.'

After which, as soon as there is tuppence in the privy purse, Braque takes the opportunity to whisper into the king's ear: 'Sire, for the sake of your honour and renown, I didn't want to leave this glaring debt outstanding, all the more so as the creditor was becoming furious and threatening to cause a scandal. For your sake, I extinguished the debt out of my own pocket.' And first in order of priority for services rendered, he is repaid in full. In addition, as Treasurer it is he who signs off all palace spending, his palms are greased with countless beautiful gifts for each order made. He gains at both ends, this honest man.

On the day of the banquet, he was concerned less with the business of securing the payment of aid hitherto refused by the states of Normandy than his negotiations with the Mayor of Rouen, Master Mustel, for the purchase of Rouennais tradesmen's debts. Memoranda dating back to the king's previous visit, and even prior to that, had remained unpaid; as for the dauphin, even before receiving the title of duke he had been the king's lieutenant in Normandy and he ordered and ordered, without ever settling any of his accounts. And Messire Braque went about his usual trade, assuring the mayor that it was out of friendship for him and the high esteem in which he held the good people of Rouen that he was to make off with one-third of their profits. Even more still, as he would pay them in *Francs à la chaise*, put differently, a thinned-down currency, and thinned down by whom? By he himself who decided on all devaluations . . . We should acknowledge that when the states complain about the great officials of the crown, they have good grounds for doing so. When I think that some time ago Messire Enguerrand of Marigny was hanged because he had been accused, ten years after the fact, of having whittled down the coinage! But he was a saint compared to the Ministers of Finance of today!

Who else was there in Rouen who deserves to be mentioned, beyond the usual servants, and Mitton le Fol, the dauphin's dwarf, who was prancing about between the tables; he too wearing a pearly hood . . . pearls for a dwarf, I ask you, is that a good way to spend the écus that one doesn't have?

The dauphin dresses him in a striped drapery, woven specially for him in Ghent . . . I disapprove of the usage made of dwarfs. They are forced to act the clown, pushed and kicked around, they become a laughing stock. They are God's creatures after all, even if God didn't make such a good job of them. Another good reason to show them a little charity. But their families, so it appears, take their birth as a blessing. 'Ah! He is small. May he never grow up. We will be able to sell him to a duke or perhaps to the king . . .'

No, I believe I have mentioned all the guests of importance, with Friquet of Fricamps, Graville, Mainemares, yes, I mentioned them . . . and then, of course, the most important of them all, the King of Navarre.

On him the dauphin lavished all his attention. Moreover, on the side of the fat Harcourt little attention was required: that one had eyes only for the platters of food set before him, and any talk was vain while he was engaged in putting away his mountains of food.

However, the two Charleses, Normandy and Navarre, the two brothers-in-law, talked a great deal. Or rather Navarre talked. They had scarcely seen each other again since their failed expedition to Germany; and it was typical of the Navarrese to seek to win over his young relative once more, through flattery, declarations of hearty friendship, joyful memories and amusing tales.

Whilst his equerry, Colin Doublel, placed the dishes before him, Navarre, laughing, charming, full of spirit and offhandedness . . . 'This is the feast of our reunion; thank you so much, Charles, for allowing me to show you how attached I am to you; I have been bored since you went away . . .'

reminded him of their finer moments the winter before, the amiable bourgeoises they played dice with, who will have the blonde? Who will have the brunette? '. . . the Cassinel girl is round-bellied now, and nobody doubts that it is yours . . .' and from there moved on to affectionate reproach . . . 'Ah! So you went and told your father all about our plans! You got the Duchy of Normandy out of it. That was well played indeed, I will give you that. But with me, you could have had the entire kingdom by now . . .' to finally whisper in his ear, taking up his refrain once more: 'Admit that you would make a better king than he!'

And to enquire, without seeming overly interested in the matter, about the next meeting between the dauphin and King John, if the date had been set, whether it would take place in Normandy . . . 'I heard that he was hunting not far from Gisors.'

And yet he found a more reserved dauphin, more secretive, than in the past. Most certainly affable, but on his guard, only responding to such eagerness with smiles or nods.

Suddenly a crash of falling tableware rose above the diners' voices. Mitton le Fol had just dropped a platter. It was the largest silver platter he could find, on which, mimicking the kitchen ushers, he was presenting a single blackbird. And he dropped it while his mouth gaped wide open and he pointed dramatically to the door.

The good Norman knights, already drunk, laughed at Mitton's most amusing stunt but their laughter immediately stuck in their throats.

Because through the door came the Marshal of Audrehem armed to the teeth and brandishing his naked sword before him, shouting in his battle voice: 'May not one of you move, whatever he may see, should he wish not to die by this sword.'

Ah! But my palanquin is stopped . . . Indeed, we are arrived; I hadn't realized. I will tell you the rest after supper.

5

The Arrest

Thank you so much, Messire Abbot, I am most obliged . . .
No, not at all, I assure you, I need nothing more . . . only that
a few logs be put on the fire . . . My nephew will keep me
company; I have things to discuss with him. That's right,
Messire Abbot, good night to you. Thank you for the prayers
you will say for the Most Holy Father and for my humble
person . . . yes, and for all of your devout community . . .
The honour is all mine. Yes, I bless you; may the Good Lord
watch over you . . .

Ooh! If I had let him, he would have kept us up until
midnight, that abbot! He must have been born on the Feast of
Saint-Garrulous[31] . . .

Let's see now, where were we? I don't want to keep you in
suspense. Ah yes, the marshal, sword raised . . .

And from behind the marshal appeared a dozen archers
who moved violently to pin the cupbearers and valets against
the wall; and then Lalemant and Perrinet le Buffle, and hard

on their heels King John II himself, fully armed, helmet on his head, and his eyes shooting fire through the raised ventail. He was closely followed by Chaillouel and Crespi, two other sergeants from his personal guard.

'I am caught in a trap,' said Charles of Navarre.

Through the door, the royal escort continued to pour forth, amongst them some of his worst enemies, the Artois brothers, Tancarville . . .

The king was headed straight for the table of honour where the Norman lords made half-hearted attempts at bowing acknowledgement to him. With an imperious two-handed gesture, he commanded them to remain seated.

He seized his son-in-law by the fur-lined collar of his surcoat, shook him, pulled him to his feet, screaming at him from deep within his helmet: 'Evil traitor! You are not worthy to sit next to my son. By my father's soul, I will not think of eating or drinking so long as you may live!'

Charles of Navarre's equerry, Colin Doublel, upon seeing his master manhandled so, was seized with a mad impulse and grabbed a carving knife which he raised to strike at the king. His intention was thwarted by Perrinet le Buffle twisting his arm out of the way of danger to the king.

Meanwhile the king let go of Navarre and, losing his composure for a moment, looked with surprise upon this mere equerry who had dared raise a hand against him. 'Take this boy and his master too,' he ordered.

The king's retinue carried itself forward as one man, the Artois brothers at the front, flanking Navarre like two oaks with a hazel tree squeezed between. The men-at-arms had completely taken over the room; the tapestries seemed to bristle with pikes. The kitchen ushers looked as though they would, if they could, disappear into the walls. The dauphin had stood and was saying: 'Sire my father, sire my father . . .'

Charles of Navarre tried to explain himself, to defend himself. 'Monseigneur, I fail to understand! Who has so misinformed you against me? May God help me, but never, I beg you to believe, have I thought of betrayal, neither against you nor against monseigneur your son! If there is a man in this world who wishes to accuse me of it, may he do so, before your peers, and I swear that I will purge myself of his words and I will confound him.'

Even in such a perilous situation, his voice was clear, and the words flowed easily from his lips. He really was very small, very slight, amongst all these men of war; but he maintained assurance in his prattling.

'I am king, monseigneur, of a lesser kingdom than yours, admittedly, but I deserve to be treated as a king.

'You are Count of Évreux, you are my vassal, and you are a traitor!'

'I am your good cousin, I am husband to madame your daughter, and I have never forsaken you. It is true that I had Monsieur of Spain killed. But he was my adversary and had offended me. I have since repented. We made peace and you accorded letters of remission to all . . .'

'To prison with you, traitor. You have played us with your pack of lies long enough. Go! May he be locked up, may both of them be locked up!' screamed the king, indicating Navarre and his equerry. 'And that one too,' he added, pointing his gauntlet at Friquet of Fricamps whom he had just recognized and who was known to have set up the assassination plot at the Spinning Sow.

The three men were dragged to an adjoining chamber by sergeants and archers while the dauphin threw himself at the king's feet. Frightened as he was by his father's furious outburst, he remained lucid enough to foresee the consequences, at least as far as he was concerned.

'Ah! Sire my father, may God have mercy, you have dishonoured me! What will they say of me? I had invited the King of Navarre and his barons to dinner, and this is how you treat them. They will say that I have betrayed them. I implore you in God's name to calm down and reorder your mind.'

'Calm down yourself, Charles! You do not know what I know. They are evil traitors, and their wicked deeds will soon be uncovered. No, you don't know all that I do.'

And thereupon our John II, catching hold of a mace from one of the sergeants, struck the Count of Harcourt a mighty blow that would have broken the shoulder of anyone less fat than he. 'Get up, traitor! To prison with you too. You will have to be smart to get away from me.'

And as fat Harcourt, dazed, didn't get up fast enough, John grasped him by his white surcoat, tearing it, pulling apart all his clothing at the seams down to his shirt.

As John of Harcourt, open-shirted, was pushed along by archers towards his fate he passed before his younger brother Louis, and said something to him that nobody could understand, but which was clearly wicked, and to which Louis responded with a gesture that could have meant any number of things . . . I couldn't help it; I am the king's chamberlain . . . you were asking for it, tough luck on you . . .

'Sire my father, insisted the Duke of Normandy, you are doing wrong thus treating these valiant men . . .'

But John II no longer heard him. He had exchanged glances with Nicolas Braque and Robert of Lorris, who silently designated certain guests. 'And that one, in prison! . . . And that one . . .' he commanded, knocking over the Sire of Graville and punching Maubué of Mainemares, two knights who had also played a part in the murder of Charles of Spain, notwithstanding they then received, two years ago now, letters of remission signed by the king's hand. As you can see, it was a deep-seated hatred.

Mitton le Fol had climbed onto a stone bench in a windowed alcove, and was making signs to his master that conjured an awareness of the dishes laid out on a sideboard, then to the king, then fluttering his fingers before his mouth . . . eat . . .

'My father,' said the dauphin, 'would you like something to eat?' The idea was most propitious; it avoided sending the whole of Normandy to the dungeons.

'By Jove yes! It is true that I am hungry. Do you know, Charles, I started out from beyond the Forest of Lyons; I have been riding since dawn to castigate these wrongdoers. Bring me some food.'

And with a wave of his hand he called for his helmet to be unlaced. From beneath it, he appeared, his hair plastered to his skull, red-faced, sweat trickling into his beard. Taking his son's seat, already he had forgotten his oath neither to eat nor drink so long as his son-in-law was alive.

So they rushed to lay the table for him, poured him wine, made the most of a near-untouched pike pâté, then presented him with a swan, whole and still warm, while new prisoners were brought forward and the valets were tearing back and forth to the kitchens . . . there reigned a wavering indecision in the room and the stairwell, whereupon the Norman lords took advantage of the moment and escaped, such as Sire of Clères who was another of the handsome Spaniard's murderers and who got away by the skin of his teeth. The archers let them by, the king not seeming to want to arrest anyone else.

The escort, too, was dying of hunger and thirst. John of Artois, Tancarville, the sergeants, all had their eyes on the platters of food. They were waiting for a gesture from the king, granting them at last permission to dine. As the gesture didn't come, the Marshal of Audrehem tore off the leg of a capon that was lying around on a table and began to eat, standing up. Louis of Orléans gave an ill-humoured pout. His brother, really, showed far too little concern for those who served him. He sat down in the seat that Navarre had occupied a moment before, saying: 'I make it my duty to keep you company, my brother.'

The king then, with a sort of disinterested benevolence, invited his relatives and barons to sit. And immediately they all sat down to eat up the leftovers of the feast, around the spattered tablecloths. Nobody worried about changing the silver platters. Everyone grabbed whatever appeared before them, the milk cake with the *confit de canard*, the fatted goose before the shellfish soup. They ate the cold remains of the fried fish. The archers stuffed themselves with slices of bread or ran off to the kitchens to get fed. The sergeants gulped down the wine in abandoned goblets.

The king, boots spread out under the table, remained shut off in a violent reverie. His anger was not appeased; it even seemed to be rekindled by the mounds of food. Yet he should have good reason to feel satisfied. He was in his role of dispenser of justice, the good king! He had finally claimed victory; he had a fine feat to have recorded by the clerks for the next assembly of the Order of the Star. 'How Monseigneur King John defeated the traitors . . . he seized at the Castle of Bouvreuil . . .' He suddenly showed surprise at the absence of the Norman knights and became worried. He was wary of them. What if they were off organizing an uprising, they might rouse the town to revolt, set the prisoners free? There he showed his true self, that clever man. First of all, driven by a fury he had long nursed, he rushed in without thinking; then he neglected to consolidate his actions; then he was subject to fantasies, always far-removed from reality, but no one could rid him of them. Now he saw Rouen in rebellion, as had been Arras a month earlier. He wanted the mayor to come. No more Mayor Mustel. 'But he was here just a moment ago,' said Nicolas Braque. The mayor was caught in the castle's courtyard. He appeared before the king, still guzzling down food, white from indigestion. He heard himself order that the town's gates be closed and that everyone should stay at home. Nobody was allowed to walk around town, bourgeois or villein, for any reason whatsoever. It was a state of siege, curfew in the middle of the day. Enemy soldiers wouldn't have acted any differently.

Mustel summoned courage enough to show his outrage. The people of Rouen had done nothing to justify such measures . . . 'Yes, they have! You refuse to pay aides, abiding by the exhortations of these evil folk that I came to confound. But, by Saint Denis, they will exhort you no more.'

As he watched the mayor withdraw, the dauphin must have thought with sadness how futile had been all his painstakingly pursued efforts to reconcile the Normans. Now he had everybody against him, nobility and bourgeoisie alike. Who could possibly think that he was not a party to this ambush? In truth, his father had given him a most unsavoury role.

And then the king asked that Guillaume . . . be summoned . . . ah! Guillaume what's-his-name . . . it escapes me, yet I did know it . . . anyway, his King of the Ribald. And everybody understood that he had resolved to proceed with the immediate execution of the prisoners, without further delay.

'For those who don't know how to uphold chivalry, there is no reason to uphold their lives,' said the king.

'Indeed, my cousin John,' approved John of Artois, that monument of stupidity.

I ask you, Archambaud, was it really chivalry to deck oneself out in battle attire to take unarmed men, and to use one's own son as bait? Navarre, most probably, had quite a record of skulduggery, but does King John, beneath his magnificent exterior, really have much more honour in his soul?

6

The Preparations

GUILLAUME À LA CAUCHE . . . There you are, I remembered
it. The name I was looking for; the King of the Ribald. His is a
curious office, which originated from an institution of Philip
II Augustus. He had set up a corps of sergeants for his close
guard, all giants, that were called the *Ribaldi Regis*, the Ribald
of the King. Inversion of the genitive or pun, the chief of this
guard became *Rex Ribaldorum*. Nominally, he has command
over sergeants such as Perrinet le Buffle amongst others; and
it is he, who, every evening at suppertime, tours the royal
household to see if all those who entered court but are not
to sleep there, have indeed left. But above all, as I told you,
I believe, he is responsible for keeping his eye on places of ill
repute in every town where the king resides. That is to say,
first and foremost, he regulates and inspects the brothels of
Paris, which are not few and far between, not to mention the
self-employed strumpets who work in the streets set aside for
them. Same goes for the houses in which games of chance are

played. All these places of evil are where one is most likely to unearth thieves, bag-snatchers, pickpockets, counterfeiters and assassins for hire; and to discover the vices of people, often in high places, who seem to have the most respectable of appearances.

So much so that the King of the Ribald has become the chief of a most peculiar police force. He has his spies almost everywhere. He maintains and supports a number of tavern vermin who supply him with information and evidence. If you want a traveller followed, his portmanteau searched, or to find out whom he meets with, you go to him. He is by no account a man loved, but a man feared. I am telling you about him for the day you will be in court. It is better to remain in his good books.

He earns a good living, as his charge is a lucrative one. Watching over the harlots, inspecting the hovels, is all good business. As well as his moneyed wages and the fringe bene-fits he gets in the royal household, he is paid a two pence weekly fee on all the brothels and all the women who work there. Now there is a fine tax, wouldn't you say, and whose collection is less problematic than the gabelle. He also gets five pence from adulterous wives . . . well, from the known adulteresses. But at the same time it is he who recruits courte-sans for the court's usage. He is paid to keep his eyes open, but he is also paid to keep them shut. And it is he who, when the king is out riding, carries out his sentences or those of the Court of the Marshals of France. He sets the rulings on the tortures and executions; and in cases of the latter, the remains of the condemned come back to him, along with all they had upon their person at the time of their arrest. As it is not usually the crimes of small fry that provoke royal wrath, but rather of the powerful and the rich, the clothing and jewellery he collects from these corpses are not inconsiderable prizes.

For him the day of Rouen was a godsend. A king to behead, and five lords all at the same time! Never had a King of the Ribald, oh! not since Philip Augustus, known such good fortune. An unmatched opportunity to gain the sovereign's esteem. And so he spared no pains. An execution is a spectacle . . . he had to find, with the help of the mayor, six carts, because the king demanded a cart per prisoner; that would make the cortège longer. So it came to pass. The carts sat waiting in the castle's courtyard hitched up to large-hoofed Percherons. But now he had to find an executioner . . . the town's executioner was not around, or there wasn't one appointed at that time. The King of the Ribald hit upon an odd villain by the name of Bétrouve, Pierre Bétrouve . . . well, I remember that name you see, don't ask me why . . . and had him taken out of the prison. Four deaths he had on his conscience, which seemed good preparation for the job he was to be entrusted with, in exchange for a letter of remission delivered by the king. He got off lightly, that Bétrouve. If there had been an executioner in town . . .

A priest also had to be found; but that is a rather less rare commodity, and they didn't go to much trouble choosing one . . . the first Capuchin friar to turn up from the neighbouring monastery.

During these preparations, King John held a privy council meeting in the partially cleaned banqueting hall . . .

The weather is decidedly wet today. It will rain all day. Bah! We have good furs, hot coals in our warming pans, sugared almonds, hippocras[32] to reinvigorate us against the damp; we have enough to hold out until Auxerre. I am delighted at the prospect of seeing Auxerre again; that will bring back memories . . .

So the king held a meeting during which he was almost the only one to speak. His brother Orléans kept quiet; as did his son Anjou. Audrehem was sombre. The king could read on his advisors' faces that even the most dogged advocates of the downfall of the King of Navarre would not approve of his being beheaded in such a way, without trial and as if in haste. It reminded everybody all too well of the execution of Raoul of Brienne, the former constable, decided on in a fit of anger, for reasons never elucidated, with which John's reign had most inauspiciously begun.

Only Robert of Lorris, the first chamberlain, seemed willing to second the king in his desire for instant vengeance; but it was more platitude than conviction. He had experienced several months in disgrace, for having, in the eyes of the king, gone too far in supporting the Navarrese in the Treaty of Mantes. Lorris needed to prove his loyalty.

Nicolas Braque, who is most skilful and knows how to manoeuvre the king towards reason, created a diversion by talking of Friquet of Fricamps. He pronounced himself in favour of keeping him alive for the time being, in order to put him to the question in due form. Nobody can doubt that the Governor of Caen, suitably treated, would give up many an interesting secret. How could they know all the ramifications of the conspiracy if they kept none of the prisoners alive?

'Yes, it is wisely thought through,' said the king. 'May Friquet be spared.'

Upon which Audrehem opened one of the windows and shouted to the King of the Ribald in the courtyard that five carts will be enough, confirming with a gesture of the hand, fingers spread wide: five. And one of the carts was sent back to the mayor.

'If it is wise to keep Fricamps, it would be wiser still to keep his master,' said the dauphin at that moment.

The first flush of emotion was behind him and he had regained his calm and his thoughtful air. His honour was at stake in the matter. He was trying in every possible way to save his brother-in-law. John II had asked John of Artois to repeat for everyone's benefit what he knew about the plot. But 'my cousin John' had come across as less sure of himself before the council than before the king alone. Whispering denunciation in one person's ear gives you an air of conviction. Said again out loud to ten people, and it loses force. After all, it was only a matter of hearsay. A former servant had seen . . . another had heard . . .

Even if, in the depths of his soul, the Duke of Normandy couldn't help but give credence to the accusations being brought before him, the presumptions didn't seem solid enough to him.

'For my evil son-in-law, it seems to me that we know enough already,' said the king.

'No, my father, we hardly know a thing,' replied the dauphin.

'Charles, are you really so obtuse?' said the king angrily. 'Didn't you hear that this evil relative, faithless and disreputable, this injurious beast, soon wanted to bleed us to death, first me, then you? For certain he wants to slay you too. Do you believe that after me you would have been a significant hindrance to the machinations of your good brother who not long ago tried to drag you to Germany, to oppose me? It is our place and our throne that he has his eye on, nothing less. Or are you still so smitten with him that you refuse to understand anything?'

Then the dauphin kept on with his defence, gaining assurance and determination: 'I have very well understood, my father; but there is neither proof nor confession.'

'And what proof do you want, Charles? The word of a loyal cousin isn't enough for you? Will you wait until you are lying, desolate, in your own blood like my poor Charles of Spain, to have proof enough?'

The dauphin persevered. 'These are strong presumptions, my father, that I cannot deny; but for the time being, nothing more. The presumption is not the crime.'

'Presumption is crime for the king, whose duty is self-protection, to protect oneself,' said John II, as red as a beetroot. 'You don't speak as a king, Charles, but as a university cleric hiding in a corner behind his big books.'

But young Charles stood firm. 'If royal duty is to protect ourselves, as kings, let us not behead each other. Charles of Évreux was anointed and crowned to rule over Navarre. He is your son-in-law. Who will have respect for royalty if kings send each other to the executioner?'

'Then he should never have begun his campaign against me,' shouted the king.

At that point the Marshal Audrehem intervened to give his opinion. 'Sire, in this case, it is you who, in the eyes of the world, will appear to have started it.'

A marshal, Archambaud, as much as a constable, is always difficult to handle. You set him up in a position of authority and then, all of a sudden, he makes use of it to contradict you. Audrehem is an old soldier . . . not as old as all that, all things considered; he is younger than I . . . but in the end a man who for a long time obeyed the king and kept quiet, witness to much foolishness without being able to say a word against it. Now he was making up for lost time.

'If only we had caught all the foxes in the same trap!' he went on. 'But Philip of Navarre is free, and is just as determined. Dispose of the elder brother and the younger one takes his place, and he will rouse his party just as well, and will negotiate equally well with the Englishman, all the more so that he is a better horseman and more ardent in battle.'

Louis of Orléans sided with the dauphin and the marshal, endorsing their points of view and impressing upon the king that as long as he kept Navarre in prison, he would keep a hold over his vassals.

'Conduct a long investigation against him, bring his black deeds out into the open, have him judged by peers of the realm; then no one will resent your sentence. Our father the king proceeded no differently than by public and ceremonious trial when our cousin John's father committed the acts known to us. And when our great-uncle Philip the Fair discovered the debauchery of his daughters-in-law, as speedy as his justice was, it was established through cross-examination and pronounced in a public hearing.'

This speech was not at all to the liking of King John, who blew up once more: 'What fine, and most beneficial, examples you present me with there, my brother! The great judgement of Maubuisson cast dishonour and disorder upon the royal family. As for Robert of Artois, to have only banished him, whether it pleases your cousin John or not, instead of properly seizing and slaying him, meant he brought war upon us from England.'

Monseigneur of Orléans, who has no love for his elder brother and who takes pleasure in standing up to him, retorted . . . I am assured that this was said . . . 'Sire, my brother, must I remind you that Maubuisson did us no great disservice? Without Maubuisson where our grandfather Valois, may God preserve him, played his part, our cousin Navarre would most probably be seated on the throne at this time, instead of us. As for the war with England, Count Robert may have pushed for it, but he only contributed a single lance, his own. Meanwhile the war has been going on for eighteen years . . .'

Apparently the king flinched under this final thrust. He turned to the dauphin, staring at him harshly, saying: 'It is true, eighteen years; and such exactly is your age, Charles . . .' as if he held this coincidence against him.

Whereupon Audrehem muttered: 'We would find it easier to rid ourselves of the Englishman if only we French weren't always fighting amongst ourselves.'

The king remained silent for a moment, looking most incensed. One has to be very sure of oneself to maintain a decision when none of those who serve you approve of it. That is how one can judge the character of princes. But King John is not determined; he is stubborn.

Nicolas Braque, who learned the art of using silence in the councils and had said nothing during this exchange, now provided the king with a way out of the situation, sparing both his pride and his rancour.

'Sire, wouldn't his crimes be expiated rather too quickly were he to die at once? Monseigneur of Navarre has been a cause of suffering to you these two years and more. And you grant him such a short punishment? By keeping him in jail you could make him feel like he is dying every day. Besides, I wager that his partisans will not fail to make some attempt or other to set him free. In that case, you will be able to capture those who today have slipped through your net. And you would have a good pretext to bring your justice to bear upon such an obvious rebellion . . .'

The king rallied round to this advice, saying that his traitor of a son-in-law indeed did need somewhat longer to atone for his treachery. 'I will defer his execution. May I not be made to regret it. But now let us make haste with the punishment of the others. Enough words have been said and we have wasted too much time.' He seemed to fear that he would be made to relinquish another head.

Audrehem, from the window, called once more to the King of the Ribald and showed him four fingers. And as he wasn't sure that the other had understood, he dispatched an archer with the message that just four carts were required.

'Make haste!' repeated the king. 'Deliver these traitors.'

Deliver . . . a strange word, perhaps surprising to those unfamiliar with this strange prince! It is his usual turn of phrase, when he orders an execution. He doesn't say: 'Deliver me of these traitors', which would make sense, but 'deliver these traitors' . . . what could that mean for him? Deliver them to the executioner? Deliver them from life? Or is it just a slip of the tongue that his confused mind clings to stubbornly, as in a state of anger he no longer has control over his words?

I am telling you all this, Archambaud, as if I had been there myself. This is because the tale was told to me in July, barely three months later, when memories were still fresh, and told by Audrehem and by Monseigneur of Orléans, and by monseigneur the dauphin himself, and also by Nicolas Braque, each one in turn, of course, remembering above all what he himself said. In that way, I pieced together, rather well I believe, this whole business, and in great detail, and I wrote about it to the pope, who had already received shorter and somewhat different versions. The detail in these affairs has more importance than one might think, as it informs us about the characters of those involved. Lorris and Braque are both above all greedy for money and immodest in their ferocity to make more; but Lorris is of a rather inferior nature, whereas Braque is a judicious diplomat . . .

It is still raining . . . Brunet, where are we? Fontenoy . . . Ah yes, I remember; it was in my diocese. A famous battle was fought here, which had important consequences for France; *Fontanetum*, by its old name. It was here, around the year 840 or 841, Charles and Louis the German defeated their brother Lothair, further to which they signed the Treaty of Verdun. And it is from that moment on that the kingdom of France would forever be separated from the empire . . . With all this rain we can't make out a thing. Anyway, there is nothing to see. From time to time, while ploughing, the yokels come across a few swords, a rusted helmet, five hundred years old . . . Let's carry on, Brunet, let's carry on.

7

The Field of Forgiveness

THE KING, HELMET once more upon his head, was on horseback, along with the marshal, who was wearing but a chainmail skullcap; the only two mounted. The danger was not so great as to require his wearing full battle attire. Audrehem is not one of those who make a show of military splendour when there is no need of it. If the king took some pleasure in displaying his crowned helmet in order to witness four beheadings, then that was up to him.

The rest of the company, from the grandest of the lords to the lowliest of the archers, were to go on foot to the site of the execution. The king had decided so, being a man who wastes a great deal of time planning parades, with a preference for bringing in minor innovations rather than letting them take place according to tradition.

There were only three carts remaining, because between order and counter-order misunderstandings had arisen, and one too many had been sent back.

Nearby stood Guillaume . . . in fact, it wasn't Guillaume à la Cauche; I was getting mixed up. Guillaume à la Cauche is a manservant; but it is a similar name . . . la Gauche, le Gauche, la Tanche, la Planche . . . I don't even know if his Christian name is indeed Guillaume; anyway, it is of little importance . . . So nearby stood the King of the Ribald and the make-shift executioner, white as a turnip further to his stay in the dungeons, scrawny, I was told, and not at all how one would imagine a miscreant guilty of four murders, and the Capuchin who was fiddling, as they always do, with his hemp cord.

Bareheaded and hands bound behind their backs, the con-demned men left the keep. First came the Count of Harcourt in his white surcoat that the king had ripped to the armholes, his shirt with it. He showed his enormous shoulder, pink like pigskin, and his fat breast. In a corner of the courtyard the axes were still being sharpened on a grindstone.

Nobody looked at the condemned men, nobody dared look at them. Everyone stared at a patch of cobblestone or wall. Who would have dared, under the watchful eye of the king, a look of farewell that spoke of friendship, or even compassion for those four who were about to perish? Even those who found themselves at the back of the crowd kept their heads down, for fear of what their neighbours should say they had seen on their faces . . . There were many who held the king to blame. But to go so far as to show it . . . Many amongst them knew the Count of Harcourt of old, having hunted with him, jousted with him, dined at his table, which was hearty indeed. At that moment, not one of them seemed to remember this acquaintance; the castle's roofs and the

April clouds had become more enthralling things for them to contemplate. So much so that John of Harcourt, looking on all sides through his fat-lidded eyes, could find not a single face to share his misfortune. Not even his brother, especially not his brother! Why yes! His concern was what the king would decide for his titles and possessions once his fat elder brother had had his head chopped off.

The man who was still, for the moment, Count of Harcourt, was made to get into the first cart. It wasn't without difficulty. A quintal and a half, and with his hands tied. Four sergeants were needed to push him on, pull him up. There was straw spread across the bottom of the cart, as well as across the executioner's block.

When John of Harcourt was at last perched in his place he turned bare-chested to the king as if he wanted to tell him something ... the king immobile in his saddle, dressed in chainmail, crowned with steel and gold, the king, Royal Dispenser of Justice, who wanted to make clear that every life in the kingdom was subject to his decree, and that the richest lord of a province, in an instant, could be reduced to nothing if such was his will. And Harcourt remained silent.

The Sire of Graville was put in the second cart, and into the third were made to climb Maubué of Mainemares and Colin Doublel, the equerry who had raised a dagger to the king. The latter appeared to say to everyone: 'Remember Monsieur of Spain's murder; remember the Spinning Sow.' As the entire audience understood that, it was revenge that was behind this fast and grim justice, if not in the case of Harcourt, then at least for the others. Punishing those to whom remission had been given publicly ... One must be able to report new grievances, and most manifest ones, to act in such a way. That should have earned remonstrance from the pope, and of the severest kind, were the pope not so weak ...

In the keep, the King of Navarre had been wickedly pushed close to a window so that he would miss nothing of the spectacle.

The Guillaume who is not la Cauche, turns to the Marshal of Audrehem ... everything is ready. A wave of the hand from the king. And the cortège set off.

At its head, a squad of archers, iron hats and leather gambesons,[33] their stride weighed down by their heavy gaiters. Then, the marshal on horseback, visibly unhappy. Even more archers. And then the three carts. And behind them, the King of the Ribald, the scrawny executioner and the grimy Capuchin.

Then the king, upright on his charger, flanked by the sergeants from his close guard, and bringing up the rear a procession of lords in hoods or hunting hats, fur-lined mantles or cote-hardies.

The town is silent and empty. The people of Rouen wisely obeyed the order to stay in their homes. But behind their thick, greenish windows their heads massing together like blown bottle bottoms; their staring eyes glinting around the edges of their half-opened leaded lights. They cannot believe it is the Count of Harcourt in the cart, whom they have so often seen pass along their streets, once more this very morning, superbly attired. Yet his portliness designates him rather well ... 'It's him; I tellin' you, it's him.' They have no doubt of the king, for his helmet almost reaches the level of the first floor of the houses. He had been their duke for a

long time . . . 'It's him, it is indeed the king . . .' But no greater
fear would have been seized if they had made out a death's
head under the ventail of the helmet. They were unhappy,
the Rouennais, terrified but discontented. Because the Count
of Harcourt had always supported them, and they were fond
of him. So they whispered: 'No, this is not fair justice. It is we
who are the afflicted ones.'

The carts bumped along. The straw slid under the feet
of the condemned, who struggled to keep their composure.
I was told that John of Harcourt, throughout the journey, had
his head thrown back, and his hair stuck out over his neck,
displaying its fleshy folds. What were the thoughts of a man
like him, going to his execution, and watching the sky flow
between the gables of the houses? I always wonder what goes
on in the mind of a man condemned to death, during his final
moments . . . Does he regret not having admired enough
all the beautiful things that the Good Lord puts before our
eyes every day? Or does he reflect on the absurdity of all that
prevents us from enjoying all these blessings? The day before,
he was discussing taxes and the gabelle . . . Or was he saying
to himself that there was foolishness in his own behaviour?
Because he, John of Harcourt, had been warned, his uncle
Godfrey had got word to him . . . 'Leave without delay . . .'
His uncle Godfrey of Harcourt had got wind of the trap early
on . . . 'This Lent banquet smells like an ambush to me' . . .
if only his messenger had got to him a little bit earlier . . . if
Robert of Lorris hadn't found him at the bottom of the stairs
. . . if . . . if . . . But it was not the working of fate, he only had
himself to blame. All he'd had to do was to give the dauphin
the slip, it was as if he had been looking for bad reasons to

stay and satisfy his greed. 'I will leave after the banquet; it is all the same . . .'

People's greatest misfortunes, you see, Archambaud, happen to them for the smallest of reasons, for an error of judgement or a decision taken in circumstances that seemed wholly without importance to them, and where they follow their natural bent . . . The tiniest of choices, and a catastrophe occurs.

Ah! How then they would love to be allowed to start again, go back in time, to the fork in the path where they took the wrong turn. John of Harcourt jostles Robert of Lorris aside, shouting: 'Farewell, messire', mounts his huge horse, and everything is different. He sees his uncle once more, his castle, his wife and his nine children, and he prides himself, for the rest of his days, on having escaped the king's dirty trick . . . Unless, unless, his day had come, so that as he fled he broke his head open in the forest, crashing into a hanging branch. God's will is unfathomable! And still, we mustn't forget . . . a fact that this bad justice eclipses . . . that Harcourt really was plotting against the crown. Well, King John's day had not come, and God was reserving yet more misfortune for France, of which the king would serve as the instrument.

The cortège climbed the hill on which stood the gallows, but its journey ended halfway up at a large square clearing, bordered with low-slung houses, where every autumn the horse fair is held; they call it the Field of Forgiveness. Yes, that really is its name. The men-at-arms lined up in ranks on both sides of the road that crossed the square, leaving a distance three lances long between their lines.

The king, on horseback still, remained in the middle of the roadway, a stone's throw from the block that the sergeants had rolled out of the first cart, and which needed to be set up on the flat.

The Marshal of Audrehem dismounted, and the royal retinue, dominated by the heads of the two brothers Artois . . . what could those two be thinking? It was the elder one who bore the responsibility for these executions. Oh! They were thinking nothing at all . . . 'My cousin John, my cousin John' . . . The retinue formed a semi-circle. Louis of Harcourt was watched carefully as his brother was made to get down; he didn't flinch.

The preparations went on and on, for this makeshift justice in the middle of a fairground. And all around the square there were eyes glued to the windows.

The dauphin-duke stood about, his head tilting forward under his pearled hood, in the company of his young uncle of Orléans; walked a few paces, came back, went off again as if trying to dispel his uneasiness. And suddenly the fat Count of Harcourt turns to him, and addresses him, and Audrehem, shouting with all of his might:

'Ah, sire duke, and you, kind marshal, in God's name, let me speak to the king, and I will find the words to apologize, and I will tell him such things that will benefit both him and his kingdom.'

Not one who heard him doesn't remember having his soul torn apart by the tone in his voice, a harrowing cry filled with final dread and malediction.

In a single movement, the duke and the marshal approach the king, who was able to hear the prisoner as well as they.

They draw so close as to almost be touching his horse. 'Sire my father, in God's name, let him speak to you!'

'Yes, sire, allow him to speak to you, and you will be better off for it,' insisted the marshal.

But John II is only an imitator! In matters of chivalry he copies his grandfather, Charles of Valois, or King Arthur of the legends. For executions he relies on what he knows about the practices of Philip the Fair: he, once he had ordered one, remained inflexible. So he copies, believing that he is copying the Iron King. But Philip the Fair would never have put on a helmet unless it was necessary. And he didn't condemn left, right and centre, founding his justice on the murky brooding of his hatred.

'Have the traitors delivered,' repeated John II through his open ventail.

Ah! How grand he must feel, he must feel omnipotent. The kingdom and the ages will remember his severity. He has just squandered a fine opportunity to reconsider.

'So be it! Let us confess,' says the Count of Harcourt, turning to the grubby Capuchin. And the king cried: 'No, no confessions for traitors!'

And there, he is no longer copying, he is creating. He is treating the crime as . . . but what crime after all? The crime of being suspected, the crime of pronouncing wicked words that were repeated by others . . . let us say the crime of lèse-majesté, like that of the heretics or the relapsed. Because John II was anointed, was he not? *Tu es sacerdos in aeternum* . . . So he thinks he is God incarnate, and can decide where souls go after death. On that point as well, the Holy Father should have, in my opinion, severely reprimanded him.

'Only that one, the equerry . . .' he adds, pointing out Colin Doublel.

Who knows what goes on in a brain as riddled with holes as a Swiss cheese? Why this discrimination? Why grant confession to the equerry who threatened him with his knife? Even today, when those who were present talk amongst themselves of that terrible hour, this oddness in the king's behaviour is still a source of wonder. Did he wish to establish that degrees of sin should follow the feudal hierarchy, signifying that an equerry who committed a crime is less guilty than a knight? Or could it be that the knife brandished at his chest made him forget that Doublel was also one of the assassins of Charles of Spain . . . just like Mainemares and Graville, Mainemares thrashing about in his bonds, a tall, raw-boned fellow, his eyes furiously darting around him, Graville stock-still, unable to sign himself, but most conspicuously murmuring his prayers . . . If God wishes to hear his repentance, He will hear it well enough without an intercessor.

The Capuchin, who was beginning to wonder what he was doing there, hurriedly seizes the soul he is left with and whispers Latin into Colin Doublel's ear.

The King of the Ribald pushes the Count of Harcourt before the block. 'On your knees, messire.'

The huge man slumps to the ground like an ox. He shifts his knees, as the gravel is probably hurting him. The King of the Ribald, passing behind him, takes him by surprise and blindfolds him, denying him the sight of the knots in the wooden block, the last thing in the world he will have before him.

It is the others who should have been blindfolded,

to spare them the spectacle that was about to take place.

The King of the Ribald ... all the same it is curious that I should not be able to recall his name; I saw him several times around the king; and I can visualize his appearance very clearly, a tall and strong fellow who sports a thick, black beard ... The King of the Ribald took the condemned man's head with both hands to place it, like an object, as was required, and arrange his hair to reveal his neck.

The Count of Harcourt continued to move his knees about because of the gravel, making life difficult for the King of the Ribald ... 'Go on, cut off his head,' he managed to say. And he saw, and everyone else saw, that the executioner was trembling. He couldn't stop weighing up his great axe in his hands, sliding his fingers over the handle, trying to calculate the right distance from the block. He was afraid. Oh! He would have been more sure of himself with a dagger in the shadows. But an axe, for this sickly individual, and in front of the king and all of his lords, and all those soldiers! After several months in prison, his muscles can't have felt that sturdy, even if he had been served a bowl of soup and a tumbler of wine to give him strength for the occasion. And he had not been given a hood, as is usually done, because there weren't any to hand. Thus, everyone would know from that moment on that he had been an executioner. A criminal and an executioner. Quite enough to terrify most anyone. To know what was going on in his head, that one too, that Bétrouve, who was about to earn his freedom by performing the same act that had put him in prison in the first place. He saw the head that he was to chop off in the place where there should have been his own, in due course, had the king not passed through Rouen. Perhaps there was more charity in this scoundrel, more of a feeling of communion, more of a connection with his fellow men than there was in the king.

The King of the Ribald was forced to repeat: 'Cut!' Bétrouve raised his axe, not straight up above him like an executioner, but sideways, like a woodcutter about to fell a tree, and he let the axe drop under its own weight. The axe fell badly.

There are executioners who behead a man with one clean stroke. But not that one, oh no! The Count of Harcourt must have been stunned, since his knees no longer moved; but he wasn't dead; the axe's blow, feeble anyway, was resisted by the layer of fat lining his neck.

Bétrouve was forced to start again. Even worse. This time, the blade only cut open the side of his neck. Blood spurted out from a broad gaping wound, which revealed the thickness of the yellow fat.

The blade of the axe had got stuck in the wood of the block and Bétrouve struggled with it; he couldn't get it out. Sweat was pouring down his face.

The King of the Ribald turned to the king with an apologetic air, as if to say: 'It's not my fault.'

Angry now, Bétrouve doesn't hear what the sergeants are telling him as he frees the axe at last and strikes again; and it looked as if the axe blade cut into a slab of butter. And again and again! Blood gushes from the block, spouting under the blade, spraying the condemned man's torn surcoat. Those watching turn away, sick to the stomach. The dauphin shows a face filled with horror and anger; he clenches his fists, turning his right hand purple. Louis of Harcourt, deathly pale, forces himself to stay in the front row, before the butchering of his brother. The marshal moves his feet to avoid the rivulet of blood meandering towards him over the ground.

Finally, on the sixth attempt, the huge head of the Count of Harcourt is severed from the trunk; encircled by its black blindfold, it hits the ground and rolls around at the base of the block.

The king doesn't move. Through his steel window, and without giving the slightest sign of discomfort, disgust or uneasiness, he contemplates the bloody pulp between the enormous shoulders, right in front of him, and the solitary head, spattered in blood and filth, in the middle of a sticky puddle. If anything showed on his metal-framed face, it was a smile. An archer fainted in a clatter of iron. Only then did the king avert his gaze. That weakling would not remain long in his guard. Perrinet le Buffle let off steam by lifting up the archer by the collar of his gambeson and slapping him full force across the face. But the lily-livered weakling, through his swoon, had done everybody a favour. They all began to pull themselves together; there was even some nervous laughter.

Three men, no fewer would have managed it, dragged the headless body backwards. 'Put it in a dry place,' cried the King of the Ribald. We mustn't forget that the clothes were his by right. It was enough that they should be torn; if they had been too bloodstained into the bargain, then he would get nothing for them. He already had two condemned men fewer than he had anticipated . . .

And for the following execution, he exhorted his sweating and panting executioner, lavishing his advice on him as if on an exhausted wrestler: 'You raise it straight above your head, and you don't look at your axe, you look where you should be striking, at the middle of the neck. And wham!' And he put some straw at the foot of the block, to dry out the ground, and blindfolded the eyes of Sire of Graville, a good Norman, rather chubby, made him kneel, put his face into the sludge of meat on the block. 'Cut!' And there, in one go . . . a miracle . . . Bétrouve slices his neck clean through; and the head falls forward while the body crumples to the side, disgorging a red stream into the dust. And the people feel almost relieved. It wouldn't have taken much for them to congratulate Bétrouve who gazes around him, dumbfounded, looking as though he wondered how on earth he had managed it.

Next it's the turn of the tall, lopsided swaying Maubué of Mainemares who has a look of defiance for the king. 'Everyone knows, everyone knows . . .' he cries out. But as the bearded one is in front of him and is putting on his blindfold, his words are smothered and nobody catches what he wanted to say.

The Marshal of Audrehem moves again because the blood is heading for his boots . . . 'Cut!' One blow of the axe, once again, a single one, firmly dealt. And that is enough.

Mainemares's body is pulled backwards and heaped with the other two. To make them easier to grab hold of, the cadavers' hands are untied, so that using all four limbs the men swing them, and heave ho! throw them into the first cart that will take them up to the gibbet where they are to be hung up on the charnel house. They would be stripped of their belongings up there. The King of the Ribald indicates to his men to gather together the heads as well.

Bétrouve is trying to get his breath back, leaning on the axe handle. His back aches; he can't take any more. And one would be inclined to pity him, if anyone. Ah! He will have earned his letters of remission! If he has nightmares till his dying day, crying out in his sleep, it would be no surprise.

Colin Doublel, the brave equerry, was tense, even though he had been absolved. He made a movement to break away from the hands that were pushing him towards the block; he wanted to go there alone. But the blindfold was intended precisely to avoid the disorderly movements of condemned men.

However Doublel couldn't be stopped raising his head at the wrong moment, and there Bétrouve ... there, he really wasn't to blame... split open his skull from one side to the other. Come on! Once again. There, it was done.

Ah! They would have some tales to tell, the Rouennais watching from the neighbouring windows, things that would be repeated from one town to the next, right to the farthest reaches of the duchy. And people would come from all over just to gaze at this square of ground that had drunk so much blood. It was hard to believe that four bodies could contain so much, and that it would make such a huge mark on the ground.

King John looked at his people with a strange satisfaction. The horror he inspired at that instant, even in his most loyal servants, wasn't, so it appeared, to his disliking; he was rather proud of himself. He looked particularly hard at his eldest son ... 'There you see, my boy, how one behaves when one is king ...'

Who would have dared tell him that he had been wrong

to give in to his vindictive nature? For him as well, that day was a fork in the road. Take the path on the left or the path on the right. He had taken the wrong one, just as the Count of Harcourt had done at the bottom of the stairwell. After six years of a difficult reign, filled with unrest, difficulties and setbacks, he was giving the kingdom, which was only too willing to follow him down that path, the example of hate and violence. In less than six months, he was to hurtle down the route of real tragedy, and take France with him.

PART THREE
THE LOST SPRING

The Hound and the Fox Cub

Ah! I am delighted, truly delighted, to have seen Auxerre again. I didn't think God would grant me this favour, nor that I would appreciate it quite so much. To see places again that were home to a moment of one's youth is always particularly moving. You will experience this feeling, Archambaud, when the years have piled up on you. Should it befall you to go through Auxerre, when you get to my age . . . may God preserve you until then . . . you will say: 'I was with my uncle, the cardinal, who had been bishop here, his second diocese, before receiving the galero . . . I was accompanying him on his way to Metz, where he was to see the emperor . . .'

Three years long I resided there, three years . . . Oh! You mustn't think that I am nostalgic for that period, nor that I felt the gift of life more intensely when I was Bishop of Auxerre than I do today. To tell you the truth, I was even eager to leave. I had my eye on Avignon, while knowing full well that I was too young; but ultimately I felt that God had put in me the force of character and the faculties of mind that could serve him well at the pontifical court. In order to teach myself patience, I pushed forward with the science of astrology; and it is precisely my mastery of that science which induced my benefactor John XXII to set the galero upon my head, when I was but thirty years old. But that, I have already told you . . . Ah! My nephew, in the company of a man who has experienced many things in life, you must get used to hearing the same things several times. It isn't that when we are old we get soft in the head; but our minds are full of memories, which come to life in all sorts of circumstances. Youth fills the time to come with imagination; old age relives the past through memory. The two things are equivalent . . . No, I don't have any regrets. When I compare what I was then with what I am now, I have reasons only to praise the Lord, and to praise myself a little, in all modesty. It is merely time that has flown from the hand of God and that will no longer exist when I stop remembering it. Except at the Resurrection, when all of our moments will be brought together. But that is beyond my comprehension. I believe in the Resurrection, I teach people to believe in it, but I don't embark upon the task of picturing it myself, and I say that those who cast doubt on the Resurrection are most arrogant . . . No, really, more people than you might think . . . because they are too infirm to imagine it. Man is like a blind person who denies the existence of light because he doesn't see it. Light is a great mystery, for the blind!

There now . . . I could preach that on Sunday, in Sens. As I will have the homily to give. I am archdeacon of the cathedral. That is why I am compelled to make this detour.

We would have shortened our journey by heading straight for Troyes, but I am obliged to inspect the Chapter of Sens.

The fact remains that I would have been most pleased to prolong my stay a little in Auxerre. These two days have gone by too quickly ... Saint-Étienne, Saint-Germain, Saint-Eusèbe, all of those beautiful churches where I have celebrated Mass, weddings and Communions ... You know that Auxerre, *Autissidurum*, is one of the oldest Christian cities in the kingdom, that it was an Episcopal See two hundred years before Clovis, who by the way ravaged it almost as much as Attila, and that a council was held there before the year 600 ... My greatest worry, all the time I spent at the head of that diocese, was to discharge the debts left behind by my predecessor, Bishop Pierre. And I couldn't complain; he had just been created cardinal! Indeed, a good See, which serves as antechamber to the Curia ... My various benefices as well as our family's fortune helped me to fill in the financial holes. My successors were to find the situation much improved. And the current bishop is accompanying us today. He is a fine prelate, this new Monseigneur of Auxerre ... But I sent Monseigneur of Bourges back ... to Bourges. He had come once again to tug at my robes so that I would grant him a third notary. Oh! It didn't take me long. I told him: 'Monseigneur, if you really need so many lawyers, then your episcopal affairs must be very muddled. I urge you to go back forthwith and put your house in order. With my blessing.' And we will do without his office in Metz. The Bishop of Auxerre will replace him most favourably ... I informed the dauphin of this by the way. The messenger I sent him yesterday should be back tomorrow, or at the latest, the day after tomorrow. We will therefore have news of Paris before leaving Sens . . . He will not give in, the dauphin; in spite of all the manoeuvring and pressure brought to bear upon him, he has kept the King of Navarre in prison . . .

What did our people of France do after the affair of Rouen? First of all the king chose to stay there a few days, living in the keep of Bouvreuil while sending his son to stay in another of the castle's towers and having Navarre under guard in a third tower. He considered that he had numerous affairs to investigate, matters pending he must conduct enquiries into. Firstly, put Fricamps to the question. 'Friquet is going to be fried alive.'[34] This *bon mot* was told by Mitton le Fol, I believe. There was no need to heat up the fire very much, nor to get out the huge pincers. No sooner had Perrinet le Buffle and four other sergeants dragged Fricamps into the vault and manipulated a few instruments before his eyes than the Governor of Caen showed himself to be of an extreme goodwill. He talked and talked and talked, turning his bag of words upside down to shake out every last crumb. Apparently. But how can one doubt he revealed all when his teeth chattered so and he showed so much zeal for the truth?

And what did he in fact avow? The names of those who took part in the murder of Charles of Spain? They had been known for quite some time, and he added no new guilty party to the list of those who had received letters of remission further to the Treaty of Mantes. But his account took up the entire morning. Secret negotiations, in Flanders and Avignon, between Charles of Navarre and the Duke of Lancaster? There was not a single European court that remained unaware of them; and that Fricamps himself took part didn't add a great deal to our knowledge of their content. The aid in war that the kings of England and of Navarre promised each other? The least astute of people could have worked it out for themselves, the previous summer, seeing Charles the Bad turn up in the Cotentin and the Prince of Wales in the Bordelais at almost the same time. Ah! Of course there was the secret treaty in which Navarre recognized King Edward as rightful King of France, and in which they divided up the kingdom amongst themselves! Fricamps did indeed confess that such an agreement had been drawn up, which gave substance to the accusations of John of Artois. But only the preliminary exchanges, the treaty hadn't been signed. King John, when this part of Friquet's statement was related to him, shouted out: 'The traitor, the traitor! Wasn't I right?'

The dauphin pointed out to him: 'My father, these plans were prior to the Treaty of Valognes that Charles signed with you, and which states the exact opposite. The one that Charles betrayed is therefore the King of England rather than yourself.'

And as the king screamed that his son-in-law betrayed everyone: 'Most certainly, my father,' retorted the dauphin, 'and I am beginning to believe it myself. But you would be wrong to accuse him of treason specifically intended to harm you alone.'

On the subject of the expedition to Germany, that Navarre and the dauphin had not accomplished, Friquet of Fricamps was unstoppable. The names of the conspirators, the rallying point, and who had gone and said what to whom, and what they had to do . . . But the dauphin had already made all of that known to his father.

A new plot hatched by Monseigneur of Navarre with the intention of seizing the King of France and slaying him? No, Friquet hadn't heard the slightest word nor detected the smallest indication of it. Admittedly the Count of Harcourt ... in charging a dead man the suspect takes no risk at all; it is a known fact of law ... The Count of Harcourt was most incensed these last few months, and had pronounced threatening words; but he alone, and speaking only for himself.

How can one not believe a man, I repeat, as obliging with his interrogators, who spoke six hours straight, without even leaving the secretaries the time to sharpen their quills? A wily one, that Friquet, very much his master's apprentice, drowning all around him in a flood of words and playing the garrulous one all the better to conceal what was most important for him to keep quiet! Anyway, in order to use his confession in a trial, it would be necessary to start his interrogation all over again in Paris, before a properly constituted commission of enquiry, as this one wasn't properly constituted in the slightest. All in all, a big net had been cast, and very few fish had been caught.

During these same days, King John busied himself going about seizing the properties and goods of the traitors, and he dispatched his Viscount of Rouen, Thomas Coupeverge, to get his hands on the Harcourts' possessions, whilst he sent the Marshal of Audrehem to invest Évreux. But everywhere Coupeverge came across unwelcoming occupants, and the seizure remained somewhat nominal. He would have had to leave a garrison in each castle, but he hadn't taken with him enough men-at-arms. On the other hand the huge headless body of John of Harcourt didn't remain exposed long on the gallows of Rouen. During the second night it was taken down secretly by good Normans who gave him a Christian burial, at the same time enjoying the pleasure of deriding the king.

As for the town of Évreux, the marshal had to lay it to siege. But it was not the only fief of the Évreux-Navarre clan. From Valognes to Meulan, from Longueville to Conches and from Pontoise to Coutances a threatening climate reigned in the towns, and the hedgerows along the sides of the road quivered suspiciously.

King John didn't feel at all safe in Rouen. He had come with troops enough to assail a banquet, but not to withstand a revolt. He avoided leaving the castle. His most loyal servants, including John of Artois himself, advised him to withdraw. His presence aroused anger.

A king who is reduced to fearing his own people is a poor sire whose reign is very likely to be cut short.

So John II decided to regain Paris; but he wanted the dauphin to accompany him. 'You will not hold out, Charles, should there be tumult in your duchy.' He feared most of all that his son proved too accommodating with the Navarrese party.

The dauphin gave way, demanding only that they travel by water. 'My father, I am accustomed to going from Rouen to Paris via the Seine. Should I do otherwise it might appear that I was fleeing. Furthermore, in moving at the slow speed of a boat, news can more easily reach us, and if I am required to return, that too will be more convenient.'

So there we have the king embarked on the great barge[35]

that the Duke of Normandy ordered specially for his own travel, since, just as I told you, he hates to ride. A large flat-bottomed boat, highly decorated, adorned and gilded, bearing the banners of France, Normandy and Dauphiny, and manoeuvred by sail and oar. The forecastle is fitted out like a veritable residence, with a fine chamber furnished with carpets and chests. The dauphin enjoys conversing there with his advisors, playing chess or draughts, or gazing at the country of France which displays much beauty all along that great river. But the king was seething with impatience at such a subdued pace. What a foolish idea it was to follow every bend of the Seine, which tripled the length of the journey, when there are routes that cut straight across the country! This confined space was unbearable to him; as far as it allowed he paced up and down as he dictated a letter, a single one, always the same one that he went over and rewrote again and again. And, at any moment, on impulse, mooring the boat, wading through the mud of the landing stage, wiping his boots in the daisies, ordering his horse brought to him, which followed with the escort along the riverbanks, to go and visit, for no particular reason, a castle he had caught a glimpse of through the poplars. 'And may the letter be copied out for my return.' His letter was to the pope, in which he would explain the causes and grounds for the King of Navarre's arrest. Was there any other business in the kingdom? One wouldn't have thought so. In any case, none that required his attention. The poor levels of aid revenues collected, the need to devalue the currency once again, the tax on cloth that had provoked the anger of the trade, the necessary repair work to the fortresses under threat from the English; he brushed these worries aside. Didn't he have a chancellor, a governor of finance, a master of the royal household, masters of requests and presidents at Parliament to deal with such things? May Nicolas Braque, who had left for Paris, go about his business, and likewise Simon of Bucy or Robert of Lorris. And indeed they did, swelling their fortunes, speculating on the price of coinage, hushing up accusations against relatives, permanently upsetting various merchant companies, towns or dioceses that would never forgive the king for the treatment received.

A sovereign who on the one hand claims to see to everything, down to the very last ceremonial detail, and on the other hand seems not to worry any longer about anything, not even the most important matters, isn't a man who will guide his people to great things.

On the second day the dauphin's vessel was moored at Pont-de-l'Arche when the king saw the prevost of the Paris merchants, Master Étienne Marcel, riding at the head of a company of fifty to a hundred lances beneath the town's blue and red banner. These bourgeois were better equipped than many a knight.

The king didn't get off the boat, nor did he invite the prevost on board. They spoke to each other from deck to riverbank, both equally surprised to find themselves face to face with one another. The prevost clearly hadn't expected to meet the king in this place, and the king wondered what the prevost could possibly be doing in Normandy with such an equipage. There was surely some Navarrese intrigue afoot behind it all. Was it an attempt to free Charles the Bad? The matter seemed rather swift in the making, just one week after his arrest. But it was possible. Or was the prevost part of the conspiracy revealed by John of Artois? The machinations he told of thus gained in verisimilitude.

'We came to salute you, sire,' was all the prevost said. The king, rather than making him talk a little, answered out of the blue and in a threatening tone that he had had to seize the King of Navarre against whom he held serious grievances, and that all would be revealed in the broad light of day in the letter that he was intending to send to the pope. King John also said that he expected to find his town of Paris in good order, and both peaceful and busy, upon his return . . . 'And presently, Messire Prevost, you may yourself return.'

A long way indeed for so few words. Étienne Marcel left, his tuft of a black beard sitting up on his chin. And as soon as the king had seen the banner of Paris disappear between the willows, he sent for his secretary to modify once more the letter to the pope . . . Ah, that reminds me . . . Brunet? Brunet! Brunet, call Dom Calvo to my window . . . yes, if you please . . . dictating something like 'And once again Most Holy Father, I have established proof that Monseigneur the King of Navarre attempted to rouse the merchants of Paris against me, making contact with their prevost who came to Norman country without warning, accompanied by a company of men-at-arms so great they could not be counted, in order to help the evil members of the Navarrese faction put the finishing touches to their perfidy, seizing my very person and that of my eldest son, the dauphin . . .'

For that matter, in his head Marcel's cavalcade was to grow by the hour, and soon would count five hundred lances.

And then he decided to move on immediately from that

mooring and, having had Navarre and Fricamps extracted
from the Castle of Pont-de-l'Arche, he ordered the boatmen
to head for Les Andelys. As the King of Navarre was following on horseback, stage by stage, surrounded by a solid escort
of sergeants who kept him on the tightest of reins and had
been given the order to run him through should he look set
to flee or should there occur any attempt to rescue him. He
should always stay within sight of the boat. In the evening, he
would be locked up in the nearest tower. He had been held
prisoner in Pont-de-l'Arche. He was to be held in Château-
Gaillard . . . yes, Château-Gaillard, where his grandmother of
Burgundy had so early ended her days . . . yes, more or less at
the same age.

How was Monseigneur of Navarre bearing up under all
this? Frankly speaking, rather badly. Now he has probably
got more accustomed to his status as prisoner, at least since
he found out that the King of France himself is prisoner of
the King of England and thus, as a result, he no longer fears
for his life. But in the early days . . .

Ah! There you are, Dom Calvo. Remind me if the word
light figures in the gospel reading next Sunday, or some other
word that evokes the idea . . . yes, the second Sunday of
Advent. It would be most surprising not to find it somewhere
. . . or in the epistle . . . the one from last Sunday obviously . . .
Abjiciamus ergo opera tenebrarum, et induamur arma lucis . . . Let
us therefore reject the works of darkness and cloak ourselves
in the light . . . But that was last Sunday. You don't have it in
mind either. All right, you will tell me later on; I would
appreciate it . . .

A fox cub caught in a trap, turning round and round in his

cage, panic-stricken, eyes ablaze, muzzle sullied, body starved thin, whining, and whining … This is how he was, our Monseigneur of Navarre. But it has to be said that everything was being done to frighten the life out of him.

Nicolas Braque had obtained a deferral for his execution by arguing that the King of Navarre should be made to feel like he is dying every day; this did not fall on deaf ears.

At Château-Gaillard, not only did King John order that he be specifically incarcerated in the chamber where Madame Marguerite of Burgundy had died, and this he was well made to understand … 'The shamelessness of his rascally wench of a grandmother it was that produced this evil breed; he is the offspring of a harlot's offspring; he must be made to think that he will end up like her …' what's more, over the handful of days that he held him there, the king announced on numerous occasions, even during the night, that his demise was imminent.

'Get yourself ready, monseigneur. The king has ordered your scaffold to be mounted in the castle's courtyard. We will come and get you shortly.' During his sorry stay, Charles of Navarre was told this by the King of the Ribald, or le Buffle, or any number of other sergeants. A moment later, Sergeant Lalemant would appear, to find Navarre with his back against the wall, gasping for breath, eyes terror-stricken. 'The king has granted you a reprieve; you will not be executed before tomorrow.' Upon which Navarre got his breath back and collapsed on a stool. An hour or so went by, when Perrinet le Buffle returned. 'The king will not have you beheaded, monseigneur. No … He wants you hanged. He is erecting the gallows now.' And then, once salvation until the morrow was declared, it was the castle governor's turn, Gautier of Riveau.

'Have you come to get me, messire governor?'

'No, monseigneur, I have come to bring you your supper.'

'Have they erected the gallows?'

'What gallows? No, monseigneur, no gallows have been prepared.'

'Nor any scaffold?'

'No, monseigneur, I have seen nothing of the kind.'

Six times over. Monseigneur of Navarre had been beheaded, and hanged, drawn or quartered as many times again. Perhaps the worst trick was leaving a large sack of hemp in his cell and telling him that during the night he would be tied up in it and thrown in the Seine. The following morning, the King of the Ribald came to recover the sack, and went away smiling when, turning it over, he saw that Monseigneur of Navarre had made a hole in it.

King John constantly asked for news of the prisoner. This helped make him wait more patiently while his letter to the pope was altered. Was the King of Navarre eating? No, he scarcely touched the meals he was brought, and his plate came back down exactly as it had gone up. He was certainly afraid of being poisoned. 'Is he losing weight? A good thing, a good thing indeed. Make his food bitter-tasting and foul-smelling, so that he thinks that we really want to poison him.' Is he sleeping? Badly. During the day, he was sometimes to be found slumped over the table, his head in his hands, starting like someone suddenly pulled from his sleep. But at night, he could be heard walking without cease, round and round his circular chamber . . . 'Like a fox cub, sire, like a fox cub.' He certainly dreaded someone coming to strangle him, just as his grandmother had been, in the same place. Certain mornings one could tell that he had been crying. 'Ah good, ah good,' said the king. 'Does he speak to you?' But of course he spoke! He tried to strike up conversations with those who entered his lodgings. And he attempted to wear them down, starting with their weaknesses. He promised the King of the Ribald a mountain of gold if he would help him escape, or just agree to sending letters to the outside. He offered Sergeant Perrinet the chance to come with him and become his King of the Ribald in Évreux and in Navarre, as he had noticed that le Buffle was jealous of the other man. To the fortress's governor, whom he had judged to be a loyal soldier, he pleaded innocence and injustice. 'I know not what they hold against me, as I swear to God that I have harboured no evil thought against the king, my dear father, nor have under-taken anything at all to harm him. He was misled about me by perfidious traitors. They wanted to send me down in his esteem; but I can bear all the punishments that he cares to inflict upon me, because I know that they are not really of his doing. There are so many things I could advise him of for his safeguarding, so many favours I could do him and that I will not be able to do him should he have me killed. Go to him, messire governor, go and tell him that it would be to his advantage to grant me an audience. And if God wishes that I return to good fortune, rest assured that I will take care of yours, as I can see that you are sympathetic to my cause as much as you are concerned about the true wellbeing of your master.'

All of this was of course reported back to the king who

barked: 'See the perfidy! See the traitor!' as if it weren't the way with all prisoners to bribe their jailers or seek to make them feel sorry for them. Perhaps even the sergeants insisted a little on the King of Navarre's proposals, all the better to sell themselves. King John threw them purses of gold in recognition of their loyalty. 'This evening you will pretend that I have ordered you to warm his jail cell, and you will light some straw and damp wood, and block up the chimney, to smoke him out.'

Yes, a trapped fox cub, the little King of Navarre. But the King of France was like a huge, raging hound circling the cage, a sly, bearded watchdog, his fur bristling, growling, howling, bearing his teeth, scratching at the dust, unable to reach his prey through the bars.

And that remained so until around the twentieth of April, when appeared two Norman knights, fittingly escorted, whose pennon bore the coat of arms of Navarre and Évreux. They brought King John a letter from Philip of Navarre, dated in Conches. Rather abrupt was the letter. Philip said how incensed he was at the great wrongs and abuse caused to his lord and elder brother ... 'Whom you took unlawfully, unjustly and without reason. But you should know that you have no occasion to think of his legacy, nor mine, in killing him through your cruelty, as you will never get your hands on a single inch of it. From this day on we will defy you, you and all your authority, and we will wage merciless war against you, as greatly as is in our power.' If these are not the exact words, they at least convey the same message. The words were stamped with just such severity; and the defiant intention was very much present. And what made the letter all the more brutal, was that it was addressed: 'To John of Valois, who calls himself King of France . . .'

The two knights that brought it saluted and, without further delay, turned their horses around and went away as they had come.

Naturally, the king didn't reply to the letter. It was inadmissible, by its address alone. But war had been declared, and one of the greatest vassals no longer recognized King John as rightful sovereign. Which meant that he would not be long in recognizing the Englishman.

One would expect such a great insult would send King John into a blinding rage. However, he surprised his people by a fit of laughter. Somewhat forced laughter. His father had also laughed, and rather more heartily, twenty years earlier, when the Bishop Burghersh, Chancellor of England, had brought him the challenge of the young Edward III . . .

King John ordered that the long-cogitated letter to the pope be immediately dispatched, yes, as it was; having been amended so many times, it didn't make much sense and proved nothing whatsoever. At the same time he ordered his son-in-law to be released from the fortress. 'I will shut him up in the Louvre.' And, letting the dauphin sail back up the Seine on his great, golden barge, he himself chose to take to the road at a gallop and regain Paris on horseback. Where he did nothing much of any importance, while the Navarrese clan got down to work.

Ah! I hadn't realized that you had come back, Dom Calvo . . . So, you have found . . . In the gospel . . . *Jesus replied* . . . what then? *Go and tell John what you have heard and what you have seen.* Speak louder, Dom Calvo. With the noise of the cavalcade . . . *The blind see, the lame walk* . . . Yes, yes, I follow. Saint Matthew. *Coeci vident, claudi ambulant, surdi audiunt, mortui resurgent, et coetera* . . . The blind see. It is not much, but it will do. It is a matter of being able to build my homily around it. You know how I work.

2

The Nation of England

I WAS TELLING YOU earlier, Archambaud, that the Navarrese party were proving themselves to be most active. From the day after the banquet of Rouen, messengers had gone off in all directions. First of all to the aunt and the sister. Mesdames Joan and Blanche; the Castle of the Widowed Queens began to hum like a weaver's workshop. And then to the brother-in-law Phoebus . . . I will have to tell you about him; he is a strange prince indeed, but by no means insignificant. And as Périgord is after all closer to Béarn than it is to Paris, it wouldn't be a bad thing that one day . . . We will talk again about this. Philip of Évreux was successfully standing in for his brother and taking matters in hand; he sent an order to Navarre to raise troops and to transport them over the sea as soon as they could. Meanwhile, Godfrey of Harcourt got together people from his clan in Normandy. And most significant of all, Philip sent to England Sires Morbecque and Brévand, who had taken part in former negotiations, to request aid.

King Edward offered them a cool reception. 'When it comes to agreements, I appreciate loyalty, and deeds that match words. Without trust between allied kings, no undertaking can successfully be seen through. Last year I opened my doors to Monseigneur of Navarre's vassals; I equipped troops, under the command of the Duke of Lancaster, which backed up his own. A treaty between us was in a late stage of preparation, but yet to be signed: we were to make a perpetual alliance, and our commitment would be never to agree to peace, truce, nor to any other accord, without the other also agreeing. And no sooner had Monseigneur of Navarre landed in the Cotentin than he took the opportunity to deal with King John, pledging him his true love and paying him homage. If he now finds himself, through an act of treachery, in jail, ensnared by this same father-in-law, the fault shall not be mine. And before rushing to his aid, I should like to know if my relatives in Évreux only come to me in distress, and as soon as I have pulled them clear they turn to others.'

Nevertheless, he made arrangements, summoned the Duke of Lancaster and with him began to prepare a new expedition, while he addressed instructions to the Prince of Wales in Bordeaux. And as he had learned from the Navarrese envoys that John II implicated him in the accusations brought against Monseigneur of Navarre, he sent letters to the Holy Father, to the emperor, and to various Christian princes, in which he denied any connivance whatsoever with Charles of Navarre, but rather, on the other hand, he strongly blamed John II for his absence of faith and for his scheming; this, 'for the honour of chivalry', he would have preferred never to see in a king.

His letter to the pope had taken rather less time than King John's, and it was considerably better phrased, believe me.

We do not like each other at all, King Edward and I; he always considers me too biased towards the interests of France and I judge him to have shown too little respect for the primacy of the Church. Each time we've met, we have clashed. He would like to have an English pope, or preferably no pope at all. But I have to recognize that he is, for his nation, an excellent prince, skilful, prudent when need be, bold when he can be. England is much in his debt. And even though he is only forty-four years old, he commands the respect that surrounds an old king, when he has been a good king. A sovereign's age is not determined by their date of birth, but by the length of their reign.

In this respect, King Edward is looked upon as an elder amongst all the western princes. The Pope Innocent has only been supreme pontiff for four years; the Emperor Charles, elected ten years ago, has only been crowned for the last two. John of Valois has only just celebrated ... in captivity, a sad celebration ... the sixth anniversary of his crowning. Edward III has occupied his throne for twenty-nine years, soon it will be thirty.

He is a man of fine stature and great presence, if somewhat corpulent. He has long blond hair, a silky, well-kept beard, rather large blue eyes; a true Capetian. He looks very much like Philip the Fair, his grandfather, more than one of whose qualities he has inherited. Shame that the blood of our kings gave such a fine product in England and such a wretched one in France! As he has got older he seems more and more prone to silence, like his grandfather. What do you expect! He has been observing men bowing before him for thirty years now. He knows by their stride, by the look in their eye, their tone of voice, what they hope to get from him, what they will ask for, what ambitions are driving them and what they are worth to the State. His orders are brief. As he says: 'The fewer the words one speaks, the fewer there are to be repeated, and they are less open to distortion.'

He knows himself to be invested, in the eyes of Europe, with great renown. The Battle of Sluys, the Siege of Calais, the victory at Crécy . . . He is the first for more than a century to have defeated France, or rather his French rival, since he undertook this war, he says, only to assert his right to the crown of Saint Louis. But also to lay his hands on prosperous provinces.

Scarcely a year passes that he doesn't land his troops on the continent, now in Boulonnais, now in Brittany, or that he orders, as he has done these two last summers, a *chevauchée* starting out from his duchy of Guyenne.

In the past he headed up his armies himself, and he acquired a fine reputation as a warrior. Now, he no longer accompanies his troops. He has them commanded by good captains who have acquired their skills on the job campaign after campaign; but I think that he owes his successes above all to his maintaining a permanent army made up for the most part of foot soldiers, always ready and always available, who, in the end, don't cost any more than dubious mercenaries called up at great expense, that are disbanded, that are called up again, become slack, never regroup in time, that are ill-assorted, often ill-equipped, and whose parts don't know how to come together to manoeuvre in battle.

It is a fine thing to say: 'Our country is in peril. The king is calling us up. Everyone must rush to his assistance!' But with what? With sticks? The time will come when all kings will model themselves upon the English example, and wage war with professional soldiers, well paid, who go where they are sent without dawdling or arguing.

You see, Archambaud, it is not necessary for a kingdom to be either vast or populous to become powerful. You need only a people capable of pride and effort, led for long enough by a wise ruler who knows how to present them with great ambitions.

From a country of scarcely six million souls, Wales included, before the Great Plague, and just four million after the scourge, Edward III has built a prosperous and feared nation, which speaks as an equal with France and with the empire. The wool trade, maritime transport, the possession of Ireland, an effective exploitation of the abundant Aquitaine, royal powers exercised, and obeyed, everywhere, an ever-ready army forever at work; this is how England has become so strong and rich.

The king himself possesses enormous wealth; it is said he can't even count his fortune, but I know that he counts it, otherwise he wouldn't have it. He started the habit of counting thirty years ago upon inheriting an empty Treasury and debts throughout Europe. Today, it is he that one consults to borrow money. He rebuilt Windsor; he embellished Westminster ... yes, Westmoutiers, if you like; I've been there so often that I've ended up pronouncing it à l'anglaise, as, strangely enough, the more they go about conquering France, the more the English, even at court, speak their Saxon language and less and less French . . . In each of his residences, King Edward has piled up wonders. He buys many things from the Lombard merchants and from Cypriot navigators, not only spices from the Orient, but also finely worked objects of every type that then serve as models for his manufactures.

Regarding spices, I will have to tell you about pepper, my nephew. It is a fine investment. Pepper does not go off; its commercial value has grown continuously these last years and everything suggests the trend will not only last but increase. I have ten thousand florins' worth stored in a warehouse in Montpellier; I took this pepper as reimbursement of half of the debt of a local merchant, Pierre de Rambert, who was unable to pay his suppliers in Cyprus. Since I am Canon of Nicosia . . . without ever having been there . . . alas, as that island has a great reputation for beauty . . . I was able to settle his business affair . . . But let us get back to our Sire Edward.

A table fit for a king is no empty promise in his household, and he who takes a seat there for the first time can but hold his breath before the profusion of gold spread out in front of him. A golden stag, almost as big as a real one, forms the centrepiece. Hanaps,[36] ewers, dishes, spoons, knives, salt cellars, everything made of gold. Then the kitchen ushers bring food to the table on golden platters, enough to mint coinage for an entire county. 'If ever by any chance we are in need, we will always be able to sell all this,' he says. But financial difficulties . . . which Treasury has never known any? Edward is always certain to find credit, because everyone knows of the treasures he possesses. He himself only appears before his subjects superbly attired, draped in precious furs and embroidered garments, sparkling with jewels, golden spurs at his heels.

In this display of magnificence, God is not forgotten. The chapel of Westminster alone is served by fourteen vicars, to which we should add the clerks, choirboys and all the servants of the sacristy. And to play tricks on the pope, whom he says is under French control, he has repeatedly increased Church employment and only wishes to see the jobs given to the English, without sharing the benefices with the Holy See, on which subject we have always clashed.

His duty to God thus served, next comes his obligation to secure the line of the royal family. Edward III has ten living children. The eldest, Prince of Wales and Duke of Aquitaine, is as you know him; he is twenty-six years old. The youngest, the Earl of Buckingham, has barely left his wet nurse's breast.

King Edward has built imposing residences for each of his sons; for his daughters he has sought out noble establishments that may serve his designs.

I wager that he would be most bored with life, King Edward, had Providence not assigned him the part he was most suited to perform: to govern. Yes, the contemplative life would have had very little interest for him, getting venerable, watching death creep up; what he lived for was to arbitrate over others' passions, and set them goals that help them forget themselves. Because men only find honour and value in living if they dedicate their acts and their thoughts to some great undertaking in which they can lose themselves, with which they can become one.

That is what inspired him when he created in Calais his

Order of the Garter, a flourishing Order, of which John II, with his Star, produced but a poor copy, initially pretentious and later pathetic.

And once more Edward is answering to this will for grandeur when he pursues his project, unavowed but observable, of an English Europe. Not that he is thinking of placing the West directly under his command, nor that he wishes to conquer all the kingdoms and reduce them to serfdom. No, rather he has in mind a free association of kings or governments in which he would have precedence and which he would dominate, and within this arrangement he would not only make peace prevail, but would also have nothing more to fear from the empire, even if he weren't to encompass it. Nor would he owe anything more to the Holy See; I suspect him of secretly harbouring that particular intent. He has already achieved as much with Flanders, which he cut loose from France; he intervenes in the affairs of Spain; he has put out feelers in the Mediterranean. Ah! If he had France, you can imagine, what wouldn't he do, what wouldn't he be capable of doing from there! His idea, by the way, is nothing new. King Philip the Fair, his grandfather, already had a project for perpetual peace to reunite Europe.

Edward takes pleasure in speaking French with the French and English with the English. He can address the Flemish in their tongue, which flatters them, and earns him much of his success over there. With others he speaks Latin.

So, you may say, with such a talented, capable king, whom fortune so clearly favours, why not join him and encourage his claims to France? Why go to such pains to keep on the throne the arrogant fool, born under unfavourable stars, that

Providence has given us ... has most probably sent to us to put this unfortunate kingdom to the test?

Ha! My nephew, it is this: indeed, we desire a beneficial understanding to be formed between the kingdoms of the West, but we want it to be French, I mean of French government and pre-eminence. If England were too powerful, we are convinced, it would quickly distance itself from the laws of the Church. It is France that is the designated kingdom of God. And King John will not last forever.

But you will also understand, Archambaud, why King Edward so steadfastly supports this Charles the Bad, who has often deceived him. It is because the tiny Navarre, and the big County of Évreux, are pieces, not only in his dealings with France, but in this long game of gathering together kingdoms that has taken root in his mind. Kings have to have something to dream about too!

Soon after the mission of our fellows Morbecque and Brévand, it was Monseigneur Philip of Navarre, Count of Longueville, who himself travelled to England.

Blond and tall and of a proud nature, Philip of Navarre is as loyal as his brother is deceitful; which means that, by loyalty to his brother, he espouses with conviction all of his brother's treachery. He doesn't have the gift of the gab of his elder brother, but he charms by the warmth of his soul. He greatly appealed to Queen Philippa, who says he looked exactly like her husband at the same age. It is no great wonder; they are cousins several times over.

Good Queen Philippa! When she wed she was a round and rosy demoiselle who promised to grow fat, as the women of Hainaut often do. She fulfilled her promise.

The king loved her dearly. But he had, with age, other impulses and desires, rare, but violent. There was the Countess of Salisbury; and at present there is Dame Alice Perrère, or Perrières, one of the queen's ladies-in-waiting. In order to soothe her pique, Philippa eats, and gets fatter and fatter.

Queen Isabella? Yes, yes, she is still alive; at least she was still alive last month. In Castle Rising, a huge and sad castle where, twenty-eight years ago, her son locked her up after he had had her lover, Lord Mortimer, executed. Free, she would have caused him far too much trouble. The She-wolf of France ... He visits her once a year, at Christmas time. It is from the Queen Dowager that he acquires his rights over France. But she it was, again, who provoked the dynastic crisis, by denouncing Marguerite of Burgundy's adultery, and providing good reason to exclude Louis Hutin's descendants from the line of succession. There is something rather ridiculous you will admit, to be found in the alliance, forty years on, between the grandson of Marguerite of Burgundy and the son of Isabella. Ah! It is enough to live in order to have seen it all!

And there you have Edward and Philip of Navarre together at Windsor, and the interrupted treaty is back under discussion, whose first foundations were set down during the talks in Avignon. Still a secret treaty. In the first drafts, the names of the contracting princes were not to appear explicitly. The King of England is referred to as *the elder brother* and the King of Navarre *the younger brother*. As if that could suffice to mask their identities, and as if the terms written didn't obviously refer to them! They are precautions of chancelleries, which fail to mislead those one distrusts: when you want a secret to be well kept, well, you shouldn't write it down, that is all.

The younger brother recognizes *the elder brother* as rightful King of France. Always the same thing; it is the first and the most essential part; it is the cornerstone of the agreement. *The elder brother* recognizes *the younger brother* his right to the duchy of Normandy, the counties of Champagne and Brie, the viscountcy of Chartres and all of the Languedoc with Toulouse, Béziers, Montpellier. It appears that Edward did not give way on Angoumois[37] – too close to Guyenne, that must be the reason; he wouldn't allow Navarre, should this treaty come into effect, may God forbid, to get a foothold between Aquitaine and the Poitou. On the other hand, he seems to have granted him Bigorre, which, if it comes to Phoebus's ears, will not be at all to his liking. As you see, when you add it all up, that makes a big piece of France, a very big piece. And one may well be surprised that a man who means to reign there would relinquish so much of it to just one vassal. But, on the one hand, this kind sort of vice-royalty that he is bestowing upon Navarre corresponds to the idea he has been entertaining of a new empire; and on the other, the more he increases the possessions of the prince who recognizes him as rightful king, the more he broadens the territorial base of his legitimacy. Instead of having to rally people to his cause, piece by piece, he can maintain that he is recognized by all of those provinces in one fell swoop.

As for the rest, sharing the cost of war, commitment to not conclude truces separately, these are habitual clauses and taken from the previous draft. But the alliance is set forth as a 'perpetual alliance'.

I was told there was an amusing exchange between Edward and Philip of Navarre because the latter requested that the settlement of the hundred thousand écus, never paid, but which featured in the marriage contract between Charles of Navarre and Joan of Valois, be included in the treaty.

King Edward was surprised. 'Why should I have to pay King John's debts?'

'But of course. You take his place on the throne; you take on his obligations also.' Young Philip certainly had quite a nerve. One has to be his age to risk saying such things. That made Edward III laugh, he who never usually laughs. 'So be it. But only after I have been crowned in Rheims. Not before the coronation.'

And Philip of Navarre left again for Normandy. He was in Normandy as long as it took to commit to vellum what had been agreed, to go over the terms article by article, to send notes back and forth across the Channel: 'the elder brother . . . the younger brother . . .' and also the troubles of war, all of which meant that the treaty, still secret, still widely known, at least to those who had an interest in knowing about it, wouldn't be signed until the beginning of September, at Clarendon Castle, barely three months ago, just days before the Battle of Poitiers. Signed by whom? By King Edward and by Philip of Navarre, who undertook a second trip to England to this end.

By now you will understand, Archambaud, why the dauphin, who was strongly opposed to the King of Navarre's arrest, as you have heard, keeps him so resolutely in prison, though as acting commander of the kingdom, he might with perfect ease and consistency release him, as he is being pressed from many sides to do. As long as the treaty is signed only by Philip of Navarre, it will be considered null and void. From the moment Charles of Navarre ratifies it, it will be another matter altogether.

At this hour, the King of Navarre, because he is held prisoner in Picardie by the King of France's son, doesn't yet know – he is probably the only one not to know – he has recognized the King of England as rightful King of France, but his recognition being by proxy, since he cannot sign it himself, it is worthless.

That adds a fine knot of confusion, even a cat wouldn't recognize its kittens in the tangle, and it's what we will try to untangle in Metz! I wager that years from now nobody will understand anything of this, except you perhaps, or your son, because you will have told him.

3

The Pope and the World

HADN'T I TOLD you that in Sens we would get some news from Paris? And good news at that. The dauphin has walked out on everyone at his turbulent Estates-General where Marcel called for the disbanding of the king's council and where Bishop Le Coq, while pleading for the release of Charles the Bad, forgot himself to the point of speaking of deposing King John. Yes, yes, my nephew, this is what we have come to: one of his neighbours had to stamp on the bishop's foot to get him to correct himself, and put on record that it was not in the power of the estates to depose a king, only the pope might, at the request of the three estates. Well, the dauphin left yesterday, Monday, taking his people with him – for Metz, he too. With two thousand horses. As an excuse he cited messages received from the emperor, obliging him to attend his Diet for the good of the kingdom. Yes, and above all, my message. He has heard me. With his exit, the estates are in a void and will break up without being

able to conclude a thing. If the town proves to be too turbulent, he could always come back with his troops. He holds
it under by threat . . .

Other good news: Capocci is not coming to Metz. He
refuses to meet me. Blessed refusal. He is putting himself in
the wrong vis-à-vis the Holy Father, and I will be rid of him.
I am sending the Bishop of Sens to escort the dauphin; that
makes two wise men to advise him, already he is accompanied by the Archbishop-Chancellor, Pierre de La Forêt. For
my part, I will have twelve prelates in my retinue. That will
suffice. It is as many as any legate ever had. And no Capocci.
Really, I cannot understand why the Holy Father persists in
appointing him to me and still stubbornly refuses to recall
him. First and foremost, without him I would have set out
earlier. Really, it was a lost spring.

In Avignon I sensed that everything was about to take
a grave turn as soon as we learned of the affair of Rouen,
and received letters from King John and King Edward, and
found out that the Duke of Lancaster was equipping a new
expedition, while the French army was convened for the first
of June. I said to the Holy Father that we had to send a papal
legate, which he agreed to. He was bemoaning the state of
Christendom. I was ready to leave that very week. He needed
three weeks to write down the instructions. I said to him: 'But
what instructions, *sanctissimus pater*? You only have to copy
out those that your predecessor, the venerated Clement VI,
drew up for a similar mission, ten years ago. They were
entirely to the point. They would instruct me how to act so as
to accordingly prevent a general resumption of war.'

Perhaps, deep down, without being fully aware, as he is

certainly incapable of a deliberately evil thought, wasn't he desperate that I succeed where he had failed, before Crécy. What's more, he admitted his failure with Edward III. 'I was cruelly rebuffed by him, and I fear that the same will befall you. He is a very determined man, Edward III; he is not easy to get around. Moreover, he believes that all the French cardinals are in league against him. I will send along with you our *venerabilis frater* Capocci.' That was his idea.

Venerabilis frater! Each pope must make at least one mistake during his pontificate, otherwise he would be the Good Lord Himself. Well, Clement VI's mistake is to have given Capocci the galero.

'And thus,' Innocent said to me, 'should either one of you fall ill . . . may God protect you . . . the other would be able to pursue the mission.' As he always feels ill, our poor Holy Father, he wants everyone else to be ill too, and he will administer you the Extreme Unction as soon as you sneeze.

Have you seen me sick since the beginning of our journey, Archambaud? But Capocci, the jolts and bumps break his back; he has to stop every two leagues to piss. One day, he is sweating with fever, another he has diarrhoea. He wanted to take my doctor Master Vigier from me, whom you will notice is not overwhelmed with work, at least not on my part. For me, the good physician is the one who every morning palpates me, auscultates me, takes a look at my eyes and my tongue, examines my urine, doesn't impose upon me too many privations nor does he bleed me more than once a month and who keeps me in good health. And to get himself ready, Capocci! He is one of those people who scheme and insist on being entrusted with a mission and no sooner they have it, can't stop making demands. One papal secretary wasn't enough, he needed two. One might wonder to what end, since of all of the letters bound for the Curia, before we were separated, it was I who dictated and corrected them. All of that meant that we only left at the time of the summer solstice, on the twenty-first of June. Too late. One does not stop wars when the armies are already marching. One stops them in the minds of kings, while the decision is still uncertain. I tell you, Archambaud, a lost spring.

The day before our departure, the Holy Father granted me an audience, alone. Perhaps he regretted a little having inflicted upon me such a useless companion. I went to see him in Villeneuve, where he resides. As he refuses to live in the grand palace that his predecessors built. Too much luxury, too much pomp for his liking, too big a household. Innocent wanted to respond to public feeling that holds the papacy lives in too much splendour. Public feeling! A handful of scribblers, for whom gall is the natural ink; a few preachers that the Devil sent into the Church to sow discord. With some of them, a good excommunication, firmly dealt out, would have sufficed; with some, a prebend, or a benefice, accompanied by some order of precedence, since it is often envy that stimulates their spittle; their intention is to set the world straight on the matter of the too small place, in their eyes, that they take up in it. Look at Petrarch, whom you heard me speak of the other day to Monseigneur of Auxerre. He is a man of evil disposition, but great knowledge and experience, we must give him that, whose opinion is valued highly on both sides of the Alps. He was a friend of Dante Alighieri, who brought him to Avignon; and he was entrusted with many missions between princes. There is someone who wrote that Avignon was the cesspit of all cesspits, teeming with adventurers, where every possible vice flourished, where one came to bribe cardinals, where the pope ran a trade in dioceses and abbeys, and prelates had mistresses and their mistresses had go-betweens . . . in short, the new Babylon.

About myself the rumours he spread were vile. As he was someone to be considered, I met him, listened to him, which seemed to satisfy him, several of his affairs were thus sorted out – it was said that he dabbled in the dark arts, black magic and other such things – I got him back several of the benefices that he had been stripped of; I corresponded with him, asking him to copy in each of his letters a few verses of the great ancient poets, that he masters to perfection, for the embellishment of my sermons, as I don't overdo things on the literary front, I have the style of a jurist; I actually put him forward for the office of papal secretary, and left it entirely up to him whether or not this would meet with a successful conclusion. Well, now he has fewer bad things to say about the court of Avignon, and about me, he writes wonders. I am a star in the firmament of the Church, a power behind the papal throne; I equal or exceed in knowledge any other jurist of this age; I am blessed by nature and refined by study; and one can recognize in me that capacity to embrace all things in the universe that Julius Caesar attributed to Pliny the Elder. Yes, my nephew; no less! And I in no way reduced my household nor my domestic staff, which used to provoke his diatribes. He has gone back to Italy, my friend Petrarch. Something in his nature prevents him from settling anywhere, like his friend Dante, on whom he has largely modelled himself. He invented an immoderate love for a lady who was never his mistress, and who died. With that, he has his grounds for the sublime. I liked him a lot, that wicked man. I miss him. If he had stayed in Avignon, he would probably be sitting in your seat, at this moment, as I would have taken him in my luggage.

But to follow the so-called public feeling, like our good Innocent? That is to show weakness, to give power to one's critics, and to estrange oneself from those who by tradition offer support, without winning over even the lesser malcontents, not one.

So, in order to give himself an image of humility, our Holy Father went to live in his little cardinal's palace in Villeneuve, on the other bank of the Rhône. But though expenses are indeed reduced, the establishment has proved to be really too small. Thus, it has had to be extended to house those who are indispensable. The secretariat of state functions poorly for lack of space; the clerks change rooms constantly as the plans evolve for the building work. Bulls[38] are written in the dust. Not only that, since many offices have remained in the Avignon palace, one constantly has to cross the river, along which a strong wind most often blows, in winter freezing you to the bone. Our affairs are falling behind, we are late in all of our business ... Furthermore, our Holy Father was elected over Jean Birel, the General of the Carthusians, who enjoyed a reputation of perfect saintliness. I wonder, after all, if I wasn't wrong to brush him aside; he wouldn't have been any more awkward, and our Holy Father promised to found a Carthusian monastery. The charterhouse is now under construction between the pontifical residence and a new defensive structure, Saint André's fort, also under construction. But here, it is the king's officers who are organizing the work. With the result that for the time being, Christendom is being commanded from the middle of a building site.

The Holy Father granted me audience in his chapel, which he hardly ever leaves, a small, five-sided apse, adjoining the great audience chamber, because he does in fact need an audience chamber, he realized, and which he had decorated by an image-maker from Viterbo, Matteo Giova something or other, Giovanotto, Giovanelli, Giovannetti . . . it is blue, it is pale; it would belong very well in a nunnery; I personally don't like it at all; not enough red, not enough gold. Bright colours don't cost any more than the others. And the noise, my nephew! Evidently, the apse is the calmest room in all of the palace, and that is why the Holy Father withdraws there! Saws grate in the stone, hammers bang against chisels, hoists squeal, cartage roll, beams bounce, workers call out to each other or quarrel, shouting. Dealing with serious matters in such a racket is purgatory. I understand that he suffers headaches, the Holy Father! 'You see, my venerable brother,' he tells me, 'I spend a great deal of money and cause myself a great deal of bother to build up around me the appearance of poverty. And then I still have to keep up the huge palace opposite. I can't just let it crumble.'

He touches my heart, Pope Aubert, when he laughs at himself so sadly, and seems to recognize his mistakes, to mollify me.

He was sitting on a wretched curule chair[39] that I wouldn't have had for a seat even in my first bishop's palace; as usual, he remained stooped throughout the meeting. A large hooked nose, in the continuation of his forehead, big nostrils, big eyebrows raised very high, big ears, the lobes sticking out from under his white cap, the corners of his mouth turned down into his curly beard. His body is powerfully built, and one is surprised that his health is so fragile. A stone sculptor is working on fixing his likeness, for his tomb's recumbent statue. Because he doesn't want a standing effigy: ostentation. But he does, all the same, allow the need for a tomb.

One day he was lamenting his fate. He went on: 'Each pope, my brother, must live, in his own way, the passion of Our Lord, Jesus Christ. My own way has been in the failure of all of my undertakings. Since God's will hoisted me up to the summit of the Church, I feel my hands are nailed down. What have I accomplished, what have I done right during these three and a half years?'

God's will, certainly, certainly; but we have to admit that it chose to express itself a little through my modest person. Which allows me a certain freedom with the Holy Father. But there are things, in spite of everything, that I cannot tell him. I can't tell him, for example, that men who find themselves invested with supreme authority should not use it to justify their elevation by changing the world. With the humble great there is an insidious form of pride that is often the cause of their failings.

Pope Innocent's projects, his high undertakings, I know them well. There are three, which are dependent upon each other. The most ambitious one: reunite the Latin and Greek Churches, under the authority of the Catholic Church, of course; bring together East and West, re-establish unity in the Christian world. It has been the dream of every pope for the last thousand years. And I had, with Clement VI, moved matters along considerably, further along than they had ever been before, and, in any case, than they are at present. Innocent took up the project once more in his own name and as if the idea had come to him, brand new, by visitation of the Holy Spirit. Let's not argue.

To achieve this, second undertaking, and a prerequisite to the first: re-establish the papacy in Rome, because the authority of the pope over the Christians of the East would only be accepted if it were expressed from the height of Saint Peter's throne. Constantinople, though at present in a state of bankruptcy, could yield only to the authority of Rome, not Avignon, without losing honour. On that point, as you know, my opinion differs entirely. Such reasoning would be true provided that the person of the pope himself should not, in Rome, be exposed as being even weaker than he is in Provence.

Now, to return to Rome, first it was necessary, as a third project, to make up with the emperor. Which was undertaken as a matter of priority. Let's see where we stand regarding these fine projects. We rushed, against my advice, to crown Emperor Charles, elected eight years ago, and over whom we had an advantage so long as we held out on his coronation. Today, we are powerless against him. He thanked us with his Bulla Aurea, that we were forced to swallow, thus losing all of our authority not only over the empire's elections, but also over the Church's finances within the empire. This is no reconciliation, it is a capitulation. In return, the emperor has generously left our hands free in Italy, that is to say he has honoured us with the chance to plunge them into a veritable hornets' nest.

To Italy the Holy Father sent the Cardinal Álvarez d'Albornoz, who is more of a captain than a cardinal, in order to prepare the return to Rome. Albornoz began by pegging himself to Cola di Rienzi, who for a while held sway over Rome. Born in a Trastevere inn, this Rienzo was one of those men of the people with the face of Caesar who spring up from time to time over there, and who captivate the Romans by reminding them that their forefathers used to hold command over the entire universe. Furthermore, he passed himself off as the son of an emperor, having found himself out to be the bastard of Henry VII of Luxembourg, but he remained alone in this opinion. He chose the title of tribune, wore a purple toga, sat in state atop the Capitoline Hill, on the ruins of the Temple of Jupiter. My friend Petrarch welcomed him as the restorer of Italy's former greatness. This Rienzo could have been used as a pawn on our chessboard, to be advanced discerningly, but not by placing all our hopes on him. He was murdered two years ago by the Colonnas, because Albornoz took too long in sending him assistance, notwithstanding his attachment. Now we must start everything all over again; and we have never been further from returning to Rome, where anarchy reigns even more so than in the past. One should always dream of Rome, but never return there.

As for Constantinople . . . Oh! We have made excellent progress in our talks. The Emperor Palaiologus is willing to recognize us; he has solemnly committed to it; he would even go so far as to kneel before us if only he could leave his cramped little empire. He made just one condition: that we send him an army to deliver him from his enemies. He has reached the point where he would happily recognize a country priest in exchange for five hundred knights and a thousand foot soldiers.

Ah! You too are astonished! If the unity of Christians, if the reuniting of the Churches depends only upon this, can't we dispatch this little army to the Grecian Sea? Well no, my good Archambaud, we cannot. Because we have neither the material to equip it nor the money to pay the men's wages. Because our fine policy has produced its results; because, to disarm our critics, we resolved to reform ourselves and return to the purity of the Church of our origins . . . Which origins? Most bold is the one who can claim to truly know them! What purity! No sooner were there twelve apostles than there was a traitor amongst them.

And to start by doing away with the commendams and benefices not contributing to the cure of souls. 'The flock should be kept by a shepherd, not by a mercenary', and to order that those who have amassed wealth should be excluded from the divine mysteries – 'Let us make ourselves in the image of the poor' – and to ban all tributes coming from prostitutes and games of dice . . . yes, we have indeed gone down deep into such details. Ah! It is because games of dice encourage the utterance of blasphemy; no impure money; let us not grow fat from sin, which, becoming ever cheaper, only grows and spreads.

The result of all these reformations is that the coffers are empty, as pure money flows in only the finest of streams; the malcontents have increased tenfold, and there are always false prophets, 'visionaries', to preach that the pope is a heretic.

Ah! If it is true that the road to hell is paved with good

intentions, the dear Holy Father will have paved a good deal of the way!

'My venerable brother, open up all of your thoughts to me; don't hide anything from me, even if it is criticism that you have in mind.'

Can I tell him that if he were to read more attentively what the Creator has written for us in the heavens, he would see that the stars form poor conjunctions and sad quadratures over almost all of the thrones, including his own, on which he is seated precisely because the configuration is ill-fated, whereas, if it were favourable it would probably be me sitting there instead? Can I tell him that when one is in such a bleak sidereal position, that it is not the time to be rebuilding one's house from top to bottom, but only to be holding it together as best one can, as it was handed down to us, and that it is not enough to turn up from the village of Pompadour in the Limousin, with the simple ways of a peasant, to be heeded by kings and to put right the injustices of the world. The tragedy of our time is that, of the great thrones, none is occupied by a man as great as his charge. Ah! The successors to these kings will not have an easy task!

He told me again, the day before my departure: 'Would I be the pope who could have reunited all Christians but who failed to do so? I hear that the King of England is assembling in Southampton fifty vessels to transport near four hundred knights and archers and more than one thousand horses to the continent.' I do indeed believe that he had heard as much; it was I who gave him the news. 'It is half of what I would need to satisfy the Emperor Palaiologus. Couldn't you, with the assistance of our brother the Cardinal Capocci, whom I know well does not have all of your qualities, and whom I cannot manage to love as much as I love you . . .' flour, flour to send me to sleep . . . 'but who in the eyes of King Edward is not seen as unworthy, couldn't you together persuade him, instead of putting this expedition to use against France . . . Yes, I can see what you are thinking. King John has also called up his army; but he is open to feelings of chivalrous and Christian honour. You have power over him. If the two kings gave up the idea of fighting each other and both dispatched the entirety of their forces to Constantinople so that it could return to the fold of the only true Church, what glory wouldn't they gain from such an act? Try to impress this upon them, my venerable brother; show them that instead of bloodying their kingdoms, and amassing suffering for their Christian peoples, they would make themselves worthy of the loyalty of the most valiant knights and saints.'

I replied: 'Most Holy Father, what you wish for will be the easiest thing in the world to achieve, as soon as two conditions have been met: for King Edward, that he be recognized rightful King of France and crowned in Rheims; for King John, that King Edward relinquish his claims and that he pay homage to him. Once these two things are accomplished, I see no other obstacle.'

'You are making fun of me, my brother; you have no faith.'

'I have faith, Most Holy Father, but I do not feel myself capable of making the sun shine at night. That said, I believe with all my faith that if God wants a miracle, He can accomplish it without us.'

We remained a moment without talking, as a cart was unloading its cargo of rubble stones in a neighbouring courtyard and a team of carpenters were having a row with the cart drivers. The pope lowered his big nose, his big nostrils, his big beard. Finally, he says: 'At least, get from them a new truce. Tell them that I forbid them to resume hostilities against each other. Should any prelate or cleric oppose your peace efforts, you will deprive him of all of his ecclesiastical benefices. And remember, if the two kings persist in warmongering, you can go so far as to excommunicate them; this is written in your instructions. Excommunication and interdict.'

Further to this reminder of my powers, I was very much in need of the benediction he gave me. Because, can you see me, Archambaud, in the state in which Europe finds itself, excommunicating the kings of France and England? Edward would have immediately released his Church from all obedience to the Holy See, and John would have sent his constable to lay Avignon to siege. And Innocent, what would he have done, in your opinion? I am going to tell you. He would have disavowed me, and lifted the excommunications. All of that was just words.

So the following day, we left.

Three days earlier, on the eighteenth of June, the Duke of Lancaster's troops had landed in La Hague.

PART FOUR

THE SUMMER OF
DISASTER

I

The Norman *Chevauchée*

NOT EVERYTHING CAN always be disastrous. Ah! You have noticed, Archambaud, this is one of my favourite sentiments. Yes! Yes, in the midst of all setbacks, of all sorrows, of all disappointments, we are always graced with some good that comes to comfort us. One simply needs to be able to appreciate it. God is only waiting for our gratitude to better prove his leniency.

You see, after a calamitous summer for France, and most disappointing, I confess, for my embassy, look how we are favoured by the season and the beautiful weather we have to continue our journey! It is an encouragement from the heavens.

I feared, after the rains we had in Berry, that we would come into a spell of bad weather, gusts of wind and the cold as we moved further north. And I was preparing to shut myself away in my palanquin, wrap myself up in furs and sustain us with mulled wine. And yet it is quite the opposite;

the air has warmed, the sun is shining, and this December is like a spring. We sometimes experience this in Provence; but I didn't expect such light, which brightens the countryside, such warmth that the horses sweat under their covers, to greet our entrance into Champagne.

It was almost cooler, I assure you, when I arrived in Breteuil in Normandy, at the beginning of July, to meet the king.

For, having left Avignon on the twenty-first of the month of June, it was the twelfth of July . . . ah! All right, you remember; I have already told you, and Capocci was sick, that's right, at the speed at which I had him travel.

What King John was doing in Breteuil? The siege, the siege of the castle, after a short Norman *chevauchée* which had not been a great triumph for him, that is the least one can say.

The Duke of Lancaster, may I remind you, landed in the Cotentin on the eighteenth of June. Pay attention to the dates; they are most important, in this instance. The stars? Ah, no, I hadn't particularly studied the stars for that day. What I meant was that in war, the weather and one's speed sometimes count as much and sometimes even more than the number of troops.

So, he lands on the eighteenth of June; over the next three days he effects a junction at the Abbey of Montebourg with the detachments on the continent: the one that Robert Knolles, a good captain, brings from Brittany, and the one raised by Philip of Navarre. How many are the three of them lining up? Philip of Navarre and Godfrey of Harcourt scarcely have more than one hundred knights with them. Knolles supplies the largest contingent: three hundred men-at-arms, five hundred archers, not all English by the way; there are Bretons there who come with John of Montfort, pretender to the duchy against the Count of Blois, who is the Valois' man. Lastly, Lancaster himself has just one hundred and fifty suits of armour and two hundred archers, but he has a sizeable remount of horses.

When King John II learned of these figures, he laughed a laugh that shook him from his belly to his hair. Did they think they could scare him with this pitiful army? If that was all his English cousin could muster, he had no great need for concern. 'I was right, you see, Charles, my son, you see, Audrehem, not to fear putting my son-in-law in jail; yes, I was right to pour scorn upon the challenges of these little Navarrese, since they can only produce such meagre insignificant allies.'

And he gave himself credit for having, from the beginning of the month, called up the army in Chartres. 'Wasn't it good foresight, what do you say, Audrehem, what do you say, Charles, my son? And you see that it sufficed to call up the ban and not the arrière-ban. Let them run, these good Englishmen, let them get deeper into the country. We will swoop down on them and throw them into the mouth of the River Seine.'

He had rarely been so joyful, I was told, and I am willing to believe it. For this perpetually vanquished man loves war, at least in his dreams. Setting off, giving orders from high up on his charger, to be obeyed, at last! For in war, people obey . . . in any case at the beginning; leave the worries of finance and of government to Nicolas Braque, Lorris, de Bucy and the others; live in the company of men, no more women in the entourage; moving, moving constantly, eating in the saddle, in big mouthfuls, or at the roadside, sheltered by a tree already laden with tiny green fruit, receiving the scouts' reports, pronouncing fine words that each one would go and repeat: 'If the enemy is thirsty, he will drink his own blood', place his hand on the shoulder of a knight who flushes with pleasure. 'Never tired, Boucicaut. Your fine sword abounds, noble Coucy!'

And yet, has he won a single victory? Never. At twenty-two, designated by his father as Chief of War in Hainaut ... ah! What a fine name: Chief of War! ... He got himself noteworthily torn apart by the English. At twenty-five, with an even finer title, as if he were inventing them himself: Lord of the Conquest, he cost the populations of Languedoc dearly, without succeeding, in four months of siege, to take back Aiguillon, at the confluence of the Lot and the Garonne rivers. But listening to him, one would think that his battles were remarkable exploits, however sad their outcomes. Never has a man acquired so much assurance through the experience of defeat.

This time, he was making his pleasure last.

In the time it took him to fetch the oriflamme from Saint-Denis and, still without hurrying, regain Chartres, the Duke of Lancaster had already crossed the River Dives, having passed by Caen in the south, and come to spend the night in Lisieux. The memory of the *chevauchée* of Edward III, ten years earlier, and particularly of the sack of Caen, was not faded. Hundreds of bourgeois slain in the streets, forty thousand pieces of cloth snatched, all the precious objects removed to the other side of the Channel, the complete immolation of the town avoided by a whisker . . . the people of Normandy had certainly not forgotten and rather seemed eager to let the English archers through. All the more so that Philip of Évreux-Navarre and Messire Godfrey of Harcourt made it known that these Englishmen were friends. Butter, milk and cheeses were abundant, the cider readily drinkable; the horses in the luxuriant meadows didn't lack forage. After all, feeding one thousand Englishmen, for one evening, cost less than paying the king all year round, his gabelle, his fouage,[40] and his eight denier in the pound tax on purchased goods.

In Chartres, John II was to find his army rather less gathered together and ready than he had thought. He had been counting on an army of forty thousand men. Scarcely a third of that number could be counted. But wasn't it enough, wasn't it already too many in comparison with the enemy he was to face? 'Aha! I will not pay those who did not turn up; all the more to my advantage. But I command that they be sent remonstrances.'

By the time he had set himself up in his fleur-de-lis-covered battle tent and dispatched those remonstrances . . . 'When the king wants, knights must' . . . the Duke of Lancaster was in Pont-Audemer, one of the King of Navarre's fiefs. He was delivering the castle that a French party had been laying siege to for several weeks in vain, and was reinforcing, though not by much, the Navarrese garrison, with whom he was leaving a year's worth of supplies, before heading south, where he was going to pillage the Abbey of Bec-Hellouin.

Time for the constable, the Duke of Athens, to bring a semblance of order to the chaos of Chartres, for those who had shown up had been trampling the fields of new wheat for three weeks now and were beginning to lose their patience, time especially to calm the discord between the two marshals, Audrehem and Jean of Clermont, who hated each other with a passion, and tackle Lancaster, who was already at the foot of the walls of the Castle of Conches and had dislodged the occupants in the name of the king. And then he set fire to it. In this way, the memory of Robert of Artois, and more recently that of Charles the Bad went up in smoke. That castle brought no good luck . . . And Lancaster headed for Breteuil. Apart from Évreux, all of the strongholds that the king had wanted to seize in his son-in-law's fief were reclaimed one after the other.

'We will crush these evil folk at Breteuil,' said John II proudly when his army was finally able to set off. There are seventeen leagues from Chartres to Breteuil. The king wanted to cover them in one single march. Already, from noon onwards, it seems that stragglers began falling behind. When the army finally reached Breteuil, exhausted, Lancaster was there no more. He had taken the citadel, seized the French garrison and set up in its place a robust defence under the command of a good Navarrese leader, Sanche López, with whom he also left a year's supply of provisions.

Quick to console himself, King John exclaimed: 'We will hack them to pieces at Verneuil; won't we, my sons?' The dauphin didn't dare say what he confided to me later, namely that it seemed to him absurd to pursue one thousand men with near fifteen thousand. He didn't want to appear any less assured than his younger brothers who all, including the youngest, Philip, only fourteen years old, modelled themselves on their father and played the ardent fighters.

Verneuil, on the banks of the River Avre; one of the gate-ways to Normandy. The English cavalcade had gone through there like a raging torrent the day before. Its inhabitants saw the French army arrive like a river in spate.

Messire of Lancaster, aware of what was sweeping towards him, was more than wary of pushing on towards Paris. Taking the spoils he had taken en route, as well as a good number of prisoners, he cautiously set off again on the westbound road. 'For Laigle,[41] for Laigle, they have left for Laigle,' indicated the villeins. Upon hearing this, King John felt singled out by divine attention. You can see why. But no, Archambaud, not because of the Eagle. Ah! You are there now. Because of the Spinning Sow, Monsieur of Spain's murder, there, where the crime was perpetrated, exactly where the king arrived to carry out his punishment. He didn't allow his army to sleep more than four hours. At Laigle, he would catch up with the English and the Navarrese, and it would be the hour, at last, of his vengeance.

Thus, on the ninth of July, having made a stop at the thresh-old of the Spinning Sow, long enough to bend his poleyn[42] of iron, a strange spectacle for the army to see, a king in prayer and in tears on the doorstep of an inn! He at last caught sight of Lancaster's lances, two leagues out of Laigle, on the edge of the Forest of Tuboeuf. All of this, my nephew, had happened just three days before the time when I was told of it.

'Lace up your helmets, get in battle order,' cried the king.

Then, for once in agreement, the constable and the two marshals intervened. 'Sire,' declared Audrehem roughly, 'you have seen how keen I always am to serve you.' 'And me too,' said Clermont.

'But it would be folly to engage the enemy straight away. You mustn't ask of your troops a single stride more. You have given them no respite for four days, and this very day you have led them more hurriedly than ever. The men are out of breath, just look at them; the archers have bloodied feet and if they didn't have their pikes to hold themselves up, they would collapse right here on the road.' 'Ah, always the rank and file that slow everything down!' said John II irritated. 'Those on horseback fare little better,' retorted Audrehem. 'A good many mounts have withers wounded by their loads, and many others limp, that we have been unable to re-shoe. The armoured soldiers, going so in this heat, have bloodied arses. Don't expect anything from your banners,[43] before they have had a rest.'

'Besides which, sire,' added Clermont, 'look at the territory we would be attacking in. Before us we have a dense forest, where Messire of Lancaster has hidden. He will easily be able to get his party out, while our archers become tangled up in the thicket and our lances charge tree trunks.'

King John had a moment of ill humour, cursing his men and the circumstances that foiled his will. Then he made one of those surprising decisions for which his courtiers call him The Good, so that their flattery may be repeated to him.

He sent his two first equerries, Pluyan du Val and Jean of Corquilleray, to the Duke of Lancaster to take his challenge to him and call him to battle. Lancaster was stationed in a clearing, his archers set out before him, while everywhere scouts observed the French army and staked out escape routes and fallback paths. The blue-eyed duke thus saw arrive before him, escorted by several men-at-arms, the two royal equerries who bore on the shafts of their lances pennons decorated with fleurs-de-lis, and who blew into their horns like tournament heralds. Flanked by Philip of Navarre, John of Montfort and Godfrey of Harcourt, he listened to the following speech, delivered to him by Pluyan du Val.

The King of France is coming at the head of an immense army, while the duke has but a small one. Therefore, he suggests to the duke that they confront each other the following day, with the same number of knights on either side, one hundred, or fifty, or even thirty, in a place to be agreed upon and according to all the rules of honour.

Lancaster courteously received the proposal of the king 'who claims to be of France', but was not any less reputed everywhere for his chivalry. He assured them he would consider the matter with his allies, whom he pointed to, as it was too serious to decide upon alone. The two equerries believed they could infer from these words that Lancaster would give his answer the following day.

It was upon this assurance that King John ordered his battle tent to be raised and fell straight into a deep sleep. And for the French the night was that of a snoring army.

In the morning, the Forest of Tuboeuf was empty. One could see that someone had been there but no sign was any longer to be seen of either Englishman or Navarrese. Lancaster had cautiously withdrawn his people to Argentan.

King John II gave free reign to his contempt for these dishonourable enemies, good for nothing but pillaging when no one was before them, and who slip away at the first signs of combat. 'We wear the star on our hearts, whereas the garter flaps around their calves. This is what sets us apart. They are the knights of flight.'

But did he contemplate giving chase to them? The marshals suggested casting the freshest banners out on Lancaster's trail; to their surprise, John II ruled out the idea. One would have said that he considered the battle won from the moment the enemy had failed to take up his challenge.

So he decided to return to Chartres to disband his army. In passing, he would take back Breteuil.

Audrehem pointed out to him that the garrison left behind at Breteuil by Lancaster was considerable in number, well commanded and well entrenched. 'I know the stronghold, sire; it will not easily be taken.'

'So why did our people let themselves get dislodged from there?' replied King John. 'I will conduct the siege myself.'

And that, my nephew, is where I met with him, in the company of Capocci, on the twelfth of July.

2

The Siege of Breteuil

KING JOHN GREETED us armed for war, as if he were going to launch the attack within the next half-hour. He kissed the ring, asked for news of the Holy Father, and, without listening to the answer, rather long-winded and florid, into which Niccola Capocci had launched himself, he said to me: Monseigneur of Périgord, you are arriving just in time to witness a fine siege. I know your family, its unfailing valour, its expertise in the arts of war. Your family has always served the kingdom most nobly, and if you were not prince of the Church, you would likely be marshal of my army. I wager that here you will find enjoyment.'

This manner of address was directed only to me, and compliments on my kinship displeased Capocci, who is not of noble lineage; he saw fit to declaim that we were not there to marvel at exploits of war, but to speak of Christian peace.

I knew at that point that things would not go at all well between my co-legate and the King of France, particularly as the latter had given my nephew Robert of Durazzo the warmest of welcomes, questioning him about the court of Naples and his aunt, Queen Joan. It must be said that he was most handsome, my Robert, superb bearing, rosy face, silky hair, grace and strength combined. And I saw stir in the king's eye that spark which usually shines in men's gazes when a beautiful woman passes by. 'Where will you be taking up your quarters?' he asked. I told him that we would make ourselves comfortable in a nearby abbey.

I observed him closely, and found him rather aged, thicker-set, heavier, his chin more ponderous beneath his thin beard, of an insipid yellow. He had acquired the habit of tossing his head back, as if he were bothered at the collar or the shoulder by some filings in his shirt of steel.

He wanted to show us the camp, where our arrival had produced quite a stir of curiosity. 'Here is His Holy Eminence Monseigneur of Périgord who has come to visit us,' he said to his knight bannerets, as if we had come specially to bring him heavenly aid. I distributed the benedictions. Capocci's nose grew longer and longer.

The king was very keen to introduce me to his chief of engineering[44] to whom he seemed to attach more importance than to his marshals or even his constable. 'Where is the archpriest? Has anybody seen the archpriest? Bourbon, bring me the archpriest ... And I wondered how the nickname of archpriest could have possibly been earned by the captain who commanded machines, mines and gunpowder artillery.

A curious fellow indeed was the one who came to us, built upon long bow-legged limbs enclosed in steel greaves and cuisses[45]; he looked as if he were walking on lightning.

His belt, tightly fastened over his leather surcoat, gave him the appearance of a wasp. Large hands with black nails that he held at a distance from his body, because of the metal cubitières[46] that protected his arms. A rather shifty face, scrawny, with high cheekbones, drawn-out eyes, and the mocking expression of someone who is always ready for a quarter of a sol[47] to volunteer himself to take another's life. And to top it all, a Montauban hat, with a wide brim, entirely made of iron, pointed forward above the nose, with two slits to enable him to look out through when he lowered his head. 'Where were you, archpriest? We were looking for you,' said the king, and then for my attention: 'Arnaud of Cervole, Sire of Vélines.'

'Archpriest, at your service, Monseigneur Cardinal,' added the other one in a mocking tone that I didn't like at all.

And all of a sudden I remember, Vélines is not far from us, Archambaud, of course, close to Sainte-Foy-la-Grande, on the borders of Périgord and Guyenne. And the fellow had indeed been archpriest, an archpriest with neither Latin nor tonsure, of course, but archpriest nonetheless. And of where? But naturally of Vélines, his little fief, he had claimed the presbytery for himself, collecting seigniorial dues as well as the ecclesiastical revenues. The only cost to him was to employ a true cleric, a pittance, to assure the work of the Church continued ... until the Pope Innocent stripped him of his benefice, as all the other commendams of the sort, at the beginning of his pontificate. 'The flock must be guarded by a shepherd ...' what I was telling you the other day. So, vanished into thin air the archpriesthood of Vélines! I had to look into the affair, one amongst one hundred others of the sort, and I knew that the court of Avignon was not upper-most in the lad's heart. For once, I must say, I was in full agreement with the Holy Father. This Cervole wasn't going to make things easy for me either, I could see straightway.

'The archpriest did fine work in Évreux, and the town has once more become ours,' the king told me, to set off his powderman in a good light.

'What's more, it is the only one you have recovered from the Navarrese, sire,' put in Cervole with quite a nerve.

'We will do the same with Breteuil. I want a handsome siege, like that of Aiguillon.'

'Except that you have never taken Aiguillon, sire.'

Gad, I said to myself, the man is well established in court to speak with such frankness.

'It is because, alas, I wasn't left enough time,' said the king sadly.

One had to be the archpriest . . . I have started to call him the archpriest too, since everyone names him thus, one had to be that man to throw down his iron helmet and murmur, before his sovereign: 'The time, the time . . . six months . . .'

And one had to be King John to cling stubbornly to the belief that the Siege of Aiguillon, conducted by him in the same year that his father was crushed at Crécy, represented a model of military art. A ruinous and interminable under-taking. He ordered a bridge to be built to approach the fortress, and in such a well-chosen place that the besieged destroyed it six times. Complicated machines had to be brought from Toulouse at great expense and with great slowness, and for a perfectly inexistent result.

Oh well! It was upon this strategy that King John established his glory, in his own eyes, and justified his experience. In truth, he was determined to settle his grudge with fate, take his revenge for Aiguillon, ten years on, and prove that his methods were the right ones; he wanted to leave in the memory of nations the imprint of a great siege.

And that is why, neglecting to pursue an enemy he could have defeated without too much trouble, he put up his war tent before Breteuil. Again addressing the archpriest, who was well versed in the new skill of destruction by gunpowder, one could have thought that he had resolved to mine the castle's walls, as had been done at Évreux. But no. What he asked of his Master of Engineering was to erect assault contraptions which would allow his men to enter by going over the walls. And the marshals and the captains listened, full of respect, to the king's orders and busied themselves accomplishing them. As long as a man is in command, be he the worst of fools, there are people around him committed to the belief that he commands well.

As for the archpriest . . . I had the impression that the archpriest didn't care much about anything. The king wanted ramps, scaffolding, belfries; well, they were built for him, and payment was asked for accordingly. If this apparatus of old, this machinery from before the time of firearms, didn't bring the expected result, the king would have only himself to blame. And the archpriest would let nobody tell him so; he had over King John an ascendancy that sometimes roughneck soldiers have over princes, and he didn't hesitate to put it to good use, once the treasurer had organized his payment and that of his companions-in-arms.

The little Norman town turned into an immense and

cacophonous construction site. Entrenchments were dug all around the castle. The earth removed from the ditches was used to build assault platforms and ramps. The noise was but the sound of spades and cartage, the creaking of axles, the cracking of whips and swearwords. I felt like I had returned to Villeneuve.

Axes rang out in the neighbouring forests. Certain villagers in the area did good business, if they were selling drinks. Others had the unpleasant surprise to suddenly see six valets demolish their barn in order to carry off the beams. 'Service of the king!' It was easily said. And with the pickaxes attacking the cob walls, and the ropes pulling on the half-timbering, soon, in a huge creaking sound, everything collapsed. 'He could have gone and put himself somewhere else, the king, rather than sending us these wicked folk who take the very roofs from over our heads,' said the yokels. They were beginning to find that the King of Navarre was a better master, and that even the presence of the English bore down less heavily upon them than the coming of the King of France.

I thus stayed in Breteuil for a part of July, to the great displeasure of Capocci who would have preferred a stay in Paris. I too would have preferred it! And who sent to Avignon missives filled with acrimony in which he would spitefully have it understood that I enjoyed contemplating war more than working towards peace. And yet how, I ask you, could I have pushed for peace otherwise than by engaging in talks with the king, and where could I talk with him but at the siege that he refused to leave?

He spent his days walking around the construction work in the company of the archpriest; he used his time verifying an angle of attack, worrying about an epaulement,[48] and particularly watching the rise of the wooden tower, an extraordinary belfry on wheels in which a good many archers could be housed, with an arsenal of crossbows and fire darts, a machine the likes of which had not been seen since antiquity. It wasn't enough just to build its floors; sufficient cowhides had to be found to cover this enormous scaffold; and then a hard, flat path had to be built to push it along. But when the tower was ready, astonishing things would be seen!

The king often invited me to supper, and there I could converse with him.

'Peace?' he would say to me. 'But it is all I desire. You see, I am in the process of disbanding my army, only keeping on what I need for this siege. Wait until I have taken Breteuil, and immediately afterwards I will gladly make peace, to please the Holy Father. May my enemies put forward their proposals to me.'

'Sire,' I would say, 'we would need to know which proposals you would be willing to consider . . .'

'Those which would not be contrary to my honour.'

Ah! It was no easy task! It was I, alas, who had to tell him, as I was better informed than he, that the Prince of Wales was gathering together troops in Libourne and at La Réole for a new *chevauchée*.

'And you talk to me of peace, Monseigneur of Périgord?'

'Precisely, sire, in order to avoid yet more misfortunes . . .'

'This time, I will not allow the Prince of England to romp about in the Languedoc as he did last year. I will call up the army once again, for the first of August, in Chartres.'

I was astonished that he should let his banners go just to

recall them one week later. I revealed my true feelings on the matter, discreetly, to the Duke of Athens, to Audrehem ... everyone came to see me and confided in me. No, the king dug in his heels, because he could save money, most unlike him, by first sending back the ban that he had called up the month before, to call them back again with the arrière-ban. Someone must have said to him, John of Artois perhaps, or another equally fine brain, that this way he would save a few days' pay. But he would have fallen behind a month on the Prince of Wales. Oh! Yes, he really needed to make peace; and the longer he made it wait, the less it would be negotiable to his satisfaction.

I got to know the archpriest better, and I must say the fellow amused me. Périgord brought him closer to me; he came to ask me to get his benefice back. And on what terms! 'Your Innocent ...'

'The Holy Father, my friend, the Holy Father,' I told him.

'All right, the Holy Father, if you like, stripped me of my commendams to put the Church to rights ... Ah! That is what the bishop told me. And what? Does he believe there was no good order in Vélines before? The cure of souls, Messire Cardinal, you think I wasn't practising it at all? It would be a sorry place where the dying depart this life without receiving the sacraments. Upon the slightest malady I sent the monk. And the sacraments must be paid for. Those who passed convicted before my justice: I fined them. Sent them to confession; and the penance tax was due. The same for adulterers. I know how good Christians should be led.'

I said to him: 'The Church has lost an archpriest, but the

king has gained a good knight.' Because John II had dubbed him knight last year.

All is not rotten in this Cervole. He has, so to speak, tender accents that surprise you, like the banks of our Dordogne, the vast river's green water in which can be seen, late in the day, the reflections of our manors between the poplars and the ash trees; the luxuriant meadows of the spring, the dry heat of the summer that ripens the golden barley; scented evenings; the grapes of September, as children we used to bite into their warm bunches ... If all men in France loved their land as much as that man, the kingdom would be better protected.

I am finally beginning to understand the reasons for the favour he enjoys. First, he had joined the king in the *chevauchée* of Saintonge, in '51, a small expedition, but it had allowed John II to believe that he would be a victorious king. The archpriest had brought him his troop, twenty men in armour and sixty foot sergeants. How could he have gathered them together, in Vélines? The fact remains that this formed a company. One thousand golden écus, settled by the War Treasury, for one year's service. That allowed the king to say: 'We have been companions for a long while, haven't we, archpriest?'

After that, he had served under Monsieur of Spain, and shrewdly never failed to mention it before the king. It was even under the orders of Charles of Spain, in his campaign of '53, that he had chased the English out of his very own castle in Vélines and the surrounding lands, Montcarret, Montaigne, Montravel ... The English held Libourne and kept a big garrison of archers there. But he, Arnaud of Cervole, held Sainte-Foy and was not willing to have it taken from him ...

'I am against the pope because he took away my arch-priesthood; I am against the Englishman because he ravaged my castle; I am against the Navarrese because he slew my constable. Ah! If only I had been in Laigle, close by him, to defend him!' It was music to the ears of the king.

And then, finally, the archpriest excels in the new explosive devices. He loves them, he tames them, he plays with them. Nothing pleases him more, so he told me, than lighting a fuse, after underground preparations, and to see a castle's tower open up like a flower, like a bouquet, throwing up into the air men and stones, pikes and tiles. Because of that, he is held in some awe, if not esteem, at least a certain respect; amongst the hardiest of knights, many are loath to approach these weapons of the Devil, but he handles them as if they were toys. There are such people, whenever new methods of waging war appear, who immediately grasp their importance and build a reputation upon their usage. While the valets-at-arms run for cover, hands over their ears, and even the barons and the marshals step back warily, Cervole watches the barrels of gunpowder roll by with an amused glimmer in his eye, gives clear orders, jumps over the fougasses, slides into the saps,[49] crawls along on his cubitières, clambers out, calmly strikes a light, takes his time to gain a blind spot or crouch down behind a wall, while thunder rumbles, the earth quakes and the walls open.

Such tasks require solid teams. Cervole has trained his own; deft louts, slaughter-loving, delighted to spread terror, to break, to destroy. He pays them well; risk deserves payment. And he goes about flanked by his two lieutenants, whom one might think had been chosen for their names:

Gaston de la Parade and Bernard d'Orgueil.[50] Between us we knew that, were King John to put these three powdermen to use, Breteuil would fall within a week. But no; he wanted his belfry on wheels.

Meanwhile, as the great tower rose up, Don Sanche López, his Navarrese and his Englishmen, shut up in the castle, didn't seem especially nervous. The guards were relieved by their fellows at set times on the battlement parapets. The besieged, well stocked with provisions, looked healthy. From time to time they shot a volley of arrows at the workers, but sparingly, so as not to use up their ammunition needlessly. These shots sometimes occurred as the king was passing and brought him the illusion of an exploit. 'Did you see? An entire volley of arrows happened upon him, and our sire did not flinch, not at all; ah! The good king . . .' and allowed the archpriest, Orgueil and la Parade to cry out to him: 'Watch out, sire, we will stave off attack!' Shielding him with their bodies against the darts that slammed into the grass at their feet.

He didn't smell good, the archpriest. But it has to be admitted that everyone stank, the whole camp stank: it was above all by the smell that Breteuil was under siege! The breeze carried the odours of excrement, because all those men busy shovelling, carting, sawing, nailing, relieved themselves as close as they could to their place of work. Nobody washed at all, and the king himself, constantly in armour . . .

Using as many perfumes and essences as I could, I stayed long enough to observe the weaknesses of King John. Ah! So much recklessness is a wonder!

There were two cardinals sent there by the Holy Father to attempt to reach a widespread general peace; he received letters from all the princes of Europe who criticized his behaviour towards the King of Navarre and advised him to release him; he learned that taxes everywhere weren't coming in, and that not only in Normandy, not only in Paris, but throughout the kingdom, the people's mood was sour and on the verge of revolt; he knew, most importantly, that two English armies were readying themselves against him, that of Lancaster in the Cotentin, which was receiving reinforcements, and that of Aquitaine ... But nothing was of the slightest importance, in his eyes, compared to the siege of a small Norman stronghold, and nothing could distract him from it. Insisting stubbornly on the detail without any longer perceiving the whole is a most unnatural vice in a prince.

For an entire month, John II only went to Paris once, for four days, and to commit there a foolishness that I will tell you of shortly. And the only edict he didn't leave to his advisors was the proclamation heard in the towns and bailiwicks up to six leagues around Breteuil that all manner of mason, carpenter, digger, sapper, hoer, woodcutter and other manoeuvrer were to come to him, without delay, bringing with them those instruments and tools necessary for their crafts, to work on components of the laying siege.

The sight of his great, mobile belfry, his assault tower as he called it, filled him with satisfaction. Three storeys; each platform wide enough for two hundred men to stand and fight on. That made a total of six hundred soldiers who would occupy this extraordinary machine, once enough faggots and fascines[51] had been brought, enough stones carted and enough earth tamped down to form the path along which it would roll on its four enormous wheels.

King John was so proud of his belfry that he had invited people to come and see it being built and then put into action. This is how the bastard of Castile, Henri de Trastamare, as well as the Earl of Douglas, had come to be there.

'Messire Edward has his Navarrese, but I have my Scottish earl,' said the king elegantly, ignoring the fact that Philip of Navarre brought half of Normandy to the English, while Messire of Douglas brought nothing more to the King of France than his valiant sword.

I can still hear the king explaining to us: 'Look, messeigneurs, this tower may be pushed to whichever part of the ramparts we wish, and look down upon them, enabling the assailants to fire all sorts of bolts and projectiles right into the stronghold, or even attack the battlement parapets themselves. The purpose of the leathers nailed to its sides is to stop dead the enemy arrows.' And I continued to insist on talking to him about the conditions for peace!

The Spaniard and the Scot were not the only ones staring at the enormous wooden tower. The people of Messire Sanche López were also watching it, with caution, because the archpriest had set up other machines which rained down balls of stone and powder darts upon the garrison. The castle had, so to speak, had its roof blown off. But López's people didn't seem that frightened. They made holes halfway up their own walls. 'To run away more easily,' said the king.

Finally the great day arrived. I was there; the matter was of interest to me. The Holy See has its troops, and towns that we need to be able to defend, and I stood nearby on a small hillock, out of the way. King John II appears, wearing his helmet crowned with flowers of gold. With his gleaming

sword he signals the launch of the attack, while the trumpets
sound. From the summit of the leather-covered tower flies
the fleur-de-lis banner; below, the banners of the troops
occupying the three storeys. The belfry is a veritable bouquet
of standards! And now it is on the move. Men and horses are
hitched up to it in clusters, and the archpriest orchestrates
with his rants. I was told that one thousand pounds' worth
of hemp rope had been used. The engine makes progress,
albeit very slowly, with a swaying motion and the creaking
of wood, but it makes progress. To see it moving forward
thus, rocking a little and festooned with flags, the image of an
attacking ship comes to mind. And the ship does indeed board
the stronghold, in great tumult. They are already fighting
on the battlements, at the level of the third platform. Swords
cross, arrows fly in tight volleys. The army surrounding
the castle, all heads up, faces raised, are holding their breath.
Up there, magnificent feats are performed. The king, ventail
raised, watches, his superb battle in the air.

And then suddenly, an enormous explosion gives the
troops a start, and a cloud of smoke obscures the banners at
the belfry's summit.

Messire of Lancaster had left the cannons in the charge of
Don Sanche López, who had carefully avoided using them up
until now. And there are the cannon muzzles poking through
the holes made in the castle walls and shooting at close range
into the rolling tower, bursting open the covering of cow-
hides, flattening rows of men on the platforms, shattering
pieces of the wooden frame.

Try as they might to join in the battle, the archpriest's
ballisters[52] and catapults cannot prevent the firing of a second

salvo, then a third. Not only iron cannonballs, but also burning pots, a sort of Greek fire, hit the belfry. The men fall, screaming, or rush and tumble down the ladders or even throw themselves into the void, horribly burnt. From the top of the noble machine flames soar upward. And then, with an infernal crack, the whole upper storey collapses; its occupants are crushed under a blazing furnace ... Never in my entire life, Archambaud, have I heard a more appalling clamour of suffering; and I wasn't even that close. The archers were trapped in a tangle of incandescent beams, their chests crushed, their legs, their arms going up in flames. The cow-hides let off an awful stench as they burned. The tower was leaning, leaning, and just as we thought it was going to collapse, it came to a halt, tilted at an angle, still flaming. Men threw water at it as best they could, they went about removing the crushed and burned bodies, and all the while the castle's defenders danced for joy on the walls, crying: 'Loyalty to Saint George! Loyalty to Navarre!'

King John, even before this disaster, seemed to be looking around him for someone to blame, though there was no one but himself. But the archpriest was there, under his iron hat, and the king's great wrath, that was to burst, for the while remained within the royal helmet. Because Cervole was probably the only man in the whole army who wouldn't have hesitated in saying to the king: 'Look at your stupidity, sire. I advised you to dig mines, rather than build these big scaffolds that haven't been in use for almost fifty years now. It is no longer the age of the Knights Templar, and Breteuil is not Jerusalem.'

The king simply asked: 'This tower, can it be repaired?'

'No, sire.'

'So break up what is left. We will use it to fill in the ditches.'

That evening, I thought it timely to speak to him seriously on the subject of the beginnings of a peace treaty. Setbacks ordinarily open a king's ear to hearing of wisdom. The horror that we had just witnessed allowed me to appeal to his Christian sentiments. And if his chivalrous fervour was hungry for exploits, the pope would give him them, him and the princes of Europe, but far more meritorious and glorious, in the region of Constantinople. I was rebuffed, which filled Capocci with joy.

'I have two English *chevauchées* threatening me in my very kingdom and cannot delay getting ready to rush upon them. That is all I care about at present. We will talk again in Chartres, if you please.'

The dangers he ignored the day before suddenly seemed to him to be of the utmost importance.

And Breteuil? What was he to decide for Breteuil? To prepare a new assault would take the besieging troops another month. The besieged, for their part, even if they hadn't used up either their supplies or their ammunition, had suffered badly. They had their wounded, their towers were roofless. Somebody spoke of negotiating, of offering the garrison an honourable surrender. The king turned to me. 'Well then, Monseigneur Cardinal . . .'

It was my turn to show him haughtiness. I had come from Avignon to work towards a general peace, not to mediate any such delivery of a fortress. He understood his mistake, and disguised his lack of composure by way of what he thought to be an amusing retort. 'If cardinal is detained, archpriest can do his job.'

And the next day, while the tower continued to burn and the workers had gone back to work, but this time to bury the dead, our Sire of Vélines, raised up on his steel greaves, and preceded by the sounding of horns, went to confer with Don Sanche López. They walked back and forth a long while before the castle's drawbridge, watched by the soldiers of both camps.

They were both professional soldiers and couldn't delude each other. 'What if I had attacked you with gunpowder mines, under your walls, messire?'

'Ah! Messire, I think you would have got the better of us.'

'How much longer could you have held out?'

'Not as long as we would have wished, but longer than you had hoped. We have water, victuals, arrows and cannonballs a'plenty.'

An hour passed and the archpriest returned to the king. 'Don Sanche López consents to hand over the castle, if you let him go free and if you give him some money.'

'So be it, give it to him and let's be done with it!'

Two days later, the men from the garrison, heads held high and purses filled, left to meet up with Monseigneur of Lancaster. King John would have to repair Breteuil at his own expense. Thus ended the siege he had wanted to be memorable. Even then he had the effrontery to maintain that without his assault belfry, the stronghold would not have come to terms so quickly.

3

The Homage of Phoebus

YOU ARE WATCHING Troyes fade into the distance? Beautiful city isn't it, my nephew, particularly bathed in sunlight, as this morning. Ah! It is good fortune indeed for a town to have been home to the birth of a pope. Because the fine town houses and palaces you have seen around the Town Hall, and Saint Urban's church which is a jewel of the new art, with its abundance of stained-glass windows, and many other buildings whose distribution you admired, all of that is due to the fact that Urban IV, who occupied Saint Peter's throne around a century ago, and for just three years, came into the world in Troyes, in a shop, just where his church stands today. That is what gave the town its glory, and a boost of prosperity, almost. Ah! If only similar fortune had befallen our dear Périgueux. Anyway, I don't want to talk about that any more, as you will think that I have nothing else in my mind.

At present, I know the route the dauphin plans to travel. He is following us. He will be in Troyes tomorrow. But he will gain Metz via Saint-Dizier and Saint-Mihiel, whereas we will go via Châlons and Verdun. First of all because I have business in Verdun: I am canon of the cathedral, and also because I do not wish to appear to be joining forces with the dauphin. But being as close as we are to each other, we could at any moment exchange messengers, all in the same day, perhaps; also our dealings with Avignon have become quicker and easier . . .

What then? What had I promised to tell you and that I forgot? Ah, what King John did in Paris during the four days he was away from the siege of Breteuil?

He had to receive the homage of Gaston Phoebus. A success, a triumph for King John, or rather for the Chancellor Pierre de La Forêt who had patiently, skilfully prepared the matter. Because Phoebus is the King of Navarre's brother-in-law and they have adjoining domains, up against the Pyrenees. Now Phoebus's tribute had been due since the beginning of the reign. To receive it precisely when Charles of Navarre was in prison could substantially change things and modify the judgement of several courts in Europe.

Naturally, Phoebus's reputation has found its way to you . . . Oh! Not only a great venerer,[53] but also a great jouster, a great reader, a great builder and what is more, a great womanizer. I would say: a great prince whose sorrow is to have but a small state. It is maintained that he is the most handsome man of our time, and I gladly subscribe to this view. Very tall, and strength enough to fight with bears, literally, my nephew, with a bear, he did it! His leg is long, hips slim, his shoulders broad, a radiant face, teeth very white in a smile. And most striking of all, a mass of hair of copper and gold, a dazzling mane, wavy, curling over his collar like a natural crown, blazing, which inspired him to take the sun for emblem, as well as his nickname Phoebus, that he writes, by the way, with an F and an é . . . Fébus . . . he must have chosen it before knowing any Greek. He never wears a hood but always goes bareheaded like the ancient Romans, which makes him unique amongst us.

I was at his home a while back. Because he has done so well, everything of importance in the Christian world passes through his little Court of Orthez, which he has turned into a great court. When I found myself there, I met a Count Palatine, one of King Edward's prelates, a first chamberlain of the King of Castile, not to mention highly reputed physicians, a famous artist, and great doctors of law. All of these people were splendidly treated.

I know of only one other such charismatic and influential court in such a narrow territory, that of King Lusignan of Cyprus; but he has far more wealth at his disposal from the profits of trade.

Phoebus has a fast and pleasant way of showing you what belongs to him: 'Here is my pack of hounds, my horses, this is my mistress, these are my bastards . . . Madame of Foix is well, thanks be to God. You will see her this evening.'

In the evening, in the long gallery that he had opened down the side of his castle, overlooking a most hilly horizon, the whole court meets and strolls a long while, in superb attire, while blue shadows fall upon the Béarn. Here and there, immense fireplaces blaze, and between the fireplaces, the wall is painted *al fresco* with hunting scenes that are the work of artists come from Italy. The guest who has failed to bring all his jewels and his finest robes, believing he is sojourning in a tiny mountain castle, cuts a poor figure indeed. I am warning you in case you happen to go there one day. Madame Agnes of Foix, which is Navarre, is the sister of Queen Blanche and almost as beautiful, her gown sewn with gold and pearls. She speaks little, or rather, one guesses as much, she is afraid to speak. She listens to the minstrels who sing *Aqueres mountanes* composed by her husband; the Béarnais love to join in singing them together.

Phoebus himself goes from group to group, greets first one, then another, welcomes a lord, compliments a poet, converses with an ambassador, finds out about the world's business as he walks, drops an opinion, gives a hushed order and governs while he chats. Until twelve, when vast burning torches carried by valets of his livery come to bid him to supper, with all of his guests. Yes, sometimes he only sits down to eat at midnight.

One evening I surprised him leaning against an arch in his open gallery and sighing before his silvery mountain stream and his horizon of blue mountains: 'Too small, too small, one might say, monseigneur, that Providence takes malicious pleasure in rolling the dice and mismatching them . . .'

We had just spoken about France, about the King of France, and I understood what he wanted me to hear. Great men often only receive small land to govern, whereas to the weak man falls the great kingdom. And he added: 'But as small as my Béarn may be, I intend that it should belong to no one other than itself.'

His letters are wonders. He never fails to inscribe all of his titles: 'We, Gaston III, Count of Foix, Viscount of Béarn,

Viscount of Lautrec, of Marsan and of Castillon,' and what else ... ah, yes: 'Seigneur of Montesquieu and of Montpezat,' and then, and then, hear how it sounds: 'Viguier[54] of Andorra and of Capir,' and he just signs 'Fébus', with his F and his é, of course, perhaps even to distinguish himself from Apollo, just as on the castles and monuments that he builds or embellishes, one can see carved in tall letters: 'Fébus made it.'

There is certainly extravagance in his character; but one must remember that he is only twenty-five years old. For his age he has already shown much skill. Equally, he has shown his courage; he was amongst the most valiant at Crécy. He was fifteen. Ah! I am forgetting to tell you, if you don't know it: he is the great-nephew of Robert of Artois. His grandfather married Joan of Artois, Robert's very own sister, who, no sooner widowed, showed such an appetite for men, led such a scandalous life, caused so much carry-on, and could cause a lot more yet, indeed, she is still alive; a little over sixty and in fine health ... our Phoebus, her grandson, had to shut her away in one of the towers of the Castle of Foix, where he has her closely guarded. Ah! It is thick blood indeed, that of the Artois!

And this is the man whom La Forêt, the archbishop-chancellor, when all is turning against King John, manages to persuade to come and pay homage. Oh! Make no mistake about it. Phoebus has thought through his decision, and is acting only, precisely, to protect the independence of his little Béarn. Aquitaine adjoining Navarre, and himself adjoining both, their alliance, at present manifest, is not at all in his interests; his short borders are threatened by their combined great power. He would like to protect himself on the Languedoc side where he had a run-in with the Count of Armagnac, governor of the king. So, let us draw closer together with France, let us end this disagreement, and to this aim, let us pay the homage due by our County of Foix. Of course Phoebus would plead for the release of his brother-in-law Navarre, it was agreed, but for form's sake, only for form's sake, as if it were the pretext for their reconciliation. It is a subtle game. Phoebus could always say to the Navarrese: 'But I only paid homage with the intent of serving you.'

In one week, Gaston Phoebus charmed Paris. He had arrived with a diverse escort of gentlemen, any number of servants, twenty carts carrying his wardrobe and furniture, a splendid pack of hounds, and part of his menagerie of wild beasts. The cortège stretched out over a quarter of a league. The smallest page was splendidly dressed, bearing the livery of Béarn; the horses were caparisoned in silk velvets, like mine. At huge expense, but designed to capture the imagination of the crowds. And Phoebus succeeded.

The great lords fought over the honour of entertaining him. All the notables of the town, those from Parliament, university, finance, and even from the Church, grasped at any manner of pretext to come and welcome him at the town house his sister Blanche, the Widowed Queen, had opened up for him for the duration of his stay. Women wanted to gaze at him, hear his voice, touch his hand. Wherever he went around town, he was recognized by his golden hair and people gathered before the doors of the silversmiths and drapers he patronized. The equerry who always accompanied him was also recognized, a giant by the name of Ernauton of

Spain, perhaps his half-brother born out of wedlock; similarly, the two enormous Pyrenean mountain dogs that followed him, held on a leash by a page. On the back of one of the dogs sat a little monkey. A most unusual great seigneur, more lavish than the most lavish, was in the capital, and everyone was talking about him.

I will tell you everything in detail; but during this un-propitious July, we were on the ladder of tragedy; and each rung matters.

You will have a large county to govern, Archambaud, and I wager the times will not be any easier than these; one cannot rise up in just a few years from a fall such as ours.

Keep this in mind: when a prince is of a mediocre nature, or as soon as he is weakened by age or illness, unity amongst the royal advisors can no longer be maintained. The king's entourage splits up, divides, because in order to do their work they take over the pieces of an authority that is no longer being exercised, or is exercised poorly; everyone speaks in the name of a master who is no longer in command; everyone fends for himself with an eye on the future. So coteries form, according to affinity along lines of ambition or temperament. Rivalries are exacerbated. The faithful regroup on one side, and on the other the traitors, who believe themselves to be loyal in their own way.

I call a traitor he who betrays the higher interests of the kingdom. Often, these men are incapable of perceiving it; they see only the interests of certain people of that kingdom; and yet, it is the traitor, alas, who generally prevails.

Around King John, two parties coexisted as they do today around the dauphin, since the same men are in place.

On the one hand, the party of the Chancellor Pierre de La Forêt, Archbishop of Rouen, seconded by Enguerrand du Petit-Cellier; they are the men whom I consider to be the best informed and the most concerned about the good of the kingdom. And on the other hand, Nicolas Braque, Lorris and above all, above all, Simon de Bucy.

Perhaps you will see him in Metz. Ah! Always be on your guard with him and those like him. A man whose head is too big for a body that is too short, is already a bad sign; holding himself up straight like a cockerel, rather ill-mannered and violent when he breaks out of his silence, and filled with an immense pride, though this he conceals. He enjoys power that is exercised in the shadows, and nothing pleases him more than humiliating or destroying anyone whom he deems to be taking to himself too much importance at court or who is gaining too much influence over the prince. He imagines that governing is the work only of cunning, lying, constructing machines. He has no great ideas, only mediocre schemes, always evil, which he most stubbornly pursues. Mere clerk for King Philip, he climbed up to where he is. First president of Parliament, member of the Great Council, by acquiring a reputation for loyalty, because he is domineering and brutal. This man has very publicly administered justice, forcing dissatisfied litigants to kneel down before him in the middle of a court hearing to beg forgiveness, or having twenty-three bourgeois from Rouen executed in one go; but he pronounces as many arbitrary acquittals, or postpones serious cases indefinitely, so as to keep his hands on certain people. He knows not to neglect his fortune; he obtained from the Abbot of Saint-Germain-des-Prés the octroi[55] of the Saint-Germain

Gate, immediately dubbed Bucy Gate, and thereby collects tolls on much of what goes through Paris.

From the moment La Forêt had negotiated the homage of Phoebus, de Bucy was against it and resolved to thwart the arrangement. It is he who went before the king, just back from Breteuil, and whispered to him: 'Phoebus is deriding you in Paris through a grand display of wealth ... Phoebus has twice met with Prevost Marcel ... I suspect Phoebus of plotting, with his wife and Queen Blanche, the escape of Charles the Bad. You must demand of Phoebus a tribute for Béarn. Phoebus does not speak well of you ... be careful not to welcome Phoebus too graciously, it will hurt the Count of Armagnac, of whom you have great need in Languedoc. Indeed, the Chancellor La Forêt is too indulgent with the friends of your enemies. And besides, what sort of man calls himself Phoebus?' And just to put the king in a truly foul mood, he gave him some bad news. Friquet of Fricamps had escaped from Châtelet thanks to the ingenuity of two of his servants. The Navarrese were flouting royal power and were regaining a most deft and dangerous man.

The result was that King John appeared haughty and aggressive at the supper that he held the day before the homage, calling Phoebus 'messire my vassal' and asking him: 'Are there any men left in your fiefs with all those escorting you in my town?'

And he even said to him: 'I would like your troops to stay out of the territory under the command of Monseigneur of Armagnac.'

Most surprised, as it had been agreed with Pierre de La Forêt that these incidents were to be considered effaced,

Phoebus retorted: 'My banners, sire my cousin, wouldn't have had to enter Armagnac if those who attacked my lands hadn't come from there and needs must be driven back. But as soon as you have given the order that Monseigneur of Armagnac's men should cease these incursions, my knights will happily keep to their borders.' Whereupon the king continued: 'I would like them to stay a little closer to me. I have called up the army at Chartres, to march upon the Englishman. I am counting on your being scrupulous enough to join them there with the banners of Foix and of Béarn.'

'The banners of Foix,' answered Phoebus, 'will be raised as a vassal's must, as soon as I have paid my homage to you, sire my cousin. And those of Béarn will follow, if I so wish.'

What a great success as a supper of reconciliation! The archbishop-chancellor, surprised and displeased, vainly went about patching things up. Bucy showed a wooden face. But deep down inside, he exulted. He felt that he was the true master.

The King of Navarre's name wasn't even pronounced, even though Queen Joan and Queen Blanche were present.

Upon leaving the palace, Ernauton of Spain, the giant of an equerry, said to the Count of Foix – I wasn't in there, but this is the gist of what was reported back to me: 'I admired your patience. If I were Phoebus, I would not wait for another insult, I would leave immediately for my Béarn.' To which Phoebus responded: 'And were I Ernauton, that is exactly the advice I would give to Phoebus. But I am Phoebus, and must first and foremost look out for the future of my subjects. I do not wish to be the one who withdraws, and thus appear to put myself in the wrong. I will exhaust every opportunity for an agreement, up to the limits of honour. But La Forêt, I fear, has led me into a trap. Unless a fact of which I am unaware, and of which he is unaware, has turned the king against me. We will see tomorrow.'

And the next day, after Mass, Phoebus entered into the great hall of the palace with six equerries to bear the train of his robe, and for once he was not bareheaded. Because he was wearing his crown, gold upon gold. The hall was filled with chamberlains, advisors, prelates, chaplains, masters of Parliament and great officers of state. But who does Phoebus notice first: the Count of Armagnac, Jean de Forez, standing close by the king as if leaning against the throne, cutting a most arrogant figure. On the other side of the throne, de Bucy pretending to tidy his rolls of parchment. He took one of them and read, as if it had been an ordinary decree: 'Messire, King of France, monseigneur, grants you audience for the County of Foix and the Viscountcy of Béarn that you have received from him, and you will become his man as Count of Foix and Viscount of Béarn according to the proprieties made between his predecessors and your own. Kneel.'

There was a moment of silence. Then Phoebus responded in the clearest of voices: 'I cannot.'

The audience showed their surprise, sincere for the most part, feigned by some, with a hint of pleasure. It is not often that an incident occurs in a tribute ceremony.

Phoebus repeated: 'I cannot.' And he added very clearly: 'One of my knees will bend: that of Foix. But that of Béarn cannot bend.'

It was then that King John spoke, and his voice was scored with anger. 'I have granted you an audience for Foix and for

Béarn.' Those gathered there quivered with curiosity. And the debate went something like this. Phoebus: 'Sire, Béarn is land of freehold tenure, and you cannot grant me audience for that which is not of your suzerainty.' The king: 'It is falsehood, what you allege, and has been for too many years subject of dispute between your relatives and mine.' Phoebus: 'It is truth, sire, and shall only remain the matter of discord should you so wish it. I am your faithful and loyal subject for Foix, as my forefathers have always professed, but I cannot declare myself your man for that which I obtained only from God.' The king: 'Wicked vassal! You are contriving for yourself treacherous means to shirk the service that you owe me. Last year you brought not one of your banners to the Count of Armagnac, my lieutenant in Languedoc here before you, and because of your failure to lend assistance, he was unable to drive away the English *chevauchée*!' Phoebus then said, superbly: 'If the fate of Languedoc depends only upon my participation, and if Messire of Armagnac is powerless to guard his province, then it is not to him that you should give the lieutenancy, sire, but to me.'

The king had worked himself into a fury, his chin was trembling. 'You are scoffing at me, good sire, but you will not do so for much longer. Kneel!'

'Remove Béarn from the homage, and I will bend my knee directly.'

'You will bend it in prison, evil traitor!' cried the king. 'Seize him!'

The play had been put on, planned, staged, at least, by Bucy, who had only to make a sign for Perrinet le Buffle and six other sergeants to promptly surround Phoebus. They already knew that they were to take him to the Louvre.

The very same day, the Prevost Marcel went about the town saying: 'King John had only one more enemy to make; that work is now accomplished. If all the thieves that hover round the king remain in place, there will soon be not one single honest man able to breathe outside of jail.'

4

The Camp of Chartres

THIS IS A FINE BUSINESS, my nephew, a fine business indeed! Do you know what the pope wrote to me in a letter of the twenty-eighth of November, though its dispatch must have been somewhat delayed, or the courier first went to find me where I wasn't to be found, as it only reached me yesterday evening in Arcis? Guess ... Well, the Holy Father, deeply concerned about the disagreement I have with Niccola Capocci, holds me to blame for: 'the lack of charity between you'. I would very much like to know how I could show Capocci any charity. I haven't seen him since Breteuil, where he promptly slipped away to establish himself in Paris. And so who is at fault for the discord if not the one who wanted at all costs to place me with this selfish, narrow-minded prelate whose only concern is his own comfort, and whose actions have no other design than to foil my own? General peace, he doesn't care for such things. All that matters to him is that I fail to achieve it. Lack of charity, a fine thing indeed! Lack of charity ... I have good reason to believe that Capocci is involved in some shady dealings with Simon de Bucy, and that he had something to do with the imprisonment of Phoebus ... let me put your mind at rest, yes, you know ... he was released in August; and thanks to whom? Me; that you didn't know, on the promise that he would join the king's army.

Finally, the Holy Father is pleased to assure me that I am praised for my efforts and that my activities meet with the approval of not only himself but also the entire college of cardinals. I don't believe he writes as much to the other one. But he wants, as he has wanted since October, to go back on his recommendation to include Charles of Navarre in the general peace agreement. I can easily guess who suggested that to him.

It was after Friquet de Fricamps escaped that King John decided to transfer his son-in-law to Arleux, a fortress in Picardie where all around the people are devoted to the Artois. He feared Charles of Navarre was receiving benefits from too much collusion in Paris. He would not have him in the same prison as Phoebus, nor even the same town.

And then, having sacrificed nearly all in the affair of Breteuil, as I was telling you yesterday, he returned to Chartres. He had told me: 'We will speak in Chartres.' I was there, while Capocci was showing off in Paris ...

Where are we now? Brunet! The name of this town? And Poivres, have we passed Poivres? Ah! Good, it is ahead of us. I have been told that its church is worth seeing. I might add that all these churches in Champagne are most beautiful. It is a land of faith.

Oh! I don't regret having seen the camp in Chartres, and I would have liked you to have seen it too. I know; you have been excused from the army in order to stand in for your sick father ... and somehow keep the English *chevauchée* in check outside Périgord. It may have saved you from laying at rest today under a tombstone in a monastery in Poitiers. Can one ever know? It is for Providence to decide.

So, imagine Chartres: sixty thousand men, at the very least, camped on the vast plain that looks down onto the cathedral and its spires. One of the biggest armies ever assembled, if not the biggest, in the history of the kingdom. But separated into two distinct parts.

On one side, lined up in handsome rows in their hundreds, the tents of silk or canvas mingled with the colours of the banners and the knights. The movement of the men, horses and carts produced a great swarming of colour and steel under the sun, as far as the eye could see; traders in arms, harnesses, wine and food had set up their stalls on wheels on this side, as well as the brothel keepers bringing cartloads of girls under the watchful eye of the King of the Ribald ... whose name I still can't recall.

And then, a good distance away, well separated, as in the images of the Last Judgement, on one side, Paradise, on the other ... Hell, those on foot, camped on cut wheat, with no other shelter than a canvas sheet held up by a stake, and that was when they had thought of bringing one; a gigantic populace spread out randomly, weary, filthy, idle, gathered in tribes by their lands of origin and not much good at obeying their makeshift chiefs. Besides, what orders would they have obeyed? They were scarcely given any tasks to carry out, they were commanded to perform no manoeuvres. All these people had to do, their only occupation, was to hunt for food. The smartest went to pilfer from the knights, or pillage the farmyards of the neighbouring hamlets, or poach. Behind each talus could be seen three beggars sitting on their heels around a roasting rabbit. Sudden scrambles erupted to get to the carts that handed out barley bread, at irregular hours. What was regular however was the king's visit, every day, amongst the ranks of the foot soldiers. He inspected the most recent arrivals, one day those from Beauvais, the next those from Soissons, the day after those from Orléans and Jargeau.

He was accompanied by, hear this, his four sons, his brother, the constable, the two marshals, John of Artois, Tancarville, who else . . . a horde of equerries.

One time, which turned out to be the last time, you will see why, he invited me as if he were doing me a great honour. 'Monseigneur of Périgord, tomorrow, should it please you to follow me, I will take you with me on the inspection.' I was still expecting to come to an agreement with him on the few proposals, vague as they were, that might be passed on to the English, to hang the beginnings of a negotiation on. I had suggested that the two kings entrust deputies to draw up the list of all the points of contention between the two kingdoms. That alone would be enough for four years of discussions.

Or, I would seek another, quite different approach. We would pretend to ignore the disputes and would commit to preliminary talks about preparations for a common expedition to Constantinople. The important thing was to begin discussions.

So I went dragging my red robe through this vast flea-ridden squalor that was camped out on the Beauce. I choose my words well: flea-ridden, as upon my return Brunet had to search me for lice. I couldn't very well push away the miserable wretches who came to kiss the hem of my robe! The smell was even more offensive than at Breteuil. A big storm had broken the night before and the foot soldiers had slept on the sodden ground; their rags and tatters steamed in the morning sun, and they stank to high heaven. The archpriest, who walked before the king, stopped. He really took up a lot of room, the archpriest! And the king stopped, as did all of his company.

'Sire, here are those from the provostship of Bracieux in the bailiwick of Blois, who arrived yesterday. They are pitiful.' With his mace, the archpriest pointed to forty or so ragged rogues, muddy, hirsute. They hadn't shaven at all for ten days; as for washed, don't even think of it. Any disparity in their clothing merged into a greyish hue of grime and earth. Some had holes in their shoes; some went barefoot; others had only rags wrapped around their legs. They straightened up to make a good impression; but they had a worried look in their eyes. Indeed, they had not expected to see the king himself suddenly appear before them, surrounded by his gleaming escort. And the beggars from Bracieux huddled together. The curved blades and the hooked spikes of a few voulges or halberds[56] stuck up above them like thorns out of a miry faggot.

'Sire,' continued the archpriest, 'there are thirty-nine of them, when there should be fifty. Eight have halberds, nine are equipped with swords, of which one is very poor. Just one possesses both a sword and a halberd. One of them has an axe, three have iron bars and another is armed with only a dagger; the rest have nothing at all.'

I would have wanted to laugh if I hadn't wondered what drove the king to waste his time and that of his marshals, counting rusted swords. That he should be seen once, so be it, it was a good thing. But every day, every morning? And why invite me to this paltry inspection?

I was surprised then to hear his youngest son, Philip, cry out in the artificial tone that youths have when trying to pass themselves off as mature men: 'It is certainly not with such levying that we will win great battles.' He is only fourteen years old; his voice was breaking and he didn't quite fill his chainmail shirt. His father stroked his son's forehead as if congratulating himself on having fathered such a wise warrior. Then, addressing the men from Bracieux, he asked: 'Why are you not better equipped with weaponry? Tell me, why? Is this how one shows up for my army? Haven't you received orders from your prevost?'

At that moment, a strapping lad who was trembling a little less than the others, perhaps the one who bore the only axe, stepped forward to answer: 'Sire, our master the prevost ordered each of us to arm ourselves according to our condition. We equipped ourselves as best we could. Those who have nothing, that is their condition, it doesn't allow them anything better.'

King John turned to the constable and the marshals, bearing the look of those who are satisfied when events prove them right, even when it is to their detriment. 'Yes, another prevost who has not done his duty. Send them back, like those from Saint-Fargeau, like those from Soissons. They will pay the fine. Lorris, you note that down.'

Because, as he explained to me a moment later, those who failed to show up for inspection, or who came without weapons, or who were unable to fight, were bound to pay reparations. 'The fines owed by all these pedestrians will provide me with what I need to pay my knights.'

A fine idea which must have been put into his head by Simon de Bucy, and which he had made his own. This is why he had called up the arriere-ban,[57] and why he counted with a kind of rapaciousness the detachments he was sending back to their homes. 'What use would I have for this rank and file?' he said to me again. 'It is because of these foot soldiers that my father was defeated at Crécy. These menials on foot slow everything down and prevent us from riding as we should.'

And everyone approved, except, I must say, the dauphin, who seemed to have a comment on the tip of his tongue, but kept it to himself.

Was that to say that on the other side of the camp, with the banners, horses and armour, everything was going wonderfully? In spite of the repeated notifications, and in spite of the fine regulations which stipulated that knights banneret and captains should inspect their men, weapons and mounts twice a month without warning in order to be always ready to make a move, and which prohibited changing chiefs or retiring without permission, 'for fear of losing all wages and being punished without mercy', in spite of all that, a good third of the knights had not turned up. Others, obliged to equip a company of twenty-five lances or more, presented only ten. Shirts of broken chainmail, dented iron hats, dried-out saddlery that could fall apart at any moment. 'Ahem, messire, how could I provide for myself? I still haven't received a penny of my wages, and it is almost more than I can do to maintain my own armour.' People fought to re-shoe their horses. Chiefs wandered through the camp looking for stray troops, passing stragglers looking, more or less, for their chiefs. From one troop to the next they pilfered as they went, a piece of wood, a bit of leather, the awl or the hammer that they needed. The marshals were beset with complaints, and their heads resounded with the harsh words the angry knight bannerets traded. King John wanted to hear nothing of it. He was counting the pedestrians who would pay reparations.

He was about to head off for the inspection of those from Saint-Aignan, when six men-at-arms arrived, riding through the camp at full trot, their horses white with foam, their own faces streaming, their armour dusty. One of them stepped down heavily, asked to speak to the constable, and having got close to him said: 'I am in the service of Messire of Boucicaut, of whom I bring you news.'

The Duke of Athens, with a sign, invited the messenger to make his report to the king. The messenger attempted a vague kneeling gesture, but his armour prevented him; the king excused him from such ceremony and urged him to speak.

'Sire, Messire of Boucicaut is trapped in Romorantin.'

Romorantin! The royal escort was for a moment struck dumb with surprise, as if astonished by lightning. Romorantin was just thirty leagues from Chartres, on the other side of Blois! They hadn't imagined that the English could be so close.

Because, during the time the Siege of Breteuil was drawing to a close, and Gaston Phoebus was being sent to jail, and the ban and the arrière-ban was slowly gathering in Chartres, the Prince of Wales had embarked upon his *chevauchée*, as you know better than anyone else, Archambaud, as you had to protect Périgueux . . . from Sainte-Foy and Bergerac, where he entered royal territory, and made his way north on the route we took, Château-l'Évêque, Brantôme, Rochechouart, La Péruse, causing all the devastation that we saw there. We were kept informed of his progress, and I must say that I was surprised to find the king revelling at Chartres while Prince Edward ravaged the country. He was believed to be, according to the latest news we had, somewhere between La Châtre and Bourges. It was thought he would continue to Orléans, and it would be there for certain that the king would do battle, cutting off his route to Paris. In view of which, nonetheless heeding caution, he had sent a party of three hundred lances under the command of Messires of Boucicaut, Craon and Caumont on a lengthy reconnaissance mission to the other side of the Loire to bring him back information. And he had received precious little of that. And then, suddenly, Romorantin! The Prince of Wales had thus cut across to the west . . .

The king encouraged the messenger to continue.

'First, sire, Messire of Chambly, whom Messire of Boucicaut had dispatched to reconnoitre the terrain, was caught near Aubigny-sur-Nère.'

'Ah! Gris-Mouton has been taken,' said the king, for that is how Messire of Chambly is nicknamed.

Boucicaut's messenger continued: 'But Messire of Boucicaut

didn't find out soon enough, and that is how we ran into the English vanguard. We attacked them so stoutly that they beat a hasty retreat.'

'As they usually do,' said King John.

'But they fell back on their reinforcements who were far greater in number than we, and they assailed us from all sides, so much so that Messires of Boucicaut, Craon and Caumont led us at speed to Romorantin, with the entire army of Prince Edward at our heels. They have shut themselves in; at the hour at which Messire of Boucicaut dispatched me, the English were beginning to lay a siege. That, sire, is what I have to tell you.'

Silence fell once more. Then the Marshal of Clermont had a fit of anger. 'Why the devil did they attack? This is not what we commanded them to do.'

'Are you reproaching them for their valour?' replied the Marshal of Audrehem. 'They had flushed out the enemy, they charged.'

'Fine valour indeed,' said Clermont. They were three hundred lances, they saw twenty, and ran at them without further ado, believing that to be some great exploit. And then one thousand suddenly appear, and they flee in turn, running to hide in the first castle they come across. Now, they are totally useless to you. That is not valour, it is foolishness.'

The two marshals continued to quarrel, as usual, and the constable let them. He didn't like to take sides, the constable. He was a braver man in body than in mind. He preferred to be called Athens rather than Brienne, because of the previous constable, his beheaded cousin. And yet Brienne was his fief, while Athens was but a distant family memory, with no grounding in fact whatsoever any more, unless a crusade. Or perhaps, he had simply become indifferent with age. For a long time he had commanded, and commanded well, the armies of the King of Naples. He looked back wistfully on Italy, because he was nostalgic for his youth. The archpriest, holding back a little, mockingly observed the marshals' argument. It was the king who put a stop to their discussion.

'And I myself think,' he said, 'that their setback serves our interests. As here the Englishman is fixed by a siege. And now we know where to run after him, so long as he is held up there.' He then addressed the constable. 'Gautier, get the army on their way tomorrow at first light. Split them into several different battalions that will cross the Loire at different points, where there are bridges, so as not to slow us down, while maintaining close contact between formations in order to regroup at the appointed place, beyond the river. As for me, I will cross at Blois. And we will attack the English army from the rear at Romorantin, or should they dare to leave, we will cut off all routes before them. Have the Loire guarded far beyond Tours, up to Angers, so that the Duke of Lancaster, who is coming from Norman country, will never be able to join the Prince of Wales.'

He surprised his people, John II! Suddenly calm and in control, here he was giving clear orders and setting out routes for his army, as if he could see all of France before him. Bar the Loire near Anjou, cross it at Touraine, be ready either to descend towards Berry, or to cut off the route to Poitou and Angoumois ... and after all of that, to Bordeaux and Aquitaine. 'And may promptness be our business, so that surprise may play to our advantage.' Everyone straightened, ready for action. A fine expedition was about to take place.

'And send back all the rank and file,' ordered John II. 'Let us not endure another Crécy. With nothing but men-at-arms we will be five times stronger than these evil Englishmen.'

In this way, because ten years earlier the archers and cross-bowmen, inopportunely engaged, hampered the cavalry's movements and made them lose a battle, this time King John was renouncing all infantry. And his banner leaders approved, as they had all been at Crécy and were still smarting from the defeat. Not to commit the same error was their biggest concern.

Only the dauphin made so bold as to say: 'In this way, my father, we will have no archers at all.'

The king didn't even deign to answer him. And the dauphin, who found himself close by me, said to me, as if looking for support, or not wanting me to take him for a fool: 'The English put their archers on horseback. But nobody here, on our side would agree to giving horses to folk of the common people.'

Look here, that reminds me ... Brunet! If the weather tomorrow stays as mild as it is today, I will complete the stage, which will be short indeed, on my palfrey. I must get back in the saddle a little, before Metz. And besides, I want to show the people of Châlons, when I enter their town, that I can ride just as well as their mad Bishop Chauveau, who still hasn't been replaced.

5

The Prince of Aquitaine

AH! YOU FIND ME again rather incensed for this stretch of road that will take us to Sainte-Menehould. It is written that I shall not stop at a large town without hearing some news there that makes my blood boil. In Troyes it was the pope's letter. In Châlons it was the post from Paris. What did I learn? That the dauphin, almost a fortnight before setting out, had signed a mandate to adjust once more the value of the currency, further weakening it, of course. But for fear that the matter be badly received he put off its promulgation until after his departure, when he would be far enough away, five days' ride, and it was only on the tenth of this month that the edict was published. In fact, he was afraid of facing up to his bourgeois, and so he outdistanced them like a stag. Really, flight is often his resource of choice! I don't know who inspired him to this dishonourable subterfuge, if it was Braque or de Bucy; but its fruits have quickly ripened. The Prevost Marcel and the biggest merchants, furious, went at daybreak

279

to give a piece of their mind to the Duke of Anjou, whom the dauphin had installed in his place in the Louvre; and the king's second son, who is only eighteen years old and hasn't a great deal of common sense, let them drag out of him a deferral of the edict, in order to avoid the rioting that threatened, until the return of the dauphin. Either the measure shouldn't have been taken, which is the view I would have been inclined to, as it is a bad expedient, or it should have been adopted and imposed immediately. He is arriving, with his numbers strengthened, before his uncle the emperor, our Dauphin Charles, but with a capital whose council refuses to obey royal rulings!

Who then, today, commands in the kingdom of France? We are entitled to wonder. This business, let us make no mistake about it, will have dire consequences. Because here Marcel has become sure of himself, in the knowledge that he has made the will of the crown bend, and he is inevitably supported by the bourgeois rabble, since he defends their purses. The dauphin played his Estates-General well, to leave them distraught at his departure; with this recent business, he loses all of his advantage. Admit that it is disappointing, really, to go to so much trouble, travelling all over, as I have been doing for half a year, in an attempt to improve the fate of princes who are so dead set on doing themselves harm!

Farewell, Châlons . . . Oh no, oh no! I do not wish to get involved in the appointment of a new bishop. The Count-Bishop of Châlons is one of the six Ecclesiastical Peers. It is business for King John or the dauphin. May they take care of it directly with the Holy Father, or may they pass on the pain to Niccola Capocci; he will make himself useful for once.

All the same we mustn't condemn the dauphin; his job is not an easy one. The guilty one is King John; and never could the son commit as many errors as the father has accumulated.

To calm my temper, or perhaps make myself even angrier, may God forgive me my sins ... I will tell you about his undertaking, King John's planned action. And you will see how a king can lose his kingdom!

At Chartres, as I was telling you, he had pulled himself together. He had stopped talking of chivalry when he was supposed to talk about finances, or thinking of finances when he should have been concerning himself with war, worrying about trifles when the fate of the kingdom was at stake. For once he seemed to emerge from his internal confusion and his ill-fated penchant for contretemps; for once his state of mind appeared to coincide with the moment. He had taken real measures to fight a campaign. And as the leader's mood is contagious, these measures were implemented with speed and precision.

First, prevent the English from crossing the Loire. Substantial detachments, commanded by captains familiar with these lands, were sent to hold all the bridges and crossing points between Orléans and Angers. The leaders were ordered to stay in close contact with their neighbours, and to frequently send messengers to the king's army. Prevent at all costs the *chevauchée* of the Prince of Wales, en route from Sologne, joining forces with that of the Duke of Lancaster, coming from Brittany. They would be defeated separately. And first off, the Prince of Wales. The army, divided up into four columns to facilitate their movement, was to cross the river by the bridges of Meung, Blois, Amboise and Tours.

Avoid engaging, whatever opportunity may present itself, before all the battle corps are assembled on the other side of the Loire. No individual exploits, as tempting as they may seem. The exploit will be to crush the Englishman all together, and to rid the kingdom of France of the fear of destitution and murder it has been subjected to for too many long years, to its shame. Those were the instructions that the constable, Duke of Athens, gave to the banner leaders gathered together before setting off. 'Go, messires, and may each of you do his duty. The king has his eyes on all of you.'

The sky was cluttered with big black clouds which burst suddenly, shot through with lightning. Throughout all of those days, Vendômois and Touraine were lashed by rainstorms, brief but heavy, soaking surcoats and the chainmail shirts beneath, saturating the saddlery, weighing down the leathers. One might have thought from the frequency of the lightning that it was attracted by all this parading steel; three men-at-arms, who had sought shelter under a huge tree, were struck down by lightning. But overall, the army braved the bad weather well, often encouraged by the clamour of the people. Because the bourgeois of the small towns and yokels in the country were most worried by the progress of the Prince of Aquitaine, of whom they told the most terrifying things. This long procession of knights in armour rushing through, four abreast, put their minds at rest ... as soon as they understood that combat would not take place nearby. 'Long live our good king! Give his enemies a good hiding! May God protect you, valiant seigneurs!' Which meant: 'May God protect us, thanks to you, of whom many will fall dead somewhere, from seeing our homes and our poor herds burnt, our flocks dispersed, our harvests lost, our girls man-handled. May God protect us from the war that you will wage elsewhere.' And they were not niggardly with their wine, which was fresh and golden. They held it out for the knights who drank, jugs raised, without stopping their mounts.

All of that I saw, because I had resolved to follow the king and go to Blois, just so, he was rushing off to war; however, I had a mission to make peace. I remained obstinate. I too had my plan. And my palanquin advanced behind the main body of the army, but was followed by detachments that had failed to join the camp of Chartres in time. They kept coming for several days more, such as the Counts of Joigny, Auxerre and Châtillon, three proud comrades who looked on the bright side of war and went unhurried, followed by all the lances of their counties. 'Good people, have you seen the king's army go by?'

'The army? We saw it pass through the day before yesterday, there were so many of them, so many of them! It took more than a couple of hours. And yet more came through this morning. If you find the Englishman, show no mercy.'

'Most certainly, good people, most certainly, and if we take Prince Edward, we will remember to send you a piece of him.'

And Prince Edward, what of him during this time, you will ask me. The prince had been delayed before Romorantin. For less time than King John had expected, but long enough to allow him to develop his battle plans. Five days, as the Sires of Boucicaut, Craon and Caumont had defended themselves furiously. During the day of the thirty-first of August alone they were stormed three times, and drove them back. And it was only on the third of September that the stronghold fell. The prince burnt it to the ground, as usual; but the following day, which was a Sunday, he had to let his troops rest. The archers, who had lost many of their own, were tired. It was the first half-serious encounter since the beginning of the campaign. And the prince had learnt from his spies – he always had intelligence well ahead – that the King of France with all of his army was readying to descend upon him; smiling less than he would ordinarily, the prince wondered if he hadn't been wrong to persist in attacking the fortress, and if he wouldn't have been better off leaving Boucicaut's three hundred lances shut up in Romorantin.

He doesn't know the exact number of King John's army; but he knows it to be stronger than his own, and by far, a huge army that will be finding ways to cross four bridges at the same time. If he doesn't wish to suffer from too much of an overwhelming disparity of numbers, then he must effect his junction with the Duke of Lancaster at all costs. The pleasant *chevauchée* is over, no longer will they enjoy the sight of villeins taking to the woods and the monastery roofs burning. Messires of Chandos and Grailly, his best captains, are no less worried; indeed, old hands accustomed to the fortunes of war, they encourage him to make haste. He descends the valley of the Cher, passing through Saint-Aignan, Thésée, Montrichard without stopping long enough to pillage them, without even taking a look at the beautiful river and its still waters, nor the islands planted with poplars that the sun shines through, nor the chalky slopes where the next grape harvest ripens in the heat. He heads west, towards relief and reinforcements.

The seventh of September he reaches Montlouis, to be told that a huge battle corps, commanded by the Count of Poitiers, the king's third son, and the Marshal of Clermont, is at Tours.

Then he weighs up his options. He waits four days, up in the hills above Montlouis, for Lancaster to arrive, having crossed the river; in short, a miracle. And if the miracle doesn't happen, in any case his position is a good one. Four days long he waits for the French, who know where he is, to bring on the battle. Against the Poitiers-Clermont corps, the Prince of Wales thinks he can hold out and even win. He has chosen his battle site on terrain traversed by thick thorn bushes. He keeps his archers busy digging entrenchments. He himself, his marshals and equerries camp out in neighbouring houses.

Four days long, from daybreak, he scans the horizon out towards Tours. The morning lays down golden mists in the immense valley below; the river, swelled by the recent rains, rolls ochre between its green banks. The archers continue to craft taluses.

Four nights long, the prince conjectures, observing the sky, what the coming dawn will have in store for him. The nights are most beautiful at that season, and Jupiter shines bright, bigger than all the other stars.

'What are the French going to do?' wonders the prince. 'What are they going to do?'

Now, the French, respecting for once the order they had been given, don't attack. The tenth of September, King John is in Blois with his battle corps gathered together. The eleventh, he moves on to the pretty town of Amboise, touching, suffice to say, Montlouis. Farewell reinforcements, farewell Lancaster! The Prince of Wales knows he must withdraw to

Aquitaine, as fast as he can, if he wants to avoid getting caught up in the net between Tours and Amboise; he cannot make a stand against two battle corps. The same day, he clears out of the hills above Montlouis and spends the night in Montbazon.

And there, on the morning of the twelfth, what does he see coming? Two hundred lances preceded by a yellow and white banner, and in the middle of the lances a big, red palanquin from which emerges a cardinal. I have accustomed my sergeants and valets, as you have seen, to go down on one knee when I step out. That always makes an impression upon those I visit. Many immediately choose to kneel as well, and cross themselves. My appearance in the English camp created quite a stir, I can assure you.

I had left King John the day before in Amboise. I knew that he wouldn't attack just yet, but that he couldn't put off the moment much longer. So, it was my turn to enter into discussions. I had gone through Bléré, where I had slept little. Flanked by the armoured knights of my nephew of Durazzo and of Messire of Hérédia, and followed by my robed prelates and clerics, I went to the prince to ask him to speak with me, alone.

He seemed to be in a hurry, saying that he would be breaking camp within the hour. I assured him that he had a moment before him, and that my words, those of our Holy Father the pope, deserved to be heard. To know, as he did from my certainty, that he wouldn't be attacked that day clearly gave him some respite; but all the time we were speaking, although he wanted to appear sure of himself, he continued to show haste, which I found to be a good thing.

He possesses a haughtiness, this prince, and as I do

too, there was not to be an easy beginning. But I have the advantage of age.

Handsome man, fine size. Indeed, indeed, it is true, I haven't yet described the Prince of Wales to you! Twenty-six years old. It is the age of all the new generation now taking command. The King of Navarre is twenty-five, and so is Phoebus; only the dauphin is younger ... Wales has a welcoming smile that no rotten teeth yet detract from. For his lower face, chin and jawline, and complexion, he takes after his mother, Queen Philippa. He has her cheerful manner, also, and will put on weight as she did. For the top half of his face, he leans towards his great-grandfather, Philip the Fair. A smooth forehead, eyes blue, large, set well apart, as cold as iron. He stares at one, in a way that belies the affability of his smile. The two parts of his face, and their different expressions, are separated by a handsome, Saxon-style blond moustache, which sets off his lips and chin. Deep down, his is a dominant nature. He sees the world only from high atop his horse.

Do you know his titles? Edward of Woodstock, Prince of Wales, Prince of Aquitaine, Duke of Cornwall, Count of Chester, Earl of Biscay. The pope and crowned kings are the only men he looks upon as his superiors. All other creatures, in his eyes, simply have differing degrees of inferiority. He certainly has the gift of command, and disregard for risk. He is hardy; he keeps a clear head in times of danger. He is lavish in victory and showers his friends with gifts.

He already has a nickname, the Black Prince, from the armour of burnished steel he is so fond of, and which makes him stand out, particularly with the three white feathers in his helmet, amongst the brilliant chainmail shirts and the many-coloured surcoats of the knights surrounding him. His glory began early in life. At Crécy, when he was just sixteen, his father entrusted him with the command of an entire battalion, that of the Welsh archers, backing him up of course with experienced captains who were there to advise him and even to lead him. Now, this battalion was so severely attacked by the French knights there came a point when those who had the charge of seconding him, judging the prince to be in danger, sped word to the king asking him to come to the aid of his son. King Edward III, who had been observing the battle from the hill of a windmill, replied to the messenger: 'Is my son dead, devastated or so wounded that he cannot help himself? No? So, go back to him, or to those who sent you, and tell them not to come and call for me, whatever adventure may befall him, so long as he remains alive. I order that this child should be allowed to earn his spurs; because I want, if God has arranged it so, that this day be his day and that he should retain the honours.'

So that is the young man before whom I found myself for the first time.

I tell him that the King of France . . .

'Before me, he is not the King of France,' the prince says.

'Before the Holy Church, he is king, anointed and crowned,' I reply; you can judge the tone for yourself. I tell him the King of France is coming for him with his army of near thirty thousand men. I overdo it a little, on purpose; and so that he understands me completely, I add: 'Others may speak to you of sixty thousand. I tell you the truth. Because I do not include the foot soldiers which remained behind.' I stop short of telling him that they had been sent home; I had the feeling that he already knew.

But it matters little; sixty or thirty, or even twenty-five thousand, a figure which was closest to the truth: the English prince had only six thousand men with him, all his archers and coutiliers included. I impressed upon him that, from now on, it was no longer a question of valour but of number.

He tells me that he will at any moment be joined by Lancaster's army. I reply that I wish it with all my heart, for his safety.

He sees that playing up his self-confidence would not make him my master, and after a moment of silence he says out of the blue that he knows I treat King John more favourably, now he had given him back his title of king, than I treat his father. 'I am only favourable to peace between the two kingdoms,' I respond, 'and that is what I have come to offer.'

But then he proceeds, with much grandeur, to lecture me on the events of the previous year: he had travelled across the whole of the Languedoc and led his knights as far as the Latin Sea without any opposition whatsoever from the king; just this season, he had carried out a *chevauchée* from Guyenne to the Loire; Brittany was as good as under English law; a large part of Normandy, brought by Monseigneur Philip of Navarre, was on the verge of changing fealty; Seigneurs of Angoumois, Poitou, Saintonge and even Limousin had rallied to him, he had the good taste not to mention the Périgord, and while he spoke he was observing through the window the position of the sun in the sky, only to finally come out with: 'After so many successes for our armies, and the ascendancy we have, *de jure et de facto*, throughout the kingdom of

France, what offers could King John possibly make us in the name of peace?'

Ah! If the king had deigned to hear me in Breteuil, in Chartres . . . Now what could I answer, what did I have in my hand? I said to the prince that I couldn't bring him any offer from the King of France as the latter, strong as he was, couldn't think of peace before claiming the expected victory; but that I brought him the commandment of the pope, who wished him to cease bloodying the western kingdoms, and who begged the kings imperiously, I insisted, to agree to come to the aid of our brothers of Constantinople. And I asked him under what conditions England . . .

He was still watching the sun climb in the sky, and broke off the audience saying: 'It is up to the king, my father, and not I, to decide on peace. I have no order from him authorizing me to negotiate on his behalf.' Then he hoped I would forgive him if he travelled on ahead of me. All he had in mind was to distance the pursuing army. 'Let me bless you, monseigneur,' I said to him. 'And I will stay close by, should it befall you to have need of me.'

You will say, my nephew, that I was taking away a most meagre catch in my nets, leaving Montbazon in the wake of the English army. But I wasn't nearly as unhappy as you might think. The situation being what it was, I had snagged the fish and left it line enough. It all depended on the eddies of the river. I just had to stay close to the water's edge.

The prince headed south, towards Châtellerault. On those days, the most astonishing cortèges moved along the roads of Touraine and Poitou. First of all, the army of the Prince of Wales, compact, rapid, six thousand men, always orderly, but a little out of breath all the same, and no longer dawdling or burning barns. It was rather the earth that seemed to be burning their mounts' hooves. A day's march later, the formidable army of King John sets off in pursuit, having regrouped, as he wanted, all the banners, almost, twenty-five thousand men, but holding together less well as he was pushing them too hard, wearing them out, and stragglers were soon falling behind.

And then, between English and French, following the former, preceding the latter, my little cortège putting a speck of purple and gold in the countryside. A cardinal between two armies, that is not oft to be seen! All the banners hurrying to war, and I, with my little escort, insisting on peace. My nephew of Durazzo stamps his feet impatiently; I sense that he is, as it were, ashamed to be escorting someone whose only prowess would be in preventing the combat. And my other knights, Hérédia, La Rue, all think the same. Durazzo tells me: 'Just let King John thrash the English, and be done with it. Besides, what do you hope to prevent?'

Deep down I am rather of their opinion, but I will not give up. I can see that if King John catches up with Prince Edward, and he will catch up with him, he can only crush him. If it is not in Poitou, it will be in Angoumois.

Everything, all appearances, announced John as victorious. But these days, the stars are bad, very bad, I know it. And I wonder how he will endure their disastrous aspect in a situation where he has such a strong advantage. I tell myself that he will fight a victorious battle, but that he will be killed. Or that a malady will overcome him on the way . . .

Also progressing along the same route are the cavalcades of

the latecomers, the Counts of Joigny, Auxerre and Châtillon, the good fellows, always joyful and taking their time, but little by little making up distance on the main body of the French army. 'Good people, have you seen the king?'

'The king? He left La Haye this morning. And the Englishman? He slept there the night before.'

John II, as he follows his English cousin, is informed most exactly of his enemy's path. The latter, feeling John hot on his heels, reaches Châtellerault, and there, to lighten his cavalcade and free up the bridge, he orders his personal convoy to cross the River Vienne by night, with all the carts bearing his furniture, his ceremonial saddlery, as well as all his spoils, the silks, the silverware, the ivories, the church treasures he looted during his *chevauchée*. And off towards Poitiers. At first light, he, his men-at-arms and his archers take the same route for a short way; then, even more cautious, he sends his people on shortcuts. He has made his calculations: bypass Poitiers via the east, where the king will be obliged to let his massive army rest; be it only for a few hours, still it will increase his lead.

What at that moment he doesn't know is that the king has not taken the road to Châtellerault. With all of his chivalry led at hunting pace, he has headed off, even earlier than sunrise, towards Chauvigny, in an attempt to outflank his enemy and cut off his escape routes. He leads from the front, straight in his saddle, chin forward, without heeding anything at all, just as he'd ridden to the Banquet of Rouen. Another stretch of more than twelve leagues in one go.

Still following on behind, the three Seigneurs of Burgundy, Joigny, Auxerre and Châtillon. 'The king?'

'To Chauvigny.'

'Go then to Chauvigny!' They are happy; they have almost caught up with the army; they will arrive in time for the kill.

They reach Chauvigny at nightfall; the huge castle looks down on the town at a bend in the River Vienne. There is an enormous gathering of troops, an unparalleled jam of carts and armour leading to the castle. Joigny, Auxerre and Châtillon enjoy their creature comforts. They are not going to throw themselves into such a crush. What was the point of hurrying? Better have a good dinner, while our pages groom the mounts. Cervellières removed, greaves unlaced, they stretch and rub their backs and calves, and then sit down to eat at an inn not far from the river. Their equerries, knowing them to like their food, found them fish, as it is Friday. Next, they fall sleep – all this was told to me afterwards in detail – and they awake the next morning, late, in an empty, silent town. 'Good people ... the king?' They're pointed in the direction of Poitiers. 'The shortest way?'

'Via La Chaboterie.'

So now Châtillon, Joigny and Auxerre, dragging their lances behind them, set out at a good pace over the heathland pathways. Fine morning; the sun cuts through the branches, without beating down too hard. Three leagues are covered without difficulty. We will be in Poitiers in less than half an hour. And suddenly, at the intersection of two trails, they come face to face with sixty English scouts. They are more than three hundred. It is a godsend. Close our ventails, lower our lances. The English scouts – who are, I might add, people from Hainaut commanded by Messires of Ghistelles and Auberchicourt – turn around and break into a gallop. 'Ah!

The cowards, ah! The cowards! Go in pursuit, in pursuit!'

The pursuit doesn't last long as, once the first copse is cleared, Joigny, Auxerre and Châtillon fall upon the main body of the English column, which closes in around them. Swords and lances clash for a moment. They fight well those Burgundians! But their enemy's number swamps them. 'Run to the king, run to the king, if you can!' Auxerre and Joigny shout to their equerries, before being forced to dismount and surrender.

King John is already in the outskirts of Poitiers when those few of the Count of Joigny's men who had been able to escape after a furious chase reach the king, out of breath, to tell him the tale. He congratulates them well. He is overjoyed. To have lost three great barons and their banners? No, of course not; but the price was not high for such good news. The Prince of Wales, whom he believed to be still ahead of him, is in fact behind. He has succeeded; he has cut him off. About turn for La Chaboterie. Take me there, my good men! In for the kill, the kill! He had just lived his finest day, King John.

And me, my nephew? Ah! I had followed the road from Châtellerault. I was to arrive in Poitiers, and stay at the bishop's palace, where I was, in the course of the evening, informed of everything.

6

The Cardinal's Approach

Don't be surprised in Metz, Archambaud, to see the dauphin pay homage to his uncle the emperor. Oh yes, for the Dauphiny, which falls in the imperial sphere of influence. No, no, I actively encouraged him to do so; it is even one of the pretexts for the journey! That doesn't belittle France in the slightest, quite the opposite; it establishes rights over the kingdom of Arles, should one decide to restore it, since the Viennois used to be a part of it. And also it sets a good example for the English, to show them that king or son of a king, without humbling himself, can consent to pay homage to another sovereign, when parts of their states fall within the ancient suzerainty of the other.

It is the first time in a long while that the emperor seems resolved to favour France a little. Because up until now, and even though his sister Madame Bonne was King John's first wife, he has rather favoured the English more. Hasn't he appointed King Edward, who proved himself most deft with him, imperial vicar? The great victories of England and the humbling of France must have led him to reflect. An English empire alongside the empire would not be at all in his interests. That is always the way with the German princes; they do whatever they can to weaken France, and then they realize that this has brought them nothing, on the contrary.

I advise you, when we are before the emperor, and if we should come to talk of Crécy, do not dwell on the battle too much. In any case, don't pronounce its name before the others. As, quite unlike his father John the Blind, the emperor, who wasn't yet emperor, didn't cut such a fine figure there. He fled, quite simply, let us not beat about the bush. But don't speak too much about Poitiers either, a subject everybody must still be mindful of, and don't think it necessary to extol the unfortunate bravery of the French knights, out of consideration for the dauphin, as neither did he distinguish himself by immoderate valour. It is one of the reasons why he has found it hard to establish his authority. Ah no! This will be no gathering of heroes. After all, he has his excuses, the dauphin; and if he is no man of war, it is not he who failed to seize the opportunity offered to his father . . .

I shall resume the tale of Poitiers, that no one can tell you more completely than I, you will soon understand why. We had got to Saturday evening, when the two armies know that they are right next to each other, almost touching, and the Prince of Wales understands that he cannot move any further.

Sunday, early in the morning, the king celebrates Mass outdoors, surrounded by fields. A Mass of war. He who is officiating wears mitre and chasuble over his coat of mail; it is Regnault Chauveau, the Count-Bishop of Châlons, one of those prelates more suited to military order than the religious orders. I see you smile, my nephew . . . yes, you say to yourself that I belong to the same kind; but I have learned to command myself, since God marked out my path for me.

For Chauveau, this kneeling army, in the dew-soaked meadows before the town of Nouaillé, must offer the vision of celestial legions. The bells of the Abbey of Maupertuis ring out in their big church tower. And the English, up on the hill, behind copses that hide them from view, hear the formidable *Gloria* that the knights of France sing out.

The king receives Communion surrounded by his four sons and his brother of Orléans, all in full battle attire. The marshals, understandably perplexed, watch the young princes, to whom they've had to give commands even though they had no experience of war at all. Yes, the princes are sources of worry for them. Haven't all of them been brought along, down to the children, young Philip, the king's preferred son, and his cousin Charles of Alençon? Fourteen, thirteen years old; what embarrassments are these dwarf-like suits of armour! Young Philip remains close to his father, who insists on watching over him personally; and the archpriest has been entrusted with the protection of young Alençon.

The constable has split the army into three large battalions. The first, thirty-two banners, is to fight under the command of the Duke of Orléans. The second, under the dauphin, Duke of Normandy, seconded by his brothers, Louis of Anjou and Jean de Berry. But in truth the command falls to Jean de Landas, Thibaut de Vodenay and the Sire of Saint-Venant, three men of war whose job is to stay close to the heir to the throne and keep him under control. The king would head up the third battalion.

He is hauled up into his saddle, onto his great white charger. He casts his eye over his army and marvels to see it so large and so beautiful. As far as the eye can see, helmets, lances side by side, in deep rows! Powerful horses, their heads nodding up and down and making their bits clink! From saddles hang the swords, the maces, the double-bladed axes. Banderoles and pennons float in glowing colours from the lances. Everywhere bright hues, painted on the shields and the targes, embroidered on the knights' surcoats and their mounts' caparisons! All of this in the rising clouds of dust gleaming, shimmering, shining forth under the morning sun.

Then the king steps forward and cries out: 'My good sires, when you were amongst your own people in Paris, Chartres, Rouen or Orléans, you threatened the English and wished to confront them, bascinets[58] upon your heads; now here you are, the time has come; I will show them to you. And I pray you will show them your talents and avenge the troubles and vexations they have caused us, because without fail we will beat them!' And then after the enormous 'May God take part! We will see Him!' which answers him, he waits. He is waiting, before giving the order to attack, for the return of Eustache de Ribemont, the Bailiff of Lille and Douai, whom he sent with a small detachment to reconnoitre exactly the English position.

And the whole army waits, in a great silence. A difficult moment when one is poised to charge and the order takes its time coming. Because it is then that each one says to himself: 'Perhaps it will be my turn today, perhaps I am seeing the earth for the last time.' And under his steel chin piece each man has a lump in his throat; everyone commends himself to God even more earnestly than during Mass. The game of war suddenly becomes solemn and dreadful.

Messire Geoffroy de Charny bore the oriflamme of France; the king had given him the honour of carrying it and he looked transformed by it, so I was told.

The Duke of Athens seemed the most calm amongst them. He knew from experience that most of his work as constable he had completed beforehand. Once the battle commenced he would no longer be able to make out anything beyond two hundred paces nor would he make himself heard at more than fifty; equerries would be dispatched to him from the different parts of the battlefield, who would get to him, or not; and, to those who did find their way to him, he would shout an order that might, or might not, be executed. The fact that he was there, that one could send dispatches to him, that he made a gesture, shouted an approval; doing this he reassured the others. And perhaps a decision would have to be taken at a difficult moment. But in this great confusion of crashes and clamour, it would no longer really be he who commanded, but the will of God. And given the number of French, it seemed that God had already reached His verdict.

King John began to get angry when Eustache of Ribemont hadn't come back. Might he have been captured, like Auxerre and Joigny yesterday? Good sense would favour sending out a second reconnaissance. But King John cannot bear to be kept waiting. He is seized with that irascible impatience that rises up inside him every time an event doesn't immediately obey his will, and which renders him incapable of judging matters soundly. He is on the verge of giving the order to attack. Never mind, we will soon find out, when Messire of Ribemont and his patrol return at last.

'So, Eustache, what news?'

'Excellent, sire; you will have, God willing, great victory over your enemies.'

'How many are they?'

'Sire, we have seen and considered them. According to our estimation, the English could be two thousand men-at-arms, four thousand archers and fifteen hundred ribald fellows.'

The king, on his white charger, has a triumphant smile. He looks at the twenty-five thousand men, or almost, drawn up around him. 'And how is their position?'

'Ah! Sire, they occupy a strong place. We can rest assured that they have no more than one battalion, and a small one at that, compared to ours, but it is well ordered.'

And to describe how the English are installed, up on the hill, on either side of a steep pathway, bordered by thick hedges and bushes behind which they have lined up their archers. To attack them, there is no other way but by this path, where horses can pass only four abreast. On all other sides there are only vines and pinewoods where riding is not an option. The English men-at-arms, their mounts kept out of the way, are all on foot, behind the archers who screen them like a portcullis. And those archers will not be easy to defeat.

'And how, Messire Eustache, do you advise us to proceed there?'

The whole army had its eyes turned towards the secret consultation which brought together around the king the constable, the marshals and the principal banner leaders. And the Count of Douglas as well, who hadn't left the king's side since Breteuil. There are guests, sometimes, that cost you dearly. William of Douglas says: 'It is always on foot that we Scots have beaten the English.' And Ribemont went one better, speaking of the Flemish militia. And here we are, at the hour of doing battle, starting to hold forth on the art of warfare. Ribemont has a proposal to make, for the strategy of attack. And William of Douglas approves. And the king invites all to listen to them, as Ribemont is the only one to have staked out the terrain, and because Douglas is the guest who has such good knowledge of the English.

Suddenly an order is cried out, passed on, repeated. 'Dismount!' What? After this great moment of tension and anxiety, during which each one prepared himself, deep down inside, to face death, we are not going to fight? There is almost a sort of wavering of disappointment. But of course you will fight, but on foot. Only three hundred armoured soldiers will remain on horseback, who will go, led by the two marshals, to break through the lines of the English archers. And the men-at-arms will immediately step into the breach and engage in hand-to-hand combat with the men of the Prince of Wales. The horses will be kept close by, for the chase.

Audrehem and Clermont are already scouring the banners' front in order to choose the three hundred strongest, boldest, most heavily armed knights, who will mount the charge.

The marshals don't look at all happy, as they haven't even been invited to give their opinions. Clermont had attempted to make himself heard and asked that they think it over for a moment. The king rebuffed him. 'Messire Eustache saw, and Messire of Douglas knows. What else could your speech bring us?' What had been chatter between a scout and a guest has become the king's plan. 'Now you have only to appoint Ribemont marshal, and Douglas constable,' mutters Audrehem.

For all those not taking part in the charge, dismount, dismount. 'Remove your spurs, and cut your lances back to a length of five feet!'

Signs of ill humour and discontent within the ranks. We hadn't come here for that, and why then dismiss the rank and file from Chartres, if we now have to do their job? And cutting down the lances broke the knights' hearts. Beautiful shafts of ash, chosen carefully to be held, wedged against the targe, perfectly horizontal, at the same time ride off like a shot! Now they were going to be walking, weighed down with iron, carrying sticks. 'Let us not forget that at Crécy . . .' said those who in spite of everything wanted to prove the king right. 'Crécy, always Crécy,' replied the others.

These men who, half an hour earlier, were exalted in their souls with honour, were now grumbling like peasants with a broken axle on their cart. But the king himself, to set an example, had sent away his white charger and stood about on the grass, his heels spurless, tossing his mace from one hand to the other.

It is into the midst of this army busied chopping off their lances with saddle axes that, coming from Poitiers, I hurtled at a gallop, under the cover of the Holy See's banner, escorted only by my knights and my finest scholars, Guillermis, Cunhac, Elie of Aimery, Hélie of Raymond, those with whom we are travelling. They are not about to forget! Didn't they tell you?

I get down from my horse, throwing my reins to La Rue; I put my hat back on my head, because it had been swept down behind my back by the ride; Brunet smoothes down my robe and I approach the king with gloved hands joined together. I tell him straight away, with as much assurance as reverence: 'Sire, I pray and beseech you, in the name of the faith, to defer combat a moment. I am come to address you upon the order and the will of our Holy Father. Would you grant me audience?'

He was very surprised by the arrival at such a moment of this intruder from the Church, but what could he do, King John, other than reply, in the same ceremonial tone: 'With pleasure, Monseigneur Cardinal. What would you care to tell me?'

I remained a moment my eyes raised to heaven as if I were praying for inspiration. And I was indeed praying; but I was also waiting for the Duke of Athens, the marshals, the Duke of Bourbon, Bishop Chauveau in whom I thought I had found an ally, Jean de Landas, Saint-Venant, Tancarville and several others, including the archpriest, to come closer. As now it was no longer a matter of words exchanged in private or conversations at dinner, like in Breteuil or Chartres. I wanted to be heard, not only by the king, but also by the most important men in France, that they may be witnesses of my efforts.

'Most gracious sire,' I continued, 'you have here the flower of your kingdom's chivalry, in their multitude, against but a handful, compared to you, of the English. They cannot hold out against your strength; and it would be more honourable for you that they put themselves at your mercy without battle, rather than chancing all of this chivalry, and watching good Christians perish on both sides. I am telling you this on the order of our Most Holy Father the pope, who has sent me as his apostolic nuncio, with all his authority, to help bring peace, according to God's commandment which seeks it between all Christian peoples. And I also ask you to allow, in the name of the Lord, that I ride to the Prince of Wales, to explain to him the danger you hold him in, and to talk reason to him.'

If he had been able to bite me, King John, I believe he would have done so. But a cardinal on the battlefield doesn't fail to impress. And the Duke of Athens nodded his head, as did the Marshal of Clermont, and Monseigneur of Bourbon. I added: 'Most gracious sire, it is Sunday, the day of the Lord, and you have just heard Mass. Would you care to postpone the work of death on the day dedicated to the Lord? At least acquiesce that I go and talk to the prince.'

King John looked at his seigneurs all around him and understood that he, the most Christian king, could not but defer to my request. If some grievous accident were to occur, he would be held responsible and God's punishment would therein be seen manifested.

'So be it, monseigneur,' he says to me. 'It pleases us to agree to your wish. But return without delay.'

I had then a flush of pride, may the Good Lord forgive me. I knew I embodied the supremacy of the man of the Church, prince of God, over the three worldly realms. Had I been Count of Périgord instead of your father, never would I have been invested with such power. And I thought I was accomplishing the task of my life.

Still escorted by my lances, still signalled by the papal banner, I headed up the hill, by the path that Ribemont had scouted, in the direction of the small wood where the Prince of Wales' base camp was.

'Prince, my fine son,' yes, this time, when I was before him, I no longer accorded him his monseigneur, to make him better feel his weakness . . . 'If you had correctly estimated the power of the King of France as I have just done, you would allow me to attempt a convention between you, and bring you to agreement, if I may.' And I enumerated the army of France that I had been able to contemplate before the town of Nouaillé. 'Look where you are, and how many you are, do you really believe that you will be able to hold out long?'

No indeed, he would not be able to hold out for long, and he knew it well. His only advantage was the terrain; his entrenchment was the very best one could find. But his men had already begun to suffer from thirst, as there was no water on that hill; they would have needed to be able to go and draw it from the stream, the Miosson, down below; and the French held it. He had scarcely enough supplies to last one day. He had lost his handsome white smile beneath his Saxon moustache, the ravaging prince! If he hadn't been who he was, amidst his knights, Chandos, Grailly, Warwick, Suffolk, who were watching him closely, he would have admitted what they were all thinking, that their situation allowed for hope no longer. Unless a miracle took place, and the miracle, perhaps it was I who was bringing it to him. Nevertheless, for grandeur's sake, he argued a little: 'I told you in Montbazon,

Monseigneur of Périgord, I am unable to negotiate without
the order of my father the king.'

'Noble prince, above the order of kings, there is the order
of God. Neither your father King Edward on his throne of
London, nor God on the throne of Heaven would forgive
you the loss of so many good lives, of the brave men put into
your protection, if you can act otherwise. Will you accept
to discuss the conditions by which you could, without loss of
honour, spare yourself a most cruel and uncertain battle?'

Black armour and red robe face to face. The three-feathered
helmet questioned my red hat and seemed to be counting the
silk tassels. Eventually the helmet made a sign of assent.

Hurtling down Eustache's path, where I made out the
English archers in close ranks behind the stockades of stakes
they had planted, there I was back before King John. I arrived
in the middle of a discussion, and I understood, by certain
looks that greeted me, that not everyone had had good words
to say about me. The archpriest rocked backwards and
forwards, raw-boned, mocking, under his Montauban hat.

'Sire,' I said, 'I have indeed seen the English. You have
no need to be too hasty in fighting them, and you will lose
nothing by resting a little, because, positioned where they
are, they cannot flee or escape you. I think in truth that you
could have them without meeting the slightest opposition.
Consequently I ask you to grant them respite until tomorrow,
at sunrise.'

Without meeting the slightest opposition . . . I saw several
of them, like the Count John of Artois, Douglas, Tancarville
himself, flinch at the word respite and shake their heads.
Opposition was what they wanted and they wanted to meet

it. I insisted: 'Sire, grant your enemy nothing if you like, but grant God His day.'

The constable and the Marshal of Clermont were inclined to favour this suspension of hostilities. 'Let us wait and see, sire, what the Englishman has to offer and what we can demand in return; we have nothing to lose.' On the other hand, Audrehem, oh! Simply because Clermont was of one opinion, he was of another, said, loud enough for me to hear: 'So are we here for battle or to listen to a sermon?' Eustache of Ribemont, because his combat strategy had been adopted by the king, and as he was keen to see it implemented, urged an immediate engagement.

And Chauveau, the Count-Bishop of Châlons who wore a helmet in the shape of a mitre, painted purple, suddenly gets restless, almost losing his temper.

'Is it the duty of the Church, Messire Cardinal, to let plunderers and traitors walk free unpunished?' There, I get a little angry. 'Is it the duty of a servant of the Church, Messire Bishop, to refuse God a truce? Please learn, if you don't know it, that I have the power to strip any ecclesiastic of his office and benefices who should impede my efforts for peace. Providence punishes the presumptuous, messire. So leave the king the honour of showing his greatness, should he so wish. Sire, you hold everything in your hands; God decides through you.'

The compliment had hit home. The king prevaricated a little while longer, while I continued to plead, seasoning my words with compliments as big as the Alps. Which prince, since Saint Louis, had shown such an example as the one he could set? All of Christendom would admire a gallant gesture and would from now on seek his wisdom for arbitration or assistance in his power!

'Have my pavilion raised,' said the king to his equerries. 'So be it, Monseigneur Cardinal; I will remain here until tomorrow, at sunrise, for your sake.'

'For the sake of God, sire; only for the sake of God.'

And I left again. Six times during the day, I had to ride back and forth, proposing the terms of an agreement to one, bringing them back to the other; and each time, passing between the hedgerows of the Welsh archers clad in their half-white, half-green livery, I said to myself that if some of them, mistaking me for someone else, shot a volley of arrows at me, I would be well stung.

King John played dice to pass the time under his pavilion of vermilion drapery. All around the army wondered. Battle or no battle? And they argued about it hard, even in front of the king. There were wise ones and braggarts, timorous natures and the quick-tempered. Each allowed himself to air an opinion. In truth, King John remained undecided. I don't think he considered himself for a single moment as the agent of the general good. He asked himself only the question of how his personal glory, which he confused with the good of his people, was best served. After so many setbacks and disappointments, what would most magnify his stature, a military victory or a negotiated settlement? Naturally, the idea of a defeat didn't occur to him, nor to any of his advisors.

And yet, the king's glory aside, the offers I brought him, with each trip, were by no means insignificant. After the first trip, the Prince of Wales consented to return all of the spoils he had taken during his *chevauchée*, as well as all the prisoners, without any demand for ransom. On the second, he accepted to give back all the strongholds and castles conquered, and to take for null and void all the homages and rallying to him and his cause. On the third trip, it was a payment in gold, as reparation for all that he had destroyed, not only that summer, but also the year before in the lands of Languedoc. One might well say that from his two expeditions, Prince Edward kept no benefit whatsoever.

And King John demanded yet more? Very well. I obtained from the prince the withdrawal of all of his garrisons located outside Aquitaine, a considerable success, and the commitment to never have any future dealings with either the Count of Foix, (while on that subject, Phoebus was in the king's army, but I didn't see him, he kept himself well out of the way) or with any of the king's relatives, which referred precisely to Navarre. The prince was giving up a great deal; he was giving up more than I thought he would. And yet, I guessed that he didn't, deep down, think that he would be exempted from fighting.

Truce does not prevent work. Consequently, all day he busied his men with strengthening their position. The archers doubled up the fences of stakes sharpened at both ends, to make defensive harrows. They cut down trees that they dragged across to block the pathways that the enemy could take. The Count of Suffolk, Marshal of the English army, inspected each troop, one after the other. The Counts of Warwick and Salisbury, and Lord of Audley took part in our meetings and escorted me through their camp.

The sun was going down as I brought King John a final proposal that I myself had suggested. The prince was ready to swear and sign that seven years long he would not take up arms nor undertake anything against the kingdom of France. We were therefore on the verge of a general peace.

'Oh! We know the English,' said Bishop Chauveau. 'They swear, and then go back on their word.'

I retort that they would have difficulty going back on a commitment taken before the papal legate; I was to be signatory of the convention.

'I will give you my answer at sunrise,' said the king.

And I went away to lodge at the Abbey of Maupertuis. Never had I ridden so much in the same day, nor had I debated so much. As exhausted as I was, I took time to pray well, with all my heart. I was woken at the crack of dawn. The sun was just beginning to shine forth when I appeared once more before the battle tent of King John. At sunrise he had said. No one could be more punctual than I. I had a bad feeling. The entire army of France was under arms, in battle order, on foot, except for the three hundred designated for the charge, and were waiting only for the signal to attack.

'Monseigneur Cardinal,' declares the king briefly, 'I will only accept to abandon the idea of fighting if Prince Edward and one hundred of his knights, of my choice, come and place themselves in my prison.'

'Sire, that is too great a demand, and one that goes against honour; it renders all of our discussions yesterday useless. I have got to know the Prince of Wales well enough to know that he will not even consider it. He is not a man to give up without a fight, and to come and give himself up into your hands with the finest of the English chivalry would be the last thing he would do. Would you do such a thing, or any of your Knights of the Star, if you were in his position?'

'Of course not!'

'Then, sire, it seems to me vain to take him a request made only to be rejected.'

'Monseigneur Cardinal, I have every respect for your offices; but the sun is up. Please withdraw from the battle-field.'

Behind the king, they looked at each other through their ventails, and exchanged smiles and winks, Bishop Chauveau, John of Artois, Douglas, Eustache of Ribemont and even Audrehem and of course the archpriest, just as happy, it seemed, to have scuppered the efforts of the pope's legate as they would be to crush the English.

For a moment, I wavered, so much wrath was welling up inside of me, hesitating to point out that I had the power of excommunication. But to what end? What effect would that have had? The French would have gone off to attack anyway, and I would only have managed to show up even more clearly the powerlessness of the Church. I only added: 'God will be the judge, sire, as to which one of you will have shown himself to be the better Christian.'

And I went back up the hill for the last time towards the copses. I was raging. 'They can all go to hell, these madmen!' I said to myself in a gallop. The Lord won't need to sort them; they are all good for his flames.'

Once arrived before the Prince of Wales, I tell him: 'Good son, do what you can; you will have to fight. I was able to find no favour for an agreement with the King of France.'

'To fight is indeed our intention,' replied the prince. 'May God help me!'

Thereupon, I left for Poitiers, embittered and greatly vexed. Now that was the moment my nephew Durazzo chose to tell me: 'I beg you to relieve me from my service, my uncle. I want to go and fight.'

'And with whom?' I cried.

'With the French of course!'

'So you don't think there are enough of them already?'

'My uncle, understand that there will be a battle, and it is unworthy of a knight not to take part. And Messire of Hérédia also asks you.'

I should have berated him forcefully, telling him that he was required by the Holy See to escort me on my mission of peace, and that, quite the opposite of an act of nobility, to have joined one of the two sides could be seen rather as an act of treachery. I should have simply ordered him to stay. But I was weary, I was angry. And in a certain way, I understood him. I would also have liked to take up a lance, and charge whomever, Bishop Chauveau. So I shouted at him: 'Go to hell both of you! And may it do you good!' Those are the last words I addressed to my nephew Robert. I regret it, I regret it terribly.

7

The Hand of God

IT IS A DIFFICULT thing indeed, when one isn't there one-self, to reconstruct a battle, and difficult even when one *was* there. Particularly when it takes place as confusedly as that of the Battle of Maupertuis. It was told to me just hours afterwards, in twenty different ways, each considering it only from his point of view and only judging important what he himself had done there. Especially the defeated; from listening to them, they would have been victorious if not for their neighbours' errors, the latter saying much the same thing.

An account that cannot be challenged is of what happened immediately after my departure from the French camp: the two marshals had an argument. The constable, Duke of Athens, having asked the king if he would care to listen to his advice, tells him something like this: 'Sire, if you really want the English to surrender to your mercy, why don't you let them wear themselves out through lack of supplies? Because their position is strong, but they will no longer be able to hold it when their bodies are weak. They are surrounded on all sides, and if they attempt to escape by the only way out, we can ourselves force them towards it, and we will crush them without difficulty. As we have waited a day, why can't we wait another day or two, all the more so that with every moment our numbers are swelling with latecomers joining us?' And the Marshal of Clermont to back him up: 'The constable is right. A little wait will give us everything to gain and nothing to lose.'

That is when the Marshal of Audrehem lost his temper. Procrastinating, always procrastinating! It should already be over, since yesterday evening. 'You will delay so much that you will end up letting them get away, as so often happens. Look at them moving around. They come down towards us to strengthen their position lower down and prepare their escape route. One might think, Clermont, that you are in no great rush to fight, and that it troubles you to see the English so close.'

The marshals' quarrel had to come out into the open. But was it the most well-chosen moment? Clermont was not a man to take such outrage on the nose. He retorted, as if in a jeu de paume[59]: 'You will not be so bold today, Audrehem, as to put your horse's muzzle up my horse's arse.'

Thereupon he joins the knights he is leading into the attack, is hauled up into his saddle, and himself gives the order to attack. Audrehem immediately copies him, and before the king has said a thing, or the constable commanded anything, the charge was under way, not at all grouped as had been decided, but in two separate squadrons which seemed less concerned with breaking the enemy than with distancing or chasing each other. The constable in turn asks for his charger and races off in an attempt to round them up.

Then the king has the attack called for all the banners; and all the men-at-arms, on foot, clumsy, weighed down by the fifty or sixty pounds of iron they carry on their backs, begin to advance through the fields towards the uphill path along which the cavalry are already rushing. Five hundred paces to cover.

High up, the Prince of Wales, seeing the French charge set off, cries out: 'My fine lords, we are but small in number, but do not be afraid. Virtue nor victory do not inevitably go to the bigger party but go where God wants to send them. If we are defeated, we will incur no condemnation, and if the day is ours, we will be the most honoured in the world.'

The ground was already shaking at the foot of the hill; the Welsh archers were ready, kneeling behind their pointed stakes. And the first arrows began to whistle by . . .

First the Marshal of Clermont charged headlong at the banner of Salisbury, hurling himself into the hedge to make a breach in it. A hail of arrows broke his charge. It was a dreadful volley, according to those who came through it. The horses that had not been hit went on to impale themselves on the Welsh archers' pointed stakes. From behind the stockade, the coutiliers and other foot soldiers suddenly appeared with their halberds, those terrible three-purpose weapons whose hook seizes the rider by his mail shirt, and sometimes by his skin to throw him down from his mount . . . whose point tears armour apart at the groin or the armpit when the man is down, whose curved blade, lastly, splits open the helmet. The Marshal of Clermont was amongst the first killed, and almost none of his people could make a hole in the English position. All undone along the route recommended by Eustache of Ribemont.

Instead of coming to the aid of Clermont, Audrehem had wanted to distance himself by following the course of the Miosson and thus outflank the English. He had run into the Count of Warwick's troops whose archers did him a lot of damage. It was quickly learned that Audrehem had been wounded and taken prisoner. Of the Duke of Athens, nothing was known. He had vanished into the fray. The army had, in just a few moments, seen its three leaders disappear. A bad start. But that made only three hundred men killed or driven back out of the twenty-five thousand that were moving forward, step by step. The king had got back on his horse to tower above this field of armour, slowly marching on.

Then a curious stirring occurred. The survivors from Clermont's charge, hurtling down between the two lethal hedgerows, their horses bolting, themselves maddened and unable to slow their mounts, collided with the first battalion, that of the Duke of Orléans, and bowled over like chess pieces their comrades-in-arms marching towards them on foot, with difficulty. Oh! They didn't knock that many over; thirty or fifty perhaps, but those in their fall overturned as many again.

As a result, there is panic within the banner of Orléans. The first ranks, wanting to steer clear of the impact, move backwards in disarray; those behind do not know why those in front are pushing back, nor under what enemy thrust; and in moments the rout takes hold of a battalion of almost six thousand men. They are not used to fighting on foot, unless in a combat area, one on one. Here, weighed down as they are, struggling to move, their vision narrowed by their bascinets, they imagine themselves already done for and with no way out. And they all begin to flee though they are still well out of the first enemy's reach. It is a wonder, an army that drives itself back all on its own!

The troops of the Duke of Orléans and the duke himself give ground where nobody is fighting them, several units seeking refuge behind the king's battalion, but most of them running straight, if one can say running, to the horses held by their pages, all these proud men with nothing, in truth, following on their heels but the fear that they had inspired in themselves.

All to be hauled up onto the saddle, to take off so soon in the battle, some leaving folded up like carpets across their mounts since they hadn't managed to straddle them properly. And disappearing into the countryside ... The hand of God, we can't refrain from thinking that ... can we, Archambaud? And only the heathens would dare smile about it.

The dauphin's battalion had also gone ahead – 'Montjoie Saint-Denis!'[60] – and having received no order to return or to surge back, carried on walking. The first rows, gasping for breath from their march, entered between the same hedges that had proven fatal to Clermont, stumbling upon the horses and the men killed there a short while earlier. They were welcomed by the same cloud of arrows, shot from behind the stockades. There was a great noise of swords struck, and cries of rage or pain. The bottleneck was extremely tight, with very few of them at the clash, all the others behind them crushed, and no longer able to move. Jean de Landas, Voudenay, the Sire Guichard too stood, as they had been ordered to, by the side of the dauphin, who would have had great difficulty, as would his brothers of Poitiers and Berry, to move or command the slightest movement. And then, once again, through the slit of a helmet, when you are on foot, with several hundred suits of armour in front of you, your field of vision is severely limited. The dauphin could scarcely see beyond his banner, held by the knight Tristan of Meignelay. When the knights of the Count of Warwick, those who had captured Audrehem, swooped down on horseback upon the flank of the dauphin's battalion, it was too late to prepare to meet the charge.

How ironic! These English, who so readily fought on foot and who had built their reputation upon it, had got back in the saddle no sooner had they seen their enemies engaging the attack dismounted. Without having to be great in number, they produced the same pile-up in the dauphin's battle corps, but tighter still than the one that had happened spontaneously amongst the Duke of Orléans's men. And with even more confusion. 'Watch out, watch out,' they shouted to the king's three sons. Warwick's knights pressed on towards the banner of the dauphin, that very dauphin who had dropped his short lance and struggled, jostled by his own men, just to keep hold of his sword.

It was Voudenay, or perhaps Guichard, nobody knows exactly, who grabbed him by the arm, shouting: 'Follow us; you must withdraw, monseigneur!' If only they could. The dauphin saw poor Tristan of Meignelay lying on the ground, blood leaking from his camail[61] as if from a cracked pot and pouring onto the banner bearing the arms of Normandy and the Dauphiny. And that, I fear, gave him the ardour to make off. Landas and Voudenay cleared a path for him through their own ranks. His two brothers followed, urged on by Saint-Venant.

That he got out of a difficult situation, is fine in itself, and one should have only praise for those who helped him get out. They had the mission of guiding and protecting him. They couldn't leave the sons of France, and most of all, the first amongst them, in enemy hands. That is all well and good. That the dauphin went to his horse, or that his horse was called to him, and that he got on it, and his companions did the same, that is still meet and right, because they had just been jostled by men on horseback.

But that the dauphin should then, without looking back, take off like a shot, should ride away, leaving the battlefield, just as his uncle of Orléans had a moment before, he will have difficulty passing that off as honourable conduct. Ah! The Knights of the Star were not having their finest hour!

Saint-Venant, an old and devoted servant of the crown, will always maintain that it was he who took the decision to remove the dauphin, having already been able to judge that the king's battalion was in a sorry state, that his priority was at all costs to save the heir to the throne with whose guard he was entrusted, and, further, that he had had to strongly insist and almost order the dauphin to leave, and he maintained that even to the dauphin himself, gallant Saint-Venant! Others, alas, have less discreet tongues.

The men of the dauphin's battalion, seeing him disappear, were not long in scattering, they too running to their horses, sounding a general retreat.

The dauphin rode a good league, as he had taken off at full

gallop. Then, considering him safe, Voudenay, Landas and Guichard informed him that they were going back to fight. He didn't answer them. And what would he have said to them? 'You are going back to the engagement, while I withdraw; I give you my congratulations and I salute you'? Saint-Venant wanted to return as well. But somebody had to stay with the dauphin, and the others forced him to take on the task, as the oldest and wisest amongst them. Thus Saint-Venant, with a small escort that quickly grew, by the way, with the terror-stricken deserters they encountered, accompanied the dauphin to the vast Castle of Chauvigny and shut him up in it. And apparently, upon arriving there, the dauphin had to struggle to remove his gauntlet, his right hand was so swollen, all purple. And he was seen to cry.

8

The Battalion of the King

THERE REMAINED THE battalion of the king ... Pour us a little more of this Moselle wine, Brunet. Who do you mean? The archpriest? Ah yes, the one from Verdun! I will see him tomorrow, that will be quite early enough. We are here for three days as we have made such good progress in this continuing spring, so much so that the trees are in bud, in December.

Yes, King John remained on the battlefield of Maupertuis. Maupertuis ... well fancy that, I hadn't thought of that. Names, we repeat them, we no longer realize what they mean. Fatal outcome, fatal period. One should be wary of waging war in a place so named.

First the king sees the banners his brother commanded fleeing in disarray, before even encountering the enemy. Then his son's banners disintegrate and disappear, when scarcely engaged. He had certainly felt great vexation, but without thinking that anything was lost for all that. His

MAURICE DRUON

battalion alone outnumbered all the English put together.

A better captain would have probably understood the danger and modified his battle strategy. And yet King John left the knights of England all the time they needed to repeat against him the charge that had just worked so well for them. They came at him out of nowhere, lances lowered, and broke his battle front.

Poor John II! His father, King Philip, had been defeated at Crécy for having cast his cavalry against the rank and file, and he himself was getting trounced, at Poitiers, for the exact opposite reason.

'Nothing can be done when one confronts people without honour who always use different weapons from your own.' That is what he told me later on, when I saw him again. Since they were moving forward on foot, the English should have, had they been valiant men, remained on foot themselves. Oh! He is not the only prince to put the blame for his failures on an enemy who has not played by the rules he himself had chosen!

He also told me that the wrath that this put him in had strengthened his limbs. He didn't feel the weight of his armour any more. He had broken his iron mace, but beforehand had battered to death more than one assailant. He preferred, for that matter, knocking out rather than setting about his adversaries; but as he only had his double-headed battle-axe left, he brandished it, he whirled it around, he brought it to bear. One might have been inspired to think of a crazed woodcutter in a forest of steel. One more furious than he on a battlefield has never been seen. He felt nothing, neither fatigue nor dread, only the rage that blinded him, even

322

more than the blood that was trickling onto his left eyelid.

He was so sure of winning, just a little earlier; he had victory in his hand. And everything collapsed. Because of what, because of whom? Because of Clermont, because of Audrehem, his wicked marshals who set off too soon, because of his constable, an ass! They can lie down and die, all of them! On that front he can put his mind at rest, the good king; that wish at least was granted. The Duke of Athens was dead; he would be found shortly after against a bush, his body gashed open by the blow of a voulge and trampled by horses in a charge. The Marshal of Clermont was dead; he was hit by so many arrows that his corpse resembled a cockerel fanning its tail feathers. Audrehem has been taken prisoner, his thigh run through.

Rage and fury. All is lost, and yet King John only looks to kill, kill, kill everything that is before him. And then bad luck, to die, his heart torn open! His blue coat of arms, embroidered with the lilies of France is in shreds. He saw fall the oriflamme, held tight against his chest by the courageous Geoffroy of Charny; five coutiliers were upon him; a Welsh bidau[62] or an Irish valet, armed with a blunt butcher's knife, took the banner of France.

The king calls his own people. 'Here, Artois! Here, Bourbon!' They were there just a moment ago. Yes! But now, the son of Count Robert, the denouncer of the King of Navarre, the pea-brained giant, 'my cousin John, my cousin John', is held prisoner, and his brother Charles of Artois as well, and Monseigneur of Bourbon the father of the dauphine.

'Come to me, Regnault, come to me, bishop! Make God

hear you!' If Regnault Chauveau was speaking to God at that moment, it was face to face. The bishop's body was lying somewhere, eyes closed under his purple mitre of iron. Nobody answered the king any more except for a breaking voice shouting: 'Father, father, watch out! To your right father, watch out!'

The king had a glimmer of hope upon seeing Landas, Voudenay and Guichard reappear at the battle, on horseback. Had the runaways pulled themselves together? Were the princes' banners riding back at a gallop to relieve him? 'Where are my sons?'

'Safe from harm, sire!'

Landas and Voudenay had charged. Alone. The king would find out later that they had died for their honour, having returned to the fight so that no one would think them cowards, having saved the Princes of France. Just one of his sons remains with the king, the youngest, his favourite, Philip, who continues to shout: 'To your left, father, watch out! Father, father, look out on your right,' and who frankly hinders him, more than he helps. As the sword is a little too heavy in the hands of the child to be truly offensive, and King John sometimes needs to push away this useless blade from his long axe, to be able to stop his assailants in their tracks. But at least he hadn't run away, little Philip!

Suddenly, John II finds himself surrounded by twenty of the enemy, on foot, in such a hurry that they get in the way of each other. He hears them shout: 'It's the king, it's the king, death to the king!'

Not a single French coat of arms in this terrible circle. On the targes and shields, nothing but English or Gascon devices.

'Give yourself up, give yourself up, or you are dead,' they shout at him.

But the mad king doesn't hear a thing. He continues to cleave the air with his axe. As he has been recognized, they hold back; why yes, they want to take him alive! And he cuts the wind to his right, to his left, especially to his right because on the left his eye is stuck together with blood. 'Father, watch out . . .' The king is hit by a blow to the shoulder. An enormous knight breaks through the throng, makes a hole in the steel wall with his body, elbow-armours his way through to the king, gasping for breath, who is still chopping the air. No, it is not John of Artois; I told you he was taken prisoner. In a loud, French voice, the knight shouts: 'Sire, sire, give yourself up.'

King John then stops hitting at nothing, contemplates all those around him, who are encircling him, and answers to the knight: 'To whom should I give myself up, to whom? Where is my cousin the Prince of Wales? I will speak only to him.'

Sire, he is not here; but give yourself up to me, and I will take you before him,' responds the giant.

'Who are you?'

'I am Denis de Morbecque, knight, but for the last five years in the kingdom of England, since I cannot remain in yours.'

Morbecque, convicted of murder and the crime of private war, the brother of that Jean de Morbecque who works so well for the Navarrese, who negotiated the treaty between Philip of Évreux and Edward III. Ah! Fate did things well and added spice to misfortune to make it all the more bitter.

'I will give myself up to you,' says the king.

Throwing his battleaxe into the grass, he takes off his gauntlet and holds it out to the huge knight. And then, motionless an instant, eyes closed, he lets the defeat sink in.

But then around him the racket starts up again, he is jostled, pulled, crushed, shaken, suffocated. The twenty fellows shout all together: 'I took him, I took him, it was I who took him!' More than all the others, a Gascon shouts: 'He is mine. I was the first to assail him. And you come along, Morbecque, when the deed is done.' And Morbecque replies: 'What are you proclaiming there, Troy? He gave himself up to me, not to you.'

Because it was sure to pay very well, the capture of the King of France, both in honour and in money! And everyone sought to cling on to him to secure their own rights. Seized by the arm by Bertrand of Troy, by the collar, the king ended up getting knocked over in his armour. They would have torn him to pieces.

'Seigneurs, seigneurs!' he shouted. 'Take me courteously, would you, and my son as well, before my cousin the prince. Do not fight any longer over my capture. I am great enough to make you all rich.'

But they wouldn't listen. They continued to shout: 'It is I who took him. He is mine!'

And they fought amongst themselves, these knights, red-faced and iron claws drawn, they fought for a king like dogs for a bone.

Let us now go over to the side of the Prince of Wales. His good captain, John Chandos, had just joined him on a hillock which dominated a large part of the battlefield, and they had stopped there. Their horses, nostrils bloodshot, bits enveloped in frothy slaver, were covered in foam. They themselves were gasping for breath. 'We could hear each other taking huge gulps of air,' Chandos told me. The prince's face was streaming beneath the steel camail attached to his helmet, which hung over his face and covered his shoulders, rose up and down with each intake of breath.

Before them, nothing but torn-apart hedges, crushed shrubs, devastated vines. Everywhere mounts and men slain. Here a horse in agony endlessly kicked in the air. There a suit of armour crawled. Elsewhere, three equerries carried the body of a dying knight to the foot of a tree. Everywhere, Welsh archers and Irish coutiliers stripped the corpses bare. One could still hear the clash of combat in some quarters. The English knights passed through the plain closing ranks on one of the last Frenchmen attempting to escape.

Chandos said: 'Thank God, the day is ours, monseigneur.'

'Yes indeed, by God it is. We have prevailed!' answered the prince. And Chandos continued: 'It would be good, I believe, that you stop here, and had your banner put up on this tall bush. In this way, your people, who are scattered far and wide, will rally around you. And you too could refresh yourself a little, as I see you are rather hot. There is no need to pursue them any more.'

'I believe you are right,' said the prince.

And while the lion and lily banner was being put up on a bush and the buglers were sounding with their trumpets the prince's call to arms, Edward had his bascinet removed, shook out his blond hair, wiped his streaming moustache dry.

What a day! It has to be said that he had really given his all, galloping relentlessly to show himself to each troop, encouraging his archers, exhorting his knights, deciding on the places where reinforcements were to be directed, well, it was above all Warwick and Suffolk, his marshals, who decided; but he was always there to tell them: 'Go on, you are doing well ...' In truth, he had taken only one decision himself, but a capital one, and which really deserved him all the day's glory. When he had seen the disorder provoked in the banner of Orléans by nothing other than the backward surge of the French charge, he had immediately put some of his men back in the saddle to go and produce a similar effect in the battalion of the Duke of Normandy. He himself had entered into the fray on ten occasions. One had the feeling that he was everywhere. And everyone who rallied came to him to say: 'The day is yours. The day is yours. It is a great date that peoples will remember. The day is yours, you have done wonders.'

His pavilion was quickly put up right there, his gentlemen of body and bedchamber hurrying to bring forward the cart, which had been hidden carefully out of the way, containing everything needed for his repast, chairs, tables, tableware, wines.

He couldn't decide whether or not to get down from his horse, as if the victory was not truly won.

'Where is the King of France, has anyone seen him?' he asked his equerries.

The action had gone to his head. He covered the length and breadth of the hillock, ready for some supreme struggle.

And suddenly he noticed, overturned in the heath, a motionless suit of armour. The knight was dead, abandoned by his equerries, except for an old, wounded servant, who was hiding in a thicket nearby . . . the knight, his pennon: the arms of France in saltire gules.[63] The prince had the dead knight's bascinet removed. I'm afraid so, Archambaud . . . it is exactly what you are thinking; it was my nephew, it was Robert of Durazzo.

I am not ashamed of my tears. Admittedly, his own honour had driven him to a deed that the Church's and my honour should have refused him. But I do understand him. And, he was valiant. Not a day goes by that I don't pray to God to forgive him.

The prince ordered his equerries: 'Put this knight on a targe, carry him to Poitiers and present him for me to the Cardinal of Périgord, and tell him that I salute him.'

And yes, that is how I found out that the victory was for the English. To think that in the morning, the prince was ready to negotiate, to return all of his spoils, to suspend fighting for seven years! He very much took me to task the following day, when we saw each other again in Poitiers. Ah! He didn't mince his words. I had tried to serve the French, I had tricked him about their strength, I had brought to bear all the weight of the Church to make him come to terms. I could only answer him: 'Fine prince, you exhausted all means to peace, for the love of God. And God's will made itself known.' That is what I told him.

But Warwick and Suffolk had arrived on the hillock, and with them Lord Cobham. 'Do you have news of King John?' the prince asked them.

'No, not that we have witnessed, but we believe that he is dead or captured, as he did not leave with his battalions.'

Then the prince said to them: 'Please, leave and ride to tell me the truth. Find King John.'

The English were scattered over two leagues all around, hunting down men, pursuing and crossing swords. Now that the day was won, every man was tracking down bounty for his own benefit. Why yes! Everything that a captured knight has on him belongs to his captor. And they were beautifully adorned, King John's barons. Many of them had golden belts. Not to mention the ransoms of course, which would be haggled over and fixed according to the rank of the prisoner. The French are sufficiently vain to let them set the price themselves at which they estimate their worth. One could rely on their misplaced vainglory. Therefore, everyone could try their luck! Those who had had the good fortune to get their hands on John of Artois or the Count of Vendôme, or the Count of Tancarville, were entitled to dream of building themselves a castle. Those who had only seized a minor banneret or a simple bachelier[64] could merely change the furniture in their great halls and offer their ladies a few dresses. And then there would be the prince's gifts, in recognition of the heroic deeds and finest feats.

'Our men are hunting the defeated up to the gates of Poitiers,' Jean de Grailly, Captal[65] of Buch, came to announce. One of the men from his banner, returning from there with four great prizes, not being able to take any more, told him that great abatis[66] of people were forming, because the bourgeois of Poitiers had locked their doors; in front of those doors, on the road, horrible slaughter had taken place, and now the French were giving themselves up from the moment they saw an Englishman. Most ordinary archers had up to five or six prisoners. Never had such a disaster been heard of.

'Is King John there?' asked the prince.

'Certainly not. They would have told me.'

And then, at the bottom of the hillock, Warwick and Cobham appeared once more, going on foot, their horses' bridles over their arms, and trying to bring peace amongst twenty or so knights forming an escort behind them. In English, French and Gascon, these people were arguing with great gestures, miming the movements of combat. And before them, dragging his feet, went an exhausted man, a little unsteady, who, with his ungloved hand, held a child in armour by his gauntlet. A father and son walking side by side, both bearing on their chests slashed silk lilies.

'Back; may nobody approach the king, unless requested to do so,' shouted Warwick to the quarrellers.

And only then did Edward of Wales, Prince of Aquitaine, Duke of Cornwall, know, understand, embrace the immensity of his victory. The king, King John, the leader of the most populous and powerful nation in Europe. The man and the child walked towards him very slowly. Ah! This moment would remain for ever in the memory of men! The prince had the feeling that the whole world was watching him.

He signalled to his gentlemen to help him get down from his horse. His thighs felt stiff, his back too.

He stood on the threshold of his pavilion. The setting sun shot the copse through with golden rays. All of these men would have been surprised to be told that the hour of vespers was already past.

Edward held his hands out to the gift Warwick and Cobham were bringing him, to the gift of Providence. John of

France, even stooped by adverse fortune, is taller than him. He responded to his victor's gesture. And also held his two hands out, one gloved, one bare. They remained a moment like that, not embracing, simply clasping each other's hands. And then Edward made a gesture that would touch the hearts of all of the knights. He was the son of a king; his prisoner was a crowned king. So, still holding him by the hand, he bowed his head deeply, and made to bend his knee. Honour be to unfortunate valour. All that glorifies the defeated further glorifies our victory. There were lumps in the throats of these hard men.

'Please take a seat, sire my cousin,' said Edward, inviting King John to enter his pavilion. Allow me to serve you some wine and spices. And please forgive that, for supper, I make you eat such a simple meal. We will sit down to eat shortly.'

As they were busying themselves putting up a great tent on the hillock, the prince's gentlemen knew their duty. And the cooks always have some pâtés and meats in their coffers. What was missing, they would go and fetch from the larders of the monks of Maupertuis. The prince also says: 'Your relatives and barons will be most welcome to join us. I will have them called. And bear that we bandage that wound on your forehead that shows your great courage.'

9

The Prince's Supper

IT MAKES ONE THINK of the fate of nations to tell you all
that, which has just taken place, and which marks a great
change, a great turning point for the kingdom, precisely here
of all places, precisely here in Verdun. Why? Ah! My nephew,
because the kingdom was born here, because what can be
called the kingdom of France stems from the treaty signed
right here after the Battle of Fontenoy, then *Fontanetum*, you
know very well, we went through it, between the three sons
of Louis the Pious. Charles the Bald's part was poorly defined,
moreover without looking at the true nature of the ground.
The Alps, the Rhine should have been the natural borders
of France, and it is not common sense that Verdun and Metz
be lands of the empire. Now, what will become of France
tomorrow? How will France be divided up? Perhaps France
will be no more in ten or twenty years, certain are seriously
wondering. They see a large English piece, and a Navarrese
piece running from one sea to the other with all of the Langue

d'Oc, and a kingdom of Arles rebuilt in the sphere of influence of the empire, with Burgundy in addition. Everyone dreams of carving up the weakest part.

To tell you my opinion on the matter, I don't believe it at all, because the Church, as long as I and several others of my ilk will live, will not allow this dismemberment. And the people remember too well and are too used to a great and united France. The French will soon see that they are nothing if no longer a kingdom, if they are no longer united in a single state. But there will be difficult rivers to cross. You will perhaps be faced with painful choices. Always choose, Archambaud, with the kingdom in mind, even if it is commanded by a bad king, because the king can die, or be dislodged, or held in captivity, but the kingdom goes on.

The grandeur of France came to light on that evening in Poitiers, in the very consideration that the victor, dazzled by his fortune and scarcely believing it, lavished on the vanquished. A strange table indeed was the one set up after the battle in the middle of a wood in Poitou, between the walls of red drapery. In the places of honour, lit by candles, the King of France, his son Philip, Monseigneur Jacques de Bourbon, who had become duke since his father had been killed during the day, Count John of Artois, the Counts of Tancarville, Étampes, Dammartin, and also the Sires of Joinville and Parthenay, served in silver; and spread out over the other tables, between English and Gascon knights, the most powerful and the richest of the remaining prisoners.

The Prince of Wales put on a show of getting up to serve the King of France himself and to pour him wine in abundance.

'Eat, dear sire, if you please. Have no regrets doing so. Because if God has not consented to your will and if the effort did not turn in your favour, you have won great renown for prowess, and your heroic deeds have surpassed the greatest. Certainly monseigneur my father will honour you as much as is in his power, and will come to such a reasonable agreement with you that you will remain good friends together. In truth, everyone here acknowledges the true worth of your bravery, as in this respect you are victorious over us all.'

That set the tone. King John relaxed. His left eye bruised black and blue, and a gash in his lower forehead, he responded to the polite remarks of his host. King-knight, it mattered to him to show himself this way in defeat. On the other tables, voices were rising. After having clashed so brutally with each other with swords or axes, the seigneurs of both sides, at present, were falling over each other with compliments.

They commemorated out loud the various episodes of the battle. They couldn't stop singing the praises of the daring of the young Prince Philip, who, sated with food after this hard day, nodded gently on his chair and slid off into sleep.

And it was the time of reckoning. Besides the grands seigneurs, dukes, counts and viscounts of which there were around twenty, they had counted amongst the prisoners more than sixty barons and bannerets; mere knights, equerries and bacheliers could not be accounted for. More than a couple of thousand assuredly; the total would only be known with accuracy the following day.

The dead? Their numbers must have been about the same. The prince ordered that those already gathered together be carried the following dawn to the Monastery of the Frères

Mineurs of Poitiers, at the head of which procession the bodies of the Duke of Athens, the Duke of Bourbon, the Count-Bishop of Châlons, to be buried with all the pomp and honour they deserved. What a procession! Never will a monastery have seen so many rich and important men arrive in one single day. What a fortune, in Masses and donations, would rain down on the Frères Mineurs! And as much again on the Frères Prêcheurs.[67]

I will tell you straight away that they had to dig up cobblestones in the nave and the cloister of two monasteries to bury beneath, on two floors, Geoffroy of Charny, Rochechouart, Eustache of Ribemont, Dance of Melon, John of Montmorillon, Seguin of Cloux, La Fayette, La Rochedragon, La Rochefoucault, La Roche Pierre de Bras, Oliver of Saint-Georges, Imbert of Saint-Saturnin, and I could go on citing more and more names by the score.

'Do we know what has become of the archpriest?' asked the king.

The archpriest was wounded, the prisoner of an English knight. How much was the archpriest worth? Did he have a big castle, a lot of land? his victor enquired shamelessly. No. A small manor house in Vélines. But the fact that the king had named him raised his price.

'I will pay his ransom,' said John II who, without yet knowing how much he himself was going to cost France, began once more to play the high and mighty.

Then Prince Edward replied: 'For your sake, sire my cousin, I will redeem this archpriest myself, and give him back his freedom, if you so wish.'

Voices rose around the tables. The wines and meats,

greedily swallowed, went to the heads of these tired men, who had eaten nothing since the morning. Their assembly had something of a court repast after the grand tournaments and of the cattle market all at the same time.

Morbecque and Bertrand of Troy hadn't stopped arguing over the king's capture. 'It was I, I tell you!'

'No it wasn't; I was upon him, you pushed me aside!'

'To whom did he offer up his gauntlet?'

In any case, the ransom, certainly enormous, would not be going to them, but to the King of England. A king's capture belongs to the king. What they were fighting about was to know who would receive the pension that King Edward would not fail to grant. It makes one wonder if they wouldn't have benefited more, at least financially if not honourably, in taking a rich baron whom they could have shared. Because prizes were being shared out, if two or three of them were on the same prisoner. Or exchanges. 'Give me Sire de la Tour; I know him, he is a relative of my good wife. I will give you Mauvinet whom I captured. You stand to gain; he is Seneschal of Touraine.'

And suddenly King John banged on the table with the flat of his hand.

'My sires, my good lords, I intend that everything between you and those who have captured us should take place according to honour and nobility. God wanted that we be defeated, but you can see the respect that has been proven to us. We must uphold chivalry. May no one take it into their head to flee or to forfeit their word, as I will hold them in contempt.'

One would have thought that he was in command, this

crushed man, and he was using all of his loftiness to invite his barons to be most scrupulous once in captivity.

The Prince of Wales, who was pouring him the wine of Saint-Émilion, thanked him. King John found him most pleasant, this young man. How attentive he was, what beautiful manners he had. King John would have liked that his sons resemble him! He couldn't resist, helped on by the drink and fatigue, asking him: 'Did you ever meet Monsieur of Spain?'

'No, dear sire; I only confronted him at sea.' The prince was courteous; he could have said: 'I defeated him . . .'

'He was a good friend. You remind me of him, his appearance and bearing.' And suddenly, with spitefulness in his voice: 'Don't ask me to release my son-in-law Navarre; that, against my life, I will never do.'

King John II, for a moment, had shown greatness, really, a very brief moment, in the instant that followed his capture. He had shown the greatness of extreme misfortune. And now he was returning to his true nature: behaviour corresponding to his exaggerated self-image, poor judgement, futile concerns, shameful passions, absurd impulses and lingering hatreds.

In a certain way, captivity would not be to his disliking, a golden captivity because a royal captivity. This falsely triumphant character had achieved his true fate, which was to be defeated. No more, at least for a while, would he have the worries of government, the struggle against all adversity in his kingdom, the grief of giving orders that are never followed. At present, he is at peace; he can call as his witness these heavens that have been adverse, wrap himself in his misfortune and pretend to bear with nobility the pain of a destiny that suits him so well. May others take on the burden of leading a restive people! We will see if they can manage to do any better.

'Where are you taking me, my cousin?' he asked.

'To Bordeaux, dear sire, where I will give you a fine house, supplies, and feasts to delight you, until you can come to an agreement with the king, my father.'

'Can there be delight for a captured king?' answered John II already mindful of his character.

Ah! Why hadn't he accepted, at the beginning of that day in Poitiers, the terms that I brought him? Has such a king ever been seen before in a position where he can win everything in the morning, without drawing his sword, who can establish his law once more over a quarter of his kingdom, simply by appending his signature and affixing his seal on the treaty that his hounded enemy offers him, and who refuses, and on that very evening finds himself prisoner.

A yes instead of a no. The irreparable act. Like that of the Count of Harcourt, going back up the stairs in Rouen instead of walking out of the castle. John of Harcourt lost his head because of it; here, it is the whole of France which may face agony.

The most surprising thing, and the most unfair, is that this absurd king, persistent only in ruining his luck, and who was unloved before Poitiers, has soon become, because he is defeated, because he is captive, an object of admiration, pity and love for his people, for a part of his people. John the Brave, John the Good.

And it all started at the prince's supper. Although they had this king to blame for everything, he who had led them to misfortune, the prisoner barons and knights exalted his courage, his magnanimity, what else? The defeated were giving themselves a clear conscience and a fine appearance. When they came home, their families having bled themselves dry, and having bled their peasants dry to pay their ransoms, they will say, you can be certain of it, with arrogance: 'You were not, like me, with our King John.' Ah! They will tell the tale of that day in Poitiers!

At Chauvigny, the dauphin, who was having a sad meal in the company of his brothers and waited on by only a few servants, was informed that his father was alive, but captive. 'It is up to you to govern, at present, monseigneur,' Saint-Venant tells him.

In the past, to my knowledge, there have been no eighteen-year-old princes who have had to take over the helm in such a sorry situation. A father taken prisoner, nobility diminished by defeat, two enemy armies camped out in the country, as Lancaster is still there above the Loire, several provinces laid to waste, no finances, grasping, divided and hated advisors, a brother-in-law in a fortress but whose most active partisans are raising their heads more than ever, a simmering capital that a handful of ambitious bourgeois is inciting to riot. Add to this that the young man is of sickly disposition, and that his conduct in battle did nothing to improve his reputation.

At Chauvigny, still that same evening, as he had decided to return to Paris by the shortest route, Saint-Venant asked him: 'Which title, monseigneur, should give to your person those who will speak in your name?' and the dauphin answered: 'The one I have, Saint-Venant, the one designated me by

God: lieutenant general of the kingdom.' Which were wise words indeed.

That was three months ago. Nothing is completely lost, but neither does anything show any sign of improvement, quite the contrary. France is coming undone. And in less than a week we are to find ourselves in Metz, where I really don't see, I must confess, what great good could come out of it, except for the emperor, nor what great work could be accomplished there, between a lieutenant of the kingdom, but who is not the king, and a pontifical legate, who is not the pope.

Do you know what I have just been told? The season is so fine, and the days so warm in Metz, where they are expecting more than three thousand princes, prelates and seigneurs, that the emperor, if this mild spell continues, has decided that he will give the Christmas feast outdoors, in a walled garden.

To dine outside at Christmas, in Lorraine, one more thing that had never before been seen!

Translator's notes and
historical explanations

1. The Holy See was in Avignon from 1309 to 1378, moved there by Clement V, a French pope who wanted to stay in France and who built a papal palace in Provence. Gregory XI left Avignon and returned the Holy See to Rome, the Vatican, where it remains today.

2. Fratricelles, Fraticelles or Fraticelli were members of the mendicant orders of Franciscan monks; Gyrovagues were also a type of wandering monk.

3. Coutiliers were knife-bearing foot soldiers or armed guards; army valets or batmen were initially referred to as goujats, the term now meaning boor or churl.

4. The Golden Seal of the Holy Roman Empire, a spherical, symbolic object, also known as the Golden Bull; both terms usually refer to the imperial ordinances, edicts or laws of the Empire.

5. My lord of Spain; the title of monsieur usually designated the king's oldest living brother.

6. Louis X, called the Quarreller, the Headstrong or the Stubborn (Hutin in French).

7. '*De jure* or *de facto*' means well grounded in law or in fact (legitimately or effectively).

8. The galero is the ecclesiastical scarlet hat worn by cardinals.

9. The County or Country of Dauphiny, formerly known as the Viennois.

10. Janissaries were soldiers of the Ottoman army.

11. Demoiselle, a maiden or young noblewoman.

12. Chatellanies or castellanies were the smallest division of land in medieval times.

13. The écu was a large gold coin similar to the franc d'or, whereas sols, deniers, pounds and gros were all silver coinage.

14. The Spinning Sow, from the French La Truie qui File, a not unusual name for an inn at the time.

15. Machine here refers to the contraptions – catapults or trebuchets for example – used in siege warfare.

16. Quarteniers commanded each quartier or neighbourhood, while cinquanteniers and dizainiers ran subdivisions of those quartiers.

17. The Langue d'Oil or the northern provinces which spoke the Oil dialect, and the Langue d'Oc, or the southern provinces, specifically the Occitan region, which spoke the Oc dialect.

18. La chambre des comptes.

19. Canons Regular were priests living under Augustinian rule, i.e. in society rather than in a monastery.

20. The ban and the arrière-ban were the components of the king's conscription army, the ban being his knights and barons, and the arrière-ban the rest of his vassals, often foot

soldiers, sometimes translated as the ward and the rear ward.

21. A limner was an image maker or manuscript illuminator; the notion of artist is anachronistic.

22. Livre tournois, or the pound of the city of Tours.

23. The three estates were the clergy, the nobility and the commoners or bourgeois.

24. Fardiers were goods vehicles, carts.

25. Perrinet le Buffle or Perrinet the Buffalo, clearly a nickname to emphasize his strength.

26. A cervellière was a close-fitting hemispherical iron skullcap, cervelle meaning brain in French.

27. An embrasure is a narrow, vertical arrow slit typical of medieval defensive architecture.

28. One quintal, sometimes translated as a hundredweight, is equal to 100 kilograms.

29. Passementerie is decorative trimming, for example, gold and silver lace and braid.

30. The mark was a unit of weight equivalent to 8 troy ounces or 249 grammes.

31. 'Le jour de la Saint-Bavard', a fictional feast day, bavard meaning talkative.

32. Hippocras, a sweet, spicy drink similar to mulled wine.

33. A gambeson was a quilted jerkin or doublet, a form of light armour.

34. 'On va fricoter le Friquet', fricoter meaning to cook up (grill), or to have shady dealings with someone, hence the pun.

35. Called a 'lin', a very grand form of barge with sails and oars.

36. A hanap is an ornate medieval drinking vessel or goblet.

37. Angoumois was a county corresponding to the modern

Charentes region; its capital was Angoulême.

38. Bulls were papal edicts or mandates. (cf. Golden Bull)

39. A curule chair is a folding seat with curved legs and no back, used mainly by high officials.

40. Fouage or hearth tax, based on the number of hearths per household.

41. Laigle, a Norman market town now called l'Aigle, 'the Eagle'.

42. A poleyn was part of the suit of armour, a metal knee-guard.

43. A banner was a company of soldiers riding under a particular flag or banner.

44. The old French engeignerie corresponds to the modern engineering, i.e. the science of building machines, for siege warfare for example.

45. Greaves were pieces of armour covering the shin and calf; cuisses were pieces of armour that protected the front of the thigh.

46. Cubitières were pieces of armour that protected the elbows.

47. There were 20 sols or sous in a pound, and 12 deniers to a sol.

48. Epaulement, parapet or breastwork.

49. A fougasse was a large, directional land mine set off by fuse; saps were covered trenches.

50. Parade as in a military parade, and orgueil, meaning pride.

51. Fascines were long faggots of wood used for lining trenches.

52. Ballisters were crossbowmen.

53. Venerer or huntsman.

54. A viguier was an officer to whom counts delegated part of their authority over their lands, and who thus administered those counties.

55. An octroi was a town or city toll, collected as one passed through one of the town gates.

56. Voulges were curved-bladed polearms also called pole cleavers; halberds were pikes with a blade combining a spearhead and a battleaxe.

57. The arrière-ban were civilians called up for military service by the king.

58. Bascinet was a type of open-faced helmet.

59. Jeu de paume, a game also called real tennis, and ancestor of the modern sport of tennis.

60. 'Montjoie Saint-Denis' was the battle cry of French soldiers, Montjoie meaning Mons Jovis, in the direction of, and Saint Denis, whose banner was the oriflamme.

61. A camail or aventail was a mail neck and throat protection attached to the bascinet.

62. A bidau was a foot soldier armed with a spear, lance and dagger.

63. Saltire is a division into four parts by a diagonal cross, gules is the heraldic term for tincture red.

64. A bachelier, or bachelor, was a young gentleman who had not yet received either land or title and was therefore obliged to ride under the banner of another knight.

65. Captal was a medieval feudal title in Gascony, meaning first chief.

66. An abatis was a system of defence consisting in stacking up trees lengthways to form a protective barrier. Here the image is of felled people rather than felled trees.

67. Frères Mineurs and Frères Prêcheurs are bodies of monks, Franciscans and Dominicans respectively.